"Bryan Litfin combines his vivid imagination [with] ... [his]tory, literature, geography, ancient languages, [...] marvelous book about 'a mysterious book.' The [...] enjoyable, quick read; it is also a great story about The Great Story—'Iesus, the Pierced One' and his past, present, and future church. Three cheers for this final volume in the trilogy!"

> **DOUGLAS SEAN O'DONNELL,** Senior Pastor, New Covenant Church, Naperville, Illinois; author, *God's Lyrics* and *The Beginning and End of Wisdom*

"In the darkness of Chiveis, where hope is a rare commodity, some dare to believe the promises of the sacred text. The adventure that follows not only grips your imagination, it also enriches your faith."

> **CHRIS CASTALDO,** author, *Holy Ground*

"The Chiveis Trilogy concludes with yet another page-turner, full of action, adventure, suspense, intrigue, and inspiration. Litfin's deep love for Scripture, reflected in his characters' passionate pursuit of the Sacred Writings, can't help but challenge and inspire readers to treasure their own Bibles and read them more often!"

> **CHRISTIN DITCHFIELD,** conference speaker; syndicated radio host, *Take It To Heart®*; author, *A Family Guide to Narnia*

"Bryan Litfin's writing is colorful, witty, and engaging. The story of Chiveis is compelling and rich. The beautiful gospel themes constantly remind me of the wonder of the True God and the power of his Word. This last installment of the Chiveis Trilogy concludes the adventures of Teo and Ana with heart racing and mind stirring pace and resolution. This is indeed the work of an artist and theologian."

> **JAY THOMAS,** Lead Pastor, Chapel Hill Bible Church, Chapel Hill, North Carolina

"The climatic conclusion of Bryan Litfin's Chiveis Trilogy does not disappoint. With his mastery of language, Litfin brings to life the struggles of Teo and Ana as they reintroduce God to a post-apocalyptic world that has forgotten Him. The cunning and captivating plot is layered with deep currents of real everyday Christian struggles. It is a thrilling novel that captured my imagination and challenged my soul."

> **JASON HUBBARD,** MD, FAANS, FACS, Neurosurgeon

THE KINGDOM

The Chiveis Trilogy:

CHIVEIS TRILOGY

THE
KINGDOM

A NOVEL

BRYAN M. LITFIN

:: CROSSWAY

WHEATON, ILLINOIS

Cover design: Josh Dennis

Cover image: Cliff Nielsen, Shannon Associates; illustrator

First printing 2012

Printed in the United States of America

Scripture on pages 7 and 8 taken from the ESV® (*The Holy Bible, English Standard Version*®), copyright © 2001 by Crossway. Used by permission. All rights reserved.

All other Scripture quotations are the author's translation.

ISBN-13: 978-1-4335-2520-9

ISBN-10: 1-4335-2520-8

PDF ISBN: 978-1-4335-2521-6

Mobipocket ISBN: 978-1-4335-2522-3

ePub ISBN: 978-1-4335-2523-0

Library of Congress Cataloging-in-Publication Data
Litfin, Bryan M., 1970–
   The kingdom : a novel / Bryan M. Litfin.
     p. cm. — (Chiveis trilogy ; bk. 3)
   ISBN 978-1-4335-2520-9 (tp)
   I. Title.
PS3612.I865K56   2012
813'.6—dc23   2012003083

Crossway is a publishing ministry of Good News Publishers.

VP		21	20	19	18	17	16	15	14	13	12
14	13	12	11	10	9	8	7	6	5	4	3	2	1

I
now
dedicate
this trilogy
to Jeff Ligon,
a loving father,
a godly husband,
a skilled physician,
and my beloved friend.
Since grad school at UVa,
until cancer took you home,
we hiked through life together.
Twice we criss-crossed Europe:
you drove, and I came up with plot,
and you let me call the Alps "Chiveis."
So rest until the Lord returns, my brother.
I'm keeping your boots until I see you again.

"O death, where is your victory?
O death, where is your sting?"
Thanks be to God,
who gives us the victory
through our Lord Jesus Christ.

1 Corinthians 15:55, 57

Why do the nations rage
and the peoples plot in vain?
The kings of the earth set themselves,
and the rulers take counsel together,
against the LORD *and against his Anointed,*
saying,
"Let us burst their bonds apart
and cast away their cords from us."
He who sits in the heavens laughs;
the Lord holds them in derision.
Then he will speak to them in his wrath,
and terrify them in his fury, saying,
"As for me, I have set my King
on Zion, my holy hill."

Psalm 2:1–6

contents

PROLOGUE

The rulers of the earth took counsel together, and the Pact they made defined the centuries to come. Jean-Luc Beaumont convened the historic meeting at which the Pact was signed. It was his second greatest achievement.

His first was still being alive.

In the summer of 2042 no one knew the world was about to end. Beaumont, the cocky young CEO of a Swiss chemical company, didn't pay much attention to the story he read in the *Tribune de Genève* about the strange virus devastating Japan. But the human race was about to learn what the murderous X-Virus could do.

The new supervirus raced around the globe like a bullet train, claiming every life it touched. Death came with agonizing cramps and a gush of vomit and blood. As the body count rose, panic set in. Citizens rioted, governments crumbled, and the horrified superpowers watched their worst nightmare come true. When a few ruthless dictators pulled the nuclear trigger against their long-hated rivals, retaliation was impossible to resist. In this way modern civilization met an ugly death under poisoned skies.

For several decades apocalyptic chaos reigned across the globe. Food was the only thing on anyone's mind. Tribal bands pursued agriculture by primitive methods while ruthless warlords guarded the communal fields. Farming and fighting—those were the two occupations in the brave new world. Each tribe was separated from its neighbors by empty spaces that eventually returned to forest, though that did not prevent raids. Brutal wars over the food supply characterized the middle decades of the twenty-first century. The anarchy devoured the weak and timid, yet it opened doors of opportunity to men with the iron will to survive—men like Jean-Luc Beaumont.

By the time he was fifty, Beaumont was king of Europe's Genevan tribe. Old Geneva was gone, of course. A ballistic missile had erased all traces of the Jet d'Eau, the Reformation Wall, and the splendid St. Pierre Cathedral on the hill above the lake. But a tribe of warriors and farmers had coalesced in the region, producing crops in the Rhône Valley to fill their stomachs and wines along Lac Léman to numb life's pain. For ten years Beaumont ruled his tribe with ruthless efficiency until a coup in 2070 forced him out.

The exiled king sailed up the Aar River with forty tough warriors and nothing to eat. The year was waning, and winter's chill was already in the air. Harassed from behind, Beaumont pressed upstream until dense wilderness finally swallowed the refugees. They approached the foothills of the Alps with little hope of survival but were surprised to discover a rabble of German-speaking peasants making a decent living off dairy cattle in the Bernese Oberland. Beaumont thanked his god and ordered his men to halt.

The winter that year was a hard one, with too little bread for supper and too much cheese, yet the refugees survived by assimilating into the mountain culture. When spring came, Beaumont knew where he would establish his new kingdom. La Nouvelle Suisse, he tried to call it, but the peasants preferred their own name: Schweiz.

Most of Beaumont's warriors were young, which meant they had no memory of the vanished world that existed before the Great War of Destruction. But as a former chemical engineer, Beaumont recalled ancient secrets he could turn to his advantage. He amassed charcoal from willow and hazel, saltpeter from stables and chicken coops, and sulfur—always the hardest ingredient to obtain—from nearby hot springs. The king picked three men to gather these substances, empowering them as archpriests of a new religious triad whose gods were borrowed from classical mythology. However, the secret of combining the ingredients into gunpowder remained unknown to each priest. Such arcane knowledge could only be entrusted to one person. For this, Beaumont chose Greta, the peasant witch he had taken as his lover.

Greta had long served her village as the mediatrix of the dawn god. She was a dark-haired vixen dripping with occult magic. Beaumont recognized Greta's beguiling power, and he used it, though not without caution. Together the king and his consort established a new religion under a divine overlord, the Bright Star, Astre Brillant. He was the Bringer of Light, or Lucifer as the Bible described him. Beaumont and Greta hated that book and hated even more the God of its pages—for Astre Brillant, the deity who supplied their power and position, hated him too.

La Nouvelle Suisse grew strong, and with it grew Beaumont's lust for vengeance against the Genevans who had evicted him. In time he made a treaty with the German tribes of the north. They were rough men who dwelled in tangled forests, but they fought with violence and vigor. In the ninth year of Beaumont's reign he ordered the troops of his Royal Guard, allied with German mercenaries, to invade the Genevan lands. The thunderous explosions and acrid stench of Beaumont's gunpowder bombs sent the Genevan warriors fleeing the battlefield. Crops were destroyed, blood was spilled, and the elderly king savored his revenge.

But then Greta brought disturbing news. Missionaries of the Christian God had arrived in Geneva, having navigated up the Rhône from Marseilles. "Astre Brillant came to me in a dream," Greta said. "He commands us to eradicate that religion once and for all." The prophetic words of Greta's decree launched Beaumont on his last great quest.

After the missionaries were rounded up and murdered, an expedition set out for Marseilles. A hundred German confederates joined the Royal Guardsmen sailing down the Rhône. At last Jean-Luc Beaumont, king of La Nouvelle Suisse and conqueror of Geneva, met the prince of Marseilles with great fanfare. In no time he managed to worm his way into the city's politics and manipulate the foolish prince into summoning delegates from the three kingdoms that ringed the nearby seas.

Soon the ships began to arrive, each bearing an important guest. Ambassadors came to Marseilles from Liguria, from Rome, and even from the Isle of Sicily, which sent as its delegate the firstborn son of the crime boss who ran the Clan. When the chessboard was laid out and the pieces were in place, Beaumont made his opening move: he summoned Greta to invoke the forces of darkness upon the momentous council. Greta's magic impressed the gathered delegates. Their awe made it a simple matter to convince them to sign a treaty.

The Pact was an alliance based on common interest. The Romans, Sicilians, Ligurians, Marseillans, Germans, and Swiss all realized they had little to gain by fighting each other. Stability had finally been achieved in the post-nuclear world. Riches flowed to the elite at the top. The iron fist of oppression ensured that the peasants' crushing poverty produced extreme wealth for the lords. To maintain this lucrative status quo, the delegates agreed not to meddle in one another's affairs, a policy that would lead to deep and long-lasting xenophobia.

Yet a nonaggression pact wasn't all Beaumont wanted. He knew a single powerful force could overthrow the wealthy rulers' reign: Christianity, the faith that dignified human beings by giving even the lowliest peasant a sense of value before God. That religion had proven it could unify people across economic, political, and social lines. Beaumont recalled how Christianity had appealed to Middle Easterners, Africans, Westerners, Latinos, and Asians alike. "The last Pope was even Chinese!" he complained to the men at the council, though most of them were too young to know what he meant. Yet when old Adolfo Borja of Rome nodded his head, the gathered rulers couldn't help but notice. Beaumont must be right: Christianity was their greatest threat.

Greta returned to the room then, resplendent in the garb of a Swiss High Priestess. Her aura was terribly exotic. The scent of the netherworld was upon her, and the men in the room were transfixed. Beaumont smiled, confident the Pact he desired would soon be achieved. Greta produced a razor, its silver blade reflecting the light from candle sconces on the wall. A single pitcher and six glass vials were placed on the table among the men. A hush fell upon them.

Beaumont offered his arm.

Greta opened a vein.

And so it was that on that fateful day each man left the room bearing a vial of intermingled blood as proof of his sacred vow. A secret society of assassins would be formed. All followers of the Enemy would be exterminated. Their scriptures would be destroyed. The name of Jesus would be blotted from the earth. At last the rulers of the nations had burst the bonds of the Creator God. Christianity had come to an end in Europe. The faith would be forgotten by everyone. And for many years it was.

But then, more than three centuries later, a young army captain named Teofil followed Anastasia of Edgeton into the Beyond to rescue her from evildoers. Teo and Ana wanted only to return to the land they called Chiveis, yet a mysterious hand seemed to lead them in the opposite direction. In the ruins of an ancient cathedral, high upon the single-spired roof, they discovered a mysterious book. Though they did not know what it was, they brought it home, opened it, and looked into its pages.

And things began to change.

PART ONE

DEPENDENCY

1

Teo set down his quill and picked up a parchment containing the words of life. Rising from his desk, he gazed out the window of the seaside convent at Lido di Ostia. A lone woman sat near the water, her head shaded from summer's rays by a wide-brimmed hat. She wore a simple cotton sundress and leather sandals. The wind blew her honey-blonde hair to one side, draping it across her suntanned shoulders. Teo smiled as he looked at the beautiful woman on the beach. Though he had loved Anastasia from the day he met her two years ago, he had only just admitted that fact last week.

And now he was about to leave her.

But not forever, he reminded himself.

Holding the parchment of new translations, Teo walked outside. The air was muggy, and the clouds along the horizon suggested an afternoon thunderstorm was brewing. He approached Ana from behind. "Need some company?"

She turned, smiling at him. "Always," she said with a wink.

Teo sat beside her on the warm, brown sand. He remained silent for a while, until at last he said, "I've been thinking about the mission the Papa asked of me." The Papa was the leader of the Christiani, so his requests could not be taken lightly.

"What about it?"

"Remember how we decided it was from Deu?"

Ana's face took on a look of concern. "You're not changing your mind, are you?"

"No, definitely not." The mission to the distant port of Marsay could be carried out by no one else. Teo knew he was uniquely qualified to journey great distances and speak the local languages. The Papa wanted Teo to be his emissary to the Knights of the Cross, collect any texts that spoke of the Creator God Deu, and explore whether other kingdoms in Marsay's vicinity might be open to the true faith. "I'm still planning on going," Teo insisted, "but I think the Papa misjudged the timing."

"How so?"

"I think I can get back here earlier than he thought. And that's important, because I believe Deu has something big in store for us."

Ana cocked her head and gazed at Teo with an amused expression. "A girl could interpret a mysterious statement like that in a lot of ways! Rather than get my hopes up, I think I'll just wait for you to explain."

"Sorry," Teo said, chuckling. "What I meant was, I think the Papa's mission won't take as much time as he supposes. He said it would take until winter, and then I'd be stuck at Marsay because the storms would close the seas. But I'm pretty sure I could return before then."

"You don't have to cut the mission short for me. I'll be fine here."

"I know. I wouldn't rush back just for you. I mean, I'll definitely miss you, but . . . there's something else."

"Another mysterious statement!" Ana's face grew serious. "What's on your mind, Teo? Be clear with me so I can know what you're thinking."

He sighed, then handed Ana the parchment. "Read this bit of the New Testament and tell me what you think. I just finished the translation. It's a letter from the preacher named Paulus."

"Oh, Paulus! His story is amazing. I've been reading it in the book of Deeds."

"This is his letter to the Ephesi. The opening of the fifth chapter."

Ana scanned the page, which was written in her native tongue. Although she and Teo were living at a convent near Roma where everyone spoke a language called Talyano, Teo had been working on a translation of the New Testament from Talyano into the Chiveisian speech. Ana enjoyed reading Teo's scriptural translations as fast as he could produce them. The parchment he had just handed her described a contrast between the deeds of light and darkness. The passage closed with an admonition to discern the will of Deu.

"It's a beautiful text," Ana said. "It calls the sacrifice of the Pierced One a fragrant offering given to us in love."

"I liked that too. But the part that caught my attention is toward the end. Look here at what it says." Teo scooted closer to Ana on the sand and pointed to the passage. "It says to 'redeem the time because the days are evil.' I think that's a message for us. Our days are evil too. Time is short. We need to be wise and discern what the will of Deu is."

"How can we know his will?"

"I'm not sure. I'm just learning to figure that out. But I've been doing a lot of thinking about . . . us."

"What do you mean?"

"Our future."

Ana remained silent as Teo stared across the sea, collecting his thoughts. At last he spoke, and when he did, he started at the beginning. He took Ana back to the day he had fallen beneath a ferocious bear attack and only her skill with a bow had saved him. Then he recalled the incredible twists and turns their lives had taken. After they found a copy of the Old Testament in a lost temple in the wilderness, they encountered severe persecution from the High Priestess of Chiveis. The only way to avoid martyrdom was to choose exile over the mountains. In foreign lands to the south Teo and Ana met other believers in Deu, including the Papa, who led the Universal Communion at Roma. Though he was a godly man, he and his followers did not possess the New Testament, for it had been lost during the Ancients' Great War of Destruction. Yet that did not stop Deu. After many battles and dangers, the one true God gave Teo and Ana the Sacred Writing. It revealed the stunning truth that Deu's executed son had triumphed over death.

As Teo reminisced about the events of the past two years he could sense Ana growing distressed. He knew why: she wanted to return to Chiveis. Ana missed her home desperately and longed for her people to hear the message of salvation. Teo considered what he should say to her. *Redeem the time*, the holy Paulus had written. *Understand the will of Deu. The days are evil!*

He glanced at Ana, who was tracing her finger in the sand. "I intend to finish the Papa's mission before the storms arrive," he announced. "I'm going to return here before winter. And then early next spring, as soon as it's safe to travel again, we'll head north."

Ana's head shot up. "*North?* You mean . . . Likuria?"

Teo nodded.

"Ulmbartia?"

He nodded again.

"And then, over the mountains?"

"Yes, Ana. It's time to go home to Chiveis. It'll be dangerous, but our people need to hear about Deu. We have to redeem the time allotted to us."

Ana leaped to her feet and yanked Teo up as well. "I agree!" she exclaimed. "Let's go home!" Brimming with joy, she hugged him around the neck.

An ocean wave rolled up, its reach longer than most. As Ana stepped back she kicked her foot to splash Teo. He bent down and tossed seawater at her with a cupped hand, eliciting a girlish squeal.

"It's so hot today!" Ana pitched her wide hat onto the sand, then flicked off her sandals. A mischievous look was on her face as she tugged Teo's arm. "Come on! Let's go for a swim!"

Teo caught her lighthearted mood. The idea of a swim in the cool water appealed to him too. He peeled off his shirt and rolled the precious parchment inside, then followed Ana into the sea. She had already waded out, soaking the hem of her knee-length dress. Her eyes shone as she waited for him to join her.

"You've made me so happy," she said, hugging him again.

Teo's only reply was to drag her with him into the choppy waves. Ana went willingly, laughing as she fell. She surfaced quickly, beaming. Her hair was slicked back from her forehead, and droplets glistened on her cheeks. Teo brushed them away with his thumb.

"I love you, Anastasia of Edgeton."

She returned his smile with a radiant one of her own. "I love you back, my Captain."

On the distant horizon a thunderclap rumbled, but the two swimmers paid it no mind.

✦　✦　✦

Dawn had not yet come to Chiveis, but the sky had lost some of its deep blackness. Far above the mountains, the morning star shone brightly, glittering like a diamond. The High Priestess stared at it for a moment, then uttered an oath and stepped through a door into the bitter predawn cold.

The giant man called the Iron Shield accompanied her, along with a gaggle of eunuch priests wearing backpacks. The party had ridden in wagons for several hours up a long, dark tunnel. At last they reached the terminus. The tunnel's exit opened onto an icy landscape at the top of the world.

Though it was late summer, the lofty elevation made heavy garments necessary. The High Priestess was swathed in a ceremonial ermine cloak, and she wore black woolen leggings instead of a long gown. She needed freedom of movement for the climb ahead.

"We are truly in the halls of the gods," the Iron Shield observed, looking around at the jagged peaks. His command of the Chiveisian speech was rough, but the High Priestess was impressed he knew it at all. As a lore-keeper of the Pact, the dark stranger had made it his business to learn the rudiments of the language for such an occasion as this. He had recently arrived in Chiveis after a month of travel from his base in Roma. Though the presence of an outsider from the Beyond drew immediate concern from the Chiveisian army and stirred up no small frenzy among the common folk, the High Priestess had readily admitted the foreigner into her inner circle. She recognized at once the dark forces that empowered him. The Iron Shield would service her in many ways.

"Indeed we stand in an exalted place," she said to the fur-clad warrior, "and yet Astrebril the Great shines down on us from above." The High Priestess motioned toward a snow slope behind her. "Come. Let us ascend."

The priestess and her followers trudged up the incline with the aid of a guide rope, then climbed hand over hand up a rocky knob. By the time they reached the silver-domed building on the summit, a pale glow had begun to edge the eastern peaks. In every direction, mountains thrust their snowy heads into the sky. A sinuous glacier wound its way through them like a white serpent with black stripes on its back.

Breathing hard in the thin air, the High Priestess entered the building and ascended to the dome. The eunuchs scurried around making their equipment ready. Long ago a telescope mirror had been discovered here and was now safely hidden in her temple. Today the dome was used for a much different purpose than studying the stars.

"Soon you shall see the awesome power of the Beautiful One," the priestess said to the Iron Shield. "This is the power that makes my subjects fear me and obey."

The effeminate priests removed a tarp from an opening in the dome. They dropped a round ball into a metal tube and aimed it through the aperture. After lighting a fuse they shrank back, though the High Priestess did not move. The string sizzled and sparked.

WHOOMPH!

A flash of light and a piercing whistle indicated the missile was away. For a moment everything was utterly silent.

And then . . .

A deafening boom shattered the morning stillness, its reverberations echoing off every peak. Blood-red sparks exploded outward, trickling down the morning sky.

The High Priestess spread her arms toward the heavens. "Astrebril's fire strikes terror in the hearts of men. It wreaks destruction upon whomever it touches."

"It is truly beautiful," the dark warrior agreed.

Five more explosions ripped the sky before the High Priestess signaled for her eunuchs to stop. "Enough," she commanded. "Leave us now." The men gathered their backpacks and exited.

The High Priestess slipped her fingernail behind a strand of her dark hair and brushed it from her forehead. Only the Iron Shield was with her in the small room. She liked how he looked as he faced her: tall, wide-shouldered, proud, erect. His complexion was swarthy, and his yellow glass eye gave him a feral appearance. He was a warrior like none she had ever met—except perhaps the army captain who served the damnable god Deu.

How did Captain Teofil survive his exile? And what trouble is he up to now, along with his impudent woman, Anastasia? Someday the High Priestess would find out. Astrebril had decreed they would meet again.

The Iron Shield spoke aloud the things that were on both of their minds. "The wider world is changing, my queen. Power is shifting. Ideas that should not be uttered are spreading here and there."

Hot fury blazed in the priestess's soul. She knew the report was true. Yet she also believed the Iron Shield could help put things right. "The Enemy has empowered a certain warrior," she said. "You know the man of whom I speak."

"Yes. I have met him in combat. And we must not forget the woman at his side. She has power too, though of a different sort."

"I want them both dead! They are spreading heresy across the land. And they have discovered the secret of Astrebril's fire. That is an art only I should know! Teofil and Anastasia must be silenced. Can you do this?"

"Yes, we can," replied the Iron Shield in a voice that resounded from deep within his chest.

The High Priestess's heartbeat quickened. *Excellent! The man is filled with a legion! He will be very potent.* She approached her new ally. "Listen to me, warrior. I must have more brimstone. And salt-stone. And iron would be useful too. But especially brimstone. I cannot get enough in Chiveis. My needs have grown. I have my eye on a new prize—a foreign one."

"And what is that, my queen?"

"The same prize obtained by the glorious Jonluc Beaumont many years ago. The Kingdom of Jineve."

"Ah! I passed through that land coming here. It is wealthy but weak. The kingdom has . . . " The Iron Shield sought the right word, then made a chopping motion as if with a pickax. "Digging, for iron?"

"Mines."

"Yes. They have mines with much iron. And they have salt-stone."

"I suspected it. What of brimstone?"

"Not in Jineve. However . . . " The Iron Shield paused, staring at the priestess. His right eye was a lump of pale yellow glass, slit with a black pupil like a cat's. "I know of a source."

The High Priestess arched her eyebrows.

"Across the sea, very far to the south, lies an island called Sessalay with a fire mountain upon it. Brimstone is found in abundance there."

"I want it. Bring it to me."

"It is a useless yellow rock."

"So it would seem. But when the dark arts are applied to it, the rock can yield the deadly fire you have just witnessed—and worse."

The Iron Shield shook his head. "I cannot imagine a more fearsome power than those thunderous blasts."

"Imagine a vapor that tortures and kills whomever it touches."

"Brimstone can do that?"

"Indeed. You must bring it to me from Sessalay in great quantities."

"The island is run by a criminal gang called the Clan. The boss may not allow it."

"The Clansmen signed the Pact, did they not?"

"Yes."

"They know better than to trifle with the power of Astrebril. But in case they have forgotten, show them this." The High Priestess reached into her garment and produced the glass vial she carried as an amulet. Seeing her action, the Iron Shield produced a vial of his own. A reddish-brown substance clung to each bottle's interior—the blood of an unholy alliance forged centuries ago.

"I will bring you the brimstone," the Iron Shield vowed. "And I will destroy the heretics from this earth."

"If you accomplish this task I shall grant whatever you desire."

The Iron Shield offered a sly grin. "You should be aware, my queen: my desire is not small."

"That is exactly as I wish."

The two servants of darkness smiled as they approached one another. Reaching out, they clasped hands. Then, to seal their purposes as one, they raised their bloody vials to the light of Astrebril's dawn.

◆ ◆ ◆

Laughter and wine flowed freely as the two young couples relaxed over an elegant Roman meal. Ana felt pretty, having put on makeup, a nice gown, and the amethyst earrings Teo liked so much. He wore a high-collared doublet in the latest aristocratic style. Ana's closest friend, Vanita Labella, sat across the table from Marco, a handsome businessman with a black goatee. *Businessman* was what Vanita insisted on calling Marco now. It wouldn't do to call him a pirate or a scoundrel or a rogue, though he was those things too—and Ana knew Vanita secretly liked it.

"More wine?" Marco refilled Vanita's glass before she could answer.

"I hope you're not trying to take advantage of me," she joked. "I'm not like that anymore."

Marco grinned. "So what are you saying? Christiani girls can't enjoy the fruit of the vine?"

Ana noted the conversation's interesting turn. She studied her friend's face, waiting for the answer.

"What makes you think I'm Christiani?" Vanita asked. "I've never said that."

"I just assumed it. You are, aren't you?"

Vanita had once mocked Iesus, the Pierced One, as foolish and repugnant. Even so, Ana had continued to bear witness to her faith, until Vanita betrayed her into the hands of murderers. That awful memory clouded Ana's mind for a moment, but she quickly reminded herself how Deu had displayed his forgiving grace. Vanita had repented deeply of her traitorous deed, even shaving her head as a sign of contrition. Now she wore her blonde hair in a long bob, so unlike the thick tresses she used to toss about her shoulders to catch men's eyes. As far as Vanita was concerned, her life as the spoiled daughter of an Ulmbartian duke was over. She claimed to be a new person, and Ana accepted that for what it was. Yet now Vanita seemed ready to go further.

"You know what?" she said after a long pause. "It's true. I am Christiani. I believe in Deu, or Deus as they call him around here. How could you deny him after what we just experienced?"

"I didn't say I deny him."

Teo leaned forward, elbows on the table. "Do you believe in him, Marco?"

"I believe in what the Christiani are trying to do in the world. I support them. I support all of you—truly! But religion just isn't for me."

Vanita touched Marco's arm. "Weren't you moved by the things that happened this summer? If our victory at the basilica didn't give you reason to believe, what will?"

It had indeed been an amazing summer. Ana could scarcely comprehend the dramatic events that had swirled around Roma in recent weeks. The Christiani had won a great battle against their persecutors. Teo and Marco had constructed a bomb to fend off an attack from mercenaries hired to destroy the Universal Communion. Though the bomb failed, Deu triumphed nonetheless.

"I guess I'll believe in Deu whenever he's ready for me to believe," Marco answered cryptically. His grin was disarming as he dropped his napkin on the table. "Come on, everyone. Let's go for a walk. The basilica is beautiful by night. On that we can all agree."

The foursome left the restaurant and strolled through the torch-lit Roman streets until they came to a promenade that led toward the basilica of the Universal Communion. As Ana approached the great building she was reminded of the first time she came here with Teo. Back then the wicked Exterminati fiercely oppressed the Christiani. Although that society of assassins hadn't disappeared altogether, their power was greatly diminished when they lost the battle in the basilica's square.

In a nearby piazza a soloist began to sing a madrigal, accompanied by a lute. "Let's go listen to it," Marco suggested.

"You two go ahead," Ana replied. "I'd rather enjoy the quiet right here."

Vanita's glance signaled she understood Ana's desire to be alone with Teo in the final days before he left for his mission. "Alright, sweetie," she said agreeably. "Have a lovely evening." Vanita followed Marco down a quaint alleyway toward the piazza, leaving Teo and Ana alone.

Ana stood still for a long time, inhaling the night air as she gazed across the open space encompassed by two curved colonnades. Moonlight gleamed on the pavement, turning the stones pale white. "Deu gave us a great victory here," she remarked.

"I know. Let's never forget it."

The pair strolled up one of the arcades, its columns looming like stone trees. Suddenly Teo slid his arm around Ana's waist and tugged her into the shadows. At first she thought he was being amorous, but his urgent whisper told her otherwise.

"See those men over there?"

Ana nodded.

"They're Clansmen."

"How do you know?"

"Something about their clothes, their build, the way they move. Marco pointed them out to me."

Ana gripped Teo's sleeve. "They're coming this way. Let's get out of here."

"Better to stay in the shadows. Hold still and we'll watch."

Ana's heartbeat accelerated as the men approached. They stopped at a dark spot in the plaza's cobbled surface.

"What are they looking at?" she whispered.

"It's the crater where I set off our weapon."

The two Clansmen rooted around in the depression in the pavement. Though their voices were muffled, Ana caught a few words as they argued. Finally one of the men uttered a cry of triumph. He held up a jagged object that glinted in the moonlight.

A shard of the bomb, Ana realized.

The man with the shard pulled out his knife. He scraped a substance from the metal fragment onto a paper held by the other man. The paper was then curled, and its contents were funneled into a bottle.

"What are they doing?"

Teo grimaced and shook his head. "Looks like they're interested in the explosive powder."

"Why would the Clan want that?"

"I don't know. But I can guarantee you they wouldn't use it for good."

Teo craned his neck to see better. The movement caused a pigeon to burst from the colonnade in a noisy flutter of feathers and wings.

"Who's that?" shouted one of the Clansmen. He and his comrade began to hurry over.

"Teo!" Ana hissed. "Kiss me—quick!"

"What?"

She slipped her arms around him. "Kiss me!"

Discerning her ruse, Teo obliged as the two Clansmen drew near.

"Hey! Have you been watching us?" one demanded.

Teo turned from Ana's embrace. "No. I was just looking for a place to be alone with my girl."

One of the Clansmen caught Ana by the arm. "Pretty little thing," he sneered.

Teo tensed, but Ana shot him a firm glance and a tiny shake of her head. Having seen him in battle she knew he could put these two run-of-the mill thugs on the ground before they knew what hit them. Yet she preferred to avoid confrontation.

"We didn't mean to disturb you gentlemen," she said, shaking her arm free.

The two Clansmen took a closer look at Teo. Something about his steely gaze made them shrink back. One of the men licked his lips, while the other flicked his hand dismissively. "Get out of here, *innamorati*," he snapped.

Teo offered Ana his elbow, and she took it gladly. *I think I'll steer clear of the Clan from now on*, she thought as she let Teo escort her away.

◆　◆　◆

The Papa sat under a shady olive tree in the gardens behind the basilica. It was a gnarled old tree that must have stood there in Ancient times before the Great Destruction. The Papa liked to think that Christiani from centuries gone by had enjoyed the tree as well.

Times were good for the Universal Communion at Roma. The Papa's grateful prayers ascended to Deus, whose recent blessings had been abundant. Enemies had been defeated. Captives had been released. New opportunities had opened up. And best of all, the second Testament of Deus's Holy Book had been recovered after forty years of searching. The Papa expected to see the first printed copy shortly.

A papal aide arrived, escorting two men. One was Ambrosius, the Overseer of a lost city far to the north. He bore a ragged scar across his forehead from a self-inflicted wound that signaled his solidarity with the broken yet beloved people under his pastoral care. The other man was named Sol, a white-haired scholar from the land called Ulmbartia. Sol's main task over the past six weeks had been to transcribe an official Latin text of the New Testament. The text came from a remarkable source: the incredible memory of Liber, a man whose mental faculties were feeble in every other way. No one had expected Deus to demonstrate his power through such a weak vessel. Blessed with this new text from the vault of Liber's mind, the Overseer had supervised the team of monks who translated it from Sol's Latin version into Talyano. The two languages were quite similar.

"Your Holiness, I believe you know your guests," the aide said, bowing. "I will leave them with you."

"Thank you." The Papa rose from his bench and welcomed Sol and the Overseer, receiving a brotherly greeting in return. "I see you come bearing a gift," he said.

"Indeed we do."

The Overseer held out a carved wooden box, and as he did, the Papa couldn't help but notice his maimed left hand. Ambrosius's fingernails had been ripped out under torture for his faith. *A steadfast confessor*, the Papa thought.

He lifted the box's lid and saw a book inside. "Marvelous!" he exclaimed as he removed the beautiful volume from its case. It had been printed on a press—a skill retained from ancient times. The Papa opened the calfskin cover and leafed through the pages. The *verso* on the left contained the Latin text of the New Testament in an elegant Roman typeface, while the facing *recto* was a translation into Talyano.

"This first edition is for you, Your Holiness," the Overseer said. "It is to be your personal copy for study, meditation, and preaching."

"I will treasure it! All praise be to Deus." The three men paused for a moment in recognition of the sacred gift that had returned to the world.

The Papa turned toward Sol. "What news from the convent at Lido di Ostia, brother?"

"As you can see, I have been very busy there with my transcription work," answered the old man with the long white hair. "I spent many hours listening to Liber chant. The Old Words are recorded in his head just as if a scribe had written them down."

"The ways of the Almighty never cease to amaze me," the Papa remarked. Forty years ago he had heard rumors of a boy with such a prodigious memory, though he never expected to meet him.

"I have also been working on a version in the speech of the Chiveisi," Sol continued. "I have some knowledge of that tongue. However, Teofil is responsible for the bulk of the labor on that project."

"Ah, yes—our brave hero Teofil is also a linguist. Some men are doubly blessed."

"And I'm grateful for it," the Overseer said as he held up his mangled hand. "It was Teofil who came to me in the dungeon and helped me escape."

"He disobeyed my orders in that matter, though I now see it was the will of Deus." The Papa looked at Sol. "What do you hear from our brother Teofil? Do you know if he intends to carry out the mission I assigned him?"

Sol nodded. "Yes, Your Holiness. He asked me to tell you he is pleased to accept the responsibility."

"Excellent! I am more than a little desirous of establishing contact with the Knights of the Cross at Marsay. And there may be other people in the vicinity who wish to hear the good news of Deus and his son."

"Teofil is just the man for that sort of thing," Sol agreed. "Harrowing adventures in faraway lands seem to be his specialty."

"Is our sister Anastasia willing to relinquish his company for so long a time? Teofil's task will occupy him until next spring. The two of them are bound together, so her cooperation is essential."

Sol cleared his throat. "Actually . . . "

The Papa shot Sol a sharp look. "The lady is obstructing?"

"No, Your Holiness! Not at all! Anastasia is a righteous woman who understands the high calling of Deus."

"What then?"

"Teofil believes he can fulfill his mission at Marsay this fall. He hopes to return here before the stormy season sets in."

The Papa let out an exasperated sigh. Deus had gifted Teofil in extraordinary ways, yet as was often the case with such men, he had a mind of his own. Certainly he was not an easy sheep to tend within the flock. "Teofil will have to learn that the plans of Deus cannot be circumvented for any reason—not for the storms of the sea, nor the much more turbulent storms of the heart."

"He's a good man," Sol said. "He will learn."

The Overseer broke into the conversation. "Holy Father, I would ask you a question if I may." Receiving a nod from the Papa, he continued. "What *exactly* is the message you intend to send to Marsay? We have received this great gift"—the Overseer inclined his head toward the new book—"yet have you digested all its teachings? Have you discerned the message we should preach far and wide?"

The Papa stared into the distance, remaining silent for so long the two visitors began to shift uncomfortably. The Overseer was right: the book needed to be studied in depth to determine its central message. Although the Papa was normally a confident man, he felt inadequate to such a great task. What if he misinterpreted the text? What if he missed a vital point? It would be a grave mistake to send out Teofil—or anyone else, for that matter—preaching a false gospel.

The sun beat down on the little garden, so the Papa returned to the shade of the gnarled olive tree as he wrestled with his problem. *How can I make certain I don't err?* A gentle breeze rustled the waxy leaves, cooling his face as it passed. Suddenly a flash of insight struck him. It was a grand idea, one that captured the Papa's imagination the moment he thought of it. He knew it could only be from Deus. Excited, he turned toward Sol and the Overseer.

"I know precisely what we need," he announced. "It must happen within a fortnight."

"Would you share your intentions with us?" the Overseer asked.

The Papa tipped his head back and laughed. "Of course! You two will be involved in the planning. Letters must be drafted. Hospitality must be arranged. The Painted Chapel must be readied. There is much to do!"

"For what, Your Holiness?"

The Papa grinned at his two visitors, amused by their wide-eyed expressions as they leaned toward him. "My friends," he said, "I have decided to call the First Council of Roma."

◆　◆　◆

The doe's ears twitched, then the animal stepped clear of the forest thicket. After a few paces it moved from a rear shot to quartering away. The time was now.

Stratetix released the sinew bowstring and let the arrow whisper from his fingers. The shot entered behind the foreleg, exactly where he intended. Though the doe jumped and ran, the broadhead did its work, and soon the animal was down. Stratetix and Shaphan went to retrieve their kill.

"I call the backstraps," Shaphan said, smiling.

"You can have them. Just save the liver for me."

Stratetix watched the olive-skinned Chiveisian youth wield the skinning knife. At times his movements were awkward. Stratetix offered a few pointers, having field-dressed more deer in his life than he could recall. He thought of Shaphan almost like a son-in-law, since the young man was married to his niece, Lina.

But not to my daughter. I've lost Anastasia.

Stratetix shook his head. Such morbid thoughts plagued him often.

The two men carried the doe on a pole for a league or two. When the smell of woodsmoke reached Stratetix's nose he knew he was nearing his campsite. Caution settled onto him now, for he was not actually in the woods to hunt, but to commit a capital crime.

Lina, a pretty girl with white-blonde curls, rose from the fire. Her mother, Rosetta, was there too, along with a third woman, Stratetix's beloved Helena.

"Have you seen anyone?" he asked his wife.

"No, my love, and there are no tracks along the trail but our own."

Stratetix nodded. The rest of the group looked at him expectantly. He glanced around at the trees, which caused everyone else to do the same. "Check the trail one more time, Shaphan."

The man with the dark wavy hair left the campfire but soon returned. "No sign of anyone, sir." He was a respectful youth who had started calling Stratetix "sir" after he married Lina.

"Very well. Let us begin." Stratetix reached into a cavity in the trunk of a hollow oak. His hand closed on a leather satchel wrapped in oilskins. He untied the thongs and opened the bundle. Inside were scrolls.

"Today we will read from the book of Hymns. I have chosen the second song in the book for our consideration."

"Good choice," Shaphan said. "It was one of the last hymns Captain Teofil translated before . . . "

Though Shaphan's voice trailed off, Stratetix knew everyone in the little group was finishing the sentence in their minds: *before Teofil and Anastasia left Chiveis forever.*

No, Deu! Not forever! I will trust in you!

Stratetix unrolled the scroll. In hushed tones he began to read:

Why this tumult among the nations,
These vain thoughts among the peoples?
Why do the kings of the earth raise themselves up,
And the princes join forces with them,
Against the Eternal One and against his anointed?
"Let us break their links,
Let us free ourselves from their chains!"
The one who sits in sky laughs.
The Lord mocks them.
Then he speaks to them in his anger,
He terrifies them in his rage.
"It is I who have anointed my king on Sion, my holy mountain!"

Stratetix paused. A squirrel skittered along a branch above, and bumblebees buzzed among the wildflowers. "Does anyone have an observation about the hymn so far?"

"The rulers of the earth are often arrogant," Shaphan said. "They join together to oppose Deu. Just like we see here in Chiveis. King Piair and the High Priestess commit great evil!"

Shaphan's emphatic assertion drew a few gasps. Lina put her hand on her husband's arm. "Don't say such things out loud, Shaphan," she urged.

"Why not? It's true, isn't it?"

"It is true," Rosetta agreed. "But Lina is right. Prudence is required."

Shaphan scoffed and folded his arms across his chest with a frown.

Beckoning the little group closer, Stratetix asked, "What else do you observe about this text? Speak your mind, yet do so quietly."

"The Lord Deu is not threatened by the kings of men," Helena said. "He sits in heaven and laughs at their pitiful attempts to rebel against him. We should remember that. Though we may feel the thumb of oppression bearing down on us, our God is not threatened by earthly rulers."

The listeners fell silent as each considered Helena's words. Like everyone in Chiveis, they could identify with her remarks about oppression. The king had become a tyrant, imposing harsh laws and restricting civil rights. Heavy taxes had been levied to fund the official cult of Astrebril and the three lesser gods. The citizens of the realm cowered in fear before the Royal Guardsmen who used to be their protectors.

"I have a question," Lina ventured. "Who is the anointed king on the mountain? Is it King David, who wrote some of the hymns?"

"I wondered that myself," Stratetix said. "I haven't read of any greater king than him in the Sacred Writing."

"We only have a small portion of it," Shaphan observed.

"Yes. Perhaps the king is another man described elsewhere in the Sacred Writing. We'll never know unless somehow Ana . . . "

Stratetix broke off, unable to endure his grief any longer. Helena intertwined her fingers with his, then lifted her face to the sky. "Let us seek divine aid," she said. Everyone joined hands as Helena prayed that Chiveis might experience a glorious return—of loved ones, of the Sacred Writing, and of Almighty Deu himself.

Helena was still speaking when Shaphan hissed, "Shh! Someone's coming!"

Stratetix's heart leaped into his throat. He heard the hoofbeats a moment after Shaphan's warning. "Get to your places—quickly!"

He dashed to the hollow tree and stuffed the satchel inside, then hurled a handful of dried leaves on top of it. Behind him, horses turned off the main trail and broke through the underbrush into the clearing.

"What's going on here?" demanded one of the riders. He wore the uniform of the Royal Guard. His insignia indicated he belonged to the Second Regiment.

"Hunting, sir," Stratetix said, sweeping his arm toward the women. They sat near the fire, their hands smeared with blood. Lina held up the skinning knife.

The guardsman prodded his horse forward. "Why are you peasants gathered out here in the woods?"

"When's the last time you saw deer roaming around Edgeton?" Shaphan shot back. Stratetix winced at his tone.

The soldier stared at Shaphan with narrowed eyes, then dismounted and strode over to the youth. His hand was on his sword's hilt. Spurs jangled on his boots. "So, farm boy! You think you're ready to take me on?"

Shaphan was about to speak when Helena approached the pair. "Sir, our friend simply meant to say we've come to the forest to hunt. It's common enough among the rural folk. We take a deer on a nice summer's day, broil some meat, enjoy some ale, and take home the rest for later."

The guardsman eyed her suspiciously.

"Would you like a few steaks?" Lina called from across the clearing. She pointed toward the carcass with her knife.

"Gimme the liver instead," the soldier answered. "And some ale."

Lina wrapped the meat in a cloth and brought it to the man along with a gourd bottle. The man uncorked the bottle and guzzled from it, then pitched it to his companion, who finished it off and dropped it on the ground.

"You say you're from Edgeton?" the first soldier asked.

Stratetix nodded. "My wife and I are. The others live in Vingin."

"Maybe you're outlaws? Robbers?"

"We'd be rather poor robbers," Stratetix said, smiling with his hands spread. "We have no weapons but hunters' tools. And where's all our loot?"

Ach! What a stupid thing to say!

The guardsman glanced around. "I don't know. You tell me, robber! Where'd you hide your treasure?" Walking to the hollow oak tree, he reached inside the hole and began to feel around.

Stratetix swallowed. His heart thudded in his chest. *Protect us, mighty Deu!*

The soldier removed a tuft of leaves and twigs. He picked out an acorn and flicked it at Stratetix. "A peasant's treasure," he said with a sneer on his face. "Grind it into flour and bake yourself a cake." He stalked off and mounted his horse.

"Don't make a habit of hiding in the woods," one of the men ordered as they turned to go. "Her Eminence the High Priestess might think you're plotting rebellion."

The little group in the forest watched the soldiers leave.

"Maybe we are," Shaphan muttered under his breath.

❖　❖　❖

Sitting before a mirror, Ana brushed out her light amber hair, then pinned it high on her head in a classic style. A few months earlier it had been cut jagged at the nape of her neck, but now it had grown out, and she was glad for that. Her gown was unadorned, though not drab, and she wore just a little color on her cheeks. Glancing in the mirror again, she decided against any lipstick.

There was a knock on the door to her guest room at the Christiani basilica in Roma. "It's time," Teo called from the other side.

Ana answered the door and found Teo grinning at her: tall, rangy, and as handsome as ever. Somehow his dark hair managed to seem tousled and combed at the same time, as if he had run his fingers through it but was too manly to do much more than that. His tunic was a dark wine color, and his black boots were newly polished. Ana decided he looked exactly like what he was: a rugged man of the wilderness who had cleaned up for a formal event.

"I brought you this," Teo said, holding out a delicate white rose. "I'm not sure why. I just saw it in a market and thought of you."

"It's lovely, Teo." She threaded the rose blossom in her hair, then took his arm. "Let's go."

In the hallway they met a warder, who escorted them to the Painted Chapel adjacent to the Christiani basilica. Other dignitaries and their attendants had gathered outside the chapel as well. Ana spotted a heavy-set man with a shaggy beard.

"Psst! Liber," she whispered, waving at him with bended fingers.

The man grinned from ear to ear and waved back energetically. "Hi, Stasia!" he called. Though a few people glanced at the feeble-minded giant, he didn't seem to notice.

A herald in formal livery rang a handbell to quiet the crowd. "Attention, ladies and gentlemen! Welcome to the First Council of Roma! You are hereby summoned into the presence of the Holy Father of the Universal Communion of the Christiani. You may now proceed to your seats."

Two dark-paneled doors swung open. The sonorous chanting of monks wafted from the chapel, accompanied by harpists. One by one the assembled dignitaries marched through the door. Most were Knights of the Cross, aristocratic men from the region around Roma who supported the Christiani faith. Yet some of the delegates were from other lands as well. The elderly teacher Sol was present, along with Vanita Labella, together representing the kingdom of Ulmbartia. The Overseer from the Forbidden Zone was escorted into the chapel by his assistant, Brother Toni. A newly freed slave, now clothed in elegant attire instead of rags, represented far-off Marsay. Even Liber had a role: not only was he honored as the man whose memory had preserved the New Testament, he also represented the Beloved—those people whose bodies or minds were frail, but whose gentle hearts were well loved by their Creator.

Teo and Ana entered last, for they represented the most distant land of all: Chiveis, a mountain kingdom unknown to any of the other council members. Ana marveled at the chapel's elaborate architecture. The floor was decorated with a series of concentric rings, while the walls and ceiling bore a stunning array of painted images. On the far wall, a beardless Iesus stood out against a blue backdrop. His arm was raised in judgment, while sinners, saints, angels, and demons swirled around him. The chanting monks gave the whole place an otherworldly feel as Ana proceeded down the central aisle. The lesser attendees sat in benches on either side, but Ana followed Teo through an altar screen to an area where high-backed chairs had been arranged in a circle. At the head of the circle, the Papa sat on a small cathedra that was, according to his custom, lower than all the other seats. The herald motioned toward the last remaining chair. When Ana sat down in it, the monks' chanting ceased. Their tones echoed away as a solemn hush descended on the hall.

The Papa stood up and spread his arms. "Brothers and sisters, I welcome you in the name of Deus and his son, Iesus Christus! Truly you have come to this place at a propitious time, and for a momentous occasion." The Papa walked in a full circle, gazing at each guest, then approached a table in the midst of them all. A beautiful chest was upon it. He reached inside and retrieved a leather-bound book, which he placed on a nearby pulpit. Flipping it open he said, "I can think of no better way to begin the First Council of Roma than by hearing from our God." Nods of agreement and even a few hurrahs erupted from the gathered dignitaries.

Lectors entered the chapel then, men and women trained to read in their clear, sweet voices. The Papa declared the entire New Testament would be read aloud to the gathered council. Short breaks were to be given for refreshments, and a light luncheon would be served at noon each day. Quills and parchments for note-taking were supplied to the participants, many of whom were hearing the words of Deu for the first time.

For two days the lectors read while the delegates listened. Ana was one of the privileged few who had already read the entire New Testament. She hadn't wanted to wait for the printed version being prepared for the Chiveisi, so she devoured Teo's translations as quickly as they came from his hand. Yet now as she heard the Sacred Writing read all at once, its words struck her afresh with their mystic power and inner beauty. The four biographies of Iesus Christus and the writings of his faithful followers recounted a divine story that the world desperately needed. For centuries the Sacred Writing had lain dormant. Now it was bursting forth once more.

On the morning of the third day the council members arrived with a heightened sense of expectation. The book had been read aloud from start to finish. What did the leader of the Christiani have planned?

"Greetings to you this hot summer morning," the Papa said after the delegates had filed into the Painted Chapel. "We have heard from Deus these past two days. Now it is our turn to speak."

The Papa explained that the purpose of the council was to determine the contours of the Christiani message. Though many topics would be discussed, the goal was to distill an essential proclamation. Later, theologians with gifted minds could spend fruitful hours exploring the details. Surely the Holy Book deserved a thorough examination. Yet here at the outset, the book's basic ideas had to be agreed upon by all.

Several participants wanted the council to produce a creed that could be memorized by the faithful. While this idea had its advocates, others thought a creed could become rote and meaningless. Ana noticed that Teo, who had remained silent during the initial discussion, now seemed to have something to say. At last he spoke up.

"My friends, I agree the council must produce a statement with fixed wording that can be memorized. However, if we make our statement too rigid it will not be flexible enough to meet the various circumstances that may arise. We need something between a formal creed and a blank page."

As Teo spoke with scholarly insight, the delegates' faces grew thoughtful. "I suggest we define a list of important words," he said. "Consider the nature of words. They are fixed in their meaning, yet only to a certain degree. Take the word *boat*, for example. It can mean a sorry little rowboat with holes in it, or it can refer to a great merchant ship. Boats come in all shapes and sizes. I propose we identify some key words from the scriptures. These would be our fixed points of consensus. Yet as we go forth proclaiming the message of Deus, the words could be explained with different nuances as the occasion may demand."

The council liked the idea. "How many words shall we choose, Teofil of Chiveis?" the Overseer called.

Teo wasn't sure. "What do you suggest, friends?"

Some delegates said seven, others ten, and a few even wanted forty. No one seemed to agree.

Off to the side, Liber fidgeted in his chair. Ana could see he had an idea but was afraid to speak his mind before such a prestigious and intellectual crowd. "Excuse me," she said, rising from her seat. "I believe we should consider the wisdom of the Beloved." Ana swept her hand toward Liber.

The big man glanced nervously around the room but finally found his voice. "This is the story Stasia told me," he announced. "Long ago the Father in the Sky chose twelve brothers to be his people. But they disobeyed. Then Iesus came. And what did he do? He picked twelve men to follow him. So I say we should have twelve words." Liber crossed his arms over his chest, nodded emphatically, and fell silent.

"Twelve words it shall be," the Papa declared.

Yet the decision to choose the Twelve Words only opened the door to more debate. For nearly a week the delegates searched the Sacred Writing as they sought to determine the essence of the Christiani message. Some council members highlighted the moral lifestyle required of Deus's followers, while others emphasized social action on behalf of the oppressed. A third group wanted to focus on the life, death, and glorious rising of Iesus Christus. Ana and Teo felt drawn to this view, yet they could not deny the importance of the other topics.

At last the council began to choose specific words. One by one they fell into place until eleven had been chosen. Only one word remained unselected. Ana wrote the words on her parchment with a few notes of clarification:

CREATION—everything made by Deu
SIN—Adam and all his children rebelled
SACRIFICE—animal blood covered the sins of Israël
IESUS CHRISTUS—his sacrifice conquered death
FAITH—all must repent, believe
WASHING—the sacred water binds us to Iesus
HOLINESS—Christiani must live righteously
REMEMBRANCE—in the Meal, we share in Iesus's sacrifice
LOVE—Deu gave it to us; we must give it to others
PROCLAMATION—the Christiani message is for all who will hear it
HOPE—never despair, Iesus will return and make things right

Having put eleven words in place, the council seemed close to finishing its task, but the twelfth word proved difficult. Ana began to grow frustrated as the productive exchange descended into wrangling. Finally she had had enough.

"Brothers and sisters," she said, "throughout this council we have followed the leading of Deus. We have prayed for his guidance. Now I believe we need to follow his will yet again."

Ana could tell the delegates thought she was going to propose another word to add to the debate, but that wasn't what she had in mind. "I suggest we call the council to a close. We have chosen eleven words. No doubt there is a twelfth, for it is a sacred number, as our brother Liber has reminded us. Yet should we demand to know all things? Does almighty Deus owe us an answer right now? We have our eleven words. That is enough for the moment, is it not? Let us commit the matter to prayer. Perhaps in the timing of the Eternal One, he will lead us to the final word."

As Ana sat down she could see her idea would prevail. It made sense to the other delegates, who had accomplished so much good work already. They voted to adjourn—but to Ana's surprise, Teo abstained from the vote.

The following morning she made a point of going early to Teo's guest room at the basilica. She brought breakfast on a tray: soft-boiled eggs, hot porridge with honey, and thin ale. He answered her knock, still a little groggy from sleep.

She smiled at him. "Something to eat?"

"Yeah, sounds good. Come in."

He closed the door behind her, and they took seats at a table, making awkward small talk as they ate. At last Ana broached the subject she had come to discuss. "Are you mad at me about the council?"

Teo paused, setting down his spoonful of porridge. "Not really. I just didn't want to give up."

"Why?"

"Leaving a task unfinished isn't my way of doing things. It feels like quitting. We shouldn't shrink back when things get difficult."

Ana thought of all the dangers she had faced at Teo's side. On more than one occasion she had saved his life. *How can he call me a quitter? Of all people, he should know I don't quit when things get difficult!*

"I don't think we were quitting," she said.

"It felt like it. We decided to identify twelve words. That's what we should have done. No loose ends."

"Maybe they're not loose ends."

"What are they then?"

"Just things we don't know yet. A mystery we have to live with for a time."

"It's hard to carry out a task when you leave unfinished business like that."

"Perhaps Deu isn't as worried about accomplishing tasks as you are." Ana intended her words to be a challenge, and she didn't back down.

Teo cleared his throat and gazed out the window. Ana waited until he turned back to her. "Deu expects us to take action," he said, "and right now my action is to go to Marsay. The ship has arrived in port. I'm supposed to leave tomorrow."

Ana felt her heart jump. Deu had given Teo a mission, and she supported it. Yet she didn't want him to depart with tension hanging between them.

"I hope you know I'm behind you," she said. "I want you to do what the Papa has asked. I want you to do it well—whatever it takes. And then I want you to . . . come back to me." Ana paused, her voice thick with emotion. "Don't ever leave me, Teo," she said softly.

His expression grew tender. He reached for her hand. The two lovers caught each other's eyes as slow smiles spread across their faces. Ana felt the tension drain away.

"I will return to you this fall," Teo vowed.

"And I'll be here waiting for you," Ana replied.

2

The Clan Boss believed there was no better time to be on the island of Sessalay than during *la vendemmia*, the annual grape harvest. Though the sun was still warm, it didn't blaze like it did in high summer. The peasants were happy, stomping the grapes with abandon. The plentiful food and drink meant dancing and feasting lasted long into the night. As the Clan Boss gazed across the orange groves and vineyards of his Sessalayan estate, he often liked to pretend he was nothing but a prosperous gentleman farmer. But then his worries would press in, reminding him he was actually the head of an international crime syndicate.

Things had been tumultuous for the Clan lately. The slave trade had been disrupted earlier in the summer by a revolt at the marble quarries on the mainland. Although that disaster primarily affected the society of assassins called the Exterminati, the disruption was felt by the Clan as well. Fortunately the excellent revenues from extortion, prostitution, and smuggling had offset the losses from the human trafficking division of the enterprise. The Clan Boss knew holy Mulciber must have been smiling on him this year.

A butler walked through the double glass doors onto the veranda where the boss was sitting in the sunshine. The crime lord had been hoping someone would show up soon with a drink, and to his delight the butler now handed him a glass of chilled marsala. Another glass remained on the tray. When the boss offered a quizzical glance, the servant said, "The district manager of Roma has come to see you with urgent news."

The boss huffed. "What kind of news? I've had far too much bad news out of Roma lately."

"He says this is good news."

"I'll hear him out. Bring him to me."

The butler went inside the villa and returned with the visitor. The man was expensively dressed like so many of the high-ranking Clansmen. *Good!* the boss thought. *Who says crime has to be uncivilized?*

After the appropriate greetings and formalities were exchanged, the district manager got straight down to business. Opening his satchel, he placed some vials and scraps of metal on a table. The boss had never seen anything like it.

"What kind of silliness is this?"

"I know it seems strange. But what you are looking at is the most destructive weapon I've ever seen. It's like a thunderstorm in a bottle. This stuff gouged a crater in a city pavement."

The boss raised his eyebrows. "One tiny bottle can do that?"

"I believe it was a more substantial quantity. Still, the same powder is contained in these vials."

"What is it?"

"I don't know. But whatever it is, we should have it."

The boss handed the district manager the glass of wine from the tray. "Tell me everything. Start at the beginning."

The district manager explained that a slave rebellion had taken place in Roma this summer. The rich aristocrat who headed the secret society of the Exterminati had been killed. His former bodyguard and chief lieutenant, a powerful warrior known as the Iron Shield, had disappeared. Now the strange cult of the Christiani was growing in influence.

"I know all that," the Clan Boss snapped. "Tell me about the powder."

"A foreign man and woman recently arrived in Roma. They aided the Christiani and the slave rebels by setting off an explosive weapon. When I heard about this I sent men to investigate. They found some metal shards in the crater, but more importantly they located the place where the weapon was manufactured. It was a remote corner of a Roman nobleman's estate."

"So what happened? Get on with it, man! I want the bottom line!"

The district manager nodded. "There was a lot of complicated equipment. Unfortunately, all the supplies had been removed. But we did find some of these." He held up a glass vial with a cork stopper.

"The powder?"

"Yes, though not much of it."

"Show me."

"I want to use it sparingly. I have a team of apothecaries trying to figure out what it's made of. But there should be enough for a demonstration."

The district manager set an empty pistachio shell on the table. He filled it with the powder, then fastened the two halves together with thread. After inserting a pine needle through a crack in the shell, he lit it and stepped back. The boss craned his neck toward the device, but the district manager pulled him to a safer distance.

Bang!

The nutshell exploded with a flash of light and a puff of smoke. The boss was so startled he dropped his wineglass, which shattered against the flagstones. He smelled a vaguely displeasing aroma as the white smoke dissipated.

"I want this!" he exclaimed.

"I knew you would. That's why I have the apothecaries working to determine the formula."

"No." The boss waved his hands dismissively. "The apothecaries are useless."

"But the formula . . . how will we discover it?"

The Clan Boss scowled at the district manager. "Think like a criminal, since that's what you claim to be."

"Um . . . we steal it?"

"Precisely."

"From who?"

"From the only people known to have it."

"The foreign man and woman?"

"Of course. Somehow they created a powerful and complex weapon. Obviously they learned it from somewhere. They must have a book of lore among their belongings." The boss gave his visitor a pained stare.

"I see," the district manager said, tapping his chin. "What would you have me do?"

"I think it's time the Clan paid these two foreigners a visit."

◆　◆　◆

Teo stood at the rail of Marco's *Midnight Glider* as it floated alongside the main pier of Roma's harbor. Normally the clipper ship's captain liked to anchor a short distance offshore in case a fast getaway became necessary. But Marco was becoming more respectable. He hadn't joined his men on their latest piracy voyage, and now the Papa had even hired him to make the trip to Marsay. Teo attributed this newfound respectability to Vanita's influence. Marco would do anything for her. *Well, almost anything.* He hadn't yet embraced the faith of the Christiani.

Surveying the crowd on the dock, Teo spotted the only woman at whom he cared to look twice. She carried a parcel wrapped in leather and twine under her arm. Teo met Ana at the top of the gangplank.

"Hello, gorgeous," he said, giving her a light kiss on the cheek.

"If I'm so gorgeous why are you leaving me?"

"Duty calls."

"No, Deu calls."

Teo chuckled at Ana's quip. "As always, you're right."

"Since when have you started admitting that, Captain?"

"Since I decided to sail away from you. I want you to remember me in a good light while I'm gone."

Ana gave Teo a playful *tsk*, then held up her parcel. "Where are your things? I have something to add to your pack."

The pair went below deck to the hold. "Marco tried to give me my own cabin," Teo said, "but I told him this little hammock is all I need." He stared at it for a moment, recalling the stormy night he had lain there and dreamed of Ana—or was it a vision? He was estranged from her then, and the dream of Ana calling out to him had spurred Teo to restore their relationship. A lot of unexpected things happened after that, things too traumatic to contemplate. Teo brushed the memories away. "What's in the package? I didn't think to get you anything."

"No need for that. It's you who's leaving. This is something for your trip." Ana handed him the parcel.

Teo untied the strings and unfolded the leather. The gift was a bear-skin cloak. Ana had made it for him long ago from the hide of the bear that attacked them at their first meeting. She had wounded the bear with arrows, then Teo killed it with his sword.

"Wow," he breathed, "it looks brand-new."

"It had gotten so ratty and dirty. I cleaned it up and repaired it."

Teo was a little puzzled that Ana would think he needed a heavy winter cloak for the trip. "It's great," he said, "but the climate is warm at Marsay."

"It's warm now," she agreed, "and it will be for a few more months. But after that . . . "

Teo frowned. "You want me to stay over the winter?"

"No, I don't *want* you to stay. But I release you to stay if necessary."

"I thought we were going to return to Chiveis! If I stay at Marsay everything will be delayed. All our plans will be thrown off."

"I'm okay with that."

"I'm not. What about 'redeeming the time'? There are tasks that need doing in Chiveis. We've wasted enough time out here in the Beyond."

Ana shook her head. "It hasn't been wasted. We discovered other believers in Deu—and we discovered the New Testament."

"All the more reason we should go home now that we have the true message."

"I agree we should go. But shouldn't we depend on Deu to determine the timing?"

"How do we know what timing he wants? It's not like he whispers in our ears."

"Maybe he does."

"Well, I've never heard it. I think Deu wants us to take action. If the doors close, we'll know it wasn't his will. Until then, we should act."

"But you *are* acting—you're going on the mission. I support that, Teo, you know I do. If you can accomplish what the Papa wants and return here this fall, I'll rejoice. But what if Deu has other plans? Be still and listen. You might hear his whisper, like you said."

Teo sighed. "I had this all figured out."

"You don't have to."

He glanced at Ana, irritated. "I don't have to what?"

"Figure everything out. What I mean is—"

"I know what you mean. You think I have to manage everything."

"No—"

"Look, somebody has to make plans or things never get accomplished. That's what I'm good at—planning. I set a goal, then strive with all my strength to achieve it. I don't stop until it's done."

"I understand," Ana soothed. "You're Captain Teofil, man of action."

Teo assumed Ana's words were an attempt to defuse the situation, yet they sounded to him like mocking. Stifling an angry response, he folded up the cloak and handed it to her. "It's a nice gift," he said more icily than he intended, "but I want you to keep it for me. I'll get it when I return here this fall."

Ana stared at him for a long moment. Finally she hurled the cloak onto the seaman's hammock, turned abruptly, and left the hold.

Teo stood with his hands on his hips, watching her go. *Good job, Teo. What a great way to say good-bye. How did things turn sour so quickly?*

He went up on deck and looked around for her. Sailors scurried back and forth, readying the ship for departure under Marco's watchful eye. Ana wasn't there.

At last the mooring lines were slipped free, and the gangplank was raised. Longshoremen pulled warps to tug the vessel so it could catch some wind and maneuver on its own. Marco came to the rail beside Teo.

"Ready for a grand adventure, *amico?*"

Teo turned to the handsome pirate, his closest friend. "It's hard to leave," he admitted.

Marco pointed. "Look there. Someone else feels the same."

Two women were on the dock. As Vanita waved her handkerchief at Marco, Ana stood next to her with a glum expression. The ship began to ease along the pier.

"Ana!" Teo shouted.

She didn't hear.

He called her name again. She looked up, her eyes wide.

"I love you," he mouthed to her.

Ana put her hand to her heart. "Me too," she mouthed back.

Suddenly she broke into a run. When she was alongside the ship she reached beneath her hair at the back of her neck and unfastened a pendant. She hurled it up, and Teo caught it above his head. It was Iesus Christus on his cross.

"May he bring you back to me," Ana called.

For a brief moment their eyes locked. Neither of them moved. Then, with a loud snap, the sails caught a gust and the ship began to turn away. Ana was quickly lost from view. Teo draped the pendant around his neck and tucked it in his jerkin.

"Ten weeks, Ana," he whispered across the water. "Just ten weeks."

✦ ✦ ✦

The luxurious coach rolled to a stop. "We have arrived, Your Eminence," the driver called down.

The High Priestess licked her lips and gazed out the window. The lonely cabin in the deep woods of Chiveis appeared deserted. It was a frontier outpost that guarded a narrow path between two hills. As an entry point into the kingdom, the path was normally watched by the Royal Guard, but tonight they had been reassigned. The High Priestess needed utmost secrecy for what she had in mind.

A decanter of wine sat in a rack on the coach's floorboard. The High Priestess removed the crystal stopper and poured herself a glass, sipping it slowly, savoring it. Her hand toyed with the iron collar around her neck. She knew that to make others wait would demonstrate her power over them. The crude outsiders could mill around in the forest a while longer. She would meet them when she was ready.

At last she stepped from the carriage. Her diaphanous robe flowed behind her as she crossed the clearing in front of the army cabin by the light of the driver's lantern. The man belonged to the Vulkainian Order, whose archpriest was responsible for obtaining precious brimstone. All the Vulkainians were fiercely loyal to the High Priestess, which made them excellent bodyguards even if they could never obtain as much brimstone as her insatiable appetite demanded.

The man with the lantern halted. "This is the boundary." He pointed to a spot where the wagon track that led to the cabin became an animal path in the wilderness.

"You're not frightened, are you?"

The Vulkainian shook his head. "No. But . . . "

"But what?"

"It's the Beyond."

"So it is," said the High Priestess as she stepped across the imaginary line between Chiveisian civilization and the terrors that loomed outside.

Men with torches waited down the path a short distance. The High Priestess approached them, then stopped short and turned to her assistant.

"Open the lantern," she said.

When he complied, the High Priestess used the flame to light a small grenade. She rolled it across the forest floor. Moments later it exploded with a loud report. The waiting outsiders yelped at the unexpected sound. They were still clutching each other and staring with wild eyes when the High Priestess stepped through the sulfurous fumes to greet them.

"Welcome to Chiveis, travelers," she intoned. "Which of you is the chief?"

It took several seconds for the men to compose themselves. They were true barbarians, swathed in greasy furs and even greasier beards. Eventually a tall man with rust-colored hair raised his hand in greeting. His pinky finger was missing. "I lead these men," he said in his vulgar dialect. "I am Prince Vlad the Nine-Fingered."

"Are you indeed? Your reputation has reached me, Vlad, though I imagined you to be a lesser man. Now that I see your virility I understand why the forest folk have made you their king."

"The gods favor me."

"No. It is the highest god who favors you."

"And who is he?"

"He is Astrebril the Great, lord of the gods you worship. I am his chosen queen."

The confident assertion made the men fall back. As they did, the High Priestess stepped into the space they vacated. Wisps of smoke clung to her, reeking of the underworld. She stared hard at Vlad, knowing her green eyes could weave a spell of lust and fear that few men could endure. When the barbarian prince broke off his gaze, the High Priestess knew he was defeated.

"Why have you called me here, queen of the high god?" he asked.

"I wish to renew an old alliance."

"We have long traded with the Chiveisi. Our brimstone for your steel. Is there something wrong with our arrangement?"

Smiling, the High Priestess came close to the prince. She noticed him swallow and shift his feet. "No, Vlad, I speak of a much older Pact."

The warrior did not answer, so the High Priestess reached into her neckline and withdrew a glass vial that dangled from a thong. When she held it up in the torchlight, several men among the outsiders let out a gasp. "The Pact of Beaumont," someone whispered in awe.

Vlad's eyes widened. "You wish to renew that ancient alliance between our peoples?"

"Yes. And I believe you know what will happen to those who disregard its invocation."

Though Vlad nodded, the High Priestess decided he could use a reminder. Closing her eyes, she raised her palm to the sky and said, "Behold! I see a vision of a blighted people. Their crops are withered and blasted. The udders of their cows dry up, and their swine are taken by the wolf and the bear. The wombs of the mothers are barren, and the fathers' manhood droops. Hunger and disease ravage the kingdom—a land of wailing and despair." The High Priestess popped her eyes open and drilled Vlad with her gaze. "Do not be deceived! Astrebril the Great can do all these things. He will curse those who disdain the Pact made in his presence long ago."

Vlad the Nine-Fingered drew his blade from his belt and dropped to one knee. "I shall not let this happen to my people, queen of Astrebril. We are your confederates." He slid the knife across his palm.

The High Priestess pinched her fingertip until it reddened, then pricked it with a needle. A crimson drop bubbled up. Seizing Vlad's hand in hers, she dipped her finger in his blood.

"I receive you," she said.

In the forest nearby someone muffled a sneeze. Every head snapped around.

"Intruder!" shouted the Vulkainian bodyguard.

The High Priestess jabbed her finger toward the sound. "Get him!"

The Vulkainian bodyguard and several of the outsider warriors crashed through the underbrush. There was a scuffle, then they returned hauling a prisoner by his arms. He was a soldier of the Royal Guard. His sword had been taken away.

"What are you doing here?" the High Priestess demanded.

"I . . . I'm stationed at the cabin, Your Eminence."

"You were supposed to be reassigned for the night."

"Yes! But I forgot my money pouch, so I returned. I heard voices . . . saw torches in the woods . . . I had to investigate."

"What did you hear?" the Vulkainian asked.

"Nothing! I swear it!"

The High Priestess approached the soldier. "Which regiment do you belong to?"

"The Fifth."

"The men of the Fifth are disloyal."

"Not me, Your Eminence!"

The High Priestess turned to her bodyguard. "He has seen us with outsiders. He cannot be allowed to talk. Dispatch him."

The terrified soldier began to struggle against the outsiders who pinned his arms. He was strong and managed to break free long enough to grapple for his sword with the man who held it.

The High Priestess grabbed a weapon from the Vulkainian's holster. It was a spray gun filled with acid under pressure. She pulled the trigger and a stream of corrosive liquid hit the guardsman in the face. Some of the acid spattered on the outsiders as well, causing them to pull back, but the soldier was no longer trying to escape. He was down on his knees, clawing at his eyes. The High Priestess pressed him to the ground with her high-heeled boot and held him there, writhing and groaning in the mud.

"I said, *dispatch him*," she snarled to the Vulkainian.

The man nodded to his queen and withdrew his knife.

❖ ❖ ❖

The *Midnight Glider* made the run up the coast in good time. The winds were favorable, and the weather was fair as the square-rigged vessel sailed north. After six days at sea, Marco ordered his crew to stop at the Likurian port of Manacho to resupply.

"Care to see the city again?" the pirate captain asked Teo as the ship floated offshore.

"No thanks. I didn't exactly have a great experience the last time I was here."

Marco offered Teo a wry grin. "You mean being sentenced to public execution doesn't make you feel welcome?"

"Not so much." Teo stared at the courthouse of Manacho, which sat atop a cliff, then looked away without saying anything more.

The next morning the ship passed the island of Hahnerat on the starboard side. Marco said everything west of the island was uncharted waters. "Are you afraid?" Teo asked him as the ship cleared Hahnerat. He knew seafarers hated going into unfamiliar territory. But Marco simply shrugged.

"You only live once," he said.

The *Glider* sailed west all day, hugging the shoreline. At nightfall the ship sheltered in a bay, then continued at dawn. Near evening a small fishing boat was spotted. As soon as the fishermen caught sight of the new arrival, they pulled up their nets and hurried off. Though the clipper could have overhauled them, Marco let them go. This wasn't a pirating expedition—and even if it were, no one was interested in a cargo of flopping tuna.

A short time later, a more imposing vessel rigged for war appeared on the western horizon. As it drew near, Marco ordered his sailors to be ready. Helmeted soldiers armed with crossbows lined the bulwarks of the warship. Several also held grappling hooks.

"Easy, men," Marco called to his crew. "Don't provoke them."

As the warship approached, a tall man with his beard waxed to a point bellied up to the rail. He shouted something across the water.

"I don't know that language," Marco said to Teo. "Do you?"

"Yes. It's a dialect of what we call the Fluid Tongue."

"What did he say?"

"He said, 'Stand down. You're in the waters of the Republic of Marsay.'"

"Tell him we're friendly."

Teo shouted a salutation, but Pointed-Beard didn't drop his scowl. "Who are you and what do you want?" he demanded.

"We are voyagers from Roma," Teo replied in the Fluid Tongue.

"You look more like pirates."

"Looks can be deceiving. We're not here for piracy but to meet the Knights of the Cross."

"For what purpose?"

Teo didn't know if the Christiani were persecuted in Marsay like they used to be in Roma, but he decided to speak the truth and see what would happen. "I am an emissary from the Papa of the Universal Communion. My mission is to make contact with the knights."

Pointed-Beard looked surprised at this, but at last he nodded. "Alright. You will follow me at a safe distance—and no tricks or my men will have your crew bristling like hedgehogs."

The warship escorted the *Midnight Glider* around a cape that put the mainland toward the east. Soon a large settlement came into view. The setting sun cast an orange sheen on the buildings along the shore.

"That must be Marsay. A nice-looking city," Teo said.

"A good spot for a harbor," Marco agreed. "They're leading us straight in."

However, instead of continuing toward the city, the warship dropped its anchor near a small island in the bay. A wall ran along the entire length of the island's coastline, and a castle loomed from its highest point. Catapults on the ramparts suggested any threatening activity would be met with force.

The night passed with no further communication between the two ships. In the morning a rowboat was lowered from the Marsayan vessel. It came alongside the *Glider* as she rode at anchor.

"Drop a ladder," shouted the captain with the pointed beard. "Your emissary will come with me."

Teo climbed down and was rowed to the island. Pointed-Beard seemed to be more at ease today. "The place you're going is called Castle d'If," he explained while his men pulled the oars. "It's the knights' base. I'll drop you there, and they can do with you as they like."

An adolescent boy with a shaved head met the rowboat at the island's dock. He spoke briefly with the captain, then ran up to the castle. Soon a group of men emerged from the fortress's main gate. They wore what Teo considered to be military uniforms: identical leather tunics with insignia, sturdy boots, and swords on their belts. Each man's hair was gathered in a ponytail at the nape of his neck. And when the knights reached the dock, Teo discovered they also had crosses tattooed on their foreheads.

One of the knights, a well-built man in his midthirties with chevrons on his shoulders, stepped forward. "I am Odo, commander of the Order of the Cross at Marsay."

Teo removed a parchment from inside his shirt. Kneeling, he proffered it to Odo. "I am Teofil. This letter from the Holy Father will tell you why I'm here."

Odo glanced at the document. Switching languages, he said in Talyano, "The people of Roma speak the tongue of the Likurians?"

"Yes. The Likurians, Ulmbartians, Romans, and Sessalayans share a common speech."

"Yet you speak Fransais. How?"

"I come from a land where it is remembered by a few scholars, of which I am one."

That seemed to satisfy Odo. "Follow me, Teofil. I will provide you a guest room while you are here." He and his men began to walk toward the castle.

Teo took the opportunity to evaluate his surroundings. The island was clearly an active military base. It had an obstacle course and a parade ground for marching and drilling. "You're training soldiers here," Teo remarked.

Odo nodded. "The men of the city comprise a powerful citizen militia. We train them on a monthly basis. Our job is to keep them in top condition. The Republic of Marsay fears no threat, for all its men are skilled in war."

"Judging from the size of your facilities, you must have quite an army."

"Thousands," Odo bragged.

The group arrived at the castle, which was protected by thick walls and rounded towers.

"Buildings like this are very old," Teo said. "This fortress was here long before the Destruction."

Odo pointed to the city across the bay. "The sky-fires of the Ancients reduced Marsay to ashes. But here on the island, the castle endured." He lovingly patted the walls, which seemed to be made out of bedrock.

Teo was led to a courtyard inside the keep. Though it was once open to the sky, a sheet of sailcloth had been drawn over the courtyard's opening several stories above. Now only a dim light came through.

"Wait here," Odo instructed. "The noon service is about to begin. You can give the knights a greeting."

A stairway led to a narrow gallery that ran around the four walls of the courtyard. An altar stood on the gallery behind a wrought-iron railing. In the center of the courtyard was a well, but it had been bricked over. A brazier sat on it now, its flames illuminating the murky chapel. Stains marked the walls where smoke had seeped past the sailcloth awning.

A bell tolled outside. Odo climbed the stairs to the altar on the gallery. Soon men began to gather in the courtyard. Most wore the leather tunics of the knights, but some were dressed in everyday clothes and carried weapons. Because they did not have ponytails or cross tattoos on their foreheads, Teo assumed they were Marsayan citizens receiving military training. A few women also mingled in the crowd—cooks and maids, judging from their attire.

Odo opened a book and began to read. The language was unfamiliar to Teo, though from the sound of it he thought it was probably Latin. None of the listeners appeared to comprehend it, for they stared into space or even talked to one another in hushed tones during the reading. Periodically Odo would break off his chant and make the shape of a cross with his hand. At other points he sprinkled water on the crowd below. Twice he lit incense sticks in a little saucer. As the ritual built to a climax, Odo's monotonous voice grew louder. Now an assistant came through a door and walked down the gallery with a chalice and a dish holding a small bun. Odo kissed the piece of bread and popped it in his mouth, then washed it down with a long draught from the chalice. Wiping his lips with the back of his hand, he stifled a burp and said: "*Tout est accompli.*" The people finally looked up at him.

The commander of the Order of the Cross surveyed the upturned faces, then started in on a speech. "Today is a momentous day, my friends! Something has occurred that surprised even me: I have received a communication from the Papa of our ancient religion." At this announcement a murmur rippled through the crowd. Odo paused to let the news sink in before continuing. "Perhaps you believed the Holy Father of the Universal Communion to be a mythical beast, like fairies and dragons. Perhaps you believed there was no such place as faraway Roma. Certainly no one in Marsay has heard from a Roman Papa in close to forty years. But now, behold! An emissary has come to us from afar." Odo jabbed an outstretched finger at Teo and looked him in the eye. "Or so he claims."

The people around Teo drew back in superstitious awe. He held up his hands, smiling to show they had nothing to fear, but they stared at him wide-eyed and open-mouthed.

Finally Odo beckoned Teo to join him on the gallery. As Teo mounted the steps he considered what he would say. His command of the Fluid Tongue—or Fransais as they called it here—was more of a translator's knowledge than a speaker's proficiency. Though his words might be understandable, they wouldn't be eloquent. Nevertheless, Teo decided he was going to do more than bring a simple greeting. He was going to preach the good news of Iesus Christus to a people who had never heard it.

Teo stood at the railing next to the altar. After introducing himself and explaining that he was indeed an emissary from the Papa, he bowed his head and offered up a silent prayer. At last he opened his eyes and met the people's gaze. "Listen to me and I will tell you a story," he said. "It starts like this: 'In the beginning Deus created the heavens and the earth.'" The opening words of the Sacred Writing seemed like the right place to begin.

While the people listened in the courtyard, Teo proceeded to proclaim the Christiani message. He used the eleven words from the Council of Roma as his outline. First he described how the goodness of the original creation became corrupted by sin. Then almighty Deus provided a system of sacrifice for his people, Israël. When that failed he sent his beloved son Iesus Christus to provide atonement. Though Iesus was killed, Deus raised him to life again. The Pierced One calls men everywhere to believe in him for salvation and be washed with water. True Christiani must live holy lives and share the sacred meal with one another. They are called to extend love to the poor and oppressed and to proclaim a message of hope to all mankind until Iesus returns.

At the end of his speech Teo examined the crowd, trying to assess the people's response. He felt thankful that his command of the Fluid Tongue had been strong enough to deliver the message. In fact, he had found himself speaking more eloquently than he would have guessed possible.

However, despite this unexpected eloquence the crowd was unmoved. Teo remembered being astounded when he first learned that Iesus Christus had come back to life after being executed by wicked men. Yet these listeners seemed unimpressed. Teo couldn't understand why his recounting of Deu's grand story failed to move the so-called Knights of the Cross. Apparently the cross was nothing to them but a meaningless symbol.

Outside, the bell began to toll again, awakening the people from their slumber. Smiles crossed their faces, and their attention perked up. Moving as quickly as possible, they exited the courtyard. Teo turned to Odo. "What's all the excitement about?"

"Can't you smell it? Roast lamb for lunch today!" Odo glanced around to see if anyone was looking, then quickly guzzled the leftover wine from the ritual before he could be noticed. When he set the chalice back on the altar it tipped over, but Odo paid it no mind. He walked toward the stairway to join the other knights for lunch.

Teo stared at the fallen chalice. A single droplet dribbled from it, staining the tablecloth red. He set the cup upright and turned away in disgust.

◆　　◆　　◆

Ana sat near the back of the chapel at Lido di Ostia's little convent by the sea. The melodious sound of the chanting sisters echoed off the stone walls and vaulted ceiling. A singer herself, Ana could appreciate the beauty of the women's combined voices. She recalled a time she had sung a ballad before a Chiveisian audience in a stone hall much like this one. Back then she had not yet encountered the Eternal God, so her song was a heartfelt lament for her spiritual emptiness and her kingdom's decadent culture. The aristocrats at the elite poetry competition had scorned her as a peasant girl until Teo burst on the scene, silencing the critics with his commanding presence. Ana smiled at the memory. She hardly knew Teo then. *Who could have guessed all the adventures I'd one day share with him?* The journey of life alongside Captain Teofil had been anything but dull.

As the service continued, Ana let the soprano and alto voices elevate her heart in worship. The glorious harmony sounded like a choir of angels. Ana was contemplating the beauty of Deu when a noise outside yanked her back to reality. A horseman had arrived at the convent. Since Ana wasn't formally removed from the world by a monastic vow, it was her job to greet visitors. She rose from the wooden pew and hurried outside.

A man stood next to his horse, tamping herbs into his pipe. His frame was stocky, and his hair was close-cropped. He wore a neat tunic and trousers in the latest style. As Ana emerged from the convent, the man turned to look at her.

"May I help you?" she asked.

"My name is Riccardo."

Ana nodded. It was a common name. "What can I do for you, Riccardo?"

"I'm a dealer in foodstuffs. Cheese, salt pork, pasta. I assume the holy sisters do not fast all the time?"

"Of course not. The fare here is simple. Much of it is produced on the property. But the housemother buys food from the market as well."

"I can cut you a deal. You can spend the money you save on luxuries for yourselves. Womanly stuff."

"Um . . . that's not really what we do . . . "

"Or you can give it to poor people. Whatever you want, I don't care. The point is, I can get you a good price on what you need."

"This is a matter for the housemother." Ana turned toward the door. "If you'll come this way I'll introduce you. A novice will care for your horse."

The man looped the reins around a post and followed Ana inside. She escorted Riccardo to a parlor and instructed him to wait.

Returning to the horse, Ana led it to the stable and left it with one of the novice girls. When she entered the main building again she saw the sisters had finished the service and begun to disperse. The housemother was in conversation with one of the senior nuns.

What's that?

Ana's head came up sharply. She smelled smoke—not the pleasant aroma of woodsmoke, but the stench of something burning that shouldn't be.

She ran to the parlor. Riccardo was there, stamping the rush-covered floor, trying to put out a bright blaze. An overturned wastebasket was on fire, and to Ana's horror, so was a decorative tapestry that hung on the wall. The flames licked the wood paneling and curled around the beams overhead. *No! Not the roof!*

"Help me!" Riccardo cried, though his ridiculous foot-stamping was accomplishing nothing.

Ana dashed down a corridor to the bell tower. She began to tug on the rope, sounding the alarm until she heard shouts and voices. Some of the sisters had followed the smoke to the parlor. The quick thinkers among them had already grabbed buckets.

"Line up in an orderly fashion," the housemother instructed. "Right down to the sea. It's the closest water."

The sisters formed a bucket brigade, and soon they were dousing the parlor wall. The wastebasket and burning tapestry had been dragged outside, but the wood paneling still smoldered. Steam hissed from the wall every time a bucketful of seawater was hurled against it. Finally the fire began to lose the battle against the determined women.

"I'm so sorry," Riccardo stammered. "I was lighting my pipe. I tossed the match away and, you know . . . "

Something about the explanation didn't sit right with Ana. The parlor had caught fire in several places. How could one careless match do that?

Vanita Labella approached Ana in the confusion and pulled her aside. "Who is that guy?" she whispered.

"He says he's a food seller who wants to do business with us."

"He's a Clansman!"

"What? How do you know?"

"Marco says they all look like him. Big beefy guys with short hair and overpriced clothes. You can tell by the way they move. Light-footed, like a cat."

Ana sucked in her breath. "You're right! Why is he here?"

"Not to sell us food, that's for sure. Is he an arsonist trying to burn the place down?"

"If so, I can't imagine he'd walk through our front door. The whole sisterhood is out here watching what's going on."

Ana and Vanita gazed at each other, considering Riccardo's devious intent. Their eyes widened in unison, and their mouths fell open as they realized what was happening.

"A diversion!" Ana exclaimed.

"Right! Let's go!"

The two women dashed upstairs to the dormitory floor. The doors to the sisters' rooms were never locked, so there was nothing to stop a thief. Yet none of them was opened. Ana glanced at Vanita. They looked down the hall toward their own room, a bedchamber designated for guests. Their door alone stood ajar.

"We need a weapon," Ana said.

"I'll get something." Vanita entered one of the bedrooms and returned with a ceramic pitcher and a mop. Ana stepped on the mop's yarn head and yanked out the handle, then led the way to her room.

They paused outside the door. Muffled sounds came from the other side. Ana's heart beat wildly. "He's in there," she mouthed as she pointed to the room. Vanita nodded. A look of firm resolve was on her face.

Ana kicked open the door and burst inside. A muscular man was rummaging through a dresser. He whirled to face the women.

"Get out of here!" Ana screamed.

She swung the mop handle with both hands. Though the man fended off the attack, the blow was hard, and he grunted as the pole struck his forearm. He barreled at Ana and rammed her into the wall, then punched her in the stomach. Ana gasped as her breath was knocked out. Nausea overwhelmed her, and her knees felt watery.

There was a loud crash. Shards of pottery flew everywhere. The thief staggered back, stunned by the blow to his head. Vanita dropped the handle of the broken pitcher and snatched a bottle of wine from the dresser. She hurled it at the man, but it missed and went sailing through the door, shattering against the opposite wall.

"What's going on?" shouted a voice in the hallway. Running footsteps sounded against the floor.

Blood trickled down the intruder's cheek. Ana mustered her remaining strength and brandished the mop handle. Vanita grabbed a washbasin and raised it over her head.

Turning toward an end table, the thief seized a book and ran from the room. Ana followed him. He fled down a stairwell just as the housemother and several other sisters arrived.

"Who was that?" the housemother cried.

Ana steadied herself against the wall, unable to answer because she couldn't catch her breath. Her stomach ached where the assailant had punched her. Bile rose up in her mouth, making her gag as she spit it out.

Vanita put her arm around Ana's shoulder and helped her stand up straight. "He was from the Clan," she said as Ana leaned against her. "I guess we can add them to our list of enemies."

◆ ◆ ◆

Though the Papa had commissioned Teo to learn more about Deu from the Knights of the Cross, the library at Castle d'If left much to be desired. Its holdings were meager, and what was on the shelves emphasized military strategy, not theology. The uncataloged books were strewn around the room in random fashion. Teo couldn't imagine a worse library than this one.

Nevertheless, he was a scholar, and that meant he had the patience for difficult research. The quest for knowledge was even more alluring when it presented obstacles, for it brought greater satisfaction when those obstacles were overcome. Teo sifted through treatises on tactics and armaments for the better part of the morning. Though he failed to find anything of spiritual value, he never knew what he might discover when he reached for the next book. Insatiable curiosity kept him going when others would have given up. He had assumed the knights wouldn't own any copies of the New Testament, a suspicion confirmed after talking with Odo. Even so, Teo hoped to find a hidden gem in the pitiful library.

Another hour slipped by. Teo had examined all the shelves but one when the noon bell signaled the daily ritual. He walked to the library door, which opened onto the gallery that encircled the courtyard of Castle d'If. People were beginning to gather down below, though Teo couldn't see their faces in the dimness caused by the awning overhead. As Odo ascended the stairs to the gallery, Teo met him by the altar.

"What's the purpose of that sailcloth up there?" he asked.

"It rains here in winter. Who likes to get wet?"

"But it's sunny much of the year. Don't you wish the chapel were brighter?"

"It doesn't need to be brighter. I know the words by heart. I could say them in complete darkness." Odo paused. "Where have you been, anyway?"

Teo jerked his thumb toward the door behind him. "Taking a look at your library."

"Interested in battle tactics, are you?"

"Yes, but that's not what I'm searching for today."

Teo could see from Odo's expression he wanted to know what his visitor was seeking. *Let him wonder.* People like Odo drove Teo crazy. They were suspicious of anything out of the ordinary. Yet somehow these conservative types always ended up with power, which they used to suppress changes for good.

"I have to conduct the ritual now," Odo said, "but afterward we must address your use of the library."

"Is that so?"

Odo nodded, then turned toward the altar and began to fill a chalice with wine. A listless crowd milled about in the courtyard. Teo hurried back to the library and finished examining the books. None of them dealt with religion. Frustrated, he was about to leave when he noticed something scrawled on the spine of a book on the bottom shelf. He bent to examine the volume, which was tucked in the room's most obscure spot. The title was *Flanking Maneuvers for Infantry and Cavalry*. But underneath the title someone had written two words: *Secret History*.

Pulling out the book, Teo opened it and perused the pages. It was a hand-copied text about warfare. At the end of the volume, several blank leaves had been sewn in. Teo flipped them one by one. His breath caught when he saw what was written on the final page. It was a reference to the Sacred Writing: Hymn 69:21, 28.

"Teofil! We need to talk!"

Teo jumped at Odo's loud voice. He stuffed the book in its place and stood up. "I'm over here," he said, dusting his hands.

"I'm afraid I'm going to have to forbid you from using the library," Odo said.

Teo frowned, though he wasn't surprised. "Can I ask why?"

"It's a long-standing policy. The library is reserved for the knights' use."

"But I have a valid reason to be here."

"Even so . . . it's our policy." Odo shrugged and held up his hands. "What can I do?"

"Perhaps you forget I'm here by direct order of the Holy Father of the Universal Communion."

A scowl darkened Odo's face. "And where is the Holy Father, might I ask?"

"In Roma, obviously."

"And where are you?" Odo countered smugly.

Teo didn't reply. He could see where this was headed. Rather than bandying crooked words with a witless fool, he walked out.

Back in his bedroom he removed his copy of the Sacred Writing from his rucksack. Teo was carrying an inexpensive Talyano version while a Chiveisian edition was being prepared at Roma. He looked up the two verses that had been written in the strange book. The first one said, "They put gall in my food, and to appease my thirst they give me vinegar to drink." A few lines down, the second verse read, "May they be blotted out of the book of life and not be inscribed with the righteous."

Teo considered the meaning of these words. The writer of the hymn was King David, whose enemies had persecuted him and made his food bitter. In response the king asked Deu to blot them from the book of life. *But what did that have to do with "secret history"? And why was nothing written on the pages added to the end of the book?* Teo decided he wasn't going to give up until he found out.

That night when the castle had grown quiet he slipped from his bed and made his way to the door that gave entrance to the courtyard. He tried the knob, but it would not turn. Unwilling to be thwarted so easily, Teo climbed a spiral staircase and emerged on the castle's roof. A crescent moon gleamed over the quiet city of Marsay across the bay. Teo crept to the sailcloth awning that covered the courtyard and peeked underneath it. Only one story down he saw the narrow gallery—and the entrance to the library.

The awning was held in place by ropes. Each ran from an iron stake through a grommet in the sailcloth and back to another stake. Teo untied one of the ropes, which made the awning droop so that a gap opened up. With the other end of the rope still secured to a stake, Teo dropped the free end into the courtyard and slid down to the gallery. The door to the library was unlocked.

After lighting a candle from the librarian's desk, Teo located the volume with the blank pages. Somehow the reference to Hymn 69 must provide a key for decoding what was written in the book. But the text about battle tactics was monotonous, and Teo could discover no hidden meaning there.

Approaching the problem from a different angle, he made a mental list of the verses' main concepts: gall, vinegar, food and drink, blotting from the book of life. What did those things have in common? As Teo racked his brain, a sudden thought occurred to him. *Gall is a substance used to make ink, and that relates to books . . . and blotting?*

In a flash everything fell into place.

The final pages aren't blank! They've been erased!

Stunned, Teo realized the text must be a palimpsest. Often when scribes were short of new parchment they simply sponged away the ink on an earlier text. Though the writing could no longer be seen, it was still there in tiny indentations. Should it ever need to be revealed again, all one had to do was rub it with a special concoction: a tincture of gall.

The librarian's desk held writing materials and jars for making ink. Teo rummaged in the drawers until he found the gall, an acidic substance drawn from bulbous growths on oak trees. He dabbed a brush in the gall and smeared it on the blank vellum pages of the book. It stained the pages brown, but it also made letters appear.

As Teo read the text he grew excited. The account described Chiveis's early prosperity under its founder Jonluc Beaumont. Yet soon the narrative took a chilling turn. The great patriarch had conquered a kingdom called Jineve, then journeyed downriver to Marsay. There he entered into a blood oath with several other rulers, all of whom swore to eliminate the religion of Christianism. The high god Astrebril guaranteed his power to those who observed the Pact—and promised the most heinous curses on those who defied it.

Teo tore the pages from the book and tucked them inside his shirt. They were far too important to leave in an obscure library like this. He returned to the rope and shimmied up to the roof, then threaded the line through the eye in the awning and drew it tight once again. As he was tying a hitch knot to the stake, someone hailed him from behind.

Teo leaped to his feet and faced the speaker. He was a stocky, powerfully built man with the characteristic cross tattoo and ponytail of a knight. His arms were corded with the muscles of a warrior. But instead of military garb he wore a coarse-spun tunic and a rope belt.

"What do you want from me?" Teo asked. He knew he wasn't supposed to be sneaking around on the roof, so he expected trouble.

The man's tone, however, was mild. "Have you come to bring good news to those who wish to receive it?"

"Is that a trick question?"

The man shook his head.

"Then yes. I have come from Roma to proclaim the message of Deus and his son Iesus."

"That is my desire too, Teofil. I did not know the full truth of my religion until your arrival. Your speech the other day made everything clear."

"I hope to make it clear to all the people of Marsay."

"Tch! Those people aren't spiritually hungry. However, I know a people who may listen. Long have I wanted to bring them the truth of Deus. Now that you've opened my eyes, I have decided to pay their mayor a visit."

"Who are they?"

"The Jinevans. And guess what else?"

Teo shrugged.

The knight in the rough robe approached until he could reach out and place his hand on Teo's shoulder. No sound disturbed the quiet night. A slow smile crept across the man's face, and a mischievous twinkle was in his eye.

"I intend to take you with me," he said.

CHAPTER

3

A light wind ruffled the waters of Leman Sea. Its blue expanse curved away to the southwest under a warm autumn sun. The Iron Shield watched his Exterminati shamans prepare two river boats for lake travel. He sat astride his horse, a sorrel with a white blaze on its nose. The animal, along with a silver-engraved saddle and harness, was a gift from the High Priestess. No doubt the fine steed would convey to the Jinevans an aura of genteel prosperity. That was exactly the impression he wanted to give.

The Iron Shield couldn't get the High Priestess out of his mind. The woman had attached herself to his consciousness like a leech—burrowing in, sucking his blood, making him itch. He could picture her raven hair cascading down the sides of her white-painted face. He could imagine her swelling curves beneath her gauzy robe. Every time she spoke, her black lips offered an invitation. Every time she moved, her lithe body made her invitations irresistible. Yet she never delivered on her promises. Despite her overwhelming sensuality, the High Priestess gave commands, not favors. Obedience was the dark queen's only aphrodisiac, and the Iron Shield found himself willing to offer it in full.

He wasn't exactly sure why. Over the years he had used many women, of course. Yet this one was different. She was dominant, alluring, unattainable. The Iron Shield considered the High Priestess worthy of respect. In fact, her direct access to the powerful god Astrebril made her worthy of fear—the highest compliment the Iron Shield could pay. He longed to provide the priestess with what she desired most: brimstone, salt-stone, iron . . .

And death.

You shall have it all, my queen.

A shaman interrupted the Iron Shield's thoughts. "Master, should I lead your mount aboard?"

The Iron Shield shook his head, preferring to do it himself. He dismounted and walked his horse up a ramp onto one of the boats. They were clinker-built vessels of the type called a longship. Each had space for sixteen rowers. With their shallow drafts they could maneuver easily on rivers and even be portaged, yet they were stable enough for travel on an open lake like Leman Sea. It would take several hours to sail from the wilderness reaches of the lake to the bustling port of Jineve at the far western end. The Iron Shield left his horse amidships and took his seat in the stern.

By evening the two boats had reached the city and were tied alongside a pier. The port authorities recognized the travelers from their previous journey though the kingdom. As before, the Iron Shield donned an expensively tailored tunic instead of his usual chain mail. He also set aside his heavy mace. Everyone in Jineve believed him to be a merchant adventurer who had come from a faraway kingdom to establish trade. Only his yellow cat's-eye might have hinted he was actually far more sinister.

A steward walked onto the pier to greet the new arrivals. "Welcome back, Antonio of Roma."

The Iron Shield gritted his teeth at the use of the ridiculous alias he had adopted. Though he preferred to be unnameable, the present circumstances required a false identity. He inclined his head politely. "I am grateful for your welcome, master steward."

"The banquet hall at Montblanc Palace is set for an evening meal," the steward advised. "Mayor Calixte would welcome your company to resume your discussion of commerce."

Fools! You invite me to supper like a hen inviting the weasel to dine. How ignorant you are! Soon you will have a new queen, and I will reign at her side!

With a slight smile the Iron Shield said, "That sounds delightful. Lead the way, if you please."

The dinner was the kind of lavish meal served by a people whose exorbitant wealth isn't matched by the virtue of self-restraint. The fish course consisted of perch fillets in a creamy fennel sauce, while the main plate was marbled roast beef. All of it was accompanied by copious amounts of wine. *These people are soft*, the Iron Shield noted. *Ripe for the picking.* As the meal progressed, Mayor Calixte described the kingdom's iron mines and salt-stone beds, and he even talked freely of national defense. Because the Jinevans spoke a language similar to the Chiveisi, the dark warrior was able to maintain his end of the conversation.

"My business partners would be interested in purchasing iron from you," the Iron Shield said, "though I need to be certain you can produce a steady supply. What assurances can you offer me?"

Mayor Calixte rose from his chair and went to a stylized map of Jineve on the wall. He was a tall man, though not a warrior, for his rotund build prevented that. "The bulk of the mining colonies are here," Calixte said, pointing to a region in the north. "The iron supply is nearly unlimited, and we maintain a good road between the city and the mines."

"Excellent. Perhaps you could have a detailed report delivered to my room?"

"Of course, Antonio. And I will also send you a report about the salt-stone fertilizer we discussed."

"Very good." The Iron Shield suppressed a smile as he took a sip of the dry, fruity wine from the vineyards along the northern shore of Leman Sea.

Back in his room that night, he handed the commercial reports to one of his lieutenants, a shaman with a red armband. The man read the reports slowly, then looked up from the parchments. "This kingdom abounds with two of the three commodities the High Priestess desires," he said.

"My mistress will be pleased."

"And their defenses are weak. I have seen no soldiers on the streets."

"They have military forces here," the Iron Shield countered, "but an invasion army will be assembled in Chiveis to overcome them. Once the Jinevans have been conquered and their resources exploited, further expansion will be possible."

"Expansion? You mean down to Marsay?"

"Yes . . . and beyond."

The shaman's smile revealed his enthusiasm. "An empire in the making! Nothing stands in the way of this glorious conquest."

"There is one thing."

The shaman peered at his master from beneath his hood, waiting for an answer.

"Her Eminence requires brimstone in great quantities," the Iron Shield said. "Everything hinges on that."

"Ah, of course. For Astrebril's fire."

"That is useful to her, but there is something even greater. The High Priestess intends to develop a new weapon from brimstone. It is a poisonous fume that burns whomever it touches. The agony is severe even for those lightly exposed. For those who receive a mortal dose, no words can describe their suffering to the end. It is beyond all endurance. Any army that wields this weapon will send the opposing force fleeing to the hills in terror."

The shaman lieutenant exhaled slowly. "Such a wondrous creation is surely a gift of the gods."

"No. It is the gift of *one* god. Astrebril the Great has revealed this weapon to his queen." The Iron Shield rose to his full, intimidating height. He pointed his finger at his lieutenant. "And I intend to make sure she gets it."

◆　◆　◆

Teo had been on the river for a week. The routine was the same every day: the sun rose on the right and set on the left, the rowers pulled the oars, and the banks of the Rone River slipped by. At times the green monotony of the forest was broken by stunning fields of purple lavender, but the fields always ended, and then the forest swallowed the travelers again.

Everywhere Teo looked he saw the relics of the Ancients. Their more recent structures, such as wire-draped poles or elevated highways, were intermingled with honey-colored ruins of an older vintage—walled hilltop towns, castles, stone bridges. At one point the travelers passed through what must have been a great city. On a hill above the river, a few surviving towers from a white temple of Deu lifted lonely crosses to the sky. Teo marveled at the wonders the Ancients had constructed and then obliterated in their colossal fires. Thick vegetation now engulfed the primordial remains. The steady progress of human culture had succumbed to the depredations of nature. Today the crumbled world of the Ancients was largely forgotten. Teo vowed that their God would not be.

The river expedition had been arranged by Brother Thomas, the knight whom Teo met on the roof of Castle d'If. Brother Thomas was what the Order of the Cross called a friar. Though he was a fighting man and a full-fledged member of the military order, he had taken additional vows of poverty and self-denial. Brother Thomas had many critical things to say about the lukewarm commitment of the knights to the principles of Christianism. Unlike them, the humble friar welcomed Teo's proclamation about Iesus Christus, who died and rose again. Excited by the idea of taking this message to Jineve—a mission that dovetailed with Teo's own plans—Brother Thomas had secured the riverboats for the expedition. Teo suspected Odo allowed the journey only because he was glad to rid Marsay of those he considered pests.

Marco came to Teo's side as he stood in the longship's narrow prow. Teo greeted him warmly, glad for the friendship of the pirate-turned-explorer. Marco's polished good looks were somewhat diminished now that his goatee had grown shaggy and his cheeks were unshaven. But when Teo jokingly commented on his friend's ragged appearance, he shot back, "Hey! Have you looked in a mirror lately, *amico?*" Teo could only laugh as he rubbed the rough whiskers on his chin. It wouldn't be long before he had a full beard.

Marco leaned on the gunwale. "Brother Thomas thinks we'll reach the outskirts of the Jinevan kingdom today."

"Good. I'm sick of river travel."

"Me too. Give me the open seas any day." Marco glanced over at Teo. "What does this little excursion do to your timetable?"

"For getting back to Roma, you mean?"

Marco nodded.

Teo thought it over. It was now late in the ninth month, which meant the ocean would close to sailing in about seven weeks. Reserving a week to return down the Rone to Marsay and another for sailing to Roma, Teo figured he could allow five weeks to accomplish the mission the Papa had assigned him. Part of that mission was already achieved: Teo had made contact with the Knights of the Cross, although they hadn't received him as warmly as he wished. The other part of the mission was to visit any nearby kingdoms that might be interested in the faith of the Christiani. Jineve seemed to be the best candidate.

"My timetable looks fine," Teo answered Marco. "In fact, I should have several weeks to spare."

The afternoon wore on as the boat traveled north up the Rone. Earlier there had been obstacles to navigate, but now the crew made good time despite the faster current. Suddenly a voice called out from upstream, "Cease rowing, strangers!" The rowers looked at each other with confused expressions. It took Teo a moment to realize why: the language was foreign to them. But it was his own native tongue.

He stood up and shouted to the boat ahead, "We're friendly! Our mission is one of peace!"

"We'll see about that," came the terse reply.

The army boat escorted Teo's party for several hours. As they traveled, the signs of civilization became more numerous: docks along the banks, other boats, even houses here and there. At last they arrived in a true city, situated at the place where the river widened into a broad lake. A sign proclaimed, "Welcome to Jineve—Jewel of Leman Sea."

The civic waterfront was indeed beautiful, lined with stately mansions and an impressive palace. A jetty protruded into the lake, capped by a majestic fountain at its tip. The army boat docked at a pier in the harbor. Brother Thomas ordered his men to moor alongside it.

A man in fine clothing met the party at the dock. "I am the steward of Montblanc Palace," he said. "Our honorable ruler Mayor Calixte welcomes new business opportunities, if that is why you are here." Teo translated the greeting for his companions.

"Tell him it's the transactions of the eternal soul we're concerned with," Brother Thomas said. Teo conveyed this back to the steward, who seemed unimpressed.

Nevertheless, the steward treated the travelers with respect. Introductions were made, with Teo serving as a go-between. The steward arched his eyebrows and nodded thoughtfully when he heard Teo had come all the way from Roma. "That is very curious," he said. "I think it will interest the mayor quite a bit."

The steward led Teo, Marco, and Brother Thomas toward the palace. The guests were shown to a comfortable bedchamber and invited to dine with Mayor Calixte in an hour.

After freshening up, the three men went down to dinner. The steward led them to the banquet hall and swung open the paneled door. Beside the table, Mayor Calixte stood in conversation with an unusually tall man.

No!

Teo's heart lurched. His hand went instinctively to his hip, though he had left his sword in his room out of courtesy.

The tall man was expensively dressed. He had a stunning physique— broad shoulders, thick arms, a narrow waist. His dark hair was slicked back against his skull. He turned to Teo, staring at him with the yellow eye of a cat.

"It's him!" Marco hissed, clutching Teo's sleeve.

"Don't back down. We have nothing to fear at the moment." Teo strode into the hall to meet Mayor Calixte.

"My, my! All of a sudden we have an influx of foreign businessmen!" The congenial mayor shook hands with his three visitors. "I hear you are from Roma, Teofil. Do you know Antonio by chance?"

Teo and the Iron Shield locked their gaze. "We've met," they said in unison.

Mayor Calixte invited everyone to find their places at the table. While the mayor prattled about business opportunities, Teo tried to decide how to handle the situation. Apparently the Iron Shield was posing as a respectable merchant from afar. Teo couldn't exactly stand up and accuse his enemy of being an occultist at the helm of an international society of assassins. Mayor Calixte had accepted the Iron Shield's story. He had no reason to believe such a wild accusation from a stranger. Teo realized he would have to win the mayor's confidence before trying to expose the facts.

And what are the facts? What is the Iron Shield doing here? The last time Teo had seen him, the man was preparing to carve out Teo's eyeballs. Now he was in Jineve. Teo wanted to know why.

Mayor Calixte turned toward the three new arrivals. "So, gentlemen, tell us about your business here."

"We didn't come to Jineve for trade," Teo explained. "We have come in the name of the Creator God with a message of hope for your people. Our faith offers brotherhood and harmony among men." Teo thought that idea might appeal to the mayor.

The Iron Shield sneered. "Who cares about warm feelings and brotherly love? What Jineve needs is wealth and prosperity."

"It's true, Teofil," the mayor said pointedly. "A prosperous kingdom is a happy kingdom, no matter what religion is embraced."

"On the contrary, the world is full of rich men who lack peace. And those who are poor often have great spiritual joy."

"That could be said about many who don't follow your faith," the Iron Shield challenged.

The wheels of Teo's mind spun as he sought to offer a well-crafted response. "I acknowledge your point," he said, "but an examination of the evidence reveals Christianism will have a greater positive effect on society than any other religion. Why? Because it's grounded in human dignity and respect for one's fellow man. When a religion advocates altruism, not domination . . . virtue, not decadence . . . order, not chaos . . . in other words, when it advocates love, not selfishness, then society will prosper." Teo turned away from the Iron Shield and faced the man at the head of the table. "That, Mayor Calixte, is what Christianism offers Jineve."

The mayor mulled over Teo's words for a long moment. At last he reached for a carafe and emptied the remaining wine into his glass. "All I want is for Jineve to get filthy rich. Come see me when you have a business proposal." He pointed at Teo's empty glass. "Do you need more merlot?"

"I'll get it for him, Mayor," the Iron Shield said.

"Thank you, Antonio."

The Iron Shield grabbed Teo's glass as he rose and went to the wine cart. Teo watched him carefully. His back was turned away from the table for several seconds before he returned, holding Teo's refilled glass in one hand and a full decanter in the other. He offered the glass to Teo. The blood-red wine glittered in the light of the chandelier.

Marco kicked Teo under the table. An urgent expression was on his face. He gave an almost imperceptible shake of his head.

Teo reached for the glass but at the last moment pulled his fingers back. The motion was quick and discreet. The Iron Shield fumbled, then the glass slipped from his hand and broke against the table. Wine dribbled into the mayor's lap. He jumped up with a displeased expression.

"Don't feel bad for spilling on the mayor, Antonio," Teo said to the flustered warrior. "We all understand you have but one eye."

The Iron Shield scowled. Marco barely stifled a laugh. Brother Thomas dipped his chin to Teo and raised his goblet as if to say, "Well played." Yet Teo took no joy in the incident.

I might have won the round, he thought, *but my enemy took the bout tonight.*

❖   ❖   ❖

Though it was the middle of the night, Ana could not sleep. Troubling thoughts churned in her mind. She huddled under her blankets, staring at the square of moonlight on the wall. Vanita breathed rhythmically in the other bed.

Ana pushed aside her covers and stood up, straightening the strap of her linen shift that had fallen off her shoulder. She thought about putting on her dress but didn't want to wake Vanita, so she wrapped herself in a shawl. It would be enough. There were no men in the convent except Liber, and he was fast asleep. Barefoot, Ana slipped out the door and closed it behind her.

She made her way to the convent's chapel. It wasn't grand like some of the temples of Deu she had seen, yet it was a holy place, sanctified by the sisters' liturgical songs that ascended daily. Ana went to the choir stalls and took a seat.

For a while she prayed in the dim chapel. The high windows of the clerestory admitted a pale glow. Everything was quiet and still. *O Deu,* Ana said in her heart, *I'm feeling sad tonight. I miss Mother and Father . . . I miss my bedroom in Edgeton . . . I miss the mountains and the sound of cowbells and the smell of new-cut hay.* Images of the pastoral Chiveisian landscape rushed through Ana's mind. Though she knew she was where Deu wanted her right now, she couldn't deny the longing she felt for the home she'd once had.

"It's so hard to wait," she whispered to her God. "Teofil has his mission to occupy him. What should I do in the meantime? What's my purpose? Will you speak to me?"

In a dark corner a cricket chirped. Ana tightened her shawl around her shoulders. Her feet were cold against the flagstones, so she pulled them up to the wooden pew with her knees bent.

Deu! I feel like an orphan! The thought seemed strange to Ana at first, but soon the comparison started to make sense. She had lost her parents. She was living in a place she couldn't call her own. The convent was much like an orphanage, an institution where the food wasn't home-cooked, the bedrooms were communal, and no one had a family. Ana told herself not to wallow in self-pity. Her situation was better than many in the world. *Yet this is how I feel right now. I'm as lonely as an orphan without a home! Will you let me be honest about that, Deu?*

As Ana prayed her eyes fell on the lector's pulpit. The housemother would often stand there to read the scriptures. Until recently that had meant only the Old Testament, but with the discovery of the Latin words in Liber's memory, the New Testament had become available to the sisters as well. In fact, a beautiful Talyano edition had just been delivered by the Papa's printers. A thought occurred to Ana. *Is the book stored inside the pulpit?* She hoped it might be. She was hungry for its words.

Ana slipped from the choir stall and crept toward the pulpit. Though she didn't believe her actions were forbidden, being barefoot and alone in the chapel gave her the strange feeling of doing something sneaky. The lower part of the pulpit was a cabinet. A lock was on it, but Ana had observed that keys were rarely used around the convent. She grasped the handle. It turned, and the cabinet opened.

A book was there.

"Come, Lord Iesus," Ana said softly. It was an invocation she had discovered at the end of the New Testament, in the closing words of the mysterious Apocalypse.

Lifting out the book, Ana set it on the pulpit's reading surface. Both testaments were in the volume. Ana marveled that the words she had spent so much effort seeking over the past year could now be reproduced in print to be spread far and wide. *It is such a privilege to live in this age of rediscovery,* she reminded herself.

Ana turned to the New Testament. The book fell open to the Fourth Biography of Iesus written by Ioannes. Her eyes alit on the fourteenth chapter:

> If you ask me anything in my name, this I will do. If you love me, keep my commands. And I will ask the Father, and he will give you another helper, so that he may remain with you forever—the spirit of truth, whom the world cannot accept because it does not see him or know him. But you know him, because he shall abide in your midst and be in you. I will not abandon you as orphans but come to you . . .

Ana's head shot up from the page.

Orphans!

She bent close and read the sacred words again. Her body shivered as she realized Deu had just spoken to her. He had impressed upon her mind the image of an orphan, then led her to a passage that dovetailed with the image. *The spirit of Deu will abide with me! Iesus will not abandon me!*

"So this is how you whisper to us," Ana said with a glance toward the ceiling. "I knew you would."

She closed the book and put it back in the pulpit. Comforted, she returned to her room. Vanita was in bed but awake when Ana arrived.

"Where have you been?" she asked as Ana closed the door.

"I couldn't sleep."

"How come?"

Ana sighed. "I guess I've been struggling in this season of waiting. Teo says we can go back to Chiveis—and I want to so much! But I also want to wait on Deu. I needed to hear from him, so I went to the chapel."

"Did you find him?"

Ana slipped under her warm covers. "Yes. He came to me."

"And what did he tell you?"

"No specific plans. But he told me very clearly his spirit would be with me."

Vanita was silent for a long moment. "Does that mean you shouldn't make plans?"

It was a good question, and Ana gave it serious thought. At last she said, "No. I definitely think I should make plans as best I know how. But then I need to listen to his spirit, and if Deu wants to change my plans, I have to be willing to let him."

Instead of answering, Vanita sat up in bed and struck a match. She lit the candle, then shook out the flame on the matchstick. Her expression was somber. "I agree. And I've been thinking about one sort of plan we ought to make."

Ana was intrigued. "What?"

"Those guys from the Clan have me worried. The fellow who called himself Riccardo, and the other guy who socked you in the gut."

"I'm still bruised," Ana said, touching the tender place above her navel.

"Clearly they were after something. Maybe we need to make it our business to thwart them."

Ana sat up on her elbow and faced Vanita. "You're right! But what can we do?"

"First let's figure out what they want. Then let's keep them from getting it."

"I assumed they wanted money."

"No. Those men weren't petty criminals. They left the other rooms untouched and came straight to this one. Why?"

Ana shrugged.

"Ours is the only room labeled for guests," Vanita said. "The others are numbered. Coincidence? Probably not, which means they were searching for something specific—something they knew we would have."

"Okay. So what is it?"

The two women considered the possibilities. An idea hit Ana. "The thief took a book! Remember? He snatched it as he left. It was just a history of the sisterhood that I was reading—nothing irreplaceable. But it shows what he was after. He was sent to find a book."

"They must want the Sacred Writing!" Vanita said.

"But that's strange. A few months ago that would have made sense, but now there are many copies of the scriptures circulating everywhere. More every day. Why would he want our particular one?"

Vanita nodded thoughtfully. "Good point. And why would a criminal gang care about a religious book? I mean, I could understand if it were the Exterminati. They were founded to stamp out Christianism. But the Clan is a different type of organization. They want money and power."

"I hear they're very superstitious. Maybe they think Christianism has magic spells they could use. Like you could put a hex on someone or conjure up evil fires if you knew the right words."

Vanita's jaw dropped. "Evil fires!"

"What?"

"Evil fires! We *do* know how to make evil fires!"

Ana shook her head, confused. "Not in the scriptures I've been reading."

Vanita rose and went to a closet. She located a sack that contained some of the belongings Teofil didn't want to take on his mission. Untying the drawstring, Vanita reached inside and pulled out a book. Ana strained to discern the title in the candlelight.

When recognition dawned on her, she gasped. The book described how to make the explosive powder. It had belonged to the High Priestess of Chiveis. Teo had stolen it from her, then accidentally carried it into exile: *The Secret Lore of Astrebril.*

"The Clan wants that deadly weapon," Vanita said.

Ana nodded. "And we have to make sure they don't get it."

✦   ✦   ✦

King Piair II stood on a balcony of his palace and gazed out over the Citadel, the capital city of Chiveis. The Citadel was constructed at a strategic location. A chain of very high mountains faced the Chiveisian frontlands, forming an unbroken wall in all but one place. There a cleft pierced the mountains, leading to a valley that branched south and east. The valley was a hospitable place to raise livestock on the rich mountain grass, or even grow a few crops in the bottomlands. The only entrance into this idyllic valley was through the cleft—a fact that did not escape the glorious founder of Chiveis, Jonluc Beaumont. He ordered the construction of a fortress whose ramparts would seal off the secluded vale. The Citadel spanned the cleft, climbing up the mountain flanks on either side. Its granite face was impenetrable, and its defensive armaments were intimidating. The Chiveisi who lived behind the Citadel's protective wall felt safe from all intruders. Even the citizens who lived on the other side—from the upscale town of Entrelac between two lakes, to the tiny village of Edgeton on the frontier—drew comfort in the knowledge they could flee to the sheltered valley in times of danger. In this way Chiveis was insulated from the outside world. And young King Piair intended to keep it that way.

The balcony doors opened, and Piair turned to see who had interrupted him. It was one of the few people in the kingdom who could barge in unannounced: his mother, Katerina.

"Good afternoon, my son," she said. "Come give your old mother a kiss." She held out her arms to him.

Piair frowned. At twenty years old he didn't want his mother treating him like a baby. He had been king for over a year now, since his father was killed. Yet no one else was around, and the palace was the highest point in the Citadel, so nobody could look down and see him. Begrudgingly he gave Katerina a kiss on the cheek, then bid her to sit at a wrought-iron table next to the balustrade.

The queen mother took a seat and poured two glasses of cider. She was a plump woman whose silver hair was streaked with the dark strands of her youth. Piair knew his own hair would look like that one day. He bore many of her features: black hair, gray eyes, strong chin. Yet Piair preferred to consider the ways he was dissimilar to his mother. She was short; he was tall. She was heavyset; he was thin. Even their ears were different: her lobes were attached to her jaw, but his hung free. Piair wanted the people of Chiveis to liken him not to Katerina but to his father, and to judge him a worthy successor. *I wish I looked more like him*, Piair thought. His sister, Princess Habiloho, had been blessed with their father's red hair, earning her the nickname "Flame of Chiveis." The thought of the deceased princess made Piair gloomy. He missed her.

"Habiloho always liked that sweet cider," he said, trying to spark a conversation. He found that talking about his sister actually eased the pain in some ways.

"She would be thirty this year. I should be bouncing a redheaded grandbaby on my knee instead of mourning."

Piair reached for his cider. "To the Flame of Chiveis," he said, raising his tumbler.

Katerina nodded and drank.

"What brings you here today, Mother? Perhaps you have news from my kingdom. What do you hear from the streets?"

"The people fear you, that's for sure."

"As they should."

The queen mother glanced at her son. "Should they?"

"Of course. They feared Father, didn't they?"

"They feared his authority. They feared his justice when they did wrong. Upstanding citizens didn't cower before him."

The implications of Katerina's statement irritated Piair. "So what are you saying? My people are oppressed by their lord?"

"There are those who believe freedoms in Chiveis have been curtailed of late," the queen mother answered.

"I wish I knew who they were. The Royal Guard would knock some sense into them."

Katerina sipped her cider. "My son, a king can be strong without dominating his people."

"The High Priestess teaches otherwise."

"The High Priestess?" Katerina scowled. "Since when was she admitted to the royal family? I have no regard for that dirty sl—"

Piair slammed his glass to the table. "I hope you weren't about to say what I think you were!"

"Oh, now you defend her too!" the queen mother spat. "No doubt she visits you as she did your father."

Piair felt his cheeks turn hot. "She is the mediatrix of the high god. Her rituals of sacred union are required of the king."

"*Rituals?* Is that what they're calling it these days? In my day we had a different word."

"You overstep yourself, Mother."

Katerina shook her head and sighed, trying to lighten the mood. "I'm sorry, Piair. You know I love you. I wish to offer you counsel, not critique."

"And what is your counsel?"

"Ease the burden upon the people. Grant freedom of religion. Let them seek their own gods—or God, as the case may be."

"A single god? You refer to the god of Christianity?"

"Perhaps. What harm would there be in that?"

Fury exploded in Piair's soul. He pounded his palm on the patio table, overturning his cider. "I will never tolerate that god! It's his fault that Habiloho and Father are dead! Astrebril hates this so-called 'Deu.' When Teofil and Anastasia introduced him to our land, Astrebril sent his deadly fire as punishment." Piair drilled his mother with a fierce stare. "Or do you so quickly forget the king's memory?"

Katerina rose from her seat. It took her a long moment to regain her composure. Piair watched her, his heart thumping hard. He swallowed nervously but tried to keep his expression firm, as befitted a man of his station.

"Piair," his mother said at last, "I think it is you who has forgotten the memory of the king."

She turned and walked inside the palace, leaving Piair alone.

◆　◆　◆

"Look at this, Marco."

Teo handed a piece of folded stationery to his friend. Only a few seconds passed before Marco's face took on an expression of surprise. "The Iron Shield wants you to visit his chambers in private?"

"Yeah. And read on. Look at the reason why."

"He says he wants to make a deal with you."

Brother Thomas sat up in his chair in the guest room at Montblanc

Palace. "We're not here to deal with him. We're here to bring a message to Mayor Calixte. I think you should leave that warrior alone."

"Me too," Marco agreed. "The man is evil. You of all people should know that, Teofil."

"I do know it. I don't plan on striking any bargains with him."

Marco frowned. "Surely you don't intend to go to his room? It could be a trap! That guy wants nothing more than to kill you—as slowly and painfully as possible."

"I know. But here in Jineve he's limited by having to keep up appearances. I don't think he'd try anything that would blow his cover."

"You don't *think* he would," Marco said skeptically, "but what if he did?"

"Things could turn ugly real quick. On the other hand, what if I missed a chance to gain some information about his plans?"

"We're not talking about verbal sparring around the dinner table here. The Iron Shield is a killer. You'd be alone in his room."

"Look, I refuse to be afraid of men like him. I intend to meet him head-on. Respect his capabilities, yes. Be cautious, of course. But I won't show fear. And I won't back down."

Marco wagged his head back and forth. "I can't decide if you're the cockiest person I know or the most courageous."

"Neither," Teo replied with a grin. "It's just that I have Deus on my side, and that makes me bold."

"Hmm, the Lord God *is* a mighty helper," Brother Thomas said thoughtfully.

Marco stared at his two companions for a moment, then went to his duffle and retrieved a little knife. He held it by its tip and offered the haft to Teo. "Put that in your boot. I'm sure the Lord God won't mind if you use it in a pinch." Teo chuckled as he complied with Marco's request.

At the appointed time the three men made their way to the palace wing where the Iron Shield was quartered. A shaman opened the door when they knocked. "We're here to see your master," Teo said.

"We know why you have come, Teofil of Chiveis. We have eyes in every head."

"And yet you cannot see."

The shaman offered a blank stare but didn't respond.

"Are you going to admit us or what?" Teo finally asked.

"Only you were invited into my master's presence. His words require privacy. The others may not pass."

"There's nothing you can say to me that you can't say to my friends."

"Nevertheless, only you may enter."

"How do we know this isn't a trap?" Marco asked with an edge in his voice.

The shaman scowled. "Such suspicions are worthy of a pirate robber like you, Marco of the high seas. But we in our ancient society are civilized. My master intends a parlay, not skullduggery."

Teo turned to Marco and Brother Thomas. "I'll only be gone a few moments. Let me see what the man wants, then I'll return. You wait here."

The shaman offered an oily smile and led Teo into the room. The second-floor salon afforded a splendid view of the Jinevan waterfront. Teo could see pedestrians strolling along the promenade that lined the docks. The fountain on the jetty spewed its water high into the air until the wind scattered the spray like a rooster-tail. Out on the sparkling lake, tiny sails dotted the waves.

A door opened, and the Iron Shield entered the salon. Instead of his customary hauberk of chain mail he wore a fashionable tunic. The man was a head taller than Teo and had tree trunks for legs, yet despite his size he moved with graceful ease. "Greetings, Teofil," he said, dipping his chin like some kind of distinguished gentleman.

"Why have you called me here?" Teo asked. He didn't intend to play polite games with a man responsible for so much death and suffering.

"I see you wish to be direct. Very well then." The Iron Shield clasped his hands behind his back and stared out the window. "It appears you and I have a common enemy."

Teo couldn't think of anything he had in common with the head of the Exterminati, so he remained silent.

"Who do you hate most in this world?" the Iron Shield asked.

You, Teo thought, but immediately corrected himself. There was one person he opposed even more.

The Iron Shield whirled to face Teo. "She is my enemy too."

What? How does he know . . .

"It's true," said the dark warrior. "The High Priestess of Chiveis is my mortal foe."

Teo was flabbergasted. The Iron Shield was based in Roma. From there he had managed to dig his claws into Likuria and Ulmbartia. Now he had even reached Jineve. *But Chiveis? How does this man know the High Priestess?*

"Explain yourself," Teo said.

"I journeyed to Chiveis and sought to ally myself with the painted queen of your land. But she would not see me. She did not want my aid. I grew angry and made threats, so she cursed my skills in battle by the immense power of her god. Now I hate her with an abiding hate."

"What does all this have to do with me?"

The Iron Shield went to a sideboard and poured a glass of brandy. He offered it to Teo, but when Teo didn't respond he put it to his lips and drank it down. Pointing at Teo with the empty glass he said, "You and I must enter into an alliance."

Teo had no such intentions. Yet he wanted to know the plans the Iron Shield had in mind, so he asked, "What kind of alliance?"

"Let us defeat the High Priestess together. Let us march against her with armies of war. And then, when she is ground beneath our heels like a cockroach, I will give you a great gift."

"You have nothing to offer to me."

"I beg to differ, Teofil." The Iron Shield's teeth were white and even as he smiled. "With my help you can have your heart's greatest desire."

"What would that be?"

"You may rule Chiveis as king. I have no interest in that frigid land of hardscrabble fields and barren peaks. Once I have my revenge, I will go on my way and never return. You could rule the realm as you see fit. Introduce your own deity if you wish. I will leave that up to you."

Teo eyed the Iron Shield. "I possess neither armies nor wealth. What would my part in this alliance be?"

"You know Chiveis better than anyone. Help me with an invasion strategy. You are the perfect man for the job."

"And if I were to say yes?"

"Then let us go immediately to my ship at the docks. I will take you to a camp on the lake, a secret place in the wilderness where we can make plans. Think of it, Teofil! This is your chance to fulfill all your dreams. You can reign supreme in Chiveis. Take the lovely Anastasia as your queen. Bring De . . . bring your god to that realm. I can make all these things happen for you! Just come with me to my ship."

Teo couldn't deny the appeal of what was being offered. *The High Priestess defeated. The Iron Shield gone forever. The Chiveisi serving Deu. And . . . marriage to Ana?*

No! Not like this!

The fantasy collapsed as Teo's inner vision clarified. He backed toward the door. "Get away from me, you tempter! Your words are devious. I would never join with you."

The Iron Shield's face fell. "I see. Well, I must say, that is most disappointing." He snapped his fingers.

The shamans attacked faster than seemed humanly possible. They ran—almost as if flying—from behind the curtains that draped the room. Teo was reaching for his boot knife when a wire encircled his neck. He struggled against the assailants who held him, but it was no use. A cloth covered his nose, filling his nostrils with a cloying scent. Dizziness fogged his brain, then everything went black.

◆　　◆　　◆

Darkness . . . jostling . . . men shouting.

Nothing.

Cramped muscles . . .

More darkness.

Teo squinted. A headache pounded in his temples. His tongue felt thick and dry. He tried to move but found he could not. Panic rose within him. He pressed the walls around, but nothing yielded.

Buried alive?

Terror seized Teo. His pulse shot up, and his breath came in rapid pants. Horrified, he thrashed as he lay on his side.

Nearby a man shouted a curse. Others responded with laughter.

Okay. Not buried. What then?

Teo felt the confining walls. They were made of wood. A few cracks let in a little light. Apparently he was in a trunk or coffin of some kind.

Teo exhaled a deep breath, fighting off the claustrophobia that threatened to overwhelm him. He put his eye to the nearest crack but couldn't see out. Bending his knee as much as he could, he reached down for his knife. It was too far, but he kept straining until his fingertips found the hilt. Gradually the knife slipped from his boot . . . and clattered to the floor of the trunk.

Easy now, Teo. Take it slow and easy.

He lowered his arm until his hand could touch the floor. His fingers probed back and forth. *There it is!* Elated, he grasped the knife with a solid grip.

Teo inserted the tip of his blade into the trunk's latch, trying to turn the bolt that would free the lid. Sweat stung his eyes as he struggled with the lock. Several times he had to calm himself before he could continue.

At last Teo felt the blade catch against the bolt. With as much torque as he could apply, he gave the knife a hard twist.

The tip of the blade snapped off, and the knife flew from his hands. *No!* Despair washed over Teo. His body went limp.

"Ready? Now!"

The lid of the trunk popped open. Numerous hands seized Teo and hauled him out, dazed and confused.

He was dragged to a clearing in the forest. Teo saw he was beside Leman Sea, though not within Jineve. The place was a deserted wilderness.

The shamans forced him to lay spread-eagle in the dirt. Two men pinned his arms and legs, while a third held iron stakes and a hammer. He brandished them at Teo with a delighted smile.

"Secure the hands first," the Iron Shield instructed. "The spikes will go through easier there than through the ankles."

Aghast, Teo felt the tip of a stake touch his palm. The shaman with the hammer raised it high. And then Teo reacted.

Curling his hand around the spike, he yanked it from his enemy's grasp and stabbed the sharp piece of iron into the man's thigh. The shaman dropped his hammer and howled as Teo withdrew the bloody spike and clubbed the second man across the skull. Wrenching his leg free, Teo kicked the third shaman in the face and bolted to his feet.

The Iron Shield held a long poker whose tip glowed red-hot. Enraged, he swung it at Teo. The blow was swift, and Teo wasn't able to dodge it completely. The poker clipped his left shoulder, knocking him to the ground.

The Iron Shield loomed over him. Teo gripped the iron stake in his clenched fist. His enemy was wearing chain mail again, and Teo knew the stake wouldn't penetrate the armor's well-wrought links.

"Prepare for *pain*," the Iron Shield sneered.

"You first!"

Teo plunged the spike through the top of the Iron Shield's foot deep into the earth. The dark warrior roared in agony. Teo scrambled up and ran.

The Exterminati clawed at him as he rushed to escape. At the edge of the forest clearing a shaman drew a bow. Teo seized one of his adversaries by his loose black robe and hurled him around. The arrow took the man in the upper back, thrusting its bloody head from his chest. Teo snapped off the arrow's shaft and dropped his human shield.

The man with the bow fumbled for a second arrow as Teo charged him. Though the shaman managed to get it on the string, he didn't have time to draw before Teo jabbed the arrow stub into his throat, knocking him backward in a cascade of blood. The bow and arrow flew from his hand, but Teo caught them both, then turned and nocked the arrow with the fluid motion of an experienced archer. Several shamans were almost on him. When Teo dropped the closest, the rest dived for cover. Teo dashed into the woods after snatching up the quiver.

He dodged through the trees, running at full speed, ignoring the branches that whipped at his face. Somewhere nearby a horse whinnied. As Teo broke into a clearing where thick grass grew, a chestnut stallion with a white blaze turned to look at him. The animal wore a fine saddle, and its flanks were sweaty. A towel, currycomb, and overturned bucket were on the ground. Evidently the shaman who was about to rub down the horse had left his post when he heard the commotion.

Teo approached the animal slowly, not wanting to startle it. The stallion was even-tempered and did not spook. It stood still, regarding Teo with what seemed like a dignified expression.

"Easy, boy," Teo said, grasping the reins. He put his foot in the stirrup and swung into the saddle. "We're going to have to see what you're made of today."

"He's stealing the master's horse! Seize him!" A bevy of shamans crashed through the underbrush. Two had bows. They halted and knelt. Others charged across the grass with their blades held high.

Teo loosed an arrow from full draw toward the shaman at the head of the pack. The man grunted and dropped to his knees, his sword slipping from his hand. His other hand clutched his chest. Directly behind him, a second shaman stumbled to the ground with the arrow protruding from his gut.

Thwock! The sickening sound of an arrow's impact against flesh was accompanied by an anguished squeal from the horse. It shivered, then bounded into the forest. Teo guided his mount onto a deer path and let it run.

For several minutes Teo rode the galloping stallion through the trees. No sounds of pursuit came to his ears. Teo had seen no other horses, and he assumed his enemies were unable to pursue.

At last the horse slowed. Teo turned in the saddle to examine its rump. An arrow had passed clean through the muscle. Teo led the animal to a river and let it drink while he washed the wound and packed it with moss. Although the chestnut stallion wasn't yet at the end of its strength, it couldn't travel much farther.

Hunger pangs rumbled in Teo's stomach. He unbuckled the saddlebags to see what was inside. The beef jerky and hardtack he found were welcome, but even more intriguing was a leather map case. Teo opened it and pulled out the map.

The crinkled paper was faded and brittle. Teo thought the words were probably in the Fluid Tongue, though it was hard to tell from place names. Colored lines that appeared to be roads were marked with letters and numbers. The topography was indicated by shading. Teo's eyes went to a large, crescent-shaped body of water called Lac Léman. At its western tip was a city: Genève. Teo sucked in his breath as he realized what he was reading.

Leman Sea.

Jineve.

A map of the Ancients!

He scanned the page, fascinated by the discovery of so precious a document. A smaller pair of lakes lay north of Lac Léman. One of them had a long, thin peninsula jutting into it. The depiction on the map triggered a memory.

No . . .

Teo slapped his forehead.

It can't be!

He had seen such a lake before. When Ana was abducted by outsiders in the Beyond, he had followed her through a lake just like that.

I entered the lake from a river on its eastern shore.

The river was on the map.

It flowed from the southeast . . . around a great bend . . . out of two other lakes.

Those features were on the map as well. One of the lakes was labeled, "Thunersee."

The Tooner Sea?

Teo swallowed hard. His hands trembled as he dropped the map.

"Almighty Deu," he whispered. "You've led me to Chiveis."

4

D o it quickly." The Iron Shield clenched his jaw. The man kneeling at his foot grasped the stake. All the other shamans stared, fascinated and horrified. The only sound in the forest was rough iron scraping against bone.

When the stake was clear of his foot, the Iron Shield demanded to see it. The gray spike was stained with his own blood. He raised it behind his head, intending to hurl it into the brush, then reconsidered. *I will keep it as a reminder of my hatred,* he decided. *Teofil of Chiveis has injured me twice. It will not happen again!*

The tall warrior turned his glare on his Exterminati henchmen. None of them spoke, fearing the rage about to burst from their master. The Iron Shield, however, was calm. Wild emotions did not drive him, unlike so many of the rabble. He was a man who controlled his fury, channeling it for his purposes. Yet those purposes now ran in opposite directions.

The shaman with the red armband broke the silence. He was a good lieutenant, quick-thinking and eager to please. "We will divide into two contingents. One will follow the blood trail. That injured horse cannot go far. The other will sail down the shoreline and set an ambush. Teofil can only go west if he expects to return to Jineve."

The Iron Shield did not answer right away. Instead he drew his knife and beckoned his lieutenant closer. Apprehension flickered in the man's eyes, but he approached. The Iron Shield grabbed a handful of the man's robe.

"My lord, I—"

The knife flashed. The shaman flinched. A hiss arose from several of the watching Exterminati.

The Iron Shield held up the swatch of coarse black material he had slashed from the shaman's garment. Wrapping it around his index finger, he bent down and tucked it into the bloody hole in the top of his boot. When the lieutenant backed away, the onlookers released their tension in a collective sigh.

"We will not be pursuing Teofil of Chiveis," the Iron Shield said.

"My lord," the lieutenant countered, "we can still apprehend him if we move now. All the trails converge along the shore to the west—"

"He will not go west."

The shaman stared at him. "But . . . there is only wilderness in every other direction."

"Do not argue with me! Teofil is well acquainted with wilderness travel. He knows we would lie in wait for him on the way back to Jineve. And even if he is inclined to return to the city, the map in the saddlebag will entice him away. He is gone from us! To pursue a mounted man while we are on foot would be folly. And besides, I cannot walk with this injury. Our mission's goals have now diverged. We must choose the greater desire of my mistress."

"The brimstone," said the lieutenant, finally understanding. He turned to the rest of the Exterminati. "Prepare the boats! We depart for Jineve at once."

"No. We will pass through Jineve by night. The circumstances surrounding Teofil's disappearance have surely raised suspicions against us." *But that doesn't matter,* the Iron Shield reminded himself. *The next time I come to Jineve, it will be to conquer!*

Most of the men scurried away to begin packing, but one shaman remained behind with a medical kit. The Iron Shield sat on the ground and let the man remove his boot. The cloth that had plugged the wound was dragged free, starting the blood flow again. The shaman lit a small fire of twigs, then began to pick debris from the wound with tweezers.

As the Iron Shield endured the procedure, the lieutenant with the red armband knelt at his side. "Send me in pursuit of Teofil," he urged. "I will find him and kill him."

"More likely he would kill you," the Iron Shield answered through gritted teeth.

"Never!"

"Regardless, I have a different mission for you."

"Then name it, master."

"We will return to Marsay. From there I shall sail to Sessalay. My mistress must have her brimstone."

"Very good. And what is my role in the mission?"

"To oversee a great host. The homing pigeons aboard my caravel will fly to the chiefs of the Exterminati in every land. I intend to summon all my warriors to Marsay. You must meet them there. Assemble them in the hidden marshes of the Camarg, and keep them in a state of readiness until my return from Sessalay."

The lieutenant could see it was a heavy responsibility, which seemed to please him. "I will do exactly as you command. And for what purpose shall I prepare our brothers?"

"Prepare them for battle. The Society of the Exterminati must join the Chiveisian army in making war on Jineve. With the High Priestess's brimstone weapon, we will be invincible."

The lieutenant's eyes lit up. "Excellent! It will be a glorious victory! All your plans will succeed, for the gods favor you!" He hesitated, glancing into the deep woods. "I only wish—"

"What?"

"I wish Teofil of Chiveis had not escaped. It galls me. I share your hatred of him, and I wish to see him suffer."

The Iron Shield stared at his lieutenant for a moment, then reached out and clasped his shoulder. "Do not fear. Soon enough we shall draw Teofil out. It will not be difficult. All we need is the right—"

"I'm sorry, master," interrupted the shaman with the medical kit, "but the bleeding inside the gash must be stopped."

Nodding, the Iron Shield said, "Do it."

Excruciating pain exploded in his foot as a hot spike was thrust into his wound. The stench of burnt flesh assailed his nostrils. His fingers clawed the earth, gouging ruts in the dirt. He held his breath and squinted until the cauterization was over. For several minutes the Iron Shield could only pant, struggling to regain his composure. At last he turned back to his lieutenant.

"As I was saying," he explained with forced calmness, "we can lure Teofil out of hiding quite easily."

"But . . . how?" The lieutenant's face was pale, and his voice quivered.

"All we need is the right *bait*."

✦　　✦　　✦

Shaphan the Metalsmith was tired of making nails. And horseshoes. And ax heads. Nevertheless, he kept doing these things because he needed to make a living—without being noticed.

It was more than a year ago now that Teofil and Anastasia were exiled and the community of truth-seekers broke up. The Sacred Writing had gone with the captain, so only the few translations he had completed before leaving Chiveis remained. Sometimes the former members of the house community met in the woods to be encouraged from the precious scrolls. Yet this was extremely dangerous. The run-in with the pair of guardsmen two months earlier proved that well enough. The High Priestess held King Piair II in her grip. Through him, she was running the kingdom as a theocratic police state in which only Astrebril and the lesser triad of Vulkain, Pon, and Elzebul could be worshipped. The one true God had been defeated in Chiveis.

Shaphan quenched a horseshoe in cold water. Steam arose as the metal rapidly cooled and hardened. He tossed the shoe onto a pile and arched his back, wiping sweat from his forehead. *There was a time I thought I'd have a different future than this.* But everything had changed when the High Priestess confronted the worshippers of Deu head-on. Though Shaphan was never accused of being a heretic, he had been Teofil's student at the University, and his wife, Lina, was Anastasia's cousin. To make matters worse, Lina's uncle Stratetix and aunt Helena had been forced to recant their faith to survive the persecution. Because of these suspicious connections, Shaphan couldn't pursue a career that would put him in the public eye. He had quit his university studies and resorted to everyday metalwork in the clifftop hamlet of Vingin. The village had burned down, so there was plenty of work to be had making nails and tools for rebuilding. But Shaphan longed for more.

Lina entered the smithy with a jug of ale and some bread and cheese. "Ready for lunch?"

Shaphan smiled at his beautiful wife with the white-blonde curls. She was a thin, pale creature with luminous blue eyes. He thought of her as a flower, perhaps the mountain-star flower that was the symbol of Chiveis. Like Lina, the ehdelveis was lovely and white and ever so delicate.

"I'm parched," Shaphan said, taking a mug from her hand. "Sit and eat with me."

They sat on a bench with the platter of bread and cheese between them. Shaphan cut off great slabs of the brown, grainy loaf and smeared it with brie. He sighed as he took a bite. "A simple life with my bride," he said with his mouth full.

Lina glanced at him. "Is it enough?"

"It's heaven's purpose, I suppose." Shaphan intentionally referred to Deu without using his name. One never knew who was listening, and rewards were available to informants.

"Do you think things will ever change?" Lina's words were vague too, but Shaphan knew what she meant. She was asking if Deu would come to Chiveis.

"Anything is possible if it's the divine will. We'll just have to wait and see."

Lina removed a fat pear from her apron pocket, then cut off a piece and handed it to Shaphan. As she did, she leaned close to him. "Do you think Ana could still be alive?"

The couple instinctively glanced around though the smithy was empty and they weren't near a window or door.

A depressing scenario ran through Shaphan's mind: *Teofil and Anastasia climbed to a frozen wasteland during a storm. Lacking food and shelter, they faced death from exposure if the crevasses didn't swallow them first. The corpse of Lina's cousin was probably locked in the ice of a glacier right now.* But of course Shaphan didn't say those things to his wife. A believer in Deu should never despair.

"Anything is possible if it's the divine will," he repeated, though he didn't feel very confident.

Lina's countenance turned gloomy. As Shaphan put his arm around her shoulder, unexpected anger rose within him. Captain Teofil had been his mentor, and Anastasia was Lina's closest friend. *Why should they be excised from the face of Chiveis like a cancer? Deu isn't an evil God—it's Astrebril who's evil! Curse the High Priestess! And curse the cowardly young king who won't stand up to her!*

Frustrated, he rose from the bench and picked up an ax. He brandished it while Lina stared at him. "What this kingdom needs is—"

"Hush, Shaphan! Don't say it!"

"Obedient, docile peasants? Is that what you want me to say? That this kingdom needs unthinking slaves to go along with every whim of a corrupt—"

"Stop!" Lina pleaded. She went to Shaphan's side. "It's okay to be angry," she whispered in his ear. "I'm angry too. But you can't say it out loud."

"Why not?"

"Because I need you."

"And Chiveis needs . . . the divine one." Shaphan used the ambiguous term for Lina's sake. Her face looked so desperate.

"We do have him," she said. "You and I, in our hearts. Let's be patient, okay? In his timing he may come to our land."

Shaphan uttered a profanity. "And I suppose your cousin is coming back too! She's going to ride in on a stallion and everything will be glorious!"

"Shaphan, please . . . " Lina's voice trembled as she spoke.

"What this kingdom needs is radical change! A rebellion, if necessary!" Shaphan slammed the ax into the wooden stump that supported his anvil.

Lina was sobbing now. Shaphan gathered his wife into his arms and held her for a long time, stroking her hair. "I'm sorry," he said at last.

"There can be no more talk like that." Lina separated from Shaphan and gave him a hard look through red-rimmed eyes. "The sacrifice would be too great."

"What do you mean? Why can't we make the kind of sacrifice that . . . they did? Couldn't we find the strength to follow in their footsteps?"

"Maybe you and I could, Shaphan," Lina acknowledged. She grasped her husband's hand and placed it on her belly. "But what about your baby?"

❖　❖　❖

The wounded horse hung its head, exhausted from its exertions and the loss of blood. Teo had ridden north on a deer path that followed a river, but for the past few leagues he had walked beside his mount, trying to conserve its strength. The noble beast had given its best, but now it could go no farther.

Up ahead a campfire twinkled in the evening shadows. Though Teo had no idea who it was, he knew it wasn't the Exterminati. They couldn't have gotten ahead of him—not to the north, at least.

The thought of those evil shamans repulsed Teo. He patted the horse's nose as it wheezed, angry that the men had inflicted such suffering on the beast. The arrow wound in its rump had stopped bleeding, but the animal was clearly in pain.

Teo thought back to the helpless feeling he had experienced when the men stretched him out for torture. There was no underlying purpose in their cruelty; they wanted no information from him. The Iron Shield only wished to see Teo suffer before murdering him. *What a fool I am*, he thought. He had pushed the limits of bravery and nearly came out on the losing end. It was clear now that the Iron Shield's lies were nothing but a trick to persuade Teo to leave Jineve quietly so he could be killed in secret. Teo hoped Marco and Brother Thomas would raise the alarm back in the city. A kidnapping might convince Mayor Calixte that the strange visitor with the glass eye wasn't the reputable merchant he claimed to be.

The sorrel nickered softly, snapping Teo's thoughts back to the present. The animal needed rest, and grain if possible. Teo figured he had no choice but to see who was camping along the river ahead. He gathered the reins and walked forward, feeling naked without his sword.

"Hail, the camp!" he shouted, using the speech of the Chiveisi.

A long silence greeted him. Then: "Who goes?"

"Just a friend looking for company over a warm fire."

"Come in nice and easy."

Teo entered the campfire's circle of light. No one was visible, so Teo seated himself by the fire and removed the lid of the pot that hung over the flames. "Looks delicious," he called as he stirred the stew. "I have a flask of fine whiskey to share with anyone who can cook something that smells this good."

Cautiously a man emerged from the shadows. He was middle-aged and scrawny, though his finger was plenty strong enough to trigger the crossbow in his hands. The man aimed it a Teo, eyeing him, taking his measure.

"I'm unarmed," Teo said, "and I can spin some great stories for someone who shares a meal with me."

At last the man seemed convinced of Teo's goodwill. He approached the fire and sat down. Soon the two forest wanderers were devouring the venison stew.

After the meal they sipped whiskey from the Iron Shield's flask and talked about trails and river courses. Teo learned that his new friend had taken up the vagabond life many years ago, so he knew the trails well. He lived off the land, doing a little fur trading on the side.

"That's a nice-lookin' horse ya got there," the man said. "Won't be able to walk in the morning with that wound. Give him a few days rest, though, and he'll be frisky again—if ya got time to wait."

"Nice saddle and harness too," Teo remarked. "Inlaid with silver."

The vagabond nodded but said nothing. Teo looked at him. Grins spread across both men's faces as each deduced what the other was thinking.

"My boat?" the man asked.

"And some food. Waybread . . . beans . . . coffee if you can spare it."

"Sure. I'll throw in a knife and hatchet as well. A little rusty, but they'll do. Plus a blanket."

"If you have any broadheads, I could hunt."

"Deal. I'm still coming out way ahead on this one."

"Yeah, you sure are," Teo said with a laugh.

The two men shook hands good-naturedly and turned in for the night. The next morning before the sun was up, Teo shoved the boat into the water. The craft was slender and light, a lapstrake canoe designed for wilderness travel. Although the way to Jineve was downstream, Teo knew the Iron Shield could easily cordon off the area and ambush him. One or two men might be evaded, but the Iron Shield had close to three dozen shamans at his disposal. Attempting to return to the city right now would be far too dangerous. Brother Thomas had intended to stay in Jineve for several weeks, working to convert Mayor Calixte—which meant poor Marco would be stuck there without a way home, hoping for the best but fearing the worst. Teo regretted that, yet nothing could be done about it. His only recourse was to disappear. And besides . . .

I have a map to Chiveis!

The idea that he was within a week's journey of his homeland had never occurred to him. Yet the more he thought about it, the more it made sense. He calculated the rough distance he had traveled south from Chiveis to Roma. Now, with the aid of the map, he realized he had journeyed that same distance north—yet not due north. He was a hundred leagues west of Chiveis. But what changed things entirely was that from his current position, no massive glaciers or incredibly tall mountains stood in the way. He had found a way around them. Teo decided that when he brought Ana home, they would use this new, relatively easy route.

Ana! Where are you right now? I miss you!

Teo's heart ached as his thoughts went to his beloved. His deep longing to be reunited with Ana only strengthened his resolve to find the way to Chiveis right now. Teo intended to make the most of this opportunity while leaving enough time to return to the port of Marsay before the winter storms closed the sea. He imagined what he would say to Ana at their reunion: *I'm back, my love, and I have so much to tell you! Yes, yes, the trip was superb. And oh, by the way, your mother and father say hello.* Teo laughed at the ridiculous fantasy and paddled harder upstream.

Over the next week he followed the route on the map. He soon reached a spot where another river swung close to the one he was on. Teo had to make the portage between them twice—first with the canoe and then with the supplies—but anticipation strengthened him. On the new river he paddled with the current until it reached a broad inland sea. He steered his canoe into a waterway that led to a second, smaller body of water.

Now Teo began to grow excited. This was the lake with the peninsula he had recognized on the map. As he paddled along the eastern shore and spotted a ruined dam, a rush of memories came flooding back. Teo had crossed that dam in a desperate attempt to catch up to the outsiders who had kidnapped Ana. Later he returned the same way with Ana safe in his boat. *How I want to bring her here again! O Deu, let it be!*

After portaging around the dam, Teo continued along the Farm River until the shadows began to lengthen. He pressed on through the evening, munching the last of his waybread as he paddled. When the sun went down he kept going under the pale light of the moon.

Teo reached a sharp bend in the river. He lifted his paddle and drifted in the lonely stillness. Everything was silent. Teo's breath made wisps of fog in the crisp night air. He looked up to his right at a high bluff—the place he first met Anastasia of Edgeton.

"Thank you, Deu," he whispered.

He was in Chiveis.

◆　◆　◆

Ana poured water into a bowl and washed with a bar of soap that smelled of jasmine. The water was cold against her skin, for the morning was chilly now that it was the tenth month. *It's a whole lot colder in Chiveis right now,* she thought as she scrubbed her face. *So why exactly do I want to go back there?* Ana smiled to herself as she considered it. Though Roma's climate was warm and sunny, she couldn't help but prefer the snow-capped peaks and flower-strewn meadows of Chiveis. *Why go back? Because it's home!*

She finished her morning ablutions and hung the washrag on a peg, then put on her gown. After opening the curtains to let in the morning sun she nudged the rumpled mass on the second bed. "Get up, sleepy," she said. "We need to make an early start."

"Mmmph," said a groggy voice from under the blankets.

Ana laughed. "I think you just said, 'Bring coffee,' right?"

The lump moaned again.

"I'll be back in a minute with breakfast," Ana promised as she closed the door behind her.

Vanita Labella was much more coherent when Ana returned with a tray of hard, sweet biscuits and a steaming mug. Vanita sipped the chicory coffee gratefully, then reached for one of the slender, almond-flavored biscuits. She dunked it in her coffee to soften it.

"The ponies are saddled and waiting," Ana said.

"Pack up," Vanita answered with her mouth full. "I'll be ready when you are."

Ana removed a book securely wrapped in leather and twine from her dresser drawer. She slid it into a nondescript satchel, then covered it with some cosmetics and a small sack of fruit. Nobody would suspect that what appeared to be an everyday handbag actually carried the secret recipe for explosive powder.

The two women set out from the convent on horseback, accompanied by Liber, whose impressive size would make any potential troublemakers think twice. In the wake of the attack by the Clansmen, Ana and Vanita had decided it was too dangerous to leave *The Secret Lore of Astrebril* unprotected. The seaside convent was shielded only by its obscurity, and the sisterhood had no means of defense against a determined thief. But the basilica of the Christiani was a large and impenetrable building. Surely somewhere within its thick walls the Papa would have a vault to guard the book from any who would misuse its deadly power.

The early morning chill wore off as the sun rose higher. Liber rode at the head of the trio, keeping a sharp lookout left and right. He was obviously enjoying his role as the women's protector.

"We're in good hands," Ana remarked to Vanita. "Look at Liber watching out for us."

Vanita nodded. "I wouldn't want to face him when he's angry and holding a heavy staff." She glanced at Ana, and the two of them grinned. They had seen Liber fight. Though he wasn't a warrior by training, his bulk made him a fearsome opponent.

The travelers arrived at a river port. From one of the docks a boat company operated a daily ferry to the city of Roma, which was situated several leagues upriver from the sea.

"The last time I rode this ferry I was with Teo," Ana told Vanita. "We were coming to Roma for the first time to find the New Testament. I remember being scared. I didn't know what to expect."

"I bet you didn't imagine you'd return a few months later when the Sacred Writing was being printed and distributed all around the city."

"I know—who could have guessed? Deu has done some amazing things."

"This way, Stasia," Liber called in his thick voice. He held out his hand toward a ramp that led onto the riverboat.

Ana and Vanita dismounted and gave the ponies to a stable boy along with a few coins. They boarded the ferry and found seats under an awning. At the appointed time the boat shoved off and the rowers began propelling it upstream. Most of the passengers appeared to be businessmen. Ana assumed they were involved in the shipping industry, which would require them to visit Roma's harbor from time to time.

The ferry docked a few hours later at a pier on the river's left bank. The place reminded Ana of the time she and Teo had eluded the shaman spies who chased them through the streets. Today, however, the only chasing Ana could discern was the shoppers' hunt for bargains.

"There's the bridge up ahead," Vanita said. The two women and their bodyguard reached it and crossed to the other side. Before long they arrived at the Christiani basilica with its impressive facade and incredible dome.

"I think that building will always amaze me," Ana remarked.

"Take a good look at it. You never know when it will be your last time."

As the threesome climbed the front steps they grew quiet. Ana knew Vanita and Liber were recalling the same thing as she: the epic battle that took place in the circular plaza. Ana and Vanita had watched it from the portico, while Liber actually participated in the fighting. Things had come so close to disaster—then Deu provided the victory. Ana felt glad those days were over.

The interior of the basilica was dark and cool. A shaft of sunlight from the dome illumined an altar canopy that stood on spiraled pillars. As the visitors proceeded down the nave, a familiar voice hailed them. Ana turned toward the man who approached.

"Anastasia of Chiveis! Liber! And Lady Vanita Labella—welcome!"

The speaker was robed in white with a gold sash around his waist. Though he wore a hood, it did not cover the self-inflicted scar on his brow that marked his solidarity with all who were broken and downtrodden. As if that were not enough, the fingernails of his left hand were missing— badges of the torture he had endured for the name of Deu. He was the blessed Ambrosius, the Overseer of the Forbidden Zone.

"Greetings, Brother Ambrosius," Ana said. The three guests exchanged the kiss of peace with the esteemed Christiani priest.

"I am surprised and delighted to see you today," said the Overseer. "I did not realize you were paying a visit to the city."

Ana held up her satchel. "We've come on secret business."

"Oh?"

"I have a book that describes how to make the explosive powder. We believe the Clan wants it, so we brought it here for safekeeping."

"That is most wise. The basilica can provide a measure of safety that your little convent cannot." The Overseer beckoned with his finger to a brown-robed priest. "Pietro, take this book and secure it in the vault," he instructed. "Try to avoid being seen by any of the servants. Not all of them are trustworthy." The man nodded and moved off with his parcel, then the Overseer turned back to his guests with a broad smile. "I must say, it is quite fortuitous you have paid us a visit today! If you will come with me, I will show you a marvel."

"Gladly," Ana said.

The visitors followed the Overseer through a series of halls and stair-wells to a room filled with bookshelves. At the far end, men with ink-stained aprons were busy setting type for a printing press that used a giant screw to make impressions on the paper.

"Hey, there's Sol!" Vanita pointed to an old man with long white hair. He hadn't seen the new arrivals, so Vanita called the name of her childhood teacher. Sol's face lit up, and he rose from his desk to greet his friends. As he bowed politely, Ana suppressed a smile. She recalled how

Vanita had once described Sol as "an overworked old geezer nearing retirement." *Times change,* Ana thought, *and so does our perspective.*

Sol's wrinkled face was animated as he talked. He described the successful distribution of several costly, high-quality editions of the Sacred Writing. Now the presses were churning out inexpensive copies that the masses could afford. It would be a time-consuming endeavor, yet Sol clearly took delight in it.

"Tell them about the other project," the Overseer prompted. "I think Anastasia will be pleased."

Sol grinned as he took Ana by the arm. "You have to see it for yourself."

Everyone moved to a writing desk by the window. Sol opened a drawer and reached inside, then glanced up at Ana before withdrawing his hand. "Close your eyes," he said.

Ana complied.

"Now open them."

Ana looked down at the desk's surface. A leaf of the finest vellum lay there. The scrollwork around the edge was extraordinary in its detail, and the typeface was elegant. The leaf was a title page that read *Versio Secunda Chiveisorum.*

"The Second Version of the Chiveisi," Sol said proudly. "A gift to the people of your land from the Papa at Roma."

"Sol, it's wonderful!" Ana understood the significance of the work right away. Teo and Sol had spent months translating the Old Testament into the Chiveisian speech, which they had named the Prima. Now Sol was making a Secunda that would include both testaments—a beautiful new edition to take back to Chiveis.

"Well done, brother," the Overseer said. "May Deus honor your labors."

Sol waved off the compliment. "It's Teofil who deserves to be acknowledged. He did most of the work. That man singlehandedly recovered the Sacred Writing in the Chiveisian speech."

Vanita leaned toward Ana and said in a low voice, "Careful there, sweetie. If you smile any wider, you'll break your pretty face."

Ana blushed and turned to her friend. "I'm really proud of him," she said.

"You should be," Vanita replied with a nod and a wink.

"I have something else to show you. Look here." Sol reached into a second drawer and withdrew an ornate book cover. It was embellished with silver filigree in a foliage pattern. In the middle of the tracery was a blank panel.

"Oh . . . it's so beautiful!" Ana ran her finger over the delicately wrought silver. "I've never seen anything like it."

"We envision an embroidered scene of Chiveis in that panel." Sol heaved his shoulders and let out a heavy sigh. "Unfortunately, the Roman embroiderers don't know what your land looks like."

"I could describe it for them, I suppose."

Sol shook his head, grinning expansively. "We have a better idea."

Ana looked around. Vanita and the Overseer were all smiles too. Even Liber seemed to be in on the joke. Heat rose to Ana's neck and cheeks. "You mean . . . ?" She put her hand on her chest.

"Yes!" Sol cried. "We want you to make it!"

"I do embroider a little bit," Ana said, taken aback. "But I'm no artist."

The Overseer gently touched Ana's shoulder. "Teofil is a master of words, but you have a gift for seeing beauty. This project requires both of your skills. Seek the spirit of Deus, my sister. Let him guide your hand."

Ana swallowed. "Alright. If you want me to do this, I will be honored to accept the assignment." She hoped her reply sounded confident, though she actually felt intimidated by the task.

Nevertheless, as the two women were getting ready for bed that night in one of the basilica's guest rooms, Ana found her mind ablaze with ideas. She sat in front of a mirror, brushing out her hair while Vanita washed her face in a basin.

"I know what scene I'm going to embroider," Ana said.

Vanita reached for a towel and patted her cheeks. "Tell me."

"It's based on a poem I once recited at a competition in Chiveis—a lament for my fallen kingdom. Teo was there that day. He quieted the crowd for me when they wouldn't settle."

"That man sure has a way of showing up when you need him."

Ana smiled and nodded. "Yeah. Always."

"What will your scene look like?"

"It'll have snowy mountains in the background. There will be milch cows in a meadow with bells on their necks. To me the sound of cowbells is the sound of Chiveis. In the grass I'll scatter the mountain-star flowers of our kingdom."

"I don't think I've seen those."

"They only grow at the highest elevations. One of the stanzas of my poem was, 'You mountain-stars, so small and white, your blossom shines like snow. Long have you been the folk's delight! Why do you cease to grow?' Old grandmothers say if the ehdelveis ever stops growing, the kingdom will fall. I often felt Chiveis had fallen into evil."

"Just remember, nothing is beyond the reach of Deu."

Ana paused, then crossed the room toward her friend. Wet strands of Vanita's hair dripped onto her shoulders. Ana took her hand and squeezed it. "Thank you for being an encouragement to me," she said.

"No, Anastasia, thank *you*. Thank you for leading me to the one true God." Tears welled up in Vanita's eyes. The sight of them made Ana choke up as well.

Vanita sniffled and gave an embarrassed laugh as she looked away. "Is there anything else in your scene?"

"Yes, one more thing."

"What?"

"My poem was called 'The Turtledove Who Could Not Fly.' It described how evil creatures that symbolized the gods had nothing to teach the little bird. Some of them even persecuted it. That's why the poem ended on a sad note. But in my scene for the Secunda, I'm going to put a turtledove soaring above the mountains."

Vanita caught Ana's eyes. "How come?"

"Because I've finally learned to fly," Ana said, "and I believe someday Chiveis will too."

◆　◆　◆

The sun was up, the sparrows were chirping, and the sky seemed bluer than normal. Teo was in good spirits, for he was home.

Well, not quite home, he reminded himself. *Remember—you're under a death sentence.*

While living in Chiveis, Teo had belonged to the Fifth Regiment of the Royal Guard, a renowned military unit posted on the frontier. As a captain he had been assigned his own rooms at the regional headquarters along the Farm River. He also had a bedchamber at the University of Chiveis, where he was a part-time professor. But now Teo was neither soldier nor scholar. He was a criminal, wanted by the state for heresy and high treason. That meant he'd have to stay anonymous.

Teo dragged the canoe into a thicket where it wouldn't be found. His waybread was gone, and the beans wouldn't last much longer. As for the coffee, he had long since finished that off. He tucked his dull knife in his belt, knowing it would be better than nothing if he found himself in a scrape. His best weapon was the bow, but carrying it around would draw too much attention. He left it behind with his hatchet and a handful of arrows. He would need to hunt meat during his return to Jineve.

Once the boat was secure Teo hiked into the woods. Somewhere near his position on the river he knew there was a rundown line cabin where Chiveisian soldiers were often posted to guard an entry point into the kingdom. Teo hoped the cabin wasn't currently being used. He needed clothing to blend in, and that was the sort of thing one could find in such cabins.

After a little scouting Teo located the deer path that approached the cabin from the wilderness. The Chiveisi called the wilderness "the Beyond," a vast and fearsome void into which they never set foot. Teo was one of the few citizens ever to venture into it. He had discovered the Beyond actually had a lot going for it.

As he followed the path between two low hills, his experienced eyes noticed footprints in the earth. They were faint now, a recent rain having nearly obliterated them. Yet Teo was able to discern an odd type of boot intermingled with those of a normal Chiveisian make. He inspected one of the tracks. It looked like the print of . . .

An outsider?

That made no sense. The barbarians of the forest were rarely encountered. When the Chiveisi did interact with them, it was to fight them off, not traipse around the woods together. Yet these prints indicated some kind of dealings with the outsiders. *Why?*

Teo followed the prints off the trail. As he picked his way through the underbrush, something white caught his eye. He took a closer look—and his breath caught in his chest.

A decayed corpse lay in the wet leaves, wearing the tattered remains of a Royal Guard's uniform. Teo knelt and examined the skull. A knife had been thrust into the back of the victim's neck, execution style.

Shocked, Teo rose to his feet and backed away. *What's going on here?* He swiveled his head, staring around the forest. Then his eyes caught a flash of movement through trees.

Outsiders!

Teo ducked behind a tree and peered around. Men had gathered a short distance away, though Teo believed they hadn't seen him.

Keeping under cover, he moved closer to the men. He eased to his belly and crept beneath a rhododendron whose branches arched just enough to provide a way through. Teo peeked between the waxy leaves. Four or five outsiders stood there: brawny, long-haired warriors whose beards were braided after the fashion of their people. The red-haired leader was taller than the rest, with a commanding presence and an arrogant swagger. He was missing a finger on his left hand.

Yet it wasn't the outsiders that startled Teo most. Other men mingled in their midst—men whose uniforms identified them as belonging to the militia of the Chiveisian god Vulkain. Teo had run into Vulkainians like these before. They were a cruel lot, unhindered by any sense of military honor. Their favorite weapon was that of a terrorist: a pistol that sprayed acid on its victims. The gun made an excellent riot-control weapon, because anyone who took a shot of acid to the face was immediately incapacitated. The Vulkainians were fond of intimidating the peasants by giving them a spritz on the arm for the smallest offense. It was this aura of cruelty and invincibility that made the High Priestess select the Vulkainians as her bodyguards and personal death squad.

As Teo surveyed the scene, another bearded outsider arrived from the trail that led toward the line cabin. He approached the nine-fingered leader. "The Chiveisi priest draws near, my lord Vlad," he said.

Vlad nodded approvingly. "Excellent. How many mules does he have with him?"

"Three, lord."

Vlad pursed his lips and shrugged. "A good start."

A few minutes later Teo saw the archpriest of the Vulkainian Order ride up on a gleaming white mare. Each of the gods of Chiveis had a color sacred to him: white for Vulkain, black for Elzebul, green for Pon, and crimson for the high god, Astrebril. The priests of these gods often dyed their horses' coats accordingly.

The archpriest looked down his nose at Vlad from the saddle. "You are in charge of this rabble?"

Vlad's face turned mean. He put his hand on his sword's hilt, but before he could reply the archpriest ordered, "Get your hand off that weapon if you ever hope to spawn another son! Do you think the gods of heaven would spare you if you committed such treachery?"

Reluctantly Vlad relaxed his grip on his sword. "We are your confederates," he grumbled. "Why do you speak to your ally as if to an enemy?"

The archpriest turned his horse away. "I do not question the decisions of my queen. Yet that doesn't mean I have to like the filth with which she deals."

"My people were good enough for your great Beaumont," Vlad retorted.

Beaumont!

Teo was astounded. *How does this outsider know about . . .*

The answer dawned on Teo at the same moment the archpriest replied to Vlad. "The Pact is a military alliance, not a friendly brotherhood," said the sallow-faced priest in the bleached white robe. Everything clicked into place as Teo realized what this forest convocation represented. It was a renewal of the ancient Pact he had read about in the palimpsest manuscript at Castle d'If.

But why? For what purpose has the High Priestess allied herself with outsiders?

The archpriest of Vulkain snapped his fingers. Several underlings led three mules into the circle of men. Vlad walked to the lead mule and untied a thong on one of the large bundles strapped to the animal's back.

He withdrew a sword and ran his thumb along its edge, then looked down the blade's length to inspect its line. He gave the weapon a few swings, appearing satisfied with its balance.

"I don't care if you call me your friend as long as you keep supplying steel like this," he said to the archpriest.

Teo grimaced and shook his head at the scene before him. The outsiders were long-standing enemies of the Chiveisi. Historic wars had been fought to defend against their invasions. Now the representatives of the kingdom were giving away fine weapons while many guardsmen had to make do with poor-quality blades. Steel was rare in Chiveis—so rare in fact that coins were minted from it. The kingdom lacked iron ore to produce new steel. To see three loads of swords being given to the rapacious outsiders felt like a betrayal of everything Chiveis stood for.

Vlad was sparring aggressively with one of his comrades, but he turned from his swordplay and addressed the archpriest. "You brought the birds?"

"Yes. New pigeons have been installed in the loft. Stay close to it, and respond right away to any directives you receive. Her Eminence is making plans as we speak. Those birds will save me further trips into this godforsaken hinterland."

"Whatever you say, Your Great and Holy Whiteness." Vlad's tone was mocking. Several of his men guffawed at their lord's sarcastic wit.

The archpriest stepped his horse close to the smug outsider. A couple of the Vulkainians put their hands on their acid guns, while the outsiders gripped their swords but did not draw them.

"Your face is ugly enough already, Vlad the Nine-Fingered," said the archpriest. "I wouldn't want my men to have to disfigure it further."

He whirled his mount and urged it into a trot with a clucking sound. Soon he disappeared around a bend in the trail. The Vulkainians filtered out of the clearing, leaving the outsiders alone.

Vlad glanced around at his warriors, brandishing his new sword. "Stay sharp, men. That black-haired vixen of the Chiveisi is up to something big."

And I'm going to figure out what it is, Teo vowed from his hiding place in the brush.

◆ ◆ ◆

Helena d'Armand gave a half turn to the skewer she had set over the hot coals of a campfire. Sizzling juices dripped from the carcass of a young wild pig. Helena's stomach rumbled as she smelled the savory aroma of the roasting pork. The meat had been on the spit for about six hours. Soon it would be ready—just in time for the other guests to arrive at the lonely camp in the woods.

Stratetix came to the fire and knelt beside his wife. "That little guy was the fattest of the herd," he said, reaching for the basting brush. He swabbed a liberal amount of sunflower oil mixed with wine and herbs over the meat. "Did you remind Lina to bring the ale?"

"Yes, love. What would a pig roast be without ale? And she's making cherry pie too."

"Good! Remember how she and Ana used to make . . . " Stratetix's jovial mood changed abruptly as he broke off midsentence.

"I remember it well," Helena said, picking up the conversation without missing a beat. "Every year at the Harvest Festival they would make those cherry pies. Those were good times, weren't they?"

Helena could see her lighthearted reminiscence had lifted Stratetix's spirits. "Yeah, life was good back then," he agreed, then glanced at his wife with a mischievous smile. "Those girls sure had different motives for their baking, didn't they?"

Helena laughed and nodded. "Lina kept hoping to attract all the farm boys to her table. If the way to a man's heart is through his stomach, our clever niece didn't want to miss any opportunities!"

"But Ana never thought like that." Stratetix wagged his head with amusement. "She didn't care about those village boys. She was just so competitive, she wanted to win the blue ribbon every time."

"I was cleaning up the other day, and I found those ribbons in a box. She won three. I'm going to show them to her if she ever . . . "

Now it was Helena's turn to falter. She swallowed awkwardly. Though she wanted to say something hopeful, the burden of her grief clogged her throat and took away her words.

"Better give that pig another turn," Stratetix muttered.

Helena sighed and rotated the spit.

A gibbous moon had risen above the trees when the rest of the group arrived. They were the former members of the Chiveisian house community that had discovered the one true God. In addition to Stratetix and Helena, the group consisted of Shaphan and Lina, Helena's sister Rosetta, and Lewth, a slender monk who was still enrolled in the Fraternal Order of Astrebril despite being a secret believer in Deu. Lewth's public denial of his faith under the threat of death preserved his good standing as a tutor at the royal palace. He now taught science and mathematics to a gaggle of aristocratic teens, though his most prominent student, King Piair himself, no longer took instruction from anyone.

"Welcome, friends," Stratetix said, rising from a log next to the fire. "It's a good night for a party of hunters to enjoy a little feast in the woods, don't you think?" He embraced everyone warmly, then spoke to Shaphan in a low voice. "Are you certain you weren't followed?"

"Yes, sir. I made sure of it."

"Good. Then come have some ribs. The meat's falling off the bone. After supper we'll commence with the real business that has brought us here tonight."

Helena distributed plates heaped with saucy pork and cornbread stuffing. She was gratified to see that everyone dug in with gusto. At last when the plates were empty and the cherry pie was almost gone, Stratetix stood up from his seat. "I think it's time to hear the words of Deu," he said.

He went to a sheltering tarp that hung suspended from the trees. Six bedrolls lay underneath it in a row, for the "hunters" planned to camp out now that the gates of Edgeton were locked for the night. Stratetix reached into his bedroll and pulled out the satchel containing the sacred scrolls. He returned to the fire and opened the satchel. Everyone gazed at him expectantly. Helena noticed his serious expression. *Mighty Deu, protect us from watching eyes*, she prayed.

"Let us allow the Eternal One to determine our reading tonight," Stratetix said. He rummaged in the satchel and removed a scroll, which he examined for a moment. "Our God has led us to the eleventh chapter of the book of Beginning. I will read it aloud so you may consider these holy words."

The text was a brief one. It described how all the people of the world had a common speech. The rulers decided to build a tower that would reach into heaven so they would not be scattered over the earth. When Deu saw this, he confused their language. For this reason the place was called Babel.

"What does Babel mean?" Rosetta asked.

"I discussed this point with Captain Teofil when he translated the scrolls," Shaphan said. "There's a verb in the Fluid Tongue that sounds like 'Babel.' It means to chatter or make nonsense sounds like children." The rest of the group nodded appreciatively as they considered Shaphan's explanation.

"Alright, friends," Stratetix prompted, "what else do you observe here?"

"The people were refusing to scatter out," Helena said. "They built the tower as a rallying point. Then the passage ends with the Eternal One scattering them anyway. It was his response to their sin."

Shaphan pursed his lips. "I don't understand why that's sinful. What's wrong with building a city?"

The group considered the question but didn't have an immediate answer. They sat quietly, staring at the glowing coals of the campfire. At last Lina said, "I think Aunt Helena was right to call it sinful. Remember the patriarch Noé who built the boat? His children were supposed to spread over the earth after the flood. But these people were doing exactly the opposite. It was disobedient."

"That's really insightful, Lina," Shaphan said, giving his bride an admiring look. She blushed at his words.

"We can also see that the people's reason for building was prideful," Rosetta said. "They wanted to make a 'name' for themselves. But doesn't the Sacred Writing tell us to magnify the name of the Eternal One instead?"

"And they built the tower into the heavens," Lewth added. "That's the realm of the gods in every religion. No doubt those people sought to commune with evil spirits."

"Just like the leaders of Chiveis!"

All eyes turned toward Shaphan, who had uttered his accusation in a loud voice.

"Caution, son," Stratetix advised.

The group fell silent as a fearful mood descended. No one wanted to speak into the awful hush.

"A new wickedness is stirring in the High Priestess's temple," Lewth whispered at last. The ominous statement only heightened the group's trepidation.

"What do you mean?" Shaphan asked.

"That witch is planning something evil. Strange deliveries are being made to her spire. I've seen it from my hovel. It's all very secret. I overheard some of the senior monks saying a new weapon is being built—a power too terrible to resist."

A frightened murmur rippled through the group. High in the trees, a night wind whispered among the branches. As Helena looked at the wide-eyed faces of her friends huddled around the fire, she resolved to offer them strength from the Sacred Writing. "'Why do the kings of the earth raise themselves against the Eternal One?'" she quoted. "'The one who sits in sky laughs.'"

"That's right!" Shaphan jumped up, stamping his foot. "The Lord mocks them! He speaks to them in his anger! He terrifies them in his rage!"

Before anyone could reply, a rustling in the bushes signaled the arrival of an intruder. Cries of alarm rose from the group as all heads whirled toward the sound. Then a tall, bearded man stepped into the light—a soldier of the Royal Guard.

Lina let out a shriek. Stratetix and Lewth leaped to their feet, converging shoulder-to-shoulder with Shaphan. The men's fists were clenched. Dread engulfed Helena. *Help us, Deu! We've been discovered!*

"What do you want with us?" Stratetix barked.

The Royal Guardsman only stared at the group in the forest. The hood of his cloak overhung his face, giving him a menacing appearance.

"We're hunters enjoying a feast," Stratetix said. "We've done nothing wrong."

Still the soldier did not speak. But he took a step closer.

Shaphan leaned toward Stratetix. "He doesn't have a sword," the young man hissed through clenched teeth. "We can take him if we have to!"

"No, Shaphan. Be still."

The guardsman closed the distance to the watchers seated around the campfire. Lina squealed, and Rosetta couldn't stifle a groan. Abruptly the man stopped short.

Stratetix stepped forward. "Why are you here? Speak!"

The soldier extended his hand. Stratetix stared at it. Then, slowly, he took the outstretched hand in his own. "Who are you?" he whispered.

The man reached to his hood and pulled it back.

"I am Teofil, and I come with good news."

CHAPTER

5

Utter silence hung over the forest clearing. Stratetix felt his legs turn watery. He collapsed to his knees, staring up at the man who held his hand.

Can it be? Almighty Deu! Can it be?

If it's Teofil . . . then that means . . .

Stratetix's breath escaped him. His eyes filled with tears. Helena rushed past him with a sob of ecstasy and relief. She threw her arms around the unexpected visitor, weeping uncontrollably. "Oh, Teofil! Is it really you? Where's Ana? Is she here? *Is she here?*"

Teo's face was laden with emotion as he returned Helena's embrace. He was visibly moved by the sanctity of the moment. "Anastasia is alive and well," he announced, "though she is far away and cannot come soon."

"She's alive!" Stratetix released Teo's hand and covered his face as he wept on his knees, rocking back and forth. The pressing weight of an immense burden rolled off his shoulders. "Thank you, Deu! Thank you for hearing me! I praise you! Oh Ana, my sweet Ana . . . you're alive!"

The rest of the group crowded close. No one could hold back the wave of euphoria that flooded the lonely forest. They could only give in to its power and be carried along. The six friends huddled around Teo, shedding tears of abundant joy as they lifted grateful prayers to the nighttime sky. They continued like that for a long time. The emotions were thick and complex and did not quickly dissipate.

At last Stratetix found the strength to speak. "What can you tell us, son? Give us the whole story, and let us know how Ana fares! Is she well? Where is she? When will she return?"

"You'd better sit down," Teo said, drying his eyes, "because this one's quite a story."

Everyone resumed their places at the fire as Teo joined them. Helena offered him the last piece of cherry pie, then reached for a coffeepot warming over the coals.

"Is this Lina's famous pie?" Teo grinned at the girl with the white-blonde curls. "It looks delicious!"

Instead of answering, Lina just smiled at Teo. She had always been a little intimidated by the dashing captain whose life had become intertwined with her cousin's. Now she regarded him with speechless awe.

"So then . . . where should I begin?" Teo asked as he wolfed down his pie.

Helena handed him a steaming mug of coffee. "Tell us everything. Start with the glacier."

"Right. The glacier." Teo gathered his thoughts for a moment, then began to recount the epic tale. The story swept the exiled pair from the stormy, icebound peaks of Chiveis to a hidden hut in which they took shelter. There they made the fateful decision to enter the fearsome Beyond. Teo and Ana stepped hand-in-hand into the unknown future with nothing but each other and the Sacred Writing of Deu. Soon they found themselves in a kingdom called Ulmbartia. From there they were led to glamorous Likuria on the salty sea. Ana suffered in that land, Teo said, though he didn't go into details.

At last Teo found Ana on a lonely island and brought her to an ancient city called Roma. Enemies converged on them, and a life-or-death battle was fought outside the magnificent temple of the Christiani. Just when all hope seemed lost, Deu won the day and delivered his people. Now the leader of the Christiani, called the Papa, had sent Teo on a mission. While journeying through distant lands Teo discovered a map that showed the way to Chiveis. He had blazed a trail to his homeland so he could bring Ana back with him next spring.

"But won't the authorities kill you if you return here?" Shaphan asked.

Teo grimaced. "I am concerned about that," he acknowledged, "but I'm wondering if things have changed since we left."

Shaphan scoffed. "They've changed alright. The laws are more brutal than before."

"Yet that has caused unrest among the people," Helena added. "The dynamic in the kingdom is different today than a year ago. There may be those who sympathize with you now. If we all join together, we might be able to resist the High Priestess's oppression."

"I don't care if I have to hide you in my barn and feed you like a pony," Stratetix said. "I just want to see my little girl!"

Teo smiled. "I'd like to aim a little higher for Ana than a barn. Maybe a nice cottage or something."

"We'll pray for a happy outcome," Lewth said. "Perhaps Deu shall grant it."

"Or perhaps not."

As Teo spoke those words he looked at Stratetix with a pointed stare. Stratetix realized Teo was asking him an unspoken question: *Do you want me to bring Ana back despite the danger? You are her father—are you sure you want me to do this?* He considered it for a moment, then said, "All of us are in Deu's hands, Teofil. We must depend on him at every moment, trusting him day by day. Nothing can happen apart from his will."

Teo gave an understanding nod. Suddenly his face lit up. "Deu! I have so much to tell you about him! We've discovered some incredible new truths."

The listeners around the fire were eager, so Teo proceeded to explain. He described how he and Ana found the New Testament in the strangest of places: locked in the mind of a simpleton with an astonishing memory.

"Oh, that's just like Deu," Helena said. "Tell us what was in the book."

"It revealed that Deu has a son."

A hush descended on the group. Stratetix could see amazement on the listeners' faces as they contemplated the announcement. "What is the son's name?" he asked at length.

"He is called Iesus Christus. Deu sent him from heaven as a man to teach us truth and heal the sick and bring a kingdom of peace. But evil-doers killed him by nailing him to a wooden cross."

The listeners shook their heads in disbelief. "No! That's terrible," Lina said mournfully.

"It is terrible," Teo agreed, "but it's not the end of the story. After three days in the tomb, Deu raised him to new life. Iesus Christus is not only the Pierced One. He is the Promised King predicted in the Sacred Writing."

The group marveled at this. "Where is his kingdom?" Shaphan asked.

"It is not yet set up on this earth. But the King will return one day. If you believe the good news of his resurrection, you will be joined to Iesus. When you die you will live, just as he lives. And when his kingdom finally comes, you will dwell in it forever."

Stratetix leaned toward Teo, awestruck by what he was hearing. "The New Testament declares all this?"

"Yes. The missionary Paulus wrote to the people of Roma and said, 'If you confess Iesus as Lord and believe that Deu raised him from the dead, you will be saved.'"

Helena d'Armand rose from her place and looked at the rest of the group. All was quiet as she met the eyes of each one. "My friends," she said at last, "I declare to you right now: I believe in the resurrection. I confess it to be true. I take Iesus as my Lord."

Stratetix stood and grasped his wife's hand. "I confess it too. This is good news indeed. I make it my own."

Lina shot to her feet. "And me!"

"I too join the Christiani," Shaphan said as he slipped an arm around Lina's shoulders. "And our child will be raised in this faith."

Rosetta likewise rose and declared her belief. Lewth stood up last of all. "I will stake my life on this truth," he said.

Teo looked at the six people standing around him. He smiled broadly and spread his arms toward them. "Welcome to the eternal kingdom, brothers and sisters of Iesus."

Somewhere in the trees an owl hooted. The spooky sound reminded everyone they were deep in the forest and the hour was late.

"We're posing as a hunting party," Stratetix said to Teo. "We planned to camp out tonight, as hunters sometimes do."

Teo shook his head. "I don't think you should. The Royal Guard is patrolling the area. But that's not the worst of it. I've seen Vulkainians in these woods."

"Vulkainians?" Stratetix felt a chill at the thought of those evil thugs. "What are they doing in such a remote part of Chiveis?"

"Somehow they're involved with the outsiders. The High Priestess is reviving an ancient Pact, though I'm not sure why."

Stratetix beckoned Lewth to come close. "Tell Teofil what you told us before."

"The High Priestess is creating a terrible weapon. It kills on a massive scale." Lewth shuddered as he spoke.

Teo put his hand on Lewth's shoulder. "Can you find out more about it?"

"I'll try, Captain."

"If Vulkainians are in these woods, we definitely shouldn't be here," Stratetix said. "It's a short boat trip back to Edgeton. We should get everyone into the village."

"I agree. Right away."

"Edgeton is locked up already," Lewth pointed out.

"The gatekeeper will let me in. We'll say we got lost while hunting. He won't like it, and it might sound suspicious, but it would be far worse to be discovered by a party of Vulkainians out here with no witnesses around."

Stratetix issued his instructions to the little group. Everyone quickly packed their belongings and made for the river. Though the moon was high and bright, ragged clouds scudded across it.

"Oh! The scrolls." Stratetix removed the satchel that hung over his shoulder. "I have to hide them before we go."

He walked to an oak at the edge of a grassy field. A hollow in the bole led to a dry cavity. Stratetix had just nestled the satchel inside when a gap in the clouds caused white moonlight to illumine the field.

"Hey there!" shouted a voice. "Halt, whoever you are!"

Stratetix started and looked up. Riders across the field spurred their horses toward him. He ducked into the shadows, his heart racing. Teo came to his side.

"Let's make a run for it!" Stratetix urged.

"No! We'll be captured. The women can't get away in time."

"We can make it!"

Teo shook his head. "They're closing too fast. It's one of us or all. You go! I'll cover for you. They don't know about the rest of us. Get to the boats and slip away."

"No, son, you can't do that."

Teo's hand gripped Stratetix's shoulder. "You must live to see your daughter again with your own two eyes. I can handle this. Now go!"

Teo shoved Stratetix into the dark forest, then turned and shouted to the Vulkainians, "I'm over here! I give up!"

◆　◆　◆

The Iron Shield stepped from his expensive hired coach and surveyed the Clan Boss's estate on the island of Sessalay. He wore a fine tunic with gold embroidery on the sleeves, and his black hair was tied in a ponytail at the nape of his neck. He rose to his full height, gazing down at the butler who met him at the portico of the manor house.

"Your ride was comfortable?" the butler asked.

The Iron Shield made no response, and the butler wilted under the stare. "This way to my master," he said timidly as he turned away.

A cobbled footpath led around the side of the manor. The Iron Shield refused to limp despite the wound in his foot, which was only partially healed. Each step stoked his lust for revenge. He clenched his jaw, trying to calm the rage that churned within his crowded soul. *Be patient*, whispered one of the voices in his head. *The captain will come to you. Drop the bread crumbs. Leave a trail. Set out the bait Teofil cannot resist.*

The Clan Boss welcomed the Iron Shield to a veranda overlooking an expansive vista of orchards and vineyards. A warm sun shone down on this southern locale even though it was late in the tenth month. The grapes had all been gathered from the vines, but the olive harvest was in full swing, and the first clementines were also coming in. "Beautiful, isn't it?" the boss asked, offering his guest a glass.

The Iron Shield nodded but did not reply as he received his cocktail of fresh-squeezed orange juice and absinthe. Such aloofness put men of power in the weaker position as they tried to discern his intent.

"So then . . . what brings you to my island?" the boss asked as the two men stood at the balustrade. "You wish to discuss religious matters, I hear."

The Iron Shield studied his host. The man who ran the international crime ring known as the Clan looked like a country squire who would rather tend olive groves than deal in extortion and slavery. He was middle-aged, balding, and potbellied. *But don't be fooled*, the Iron Shield reminded himself. *This man sits atop a powerful empire.*

"My name is Antonio of Roma," he said, adopting his alias again. "I have high-level connections to the Society of the Exterminati."

The Clan Boss's face remained neutral. "Interesting," he remarked.

He knew that already. The Clan is almost as good as we are at obtaining information.

The Iron Shield pressed on. "We in our society have come to believe the heavens are disrupted. Where the gods once favored our endeavors, they now withhold their beneficence."

"Our business was upset this summer as well," the Clan Boss acknowledged. "A foreign deity is aroused against us."

"Yes. And it is time to retaliate. We must cooperate to bring him down."

"We?" The boss laughed gently. "Our family enterprise does not enter into alliances with brotherhoods such as yours, Antonio."

"You are mistaken."

The statement was bold, almost rude, and the boss noticed it. Before he could respond the Iron Shield withdrew a leather thong from around his neck. He held up a vial of dark blood. "Your people and mine are already bound together."

The Clan Boss sucked in a breath and stepped back. "The Pact? That agreement hasn't been invoked for centuries. I almost thought it was a legend."

"I can assure you it is no legend. I stand before you today as an emissary from the High Priestess of Chiveis. That is the kingdom whose leader sponsored the Pact."

"I know. Beaumont, he was called. A man with access to high-level powers."

"The very highest. And that same power now undergirds the priestess."

"Can she rebalance the heavens? We can't afford to take another hit like the affair in Roma this summer. Revenues from the trafficking division plummeted."

"There is little the High Priestess cannot achieve."

"What would it take? It seems our interests may converge after all."

"Indeed they do. Fortunately, I have a solution that is mutually beneficial."

"Go on."

"Chiveis and Sessalay share a deity in common. The Chiveisi know him as Vulkain—the god of the fiery underworld."

"Mulciber?"

"That is your name for him. He is provoked by the disregard we have shown him of late."

"He needs a tithe perhaps? A generous one?"

"His hunger is more voracious than that."

The Clan Boss glanced up from his cocktail, eyebrows raised. "What else is there?"

For a long moment the Iron Shield did not answer. At last he uttered a single word: "Virgins."

Silence hung over the veranda. When the Clan Boss finally spoke, uncertainty tinged his voice. "You mean . . . like the old days?"

The Iron Shield nodded. The ways of the ancient pagans at Sessalay ran deep in the people's bones. The old rites could easily be revived. "Like the old days," he agreed. "Swallowed by fire on the sacred equinox, when dark and light are in perfect balance. You know how fragrant this gift would be to the god."

"Of course. But where would we get the girls? The peasants would revolt if we snatched their daughters."

"We could raid the houses of Christiani sisters along the coasts."

"The Christiani! They're the ones causing all these problems!"

"So this would be a fitting gift, would it not?"

The Clan Boss rubbed his chin as he considered the proposal. "I have hit men working for me," he mused, "but the Clan thrives on being invisible. Large-scale abductions aren't really our specialty."

"Never fear," the Iron Shield said drily. "The Exterminati have a little experience in this regard." The warrior's laughter came out as a deep, reverberant echo.

"It will be expensive. You'll need several ships. The raids will have to be perfectly coordinated or you'll have the local militia on your hands. This is no simple undertaking."

"Leave that to me. We'll hit the convents all at once, then rendezvous for resupply in Napoly after we have the women. It's the nearest large port, and the authorities there are corrupt. They won't bother us."

"The Exterminati will pay for all this?"

"I was thinking Sessalay could defray the costs with some of its natural resources."

"What resources? Olive oil? Blood oranges? The profit margins in agriculture are thin."

"You have abundant brimstone in the interior. It could be mined and sold on the black market."

"Brimstone? You can't be serious! That yellow rock has no value except to launderers and quacks."

"I have outlets I could exploit."

"Is that so? Well, there's plenty of brimstone on this island. You're welcome to as much of it as you want."

The Iron Shield put his drink to his lips to cover his smile. *You fool! You have no idea of its power!* He finished his cocktail and set down the glass. "My men will mine the brimstone over the winter. Meanwhile I will prepare a coordinated strike against the Christiani convents in time for the equinox next spring. Sixty-six women will be devoted to the great Mulciber—a holy number. And the centerpiece of our gift will be the woman the god hates most."

"Who is that?"

"Her name is Anastasia of Chiveis."

"Anastasia?" the Clan Boss exclaimed, then abruptly fell silent.

The Iron Shield flicked his glance toward his host. "You know of her?"

"No—I've never heard of her before in my life."

"Are you sure?"

"Of course I'm sure! But if this woman is important to the god, let her be brought here for the sacrifice. Do you know where to find her?"

"We know whatever is important. The Exterminati have eyes in every head."

"In that case you can spare a few eyes to watch Anastasia's convent until next spring."

"Her convent?" the Iron Shield asked mildly. "I thought you said you didn't know the woman."

"I—I assumed she is one of those Christiani sisters you mentioned."

"Ah. Of course."

The Iron Shield turned away and stared across the orange groves. "The woman does indeed follow that wicked religion," he said, leaning on the balustrade. "But she shall learn to appreciate a fierce new love when Mulciber takes her as his bride."

✦　✦　✦

On the third day, Teo thought he might die.

The Vulkainians had taken him straight to the High Priestess's temple. It was high in the mountains of Chiveis, nestled against one of the three great peaks of the kingdom. A spire rose from the temple complex, a sheer spike of granite that thrust upward like a finger pointing the way to Astrebril. Teo's cell was about halfway up the spire's immense height. He had been provided with a cot, a straw pallet, and a blanket.

But he had been given no food or drink.

The first day had been uncomfortable. By the end of it Teo found himself fantasizing about a cool glass of water and a hearty meal. His stomach rumbled, and he swallowed often, trying to moisten his mouth. Restless sleep claimed him at last.

The next morning Teo knew he was in trouble. His thirst had intensified overnight, making his tongue feel like a wad of cotton stuffed in his mouth. His eyes were dry and scratchy. Though hunger pangs tore at his gut, the raging thirst tormented him even more. He couldn't stop thinking about water. His whole body was parched. Trapped in the tiny room, he felt frantic and desperate, like a man in the desert with an empty canteen.

Now on the third day Teo could only lie on his bed and stare out the window. His cracked lips were bleeding. The skin on his hands was shriveled, making his fingers feel like sandpaper. His only comfort was that he didn't have to get up to use the chamber pot anymore. Periodically he would doze, but his dreams were plagued by strange visions of terrifying monsters. Perhaps they weren't even dreams, for sometimes the monsters appeared in his room while he was awake. The hallucinations blended into the nightmares to create an endless ordeal.

The shadows lengthened as the third day wore on. Teo sighed, feeling listless and weak. His heart fluttered, and his respiration was rapid. He tried to picture Ana's face but couldn't. The mental clock that had been ticking in his mind since he departed for his mission had begun to slow down. Though Teo initially experienced frustration at his confinement, knowing the window of opportunity for returning to Roma before winter was closing, he now thought it didn't matter so much. Maybe it would be better to die. Then at least the agonizing thirst would be over. He closed his eyes . . .

A distant thunderclap yanked Teo from the black void. He stared around the cell, trying to get his bearings. It must have been near dawn, for a little light came through the eastern window.

Someone jiggled a key in the lock, then the door swung open. Two beefy men hauled Teo from his cot. Manacles connected by a rusty chain were snapped onto his wrists. He did not try to resist the Vulkainians but only shuffled where he was led.

Teo was forced to trudge up a spiral staircase. Cramps seized his calf muscles, and he stumbled. The guards mocked him, kicking his ribs as he tried to stand. Teo dragged himself to his feet and continued the climb.

At last he reached the top. An oaken door was opened, and Teo was shoved inside. The circular room had four windows and a table with some implements on it, yet its most prominent feature was the great pit at its center. Smoke rose from it, exiting through a hole in the roof. A chain hung from a pulley on the ceiling. The guards hooked Teo's handcuffs to an iron bar that dangled from the chain, then cranked a windlass on the wall so that his arms were drawn above his head. The door slammed shut behind him.

Teo glanced around. He could feel his heart thumping in his chest. Everything was quiet . . . until a silky voice broke the stillness.

"Welcome home, Captain Teofil." The words out of the darkness were melodious and enticing. Teo knew who spoke them. He steeled his mind against the wiles of Astrebril's favorite queen.

A torch flared on the wall. Teo watched the High Priestess walk over and light a second one. Her movements were sensuous even as she performed this mundane task.

"You have no right to imprison me," Teo said.

The priestess turned away from the wall, gazing at Teo with beguiling eyes. A smile was on her black lips. Because she was backlit by the torch, Teo could see her voluptuous figure through her gauzy robe. He wanted to tear his eyes away but could not.

"Am I imprisoning you, Teofil? Or have you come here of your own accord?"

The suggestion seemed reasonable to Teo's dulled mind. He fought to grasp the truth. "I . . . I chose to come to Chiveis. But you . . . your guards . . . they brought me here. They gave me nothing to drink."

"Is that so? Then you must be incredibly thirsty." The priestess slinked closer. Her expression was mischievous. The dancing torchlight cast an orange glow on her white-painted cheeks. She came on steadily. Teo stared at her, fascinated. She stopped a short distance from him, then held up a carafe. Ruby liquid sparkled inside it.

"Drink with me," she whispered.

Teo shook his head.

"Do it," she insisted. "Drink deeply with me."

The High Priestess put the carafe to her lips and tipped back her head. Her long dark hair cascaded down her shoulders. She lowered her head and caught Teo's eye, holding a mouthful of wine in her cheeks. Her lips were pursed. Redness dribbled down her chin. She hurled the bottle into the pit at the center of the room, but the sound of breaking glass never came.

"Wh-what do you want with me?" Teo felt ashamed that his voice trembled.

The priestess approached him until their bodies touched. Her hand went to the back of his head. Black fingernails stroked his neck behind his ear, raising gooseflesh. Teo's heart was beating wildly. The temptress tilted her chin and brought her face close.

Teo closed his eyes. He turned his head away, but not enough. As the woman's lips met his, honeyed wine flooded his mouth, moistening his parched tongue. Teo urgently swallowed the liquid, longing for more. But the High Priestess backed away.

"Let the turning commence," she said.

Strange colors flashed and swirled before Teo's eyes. At the wall a eunuch priest in a white tunic cranked the windlass. Teo felt himself hauled into the air by his wrists. He swung out over the pit, dangling above the abyss. The manacles pinched his flesh without mercy. Pungent smoke wafted around him. Far below, an orange light danced in the darkness. Then the chain began to unwind as Teo descended into the gloom of the nether world.

A glowing green streak coalesced into a serpent. It stared at Teo with lidless yellow eyes. "Come higher with me," it hissed, then slithered away.

Next a hideous, scaly imp appeared. Its sneer was malicious. Reaching out a clawed hand, it grabbed Teo's ankle. Teo tried to kick it away, but the creature's claws dug into his skin and would not let go. "My master awaits at the next level," it said in a raspy voice. "Let us go up to him."

Ten more creatures appeared, each larger and scarier than the last. Teo had never felt so afraid. He had faced danger before; he had stared death in the eye. But this was different. The wraiths in this underworld pit were spirits from a different dimension. They berated him, jeered at him, enticed him, tormented him. Teo thrashed as he hung suspended from the iron bar. The rising fumes felt like a suffocating blanket. Nothing would stop the parade of terrors.

A cold draft seeped from the deep, signaling the arrival of a malevolent presence. Though Teo's eyes were clenched shut, he could see the apparition in his mind. The rising angel had wings like a bat and a pointed beard. Its tongue lolled between its fangs. A resonant voice spoke from the shadows. "Turn to meeeee," it droned.

"No!" Teo cried.

"You muuuust. It is decreeeed." The angel's drawn-out words were thunderous and deadly and very beautiful.

Teo shook his head. "Never!"

"My yoke is eeeeasy. My burden is liiiight."

"It's tyranny!"

"I offer you freeeeedom."

Teo could not answer.

"Cooooome, Teofil. Serve meeeeee . . . "

The chains rattled. Teo felt himself being raised into the High Priestess's chamber again. His wrists ached. The eunuch drew Teo to the edge of the pit with a pole, then unhooked his manacles from the iron bar. Teo's knees sagged as he stared at the floor. The High Priestess took him by the hand and led him to a table next to a window. She picked up a knife.

"Sign here and the turning will be complete."

Her hand flicked across Teo's chest. Though he felt a hot burn, the pain was sweet and delicious. Blood trickled from the wound, soaking into the military uniform he had taken from the line cabin. The High Priestess dipped a quill into the fresh cut and pressed it into Teo's hand. He held the feather and gazed at the parchment on the table. In his stupor, the words were illegible.

"Sign it, Teofil. Sign now and I will give you . . . everything."

If I sign, maybe this nightmare will end. Just do it!

Teo's eyes focused on the words scrawled across the page:

I give you my heart, and my soul, and my mind, and my strength, O Astrebril my only lord.

Teo reeled backward. Horror flooded him as he realized what was happening. The evil god was making a claim on his eternal soul. Teo threw back his head and raised a shout to the heavens: "Iesus Christus! I call upon your name!"

Teo yanked his arms apart and flexed his shoulder muscles. Gritting his teeth, he strained with fierce exertion against the handcuffs that bound his wrists. Suddenly the chain snapped as a rusty link gave way. The abrupt release of tension made light explode in Teo's brain. He felt as if a bright whiteness had flashed around him.

The High Priestess snarled and came at Teo with the knife. He caught her hand as she attempted to thrust the blade into his belly. The two opponents stared at each other, locked in a death grip as each struggled for supremacy. Teo was amazed by the priestess's strength. He had never encountered power like that in a woman before.

"Get the guards!" she screamed to the eunuch. The terrified servant ran from the room.

Teo knew he didn't have much time. Calling on his last reserves of strength, he gave the knife a tremendous heave. The blade shot up, catching the priestess across the cheek as it flew past her head. She screamed and dropped the weapon. Crimson droplets trickled from a slice in her white-painted face.

"How dare you defile me!" she shrieked.

The priestess pressed her hand to the cut as she backed away. Crouching low, she eased toward the door. Blood oozed between her fingers. Then, like a wisp of fog caught in a breeze, she slipped from the room.

Outside it was raining hard. Teo threw open the casement window. Water had gathered in a depression in the stone sill. He thrust his lips into the pool, drinking greedily.

The door banged open behind him. Teo whirled. Two Vulkainians burst into the room, drawing their acid guns as they charged. Teo snatched the priestess's knife from the floor and hurled it at the first Vulkainian, burying the blade in his chest. The second man dodged around his fallen partner, but before he could bring his gun to bear Teo stopped his advance with a high kick. The heel of Teo's boot smashed the Vulkainian's gun, breaking open its reservoir of sulfuric acid. Teo felt a sting against his calf, but most of the liquid splashed the Vulkainian. The man squealed and stumbled backward, his tunic soaked with the burning fluid. As he flailed and reeled about, his foot stepped back into empty space. For a brief moment Teo saw shock cross the man's face—then he plunged into the priestess's pit with a terrified, fading scream.

More shouts and footsteps echoed up the staircase. Teo couldn't bar the door against the intruders nor fight them in his weakened condition. To be captured now meant certain death. He glanced around the room. There was only one way out. He ran to the windlass bolted into the wall. Its chain ran over the pulley to the iron bar that dangled above the pit. Teo broke off the pawl that prevented the ratchet gears of the windlass from sliding.

The Vulkainian militiamen reached the top of the stairs. They wore leather helmets and were more heavily armed than the first two guards. "Kill him now!" shouted the squad's sergeant. He knelt and aimed his crossbow.

Sprinting across the room Teo snatched the iron bar without slowing down. The chain clattered as it rolled off the loose windlass behind him. Crossbow bolts whizzed through the air, ricocheting off the walls. And then, with a wild yell, Teo leaped from the window of the High Priestess's holy spire.

Rainwater pelted Teo as he plummeted toward the earth. Though he didn't know the length of the chain, he knew it was going to jerk to a stop at any second. He clenched his fists and determined to hang on no matter what. The chain went taut at the end of Teo's outstretched arms, yanking him out of his free fall. He kicked his legs wildly to spin around so he could face the spire wall. Its granite face rushed to meet him as he swung toward it like the pendulum of a giant clock. The impact was going to be tremendous; it might even knock him loose. Rather than risk it, Teo released his hold on the iron bar at the last second, letting his momentum carry him through an opening in the wall.

Teo sailed feetfirst through a window covered by a curtain. He crashed into a flimsy structure that exploded in a profusion of feathers and wood shavings. Birds flew in every direction amid a cacophony of squawks. Teo tumbled across the floor, tangled in the curtain. He shook his head, trying to regain his senses. The rancid smell of bird droppings hung in the air.

In a corner of the room a skinny scribe cowered with his mouth agape. Teo scrambled up and grabbed the man by the elbow, then shoved him into a closet and wedged a chair under the doorknob. He crossed to the man's desk. A bowl of gruel was on it, along with a full tankard of ale. Teo gulped down the food and drink, which immediately started cramps roiling in his gut. He gripped his stomach and was about to lurch out the door when something on the desk caught his eye. The scribe had been copying messages onto the tiny slips carried by the homing pigeons. Teo grabbed the document he had noticed, his eyes widening in disbelief as he read:

Her Eminence the High Priestess, Mediatrix of the Beautiful One; To Vlad the Nine-Fingered, prince of the Germani; Greetings and salutations to you in the name of Astrebril.

The lord god has revealed his will. Jineve shall be ours before the summer solstice. Return to your people and muster your army. Encamp in the wilderness at the edge of Chiveis next spring. You will be met by the Royal Guard to march against our enemy. All iron and salt-stone captured in Jineve shall be mine. Your spoil in war shall be every woman in the realm. May the blessing of the high god be upon you, my blood-sworn confederate. Farewell.

Teo staggered from the desk, unable to comprehend what he had just read. *An invasion of Jineve by the Chiveisian army! And in cooperation with outsiders!* Such a force would be unstoppable, especially if the High Priestess possessed a secret weapon, as Lewth seemed to believe. With Jinevan iron for making swords, and plentiful ingredients to produce Astrebril's fire, the High Priestess was poised to solidify her power base beyond any chance of resistance. Teo folded the paper and tucked it in his pocket. He needed proof of the High Priestess's nefarious intent.

Out in the hall Teo made his way to a staircase and reached the ground floor. The whole temple was in pandemonium. Eunuch priests scurried everywhere. Some of them noticed Teo, but they didn't have the brass to face him.

He emerged from the temple and ran to a hitching rail, where he untied the best horse of the bunch. It was long-legged and proud—the kind of horse born to run, then run some more. Teo swung into the saddle and headed for the gate.

"Hey, stop!" The guard at the gatehouse wasn't a Vulkainian, just a mean-faced monk in a dirty robe. Teo charged the man, forcing him to dive out of the way.

Once he was clear of the gate Teo urged his horse into a full gallop. The High Priestess's temple was situated above the treeline, so the land around it was an alpine pasture. As Teo sped across the meadow in the driving rain he glanced over his shoulder at the granite spire, a symbol of everything he loathed. From this place the priestess had cast her shadow over the kingdom. Fierce anger rose within Teo, an outrage that couldn't be contained.

"Deu!" he cried aloud. "Come to Chiveis! Bring your truth to my people—and set a new ruler over this land!"

❖ ❖ ❖

As the sailing season came to a close, the ships of Roma returned one by one to the safety of the harbor. The smaller boats were dragged out of the water, and even a few of the larger vessels were dry-docked to undergo major repairs. The rest of the ships were brought deep into the port and tucked into sheltered slips along the river where they would be safe from the winter storms. The sails and rigging were stowed, the bilges were pumped out, and the hulls were caulked as needed. The good weather was about to end, and the people of Roma knew it.

But Teo wasn't home.

Ana browsed the seaside market with Vanita, picking up a wheel of cheese, some bread, a jar of sardines, and a bottle of the zesty fish sauce called garum. As she ticked off the items on the housemother's list, her eyes kept roving over the ocean.

"They'll come," Vanita said.

"What?" Ana's attention was snapped back to the present by her friend's remark.

"I said, 'They'll come.' Marco is a great sailor. Teofil will finish his mission, and they'll be back any day now."

"Oh, right . . . the mission." Ana gave a little laugh. "So you could read my mind, huh?"

"It's not hard when you're staring at the horizon with puppy-dog eyes." Vanita squeezed Ana's forearm. "Don't worry, I feel the same as you. We're like two women whose men have gone off to war."

"Except nobody's trying to kill our men," Ana pointed out.

"As far as we know."

The statement disturbed Ana, but she shook away her troubled thoughts and gave her friend a closer look. Though the chemistry between Vanita and Marco was obvious, Ana had never heard her speak so affectionately about him. She smiled mischievously. "You called Marco your man. Do I sense a romance developing here?"

Vanita couldn't suppress a smile, but she kept her eyes down as she examined a jar of honey. "He's a handsome rogue, that's for sure."

"And he's clearly attracted to you."

"I guess."

"What's taking so long then?"

Vanita glanced up from the honey with an expression of surprise. She poked Ana's shoulder. "You're one to talk!"

"What do you mean?" Ana felt heat rise to her cheeks. "Teofil and I have made our feelings clear to each other."

"Yeah . . . after two years of dithering around!"

Ana dipped her chin and caught Vanita's eye. "Maybe I dithered because somebody advised me Teo wasn't good enough for me."

The accusation made Vanita wince. "Alright, fair enough. You got me." She set down the jar of honey. "Teofil is a great man. I realize that now. Any girl would be lucky to have him."

"The same is true for Marco."

Vanita shrugged. "In most ways."

"What do you mean?"

"Well, he's not . . . you know . . . "

Ana thought Vanita might conclude her statement with something like "respectable" or "upstanding." Marco was a pirate—one who robbed rich profiteers and offered bargains to the poor, but a pirate nonetheless. To some women that would be a problem.

Vanita, however, was thinking along very different lines. "He's not Christiani," she said.

"Oh. Right. Of course." *Why didn't I think of that?* Ana looked at her friend. "Has he grown more open to it?"

"Not really. You know how he is. He's not hostile. He's happy that I believe. But he just doesn't want religion for himself."

"Teo used to be like that."

"Really?" Vanita's face was hopeful. "What did you do to change it?"

"I tried badgering him, until I realized that doesn't work at all."

"I've tried that too," Vanita admitted. "And you're right. It's counterproductive." She sighed deeply.

Ana sensed her normally confident friend was at a vulnerable place. "Come with me," she said, taking Vanita's arm.

The two women walked to the end of a pier that jutted into the ocean. Ana reached into her basket and tore a chunk from a loaf. She tossed it to the nearest seagull, which swerved midair to catch the bite. Soon several gulls were hovering overhead.

"Look at how those birds fly," Ana said. "They have to flap their wings a little, but for the most part they're simply adjusting themselves to the gusts."

Vanita nodded as she stared at the seagulls. Because the Ulmbartian aristocrat was so glamorous, people often assumed she was empty-headed, but she was actually very intelligent. Ana could see she understood the illustration.

"You're saying I can't change the wind, but I can adapt to it," Vanita observed.

"We can either resist what Deu is doing, or we can catch his breeze and ride it."

"And what does that mean for me and Marco?"

"You can't convert him. You can only pray hard and wait to see what Deu has in store."

"Do you remember what Iesus told Nicodemus about that?"

"No," Ana admitted. "What was it?"

"It's in the book of Ioannes. 'The wind blows wherever it wishes. You can hear it, but you don't know where it comes from or where it goes. That's how it is with everyone born by Deu's spirit.'"

The quotation brought Ana a sense of hope, though mingled with trepidation. "What if Deu doesn't bring Marco and Teofil back to us?"

"And even if they do come back—what if Marco never believes?"

There wasn't an easy answer to that heartfelt question, so Ana didn't offer one. Instead she slipped her arm around her friend's shoulder.

Vanita leaned her head against Ana's. "Sorry to be so gloomy. I'm just *lonely*." Vanita's voice cracked as she spoke, and she scrunched her eyes shut. Though she put her hand to her mouth, she couldn't stifle the disconsolate shudder that escaped her lips.

Vanita's sadness made tears gather in Ana's eyes as well. A deep longing overwhelmed her—the longing to be in Teo's arms again, to be under his covering protection, to be supported by his masculine strength.

"I'm lonely too, Vanita," she murmured.

The seagulls drifted away as the two friends stood on the pier. They remained motionless for a long time, clinging to each other, exchanging no words—for nothing could be said that wasn't already being voiced by the vast and empty sea.

✦　✦　✦

Teo returned to Jineve three weeks after being kidnapped by the Iron Shield. After fleeing the High Priestess's temple he had headed straight for the Citadel and passed through the gate before an alarm could be sounded. Most of that ride was an act of sheer endurance as his weakened body came down from the adrenaline rush of his daring escape. He swayed in the saddle and sucked rainwater from his cupped hands.

Once clear of the Citadel, Teo made for the deep woods of Chiveis. He was too exhausted to go far, so he camped in a lonely apple grove on the northern shore of the Tooner Sea. The place stirred up bad memories of the time he had taken Ana to a decadent party near there, before either of them knew Deu. Teo slept fitfully on his dinner of tart apples, his nightmares denying him the rest he so desperately needed.

He traveled slowly the next day, grazing like a wild animal on chard, chestnuts, and mushrooms. Pine resin closed his chest wound, which was bloody but not deep. His only stop was to visit a shed on one of Stratetix's wheat fields along the Farm River. Teo used a sharp rock to carve the words "will return" on the door. As an afterthought, he added the word "we," which he now considered a solemn oath to Ana's father.

The line cabin on the frontier was unlocked. Teo had no reservations about helping himself to the meager supplies. He turned his horse loose, recovered his canoe, and began to backtrack along the path he had blazed to Chiveis. Neither the weather nor the hunting was favorable. Teo lost precious time searching for food under cold, dreary skies. Even with his map, he lost his way twice and had to double back. When he finally arrived at Leman Sea he was a filthy, ragged mess. His bushy beard and long hair made him feel like some crazed trapper from the wilderness.

At last Teo paddled his canoe alongside Brother Thomas's riverboats in Jineve's harbor. Marco met him on the dock, overjoyed and relieved after several weeks of agonized worrying about his friend. Though he tried to scold Teo for subjecting him to such grief, in the end Marco had to laugh as Teo recounted the tale of his adventures in Chiveis.

"That God of yours certainly watches over you, *amico*," he said with a shake of his head.

A locksmith was summoned to remove the handcuffs from Teo's wrists, and a barber provided a haircut and shave. Even when he was cleaned up, though, Teo found he was no longer welcome at Montblanc Palace. Brother Thomas's religious enthusiasm, along with his heated accusations against "Antonio" and the Exterminati, had soured Mayor Calixte on the two groups of foreigners. Now the Iron Shield was long gone, and Teo's expedition had fallen out of favor. His warnings about an imminent invasion were met by disdain from the palace steward. Even the note from the pigeon roost was dismissed as nonsense. At this rebuff Brother Thomas decided to leave. "Jineve isn't ready for Deus," he declared. "It's time we returned to Marsay."

The day of departure from Jineve arrived none too soon for Teo, who was anxious to set sail for Roma. It was the twenty-seventh day of the tenth month, and sailors rarely plied the seas in the eleventh.

Teo stood at the prow of the lead boat, looking downstream along the Rone River. Marco was in the stern conferring with Brother Thomas and the pilot. *He's a true friend*, Teo thought, then was pricked with remorse. *I sure gave him a scare!*

Once the riverboats found their course, Marco joined Teo in the prow. "Ready to go home?" Teo asked him.

Marco shrugged noncommittally.

"I hate to leave the Jinevans vulnerable," Teo said, "but they just won't listen. They're oblivious to the forces being mounted against them."

"Even if they wanted to resist they couldn't. Their army isn't strong enough on its own."

"The Knights of Marsay will help," Teo predicted. "They won't want Jineve to be conquered by a hostile dictator with expansion in mind."

"We'll know within a week."

The journey downriver actually took six days, one fewer than the trip upstream. Teo thought that was a good sign. The riverboats meandered through the broad, marshy delta of the mighty Rone. White horses called *camargs* roamed the wetlands. Finally the travelers reached the open sea. They crossed a bay, and soon the rocky isle of Castle d'If appeared in the distance.

"Odo will be so excited to see us," Teo said with a wry grin.

Brother Thomas folded his arms across his barrel chest. "Don't count on it."

The boats reached the island, and the travelers disembarked. As Teo climbed onto the dock, he saw the trim commander of the Order of the Cross approaching from the castle.

"Hail, adventurers," Odo said. "I trust your trip wasn't a fool's errand?"

"Nothing done for the glory of Deus can be called such," Brother Thomas replied.

"Hmm. Yes, of course."

"We have much to report," Teo said.

"Very well then. Follow me to my chambers and tell me all about it."

Odo led Teo and Brother Thomas to his private rooms in the castle. The space was decorated with tapestries of hunting scenes. Thick carpets covered the floor. Odo went to the hearth and added a log, then swung a cauldron away from the fire. He ladled mulled wine into cups and handed them to his guests. "What did you learn about the Jinevans?" he asked when everyone had taken a seat.

"They're going to be attacked by a foreign army," Teo announced. "Next spring sometime."

Odo arched his eyebrows as he took a sip from his steaming cup.

"The army of my homeland is being stirred up by a pagan priestess," Teo continued. "She has allied herself with forest tribes called Germani. And she's developing an evil weapon against which no one can stand."

"How unfortunate for the Jinevans."

"If they are unaided, they will fall," Brother Thomas declared.

"Do they not have allies of their own?"

Teo set down his cup and leaned forward with his elbows on his knees. "They have us."

"Us!" Odo choked on his wine, which made him cough and sputter for a moment. When he finally got control of himself he looked at Teo and said, "Why in the world would the Marsayans want to rescue the people of Jineve?"

Anger flared in Teo's heart. "Don't you see? The High Priestess is making a move to expand her power! Once she has control of Jineve's natural resources, she'll be in position to make a move downriver!"

"We'll worry about that when it happens."

"If you wait, she'll only grow stronger. She'll have a well-rested army. She'll have her Germani confederates. She'll probably conscript Jinevan forces. And she'll have her deadly new weapon. You need to act now—before she becomes too powerful to stop!"

"Brother Odo, I implore you," Thomas put in, "the matter is urgent. This woman is an enemy of Deus."

"Is that so?" Odo leaned back in his overstuffed chair and crossed his legs. "Then we should really have the Papa's wisdom on this matter, shouldn't we?"

"The Papa!" Teo jumped to his feet. "He's in Roma!"

"I know where the head of my religion dwells, Teofil," Odo said icily. "Now sit down."

Teo remained standing. It was all he could do not to slap the smug expression off the commander's face. "Can't you see your inaction is going to have terrible consequences?"

"That will be the will of Deus, I suppose."

"Deus calls us to act! He has given us freedom to choose one course over another!"

"Then I choose to consult the Holy Father. Unless I receive a directive from him, my troops stay here."

Teo towered over Odo, staring into his eyes for a long moment. At last he bent at the waist and extended his hand. "You may have the cross here"—he flicked Odo on the forehead, eliciting a startled yelp—"but you don't have it *here*." Teo poked the man in the chest, then turned and left without another word.

Outside in the cold drizzle, Teo marched to the island's dock with one goal in mind. At least now his next steps were clear. The way forward meant getting to Roma—right away.

The ferryman took Teo to Marsay's main harbor. The *Midnight Glider* was anchored there, its men having enjoyed several weeks of shore leave while their captain was away. As Teo approached the ship, Marco called down to him from the bulwark. "How'd it go?"

"He wants orders from the Papa before he'll move."

"From Roma."

"Right."

Marco motioned toward the gangplank. "Come up here and we'll talk."

Teo met his friend on deck. As they walked toward the staterooms Teo noticed there was little activity aboard the ship. The sails were furled, and no one scurried around loading fresh water or supplies. "Marco, you're planning to leave, right?"

The captain frowned and sighed. "Teofil—"

"Marco! We have to go!"

"Look around, *amico*. The skies are dreary. This time of year the winds are all wrong. Gales can blow up out of nowhere. You don't know what it's like to be caught in a winter storm. You can be driven along for days. Ships sink and men die in weather like that."

"But Deu is with us! He controls the wind and rain."

"Does he dole out good weather at our command?"

"As a matter of fact, Iesus can do exactly that."

"*Can* and *will* are two different things."

"Listen, I know you're concerned about the weather. But Deu takes care of his people in storms. There's a story in the book of Deeds about this. Paulus was going to Roma just like we are. He was caught in a storm, but Deu got him through it."

Marco shook his head. "It's rash."

"No, it's bold. There's a difference."

"The sailing season has ended. I'm sorry, but that's just the way it is."

"Okay, let me ask you this." Teo put his hand on Marco's shoulder. "Does a spell of fine weather ever occur before winter sets in for good?"

"It's been known to happen."

"Then here's what I'll do. I'm going to ask Deu for that. I'm going to rattle the gates of heaven until he hears me. Meanwhile you lay in provisions. Get your sailors ready. If Deu gives us the window, we'll go."

Marco grinned and shook his head. "If Deu answers that prayer, Teofil, I just might have to convert."

"You wait and see," Teo replied.

The next morning Teo jumped from his hammock at dawn, but the weather was gusty and cold. The local wind known as the mistral buffeted the city of Marsay. The following day was the same. The third day, however, dawned bright and clear. Marco agreed to leave.

"I hope you know what you're doing," he said as he stood next to Teo on the deck. "Weigh anchor!" he shouted to his crew.

The ship sailed several leagues from the city under sunny skies. Teo felt his spirits soar. Then a heavy overcast began to roll in. Black clouds gathered on the horizon.

"Come about," Marco ordered the helmsman. "Return to the port!"

The ship turned, but it couldn't outrace the wind. The seas grew choppy. A fierce gale snapped the sails. The sailors desperately hauled on the ropes as they attempted to maintain a steady course, but the wind only grew stronger. Sleet pelted the *Midnight Glider* as it tried to race to safety.

"Look out!"

A yard on the mainmast broke loose and plummeted to the deck, bringing with it a web of rigging and canvas. The fallen spar barely missed several of the sailors. Now the ship was even more unstable. All hands struggled to reach the lee of the shore.

At last the *Glider* neared Marsay. Proud but wounded, it limped into the harbor. Marco met Teo on deck. "I'm sorry," he said.

Teo went below and retrieved his rucksack, then returned topside. The wind's icy fingers clawed at him. Sleet stung his face. He knelt and rummaged in his pack. Standing up again, he slung his bearskin cloak around his shoulders and drew it close at his neck. Its familiar smell elicited a rush of memories, though he could take delight in none of them.

"Alright, Deu," he whispered to the turbulent skies. "I'll wait."

PART TWO

MINISTRY

CHAPTER

6

Count Federco Borromo had lost his fortune. One million scudi—gone to pay for mercenaries to save the Universal Communion. Now Federco's palatial estate on Greater Lake had fallen into foreclosure. His fields lay fallow. His beautiful gardens had become overgrown. Even his expensive thoroughbred horses had been auctioned off. The count was pitied by the Ulmbartian aristocracy. He had lost everything a man could lose.

Yet he was having the time of his life.

Count Federco lived on his last remaining property, a chateau in a rugged and remote part of Greater Lake. The place had been raided by barbarians not long ago. The Rovers attacked during a party of the Ulmbartian elite, and only the quick thinking of Teofil of Chiveis saved everyone from a massacre. That event had given Count Federco an idea. He had improved the fortifications of the lakeshore chateau and turned it into a comfortable place to live in solitude with his baby boy, Benito. A few old servants tended the house, freeing the count for a much more urgent concern: war. Count Federco was determined to rid Ulmbartia of all Rovers. He had reenlisted in the Ulmbartian army, and now the Rovers who raided the frontiers were squarely in his sights.

He crouched atop a rocky knob, watching a cohort of warriors advance through a mountain defile. They were swathed in thick furs, for it was the third month of the new year and snow still lay thick on the ground. Freezing rain had fallen all morning before the clouds finally cleared. Normally the Rovers wintered on the far side of a mountain pass that led to uncharted wilderness, but this year a war party had remained in the sparsely settled forests of Ulmbartia. Count Federco glanced up at the pass. The Ancients had named it "Simplon," but the Ulmbartians now called it Eagle Pass because of the stone monument that marked its crest. Once the Rover presence was eliminated in Ulmbartia, Federco intended to occupy the pass and prevent further incursions. This would be the last year his people would be harassed by the vicious barbarians.

An Ulmbartian lieutenant crawled to Federco's side while the Rovers approached. "What are your orders, sir?" The man's voice contained a hint of urgency.

Unlike the young soldier, Federco felt calm. It was a trait that had marked his first military enlistment, and it had also come in handy during the high-stakes business negotiations of his middle age. Now, as a commander of a squadron of untested recruits, Federco once again relied on his uncanny ability to keep a cool head. "Remain in your positions until I give the signal to attack," he said.

The soldier nodded, though a disconcerted look crossed his face. "But, sir . . . shouldn't we move our men down from the ridgeline? We have only a few archers here. We can't defend this little knob without reinforcements."

"I'll call for them when necessary," Federco replied crisply. "Prepare your archers. Be ready to shoot on my command."

The soldier saluted and moved off.

Federco watched the Rovers draw near. They were traveling through a narrow vale with steep snow-covered mountain flanks on either side. It was the perfect location for the plan Federco had in mind. The enemy was on foot, forty warriors armed with battle-axes, swords, and spears. A few weeks earlier they had raided an Ulmbartian village, killing all the men and carrying off the young women and boys. Federco felt sick at what those unfortunate captives had endured since the raid. *Give me victory, mighty Deus,* he prayed, for he was secretly a Knight of the Cross. *Then help me find the prisoners!*

When the Rovers entered an open snowfield Federco raised his bugle to his lips. He took a deep breath and sounded the attack. The Ulmbartian archers rose from their hiding places on the rocky outcrop. Down below in the open area, the Rovers bunched together and drew their weapons. Though the barbarians were still a quarter-league away, Federco's archers raised their bows to the sky and sent their arrows arcing toward the enemy. Little damage was done, but the volley kept the warriors from advancing any farther. They jeered at the Ulmbartian soldiers, yet hesitated to charge for fear of the deadly missiles.

Now Federco blew another blast on his bugle. "Remain in position!" he yelled to the archers, who looked around in confusion. They did not know the meaning of the second bugle call because it wasn't intended for them. It was a signal to the troops stationed on the mountainside above the Rovers.

Before the bugle's echo died away, an answering call resounded from the top of a steep white slope. The notes were low and sustained, for they weren't played on bugles but on long alpenhorns taken from a herder's barn. While some of the soldiers blew the deep-throated horns, others began to dislodge huge boulders and vibrate ropes stretched in the snow. Federco could see his men like tiny black dots moving along a snowfield that was exposed to the afternoon sun. It was an avalanche zone if ever there was one.

The Rovers turned around and began shouting and pointing up the slope. The danger to them was clear, yet so was the risk of advancing inside the archers' range.

A jagged line materialized across the head of the snow slope, then the mountain itself seemed to crumble. Though Federco knew his men were deployed along the slope's upper edge, when the snow began to move he offered a quick prayer that they had all scrambled high enough. A huge slab broke off, sending swirls of powder curling into the air. The leading edge of the avalanche began to speed down the slope like a wolf streaking toward its prey. As the snow raced into the valley, it picked up other streams until it formed an implacable wall of white death.

Now the terrified Rovers charged toward Federco's archers. Though several fell to arrows, the rest pressed on. But the oncoming snow was moving much faster than a man could run. It whooshed into the valley, billowing and roiling as it engulfed the Rovers in its freezing embrace.

Even Federco's archers, who stood on high ground, were so intimidated by the spectacle that they scurried back from their positions.

At last the avalanche's force was spent. The valley was now a jumbled expanse of churned-up snow. Nothing moved in the awful hush.

Federco stood up from the ledge that was his vantage point. He knew the Rovers' camp must be within a few hours' march. The Ulmbartian captives would be there, lightly guarded now that the forty warriors were gone. It was a great victory.

The lieutenant approached Count Federco, visibly shaken. "I'm f-from the plains," he stammered. "I've never seen anything like that! Danger lurks everywhere in these mountains!"

Federco stood with his hands on his hips, appraising the young recruit. He was a good man, though inexperienced and in need of courageous leadership. The count gave a hearty laugh.

"Well, get used to it, soldier," he said. "Our next assignment is to capture Eagle Pass."

◆　◆　◆

Ana stood on a grassy bank with the sparkling Tooner Sea behind her. It was high summer, so the fields were awash with bright red poppies. Teo faced her, handsome and smiling. A lock of his tousled hair hung over his forehead. He wore the Royal Guard's dress uniform, and his boots were polished to a shine. Ana smoothed her white gown as the march began to play. All eyes were on her: Father, Mother, Lina, Aunt Rosetta . . .

A black alpine chough circled in the sky. Suddenly it folded its wings and dived. Its yellow beak was razor-sharp. It pecked at Ana, seeking her eyes. She covered her face, crying, "Teo! Help me! Get it off!" But Teo did not come.

The bird seized her eyeball and plucked it out, then flew to the Iron Shield and landed on his shoulder. He stood there laughing at her.

"Give it back!" Ana demanded.

The warrior held out his hand. In his palm was a glass eye like a cat's. "A gift for you, my love," he said.

Ana inhaled a huge breath and bolted upright in her bed.

The room was dark. Her heart raced. Pain stabbed her eye. She grasped her eyelid and pulled it down by the lashes to produce tears. Wiping her eye with the heel of her hand, she blinked furiously until the eyelash or whatever had caused the irritation washed free.

Ana slowed her breathing and collected herself in her bedroom at the little convent by the sea. Eventually the nightmare receded. *A wedding?* Ana lay back on her pillow and considered that. Like every girl, she had daydreamed about her wedding before. Now that she and Teo had acknowledged their love, she thought about it quite often. But tonight's dream was much more vivid than those fantasies. She felt as if she had actually experienced the emotions of her wedding day. Ana smiled at how thunderstruck Teo had looked as she walked toward him . . .

Abruptly the wisps of the dream that lingered in Ana's mind vanished, and the real world rushed to take its place. Sadness filled Ana's heart as she realized how far she was from an idyllic wedding in Chiveis with her family and friends. Physical distance from her homeland was only part of the problem. So many other things had to change if this particular dream was to come true. *I'm a condemned criminal*, Ana recalled. *And Teo is across an ocean!* He had not come home for the winter, and the seas were just now beginning to open again.

She glanced over to the second bed. Vanita was there, a sleepyhead who rarely awakened at night. Ana, in contrast, often found herself sleepless. Now wide awake, she decided to visit the chapel to seek the face of Deu. Grabbing her shawl, she tiptoed from the room.

The convent was quiet. Ana clutched the shawl close to her neck, glad for its warmth over her thin nightshift. Now that it was the third month, the daytime temperatures had begun to warm up, but the nights along Roma's coast were still cool.

She reached the staircase and descended to the main floor. The chapel door creaked as she pushed it open. The moon was new, so no light filtered through the clerestory windows. Ana lit a couple of tapers in a candelabra by the door, then carried one of them with her as she walked down the dark nave. The table at the front was set for the Meal that the sisters celebrated. Ana had never partaken of that solemnity because she had not yet undergone the Washing. After setting the taper in a candlestick on the table, she retrieved the Sacred Writing from the reading pulpit. She was about to open it when something caught her eye. High above, through the window of the apse, a bright light gleamed against the night sky: the morning star.

Ana shivered. A memory rushed through her mind of the time she had fled from a chapel much like this one as a demon pursued her. *Was that real or just a hallucination?* Ana didn't know, though she certainly believed in evil spirits. They masqueraded as gods for men to worship, sharing their power with their most devoted followers. According to the fourteenth chapter of Isaias, the morning star was the symbol of Astrebril: "Behold, you are fallen from heaven, Brilliant Star, son of the dawn!" Teo had told Ana that the words for "brilliant star" in the original Fluid Tongue were *Astre Brillant.*

And yet, as Ana considered the pinpoint of light glistening through the window, a new testimony came to her mind. She opened the Sacred Writing and flipped the pages by the steady light of the candle on the table. At last she found the passage she sought in the book of the Apocalypse, the twenty-second chapter: "I, Iesus, have sent my angel to declare these things to you in the churches. I am the root and descendant of David, the bright Morning Star."

Iesus is the true Morning Star!

It made sense, for the star signaled the coming of sunrise. Though Astrebril posed as a dawn god, it was Iesus alone who provided new life. The glory of the morning—light triumphing over darkness—belonged to the one who had defeated death. Ana felt glad to be joined to the new life of Iesus, though it angered her that Astrebril sought to usurp his glory. She pointed her finger at the star. "Impostor!" she accused. "I see you for what you are! I'm not afraid of you!"

"You should be, Anastasia."

Who said that? Ana spun around, but no one was in the chapel. *Was it a voice in my head? It sounded so real!*

The door to the chapel began to ease shut, creaking as it moved.

Leave me alone!

Ana hurried to the door, wanting to catch it before it closed and locked her inside, but she couldn't reach it in time. A gust of wind swirled about the room, extinguishing the candles and plunging the chapel into darkness. Then the door slammed shut.

Ana's heart thrummed in her chest, but she forced herself to remain calm. *That was normal*, she decided. *Doors often move when air pressures are altered, like when someone opens a window . . .*

A window?

What's going on here?

Ana reached for the knob and was relieved to feel it turn in her hand. She peeked into the hallway. A cold breeze stirred her nightshift against her calves.

Behind her something cackled.

The sound made Ana cry out. She whirled, terrified of what she would see. The hair on the back of her neck stood up. Gooseflesh broke out across her forearms.

But the chapel was dark and silent.

Ana backed through the doorway into the corridor. Her legs felt shaky. A sense of foreboding weighed on her. She knew something terrible was about to happen.

The door to the chapel started to move again, groaning on its hinges. Ana had seen enough. She started to flee to her room—but what she saw when she turned caused fear to convulse her body. At the end of the corridor, a tall shadow darted from one door to the next.

Ana staggered, terrified by the strange presence in the convent. This time her legs gave way, and she collapsed to the floor. Her shawl fell from her shoulders.

Who's there?

Though she wanted to scream, no words would form in her mouth. All her senses were on high alert. Perspiration beaded on her brow. Her hands trembled like leaves in the wind.

Someone is sneaking around the convent!

Ana had no weapon. She felt naked and exposed. The overwhelming urge to get behind a locked door propelled her to stand. She sprinted down the corridor, her bare feet padding against the cold stones. The stairwell to her second-floor room was only a few paces away. She was almost there . . .

And then the shadow stepped in front of her.

Ana shrieked as she collided with the figure. Cruel arms seized her by the shoulders. Fingernails dug into her skin. She wrestled with her assailant, yelling for help. The man cuffed her across the head, hard enough to stun her. Ana stopped shouting and drooped in her enemy's grasp. A hand grabbed her by the throat and began to squeeze. Ana clawed at the hand but couldn't loosen the iron grip. Dizziness made her head swim.

"Let go of her!"

The voice was like the roar of an enraged bear. A huge shape exploded from the stairwell and sent Ana's attacker flying. She fell to her hands and knees, gasping for breath while two men careened back and forth, slamming against the walls of the corridor. Curses and grunts resounded in the narrow space.

Several of the sisters arrived, followed by the housemother with a flaming torch. She thrust it at Ana's assailant. "Get out of here!"

"Arrrgh!" A scream of terrible pain filled the hallway.

Then everything fell still.

Ana stood up, breathing hard. Her nightshift was ripped, but she held it close to cover herself.

"He's gone," shouted the housemother from an adjacent room. "He went out through a window and took off down the beach."

"Help him!" squealed one of the sisters, pointing.

Ana looked to the floor. A giant man was slumped against the wall, his eyes squeezed shut. A grimace contorted his bearded face.

Liber!

Ana ran to her friend. "Stasia . . . " he moaned. His arm was nestled against his side. The place was slick with glossy blood.

Carefully lifting Liber's arm, Ana inspected his injury. The hilt of a knife protruded from his side. It had been thrust into the fatty tissue of his belly just above his hip bone. Ana was relieved. Though it was a deep flesh wound, no internal organs would be affected.

The housemother turned to the gaping nuns. "Bring hot water—quick! And fetch Sister Deidre at once!"

"It hurts, Stasia," Liber said, whimpering.

"I know. But the sisters are going to take good care of you."

Liber searched Ana's face. "Will you take care of me?"

Ana intertwined her fingers with Liber's. Holding his fist to her chest, she patted it with her other hand. "Liber—it's you who takes care of me."

A smile spread across the big man's face despite his pain.

"I love you, Stasia," he said.

✦ ✦ ✦

Teo stared at the note written on a scrap of parchment:

DANGER TO THE CHRISTIANI! IMPORTANT INFORMATION AT CASSEE.

He had left the tavern's common room to use the outhouse. When he returned, the note was protruding from underneath his empty breakfast plate. The letters were nondescript, and there was no signature. He glanced around. All the patrons were going about their business. No one was looking his way. Teo put the slip in his pocket and waved the barmaid over.

"Did somebody stop by my table while I was out?"

The barmaid shook her head. "Didn't see nobody."

Teo turned and caught the attention of a sailor sitting nearby with a bowl of porridge. "You see anyone at my table in the past few minutes?"

"Lots of people passing by. The place is crowded."

"No one stopped though?"

"Not that I saw."

Teo frowned and turned back to the barmaid. "How much do I owe you?"

"Two livre."

"Here you go." Teo handed her three coins, then put his cloak around his shoulders and left the tavern.

The *Midnight Glider* was anchored at the far end of Marsay's Old Port. Teo walked down the pier until he reached the ship. "Hail, pirate!" he called up to Marco.

Marco grimaced and held his finger to his lips. "Shh! Don't let my secret out!" He chuckled, then beckoned Teo to come aboard.

Brother Thomas was standing with Marco when Teo climbed the gangplank. The friar had become something of a fixture in Teo's life over the winter. They had spent long hours discussing the meaning of the holy writings. Teo's command of spoken Fransais had grown much stronger, while Brother Thomas's new insights into Christianism had deepened his nascent faith. The friar clearly had the inclinations of a reformer, but Odo controlled the knights at Castle d'If and marginalized anyone who proposed changes.

"You'll be happy to know I've started to provision the ship," Marco said as Teo approached. "Give me a few more days and we'll shove off. It's earlier than I'd like, but the weather has been mild, so I think we can risk a voyage."

"Just say the word and I'll be the first to cast off the hawsers." Teo reached into his pocket and pulled out the parchment. "What do you make of this? Somebody put it on my table when I wasn't looking."

Marco and Brother Thomas examined the slip. "What danger is it referring to?" Marco asked.

"I'm not sure."

"It's written in Talyano," Brother Thomas pointed out. "Other than a few of the knights, nobody around here speaks that language."

"I know. It makes me suspicious."

"Of the knights?"

"No. I suspect this involves foreigners. I just can't figure out who would want to warn me about danger."

"So what are you going to do?"

"Obviously I'm going to have to check it out."

Brother Thomas frowned. "It could be a trap."

"I know. I've learned to be careful with things like this. But I'm not backing down."

"Somehow I thought you might say that," Marco said with a knowing smile.

Teo turned to Brother Thomas. "Any idea where Cassee is?"

"It's a little fishing village about twenty-five leagues from here. Technically it's outside the jurisdiction of the Republic of Marsay. You can get there in four hours if you'll let me show you the way."

"Alright. Let's go."

"Want me to come along?" Marco asked.

"You focus on the ship," Teo replied. "We can handle this. We'll be back late tonight."

The ride to Cassee took closer to five hours—not only because the best rental horses were a couple of swaybacked mares past their prime, but also because of the rough terrain. In the time of the Ancients, the city of Marsay had been much larger than its current size. The Great War of Destruction had vaporized the city's center in a giant conflagration, but many ruins remained on the outskirts. Eventually the two travelers left the tangled urbanized area and reached a land of rugged hills covered in scrub oak and aleppo pine. A winding trail brought them to the village of Cassee, a seaside community with a splendid view of a headland whose cliffs plunged into the ocean.

"That's called Scoundrels' Cape," Brother Thomas said, pointing to the cliffs. "This must be a good place to find danger, eh?"

"I guess we're about to find out." Teo nudged his horse forward.

It didn't take long to discern that Cassee wasn't just a quaint village of pastel cottages clustered around a picturesque harbor. Several of the taverns catered to the type of sailor whose idea of a "catch" didn't mean tuna. The two travelers approached one of the seediest of the pirate establishments, a place called *The White Rocks*.

The sailors inside hunched at the bar or sat at tables playing cards. It was midafternoon—too early for anyone to be intoxicated, but just right for the first stiff drink of the day. A sense of restlessness pervaded the room. Teo knew these men were ready to get back to the sea.

"Ale for us both," Teo said, putting a silver coin on the counter. The bartender drew two drafts with foam spilling down the sides, then collected the coin.

As the bartender started to turn away Teo waved him closer. "I'm looking for information from anyone who might be in the know," he said in a low voice.

The bartender shrugged. "Anything can be bought here. Liquor . . . women . . . contraband . . . and information."

"Who should I talk to?"

"The man in the back room might be able to help."

"Maybe you could introduce me." Teo flipped a second coin to the bartender, who caught it in midair.

"Knock on that door in half an hour."

As the bartender moved off, Brother Thomas looked at Teo admiringly. "You're always so confident," he remarked.

Teo set down his mug and wiped foam from his lips. "It's just a show," he said with a grin.

At the appointed time Teo left Brother Thomas at the bar and knocked on the door to the back room. A gruff voice commanded him to enter. Four pirates were seated around a table, smoking the *tabako* weed and playing a game with Marsayan tarot cards.

"You must be Teofil," said the leader, a stout fellow with a mean scar along his cheek.

Teo was taken aback. "You know my name?"

The scar-faced man laughed. "You came to me for information, didn't you? Why are you surprised that I have it?"

"I thought you'd know what's happening around Cassee. I didn't imagine your knowledge would extend to a nobody like me."

"To some people, you ain't a nobody," the pirate said cryptically.

What does that mean?

Teo shook off the perplexing comment and pressed forward with the reason for his visit. "I'm looking for information about any strange activity involving the religion of Christianism. Something unusual or out of the ordinary. In particular I think it might involve the Clan, or maybe—"

"The shamans?"

Teo paused. *How did he know I was going to say that?* The situation here was unclear, but Teo sensed trouble was brewing. "Yeah, the shamans," he said evenly. "What can you tell me about them? I'll pay."

"Keep your money. I've already been paid plenty to pass you a message."

"Someone paid you? Who?"

"The man said he was a friend of the Christiani. That's all I know."

Though Teo wanted to inquire further, he didn't think the pirate would divulge the information, so he said, "Speak up then if you have something to tell me."

The other three men shifted uncomfortably at Teo's brusqueness, but the scar-faced leader was unperturbed. "The shamans are planning an attack. A raid, if you will."

"Where? Cassee? Marsay?" Teo tried to imagine why the Iron Shield would want to attack this area. *To prevent reinforcements from going to Jineve? To reestablish the Pact in its original locale?*

The pirate waved his hand. "No. That would be foolish. The Knights of the Cross have a powerful militia at their command."

"Where then?"

"A coordinated attack on religious houses."

"Religious houses? What do you mean?" Apprehension seized Teo.

"The Christiani have houses of devoted virgins along the coast around Roma. The shamans are planning to take those women captive. For what purpose, I don't know."

Teo couldn't speak. For a moment he couldn't even think. The pirate's announcement struck him like a club to the head. He felt his knees go weak, and he had to steady himself against the doorframe to stay upright.

Through the haze of confusion and alarm, a single word formed in Teo's mind. He tried to get it out twice but could only manage a breathy stutter. Finally he said, "When?"

"Sometime before the equinox."

The equinox!

Teo's jaw hung slack. He put his hand to his forehead.

That's two weeks from today!

◆　◆　◆

The Astrebrilian monk fidgeted as he faced the High Priestess in her private rooms. "It is finished, Your Eminence," he said, his gaze cast down. "Early this morning we were able to produce a purified sample at last."

"Excellent!" cried the High Priestess. "Do you have it with you?"

"No, my lady. It is considered too dangerous to move."

"That shall have to be remedied or the substance will be of no use to me."

"We know. Men are working on that."

"Copper tanks?"

"Yes, tanks to hold the fluid, with pressurized air to eject it in a mist."

"I assume you have followed the exact specifications I gave you."

"Of course, Your Eminence. You speak as the mouthpiece of the high god. We would never disobey your orders."

"Even so, I would like to evaluate your progress." The High Priestess waved the visitor away with the back of her hand. "Return to the laboratory and prepare a demonstration. I will be there shortly."

"As you wish." The Astrebrilian monk bowed and left the room.

Leaning back in the chair behind her desk, the High Priestess stroked her iron collar as she considered the important milestone she was about to pass. Her best men of science had been experimenting with chemicals for years. Though the explosive powder of Astrebril was fearsome and deadly, the priestess had long wanted to develop a second weapon, one that could be sprayed across a battlefield to inflict widespread suffering. The founder of Chiveis, Jonluc Beaumont, had left instructions on exactly how to do this, yet no one had attempted it until the High Priestess came to power. It didn't take long for her scientist monks to realize how difficult it would be to replicate the machines and devices of the Ancients. Years of vigorous effort had been invested to reach the goal. Now the day of victory had arrived.

The High Priestess rose from her desk and went to a chest. She knelt and unlocked it, then lifted the lid. Books were stacked inside, most of them old and tattered. She hissed as she noticed the sacred book of Christianism lying among the others. It recited mythical stories about the creator god Deu and his son, the crucified criminal. The High Priestess uttered a raspy imprecation as that god came to her mind. His self-righteous pretenses at holiness disgusted her. She knew Astrebril hated that god—and feared him too, which made his hate all the more intense. The High Priestess owned the only copy of Deu's book in Chiveis. Sometimes she forced herself to read it to understand her adversary, and she also used it for her rituals of desecration. But today she wasn't interested in that book. Her mind was set instead on the important text that Jonluc Beaumont had bequeathed to his consort Greta the Great.

The original manuscript was long gone, of course, but scribes had preserved a single copy over the centuries. The High Priestess lifted the codex from the chest and took it to her desk. It was brittle, and its illuminations were now faded, yet the words remained clear enough to read. The title was written in a bold, flowing script: *Weapons for a New World*.

"I thank you, great lord," the High Priestess intoned as she thumbed the pages. "You have brought us to this momentous day by the dominance of your power." Awe filled her as she considered the supremacy of Astrebril.

The book contained detailed drawings of scientific apparatus: beakers and vials and tubes and vats, much like the equipment at a distillery. Beaumont's explanations were clear and concise. He was a master of the Ancients' chemical lore. Few who survived the Great War of Destruction possessed such knowledge, and fewer still had the ingenuity to win power with it. That combination made Beaumont a great man.

The explosive powder of Astrebril was only the beginning. Beaumont's book went on to describe how to render brimstone and other chemicals into a liquid that could be spread as a cloud of gas. An entire battlefield could be enveloped in a toxic yellow fog that smelled of mustard. The gas didn't seem particularly harmful at first. For several hours the afflicted soldiers wouldn't even know they were injured. Then all the powers of hell would break loose.

The High Priestess smiled as she read about the effects of the noxious gas. The victim's eyes would swell shut as tears and mucus flowed from them in great quantities. Blisters would develop on the skin, bulging like fat tumors filled with yellow bile. The enemy soldiers would writhe in agony, unable to stop screaming at their continuous torture. Yet as horrible as the external symptoms were, what was happening inside the body was even worse. The burning gas penetrated the throat and lungs, stripping away their delicate linings. Every choking gasp produced searing pain. Those who received a mortal dose of the gas would die after weeks of unbearable suffering. Nothing could be done for them except to look on with horror, and that was the weapon's most powerful effect. Though it might not produce mass casualties on the battlefield, the intensity of its torments would produce something even better: abject terror at the prospect of being gassed.

A vial on the High Priestess's desk contained the explosive powder of Astrebril. She poured some of the black granules into a dish, then struck a match. The powder flared up in a flash of light and smoke. "Ahhhh, yes, my lord," the priestess said as she inhaled the acrid vapors with her eyes closed. "The good bounty of thy hand knows no end."

With the aroma of Astrebril still upon her, the High Priestess rose and went to the door. She descended a spiral staircase to the ground floor, then exited her spire and walked toward a low building constructed against the wall that surrounded her temple complex. Snow crunched under her feet as she walked. A cowled monk met her at the door.

"Welcome, Your Eminence," he said. "We have been hard at work for you here."

"We shall see if your labors have paid off." The priestess handed her embroidered cloak to the monk.

The laboratory was filled with equipment for distilling chemicals and pumping gasses. An oaken door at the back of the room led to an inner sanctum where the demonstration would take place. A transom window above the door opened toward a grate in the ceiling, a means of escape for the poisonous fumes concocted in this place.

Most of the room was occupied by a table. Lead figurines of miniature soldiers had been spread out to imitate a battlefield. Several wicker fans on long rods lay on the table as well. And in the midst of everything was a small metal cylinder set into a tiny wheeled cart made to fit it.

"That cylinder has been filled with an inert substance," said a hump-backed scientist standing by the table. "Compressed gas forces it out. The machine worked just as your instructions suggested it would."

"That is because my instructions came from the great Beaumont himself," answered the High Priestess. The handful of monks in the room murmured at this.

The senior scientist beckoned to his assistants. The men came forward and took up the fans, waving them briskly to create an air flow. "Pretend that is the wind," the scientist said. He rolled the little cart into position and opened a valve on the cylinder. White vapor began to spew from it, wafting across the figurines in the breeze from the fans.

"You are sure this substance is harmless?" the priestess asked.

"Quite sure. Look." The old scientist bent over and breathed it with no ill effect.

Cautiously, the High Priestess approached the table. With her finger she flicked each figurine until all of them were toppled. She turned to the leader of the monks. "Show me the actual sample."

After waving the other men from the room he escorted the priestess to a wooden chest on a bench. After opening it, the scientist donned thick leather gloves and removed a glass vial. The stuff inside was an ugly yellow-brown, like the contents of a chamber pot.

"The poison is very potent," the scientist said. "We sprayed it on rabbits, and they nearly clawed out their eyes. All of them died thrashing in a mess of vomit and blood."

"Very good. How much of this substance have you been able to manufacture?"

"Only what you see there, my lady."

The High Priestess raised an eyebrow. "Your abilities disappoint me. No doubt Astrebril is displeased as well."

The humpbacked scientist cringed. "Your Eminence, we could make more now that we've perfected the process, but one thing holds us back."

"And what is that?"

"We need more brimstone. Supply us with that and we can make many barrels of this poison—enough to cover a battlefield."

"Brimstone, you say? That is your only obstacle?"

"That's right, my lady. I know it's precious and rare, but perhaps you could obtain some."

The priestess walked to the door and gazed up through the grate in the ceiling. She stood silent for a long moment, hands on her hips, praying to the god of the dawn. At last she turned back to the nervous scientist.

"Soon," she vowed, "soon you shall have what you need."

✦ ✦ ✦

The *Midnight Glider* was ready to sail, but the winds were adverse. Teo stamped his foot on the deck, fighting to remain calm.

"The gale will pass," Marco said. "I want to get out of here as much as you do. We'll weigh anchor the moment we can."

Teo clasped his friend's shoulder. "I know. It's just so hard to wait." Marco nodded understandingly.

The news from Cassee that the Exterminati were planning a raid on the convents had thrown Teo into action. He had nearly killed his old nag rushing back to Marsay's harbor. Though the *Glider* wasn't fully provisioned yet, Marco had ordered an immediate departure. He was as concerned for Vanita's safety as Teo was for Ana's.

Unfortunately the weather didn't cooperate. A gale had blown up that lasted into the next morning. Marco claimed the system would clear out before midday. In the meantime Teo struggled to be patient. Every moment of delay was an agony.

At last the ship left Marsay beneath overcast skies. Brother Thomas was aboard, along with ten friar-knights under his command. All were warriors, and Teo had a hunch their skills would be needed before this business with the Exterminati was over.

Despite the late start the ship made good progress. There was a delay at Manacho when the authorities demanded to board for an inspection. Teo hid in a crate below deck because he had been banished from Likuria forever. The inspectors didn't find him, and the journey resumed. Marco ordered his men to sail at top speed. The days slid by, and after a week the *Glider* arrived at the harbor where Roma's river met the sea.

"Have your men arm themselves," Teo told Brother Thomas. "Captain Marco's crewmen are fighters too, so they'll come with us. We'll be a strong force. I just hope we can get to the convent in time to prevent disaster."

Brother Thomas closed his eyes and touched the cross tattoo on his forehead. "Let it be so," he said.

✦ ✦ ✦

The day the shamans came was rainy and cold.

Ana rose early to check on Liber, whose knife wound had become infected. Sister Deidre had numbed it with a tincture of poppies and stitched it shut, but instead of healing the cut grew red and swollen.

Although the big man with the childlike mind had received the best pos-sible treatment at the convent, everyone agreed it was time for him to go to the Christiani basilica. The doctors there would have bread-mold elixir to deal with the infection. Two young nuns were appointed to escort Liber to the river, where a ferry would take them to Roma. A message had been sent ahead to the Papa, who held Liber the Beloved in high regard as Deu's chosen vessel to preserve the New Testament.

Once Liber was safely off, Ana went to the kitchen to see if she could assist with breakfast. She had always enjoyed cooking, but her twenty-one-month exile from Chiveis had given her little opportunity for that. She tried to help out in the convent's kitchen whenever she could.

As Ana diced potatoes for a breakfast hash, she offered a prayer for Liber's safety. Tension had been high ever since the break-in and stab-bing a week ago. Although the incident of arson and theft last autumn had been dismissed by the nuns as an aberration, it was clear to Ana that nefarious forces in the outside world had their eye on the little convent. The housemother tried to suggest a third break-in was unlikely. She held out hope that the two crimes were unrelated—just petty thieves looking for easy loot. But Ana and Vanita had a different theory about the recent attack. Though the nighttime intruder didn't wear the traditional robe of the shamans, the women sensed he was a member of that evil sect. Certainly he was no thief—nothing in the convent had been stolen or disturbed. On the surface things appeared to be back to normal. Yet as Vanita liked to say, "Just because you don't see the cockroaches doesn't mean they're not there." That repulsive thought was running through Ana's mind when she heard the loud crash that changed everything.

It was a thunderous boom, like something heavy striking something equally resistant. Several of the kitchen workers let out a cry and huddled together. Ana told them to wait in the kitchen until she had discovered what was happening.

The boom came again, and this time it was followed by a terrible splintering sound. Ana felt a chill of fear grip her stomach. This wasn't some kind of accident. The convent was under attack. Its front door was being battered down.

"Grab those knives!" she shouted to the frightened sisters. When one of the wide-eyed girls picked up a mixing spoon with a trembling hand, Ana realized they were all in deep trouble. She snatched a meat cleaver and ran from the room.

Shouts resounded from the convent's main entryway—male voices, aggressive and harsh. Ana ran to a window, then froze as she looked out. Two ships were anchored a short distance offshore. Boats had landed on the beach. Raiders were running toward the convent in the driving rain, weapons in hand.

Exterminati.

"Deu, help us," Ana whispered.

Women's screams now mingled with the shouts of the attackers. A man rounded a corner and glanced down the corridor. Instead of loose robes he wore black fitted trousers and high boots. He held a club in one hand and manacles in the other. His expression was full of malice. Ana gripped the meat cleaver in her strong, sweaty hand. The shamans would not take her without a fight.

When the man charged at Ana, she spun away and ran. She assumed that was what all the sisters were doing, but she had a different plan. The man's club and manacles told her this was a kidnapping raid, not a mass murder. Ana knew her pursuer wasn't going to run a blade through her back; the clubs were for knocking the women to the ground where they could be chained into submission. As she dashed past a decorative vase on a pedestal she tipped it over behind her. The shaman cursed as he stumbled on the broken shards. Ana turned. Off balance, the man tried to bring his club around in a wide arc. Ana stepped inside the attack and buried her cleaver in the shaman's skull.

The blow hurled him backward, wrenching the cleaver from Ana's grasp. The shaman's eyes bulged in surprise. The thick blade had sunk deep, so the handle protruded from his forehead like the horn of a grotesque beast. Surprisingly, there was little blood. He clawed at the handle as if to pry it from his cloven skull. Then his eyes closed, and he fell to the floor.

Someone shoved Ana hard. She went flying across the hallway, careening off a wall before hitting the ground. Another shaman ran at her, brandishing his club. Ana shielded herself with her arms.

"Not the head!" shouted an authoritative voice. "No visible marks!"

"But this one killed one of ours!"

"You heard me!" the first voice roared. "No marks!"

The club whacked Ana across the shoulders. It hurt, but she bit back her cry. A boot pressed her roughly to the floor. Her arms were pinned behind her back, then manacles were slapped on her wrists. Ana was hauled to her feet.

"You'll die soon enough," said the sneering shaman who gripped her arm, "by a death far worse than a club to the head." He forced her to march into the chapel.

Most of the other sisters were there, whimpering as the shamans harassed them. A few women still screamed in the halls, but gradually they were rounded up and brought to the chapel with the rest.

Ana spotted Vanita across the room. Like everyone else she was bound with chains. A shaman was making lewd faces at her and tickling her chin with his finger. Vanita turned away, repulsed. Ana edged toward her in the mayhem.

A lightning bolt flashed outside, accompanied by an explosive thunderclap. The room fell silent as the babbling voices died away one by one. The only sound now was the rain drumming on the chapel's roof. Everyone stood still. No woman dared moan, no man dared speak, for the Iron Shield stood silhouetted in the doorway.

He stalked into the room, his booted footsteps loud in the hush. Suddenly his hand shot out and grabbed a shaman who was locked in a lusty embrace with one of the sisters. The tall warrior wrenched the man's arm, forcing him into a submissive posture. Staring down into the shaman's face he asked, "You dare to assault a bride of Mulciber?"

"N-n-no, my lord. I was . . . arresting her escape."

The Iron Shield uttered a growl and hurled the shaman away from the terrified nun. He turned and surveyed the room. "How many are there?" he demanded.

One of the shamans stepped forward. "Twenty-three, master."

"Listen! Any man who violates one of these women will answer to me! They are devoted to the god and must be kept as virgins."

Vanita moved to Ana's side and leaned close. "It's been a while since I've been called that," she whispered. "Think they'll let me go?"

Ana gave her friend a rueful smile, admiring her defiant spirit.

"Round them up and take them to the ships," the Iron Shield ordered.

"What about this one?" A shaman pointed to the housemother.

The Iron Shield took the woman's jaw in his hand and examined her. "Mulciber does not wed old hags like this." He pushed her face away so he wouldn't have to look at it.

"What is to be done with her then?"

"Whatever you wish."

No!

Ana was horrified. The housemother was a righteous woman. Ana worked herself through the crowd and tried to intervene, but with her arms cuffed behind her back there was nothing she could do. Two men seized Ana and pulled her along. Meanwhile the housemother was dragged to a different room. Though she did not speak aloud, her head was bowed, and her lips moved in silent prayer.

A martyr for Deu, Ana realized. Tears welled up in her eyes.

"Feeling weepy, are you?"

Ana whirled to confront her tormentor. The Iron Shield's one good eye was locked on her face.

"Fiend!" she accused.

"No. *Fiends*," he answered, then laughed in a strange, echoing way.

"You disgust me. I reject you in the name of—"

The Iron Shield seized Ana's face, squeezing her cheeks in his gauntleted fist. "Don't say it," he snarled.

Ana couldn't speak even if she wanted to. The Iron Shield's tight grip on her face puckered her lips shut.

"I killed him, you know." The dark warrior's voice was arrogant.

What?

"That's right. I captured Teofil in the wilderness and made him suffer. He screamed for you, and every time he did I hurt him worse. He wasn't even a man anymore by the time I was finished with him."

No! He's lying!

"I'm not lying," the Iron Shield said. "Teofil died the most horrific death imaginable—just like the one I have planned for you." He released Ana's cheeks, then turned to address the crowded room. "To the ship now, brothers! Quickly!"

The Exterminati led the women into the pouring rain. As a shaman dragged Ana to the waiting boats, she found her will to resist had dissolved. The gruesome killing of her attacker . . . the housemother's plight . . . the Iron Shield's taunts . . . it was all too much. Raindrops mingled with Ana's tears as she plodded across the beach.

Teo isn't coming?

It can't be true . . .

Can it?

◆   ◆   ◆

The *Midnight Glider* barely had time to drop its gangplank onto the dock before Teo went ashore at the head of a fully armed war party. Rumors would no doubt fly along the waterfront of Roma's harbor, but Teo didn't care about that. He only wanted to reach the convent before the Exterminati.

It took an hour to round up thirty horses from the hostlers at the local taverns. Brother Thomas gladly paid the fees. Though the Knights at Marsay might be lacking in piety, the monastic order seemed to have no shortage of money. By the time the party of warriors set out, a gray dusk had begun to gather.

The convent lay a few leagues south of Roma's port. Teo led the men through the overgrown ruins of the Ancients until he came to a rusty sign that marked the turnoff. "Lido di Ostia," it read. Teo had just guided his mount onto a faint trail when he smelled something that caused the weight of dread to settle on his shoulders.

Smoke.

He urged his horse into a gallop with Marco close behind. As Teo raced down the trail, the smoky stench grew stronger.

Must be cooking fires, Teo decided. *It's chilly and rainy today . . . the sisters are keeping warm.*

175

But Teo knew he was kidding himself. When he reached the convent his worst fears were confirmed. The building was a smoldering ruin, a complete devastation. Nothing remained but scorched stone walls. The roof was gone, and soot smudged every gaping window. A column of black smoke rose to the sky as if from a pagan altar.

"No!" Teo screamed, leaping from the saddle. He ran to the convent. Its stones were still hot to the touch.

Marco stared at Teo with a stunned expression. "Are they . . . dead?" His eyes were large and round.

Teo pushed away his shock and grief, forcing himself to think like the wilderness scout he was. The first thing he noticed as he scanned the ruins was the lack of charred corpses. "They're not dead," he told Marco, pointing to the churned-up sand of the beach. "They've been taken away in ships."

"Where?"

Teo sighed heavily. "The sea leaves no tracks." A feeling of helplessness washed over him as he realized Ana had gone where he could not follow.

Marco picked his way through the blackened debris. "Let's go up to their room."

"Careful. Everything is unstable."

"I'll follow you."

The two men made their way to the stairwell, where the stone steps had not been destroyed by the flames. In several places the upper floor had caved in, but the fire had burned erratically, so other parts of the convent still stood. Most of the dormitory rooms were intact, though their furnishings had been consumed in the blaze.

"This is it." Teo kicked aside the remains of the door and entered the women's bedroom. Everything reeked of burnt wood. The two beds were reduced to ashes, and the roof gaped open to the evening sky. Tendrils of smoke wafted in the breeze.

"Gone! Everything is just . . . gone." Marco clasped his forehead in his hand.

Teo crossed to a closet and peered inside. The remains of a burlap sack lay on the floor. As he knelt and inspected its contents, a new wave of grief struck him. His books were there, crumbling in his hands like dried leaves. The lexicon he had used to translate the Prima was no great loss, but underneath it was a book whose ruined pages made tears rise to Teo's eyes.

The Sacred Writing, written and preserved in the Fluid Tongue.

Teo's mind flashed back to the day he had discovered it with Ana. They had broken into a mysterious cathedral in a lost city of the Ancients. A secret message encoded in wall murals had led them to the roof. There they found the holy scriptures of Deu, hidden long ago by a man named Jacques Dalsace. That discovery had launched Teo and Ana on an incredible adventure—not only a physical journey, but an odyssey of the soul.

Treasure, they had called the book that day.

And now it was destroyed.

Horrified, Teo let the charred volume slip from his hand. It fell apart. His eyes caught a flash of pale yellow in the midst of all the blackness.

"A page in the middle has survived," Marco said.

Teo plucked the sacred page from the ashes. Though its edges were singed, the words were still legible. Having spent all winter speaking the Fluid Tongue at Marsay, Teo could read the text as easily as if it were his native speech.

"What does it say?" Marco asked, his voice touched with awe.

"It's Hymn 143," Teo replied, then began to translate:

The enemy pursues my soul, he tramples my life to the ground.
He makes me live in the darkness like those long dead.
My spirit is slaughtered within me, my heart is troubled in my breast.
I remember the days of old,
I meditate on all your deeds,
I reflect on the work of your hands.
I spread my hands toward you; my soul thirsts for you like a dried-out land.
Hurry to answer me, Eternal One! My spirit is consumed.
Do not hide your face from me, or I will be like those who descend
    into the pit.
Let me hear of your goodness in the morning, for I confide in you.
Let me know the road I must walk, for I lift up my soul to you.
Deliver me from my enemies, Eternal One.

I seek refuge next to you.
Teach me to do your will, for you are my God.
May your good spirit lead me the right way.

Teo raised his eyes to the night sky. "May your good spirit lead me the right way," he repeated.

Outside, Brother Thomas's voice rang out. "Heads up, men! Someone's coming!"

CHAPTER

7

S tratetix carried an armload of firewood up to the quiet bedroom. He knelt in front of the hearth and arranged the logs, then added some kindling. A box of the little fire sticks made by the priests of Vulkain was on the mantel. But Stratetix didn't need any matches—not yet anyway.

"What are you doing?"

The voice startled Stratetix. He turned to see his lovely wife standing in the doorway. She was in her midforties but still as beautiful as the day he married her. Helena's ash-blonde hair and delicate features gave her a youthful appearance. She smiled at him, amused and perhaps intrigued by his actions.

"I thought I'd better lay a fire," he said.

"Just in case?"

"Yeah . . . you never know . . . today could be the day. It's still chilly this time of year. Can't hurt to be prepared."

Helena entered and sat down on the sleigh bed. Ana's room was furnished simply: a carved dresser with a ewer and bowl on it, a wardrobe in the corner, a mirror on the wall, a wooden bathtub. Green shutters were at the window, and a door led to a balcony that overlooked Edgeton's village square.

"It actually seems real now, doesn't it?" Helena remarked.

Stratetix straightened from the hearth and nodded. "Ever since Teofil came back, a gloom has lifted from me." The Chiveisian farmer recalled the words he had found carved into his shed: *we will return*. Since then, not a day had passed that he hadn't cherished the promise.

Helena's eyes twinkled as she glanced at her husband. "You'd better save some wood for heating water. She'll probably want a long soak."

"She can have all the wood she wants! Never again will I complain about how much hot water that girl uses!" Stratetix and Helena chuckled, sharing the kind of joke that only parents can understand.

After a bit Stratetix's mood grew more serious. For the past several days he had been considering some matters he wanted to discuss with his wife. Now things were quiet, and the subject of Ana had come up. Stratetix decided the moment was right.

"We denied Deu," he said.

Helena's gaze fell to her lap. She frowned and nodded but didn't speak.

"I'm not proud of that," Stratetix continued, "but we did what we felt we had to do. Perhaps it was weakness on our part. Perhaps it was necessity. In any case, I'd like to do what I can to make it right."

"We've begged Deu's forgiveness many times."

"I know. And I'm sure he has forgiven us. But I want to be able to hold my head high when Ana comes home. I want to regain my honor before Deu."

Helena's face grew uneasy. Stratetix knew she was a courageous woman, yet the times were evil and caution was required. "What are you thinking?" she asked.

"The men of the Fifth Regiment are growing dissatisfied with the current regime."

Helena rose from the bed and went to the window. After closing the shutters she sat down again. "That's dangerous talk, love."

"I'm not trying to incite a rebellion. I'm not even saying we should mention the name of Deu in public."

"Good. Because I think you know where that would lead us."

"I do. But maybe we could drop a few well-placed hints about recent encroachments on civil freedoms. You know how patriotic the soldiers are. They signed up to protect the people of Chiveis, not to enforce a theocracy on behalf of the High Priestess. They have to be frustrated by what's been going on lately."

"I believe there is some unrest in the Fifth Regiment," Helena agreed.

"Exactly! All they need is a spark."

"But would they listen to you, Stratetix? You're a respected villager, a loyal farmer of Chiveis, but that doesn't mean the soldiers would pay you any mind. The military has its own way of doing things."

"They might not listen to me, but they would listen to . . . "

"To who?" Helena pressed.

"The daughter of Armand."

"Oh, Stratetix . . . no."

"Why not? There are men in the Fifth who hold your father in the highest regard. The name of Armand would open some doors."

"I've lived in anonymity all these years. When I married you I left the military world behind."

"Your father's name isn't forgotten though."

Helena sighed, turning her face toward the wall. Stratetix thought he saw her lip quiver, which surprised him. He knew his suggestion was audacious, yet he hadn't realized it would strike such a deep emotional chord in his wife. He sat down on the bed and took her hand. "What is it?"

"There are some things you don't know. Things I've never told you."

Helena's ominous words and the tears that had gathered in her eyes made Stratetix's heart begin to thud in his chest. He swallowed. "Can you . . . tell me what they are?"

Helena removed her hand from her husband's and stood up. She kept her back to him with her head bowed for what seemed like an eternity. Finally she turned around again, her face laden with emotion. "I think it's time I told you about my youth."

Stratetix nodded nervously. "Go ahead. I'm listening."

"Some things happened to me before I met you, when I was just a girl." Helena lifted her chin and wiped her eyes as she regained her composure. After taking a deep breath she said, "I was seventeen when I met a man. He was more than a decade older than me. His name doesn't really matter, but what I can say is, he was a rising star in the army. He had climbed quickly through the ranks of the Second Regiment."

Stratetix did the math. "That would have been thirty years ago. Your father was still alive then, right?"

"Yes. He was the Warlord at the time, after coming up through the Fifth Regiment. He fought many battles at King Piair's side. The first King Piair, I mean."

"I don't think the current King Piair is much of a fighter."

"No, but his father certainly was, and my father was his most trusted commander. The king gave him the fine sword that Teofil now carries."

"What about this mysterious man you knew?" Stratetix wanted to get back to that subject, though he dreaded what he might hear.

"I thought I was in love with him."

"Okay," Stratetix said through gritted teeth.

"He pursued me," Helena went on. "Truth be told, he tried to seduce me, but I was too young and inexperienced to realize it. At that time my family was living in the Citadel near the royal palace. One day this man caught me alone. He pressured me in the way that men do. Though I resisted him, I won't lie and say I wasn't tempted."

Stratetix clenched his jaw. Jealousy stirred in his gut, but he suppressed that unbecoming response and motioned for Helena to continue.

"My father walked in unexpectedly and caught us in a compromising position. I was humiliated even though I had done nothing wrong. But it was much worse for that young captain. He had tried to violate the Warlord's daughter in his own home. My father's morals were very traditional. He was outraged. Things nearly came to blows. In the end he had the captain severely flogged, then demoted him to the rank of private with no hope of advancement. Of course that angered everyone in the Second Regiment. There were riots. Men died. For a while there was talk of civil war."

"That explains why the men of the Fifth revere Armand but the men of the Second don't."

"Perhaps, although no one remembers the details of those days anymore. It was three decades ago. If rumors still circulate about my involvement, I don't know what they are."

"So what happened next?"

"The Battle of Toon."

"Oh, of course. Your father was killed there." Every Chiveisian school-boy knew about that epic battle. It was the last time outsiders had invaded Chiveis. Many soldiers had been lost, but the invasion was repelled in the end.

"His death shocked me," Helena said. "He was always so strong, like a rock. Soon after that my mother caught a fever and died. Rosetta had already started her own family by then. I was nineteen years old and all alone."

"What did you do?"

"Queen Katerina provided me a small endowment to live on."

"Queen Katerina! You knew her *personally*? I can't believe you never told me!"

"I just wanted to close off that part of my life. But yes, I knew her, though she's probably forgotten me now. When we lived at the Citadel I used to visit the palace from time to time. I was a precocious teenager, and I struck up a conversation with the queen that led to some regular discussions. We used to speak about religion, though we could never find any good answers."

"Just you and the queen, talking back and forth about your beliefs?"

Helena paused for a moment, then said, "Actually there was one other person."

"That army captain?"

"No!" Helena waved her hands. "Not him. He wasn't interested in that sort of thing. It was someone else—someone you once knew."

Stratetix shrugged. "I have no idea."

"Master Maurice."

"Maurice!" The announcement shocked Stratetix. Master Maurice was the wise university professor who led the house community when Teo and Ana brought the Sacred Writing to Chiveis. The High Priestess killed the elderly Maurice as part of her persecution against the followers of Deu.

"It's true," Helena said. "When you introduced him to me in Vingin, it wasn't the first time we'd met."

"I remember that day. Maurice's words to you were strange. He said, 'You of all people will be happy to hear my news.' It was like he already knew you."

Helena laughed lightly. "Yes, he did. He was well aware I was an inde-pendent thinker who longed to discover the meaning of life."

"And yet you never told me any of this?"

"I'm truly sorry, love. I wasn't trying to keep secrets. I felt I had to forget my past so I could build a new life with you. I didn't want to be the daughter of a war hero. I didn't want to be the woman who almost caused a civil war between two regiments. I just wanted peace and quiet. I returned to the village where I was born, the farthest settlement on the edge of the frontier. And it was in Edgeton that I met the love of my life. Since I met you, Stratetix, I've never wanted anyone else."

At those words Stratetix rose from the bed and held out his arms. Helena gratefully allowed herself to be folded into his embrace. He stroked her hair. "I know that was a hard story to tell," he said.

Helena rested her head on her husband's chest. "Do you see now why I'm reluctant to use my name to gain a hearing with the army?"

"I do understand." Stratetix separated from his wife and held her by the shoulders, gazing at her face. "Helena, I won't ask you to do it."

"I know. You're so protective of me." She sighed deeply and lowered her head, her expression downcast.

"What's the matter? I said you don't have to talk to any soldiers. We'll just drop it."

"No. Even though you might not make that demand of me, there's someone who would—without hesitation."

"Who?"

Helena didn't answer. Stratetix stared into her blue-green eyes as he tried to discern her meaning. At last it dawned on him.

"You're right," he said. "She would."

◆　◆　◆

The sea churned, the ship rolled, and the frightened sisters cried out in their dismay. Ana was among them, fighting to remain calm. In the dark hold of the Exterminati slave ship, peace was hard to come by.

The women had been loaded onto a single ship. After their manacles were removed, they were forced below deck. Though the weather was bad and the seas rough, the shamans left the convent immediately. They had struck with lightning speed like a snake. Now the serpent was slithering away. Ana had no idea where the captives were being taken.

And if I don't know, how can . . . ?

Ana knew the exact words that would complete her thought. It was one of the first things that had crossed her mind when she was taken prisoner. Yet it seemed impossible. Teo was far across the ocean. How could he follow her? How could he come to her in her moment of need like he always did?

Is he even alive? Or was he tormented by the Iron Shield until . . .

Wincing and shaking her head, Ana rejected what the evil warrior had said. The man was a liar. He would say anything to induce hopelessness. Teo was strong and capable. He would not easily be captured by the likes of the Iron Shield.

But maybe this time . . .

No!

Ana struggled against despair. *Help me, Deu! Help me trust in you!*

The hatch to the ship's hold banged open. Several of the sisters whimpered as a shaft of light flooded the dim space. A shaman descended the steps, club in hand. Several burly thugs followed him, seamen who didn't have the same occult aura as the shamans, yet were brutes nonetheless.

"Greetings, ladies," the leader said in an oily voice. "I trust you are having a pleasant voyage so far."

No one responded, so the shaman motioned to some men above deck. A large barrel was lowered into the hold. "Here's how it's going to work. Water in the morning, one ladle for each of you. Then water in the evening with some barley porridge. The stuff's infested with weevils, but you'll get used to the taste." The shaman snickered at this last remark.

Vanita stood up. "Where are we headed? What do you want with us?"

The shaman approached Vanita, tapping his club in the palm of his hand. "You're a bold one," he said.

Vanita didn't back down. "We have a right to know."

"Do you?" The shaman spit in Vanita's face, making her grimace and turn away. "You have no rights! You belong to my master now. The Iron Shield has plans for you—plans for a marriage that is truly horrific."

The way the shaman used the word *plans* jogged Ana's memory. Holy words rushed to her mind. When she was leaving Chiveis nearly two years ago, Teo had read a passage from the Sacred Writing that Ana claimed as her own: "'For I know the plans I have for you,' declares the Eternal One, 'plans for peace and not misfortune, plans to give you a future and a hope. You will go away. You will pray to me. You will seek me and find me when you seek me with all your heart. Then I will gather you out of the place I have sent you, and bring you back to the place from which I made you go.'" At the time of Ana's greatest trial, when she was leaving her homeland to venture into the vast Beyond, Deu had comforted her with those words from the prophet Jérémie. Now Ana embraced that promise anew.

The Exterminati leader ordered his thugs to get on with their task. They opened the barrel and began to spoon water into the sisters' parched mouths as they crowded around. A cauldron was brought, and the women were given thin gruel in clay bowls. Bits of debris floated among the lumps, but Ana decided she was better off not trying to discern what it was. The women slurped the gruel and scooped out the last bits of moist barley with their fingers. Finally the shaman and his henchmen left. The hatch slammed shut behind them.

Though no one felt at ease, the food had taken the edge off the women's fears. A little light came through the gaps in the ship's planks, giving the hold a desolate and gloomy appearance. Each of the sisters brooded in silence. After a while Vanita stood up again.

"My friends, we can't let those evildoers get us down," she said.

"What hope do we have?" called a tenuous voice. "We're helpless here."

"You heard that man," said another sister. "They're going to force us to marry the shamans!"

Vanita held up both hands. "Hey! Don't you remember the lection from last night? You girls sang the reading in your service. Apparently you need to sing it again—and this time sing it like you mean it." No one responded, so Vanita said, "I'm serious. I want you all to sing it right now."

"The housemother used to start us," said one of the younger nuns.

Vanita nodded confidently. "I'll start you this time."

A hush descended on the ship's hold. The only sound was the crash of the waves against the hull. Ana leaned forward. Since she had not attended the evening service, she was curious to hear what scripture passage would be sung.

Vanita widened her stance as the vessel rolled through the turbulent sea. Ana knew her friend had a beautiful voice, for the art of singing was taught to every Ulmbartian aristocrat. Vanita took a deep breath, then began to chant in high, clear tones.

"I will awaken over you my good word . . . "

Ana's mouth fell open. *Deu!*

" . . . to bring you back to this place . . . "

Tears flooded Ana's eyes. She shivered as a powerful emotion washed over her, making her weak and strong at the same time. *Oh, my Deu . . . thank you! Thank you for speaking to me!*

Emboldened, the sisters began to join Vanita's sacred hymn. One by one their voices united to form a delicate harmony that echoed around the hold. "For I know the plans I have for you," they sang, "plans for peace and not misfortune, plans to give you a future and a hope . . . "

Ana bowed her head, overcome with awe. She knew the singing of this particular passage was no coincidence. Tears flowed freely down her cheeks. Though she could not sing aloud, her heart resounded with worship.

Do not fear, daughter, whispered a serene and mighty voice.

"I will not fear," Ana vowed to her God.

"Halt!"

Brother Thomas's knights shouted the order and emerged from the brush outside the convent at Lido di Ostia. Arrows were nocked in their bows. Two startled riders reined up abruptly, their horses snorting and stamping.

Teo stepped forward and spoke to the knights. "It's okay, everyone. Put down your weapons. These men are friends."

"Teofil!" said one of the riders. "What's going on here?"

"A tragedy," Teo replied in answer to Sol's question.

Sol and the Overseer dismounted. "What tragedy?" the Overseer asked.

"Come and see."

Teo led his friends to what was left of the convent. It was dark out now, but the clouds had cleared, and the rising moon illuminated the smoldering remains. When the two men saw the devastation they were speechless.

"It was the Exterminati," Teo said grimly. "They carried away all the sisters."

"What about the housemother?"

"We found her body. She was mistreated and put to death."

"Bring vengeance upon this heinous evil, O Deus," the Overseer said under his breath.

"Perhaps through human hands," Teo agreed.

"Will you follow them?"

"In the morning I'll scout for clues. But there may be nothing to find."

"And if not?"

Frustration blazed in Teo's heart. He wrinkled his nose and ground his teeth, clenching his fists at his side. It infuriated him to stand still while Ana was endangered. Yet he had to remain here until morning to make a thorough search for clues that might reveal the ship's destination. *And if that's a dead end, then what?*

"I'll make inquiries around the harbor," he told the Overseer. "Perhaps someone along the docks will know where the Exterminati were headed."

Sol hung his head. "This is not the joyous occasion we hoped for."

Teo turned toward his scholarly friend with the long white hair. "Why *are* you here, anyway?"

"Let's go sit by the fire and I'll show you."

Marco's crewmen had returned to their ship, but the Knights of the Cross had kindled a campfire on the beach. A cookpot was over the flames. When Teo introduced Brother Thomas to Sol and the Overseer, the two men were fascinated to meet a Knight of the Cross from such a faraway land.

"We at Roma hoped the brotherhood still existed at Marsay, but we weren't sure of it," the Overseer said.

Brother Thomas turned up the corner of his mouth. "It exists alright, though at times I wonder if it's in name only."

Everyone sat down by the fire and received a bowl of stew. As they ate Teo described his adventures in Marsay and also his journeys to Jineve and Chiveis. The Overseer smiled as he heard the story. "The Papa certainly picked the right man for this daring mission," he said.

Mentally Teo disagreed. *I should never have gone*, he fumed. *Then I would have been here to protect Ana!*

Sol laid a leather satchel on the sand. "You asked about our reason for coming here. This is it." He opened the satchel and brought out a plain wooden box, which he handed to Teo.

"What is it?"

"Open it and find out."

When Teo raised the lid, his eyes fell upon a marvel: the most beautiful book he had ever seen. The cover was adorned with delicate silver filigree. The words *Versio Secunda Chiveisorum* surrounded a central panel with an embroidered inset. The scene depicted jagged snow-capped peaks, wooden chalets, and cattle grazing in meadows strewn with the star-shaped flower called ehdelveis. At the top of the embroidery, a graceful turtledove soared in the blue sky.

"This is Chiveis!" Teo exclaimed. "How did you know how to—" He paused, then glanced at Sol. "Did Anastasia make this?"

Sol nodded.

Teo touched the embroidery with his finger. "Has she ever . . . seen it like this?"

"We planned to deliver the finished book to her today."

Swallowing his grief, Teo said, "She *will* see this book. She will admire its great beauty. We will take it to Chiveis. I swear it."

Sol put his hand on Teo's shoulder. "I know."

The mood around the campfire grew melancholy as the mist-shrouded moon rose higher in the sky. Eventually the men began to pull blankets over themselves for the night. Teo fell asleep wrapped in his bearskin cloak. It kept out the chill, but not the nightmares that assailed his mind.

At first light he was awake and casting for signs along the beach. Unfortunately the rain and the tides had erased most of the tracks. Teo walked down the shore a ways until he noticed a deep groove in the sand. A boat's keel had been dragged onto land. Teo left the beach to inspect the coastal forest.

Under the trees, the rain that had been his enemy turned to his favor. The ground was wet enough to hold an impression but not so wet that all tracks would be washed away. Teo spotted several partial boot prints and began to follow them through the woods.

He came to the remains of a camp. Matted grass and broken stems indicated where eight men had slept. Teo surmised it was an advance scouting party. No doubt the Exterminati would have sent men ahead to learn the convent's daily routine and its vulnerable points of entry. In all likelihood they had sent stealthy shamans inside the building at night to ascertain the floor plan. Good assault tactics would demand such reconnaissance.

As Teo surveyed the enemy camp, a glint in the underbrush caught his attention. He crossed the clearing and knelt down. A clear bottle lay in the dirt, its glass clean enough to prove it hadn't been there long. Some of the bottle's contents remained at the bottom—a liquid so bright and yellow it was almost chartreuse. Teo's heart began to beat faster.

If that's what I think it is . . .

Tipping the bottle, he let a droplet fall on his finger then raised it to his tongue. The taste was sweet and lemony, and the liqueur was highly alcoholic.

Yes! Thank you, Deu!

Relief coursed through Teo as the pieces of the puzzle fell into place. The shamans had made an unbelievably foolish error. They had left behind a clue that announced in no uncertain terms the identity of their home port: Napoly, the only city where the yellow liqueur called *limoncello* was consumed.

Napoly was a dirty metropolis of thieves and racketeers controlled by the Clan. Its reputation for human trafficking was well known. Now the abduction made perfect sense. There could be no better place than Napoly to turn a cargo of innocent young women into lifetime prostitutes. With deep revulsion, Teo considered what the Exterminati had planned for

Ana, Vanita, and the holy virgins of Deu. An endless cycle of disgusting encounters with dirty men was the fate that awaited the Christiani sisters.

Unless good men intervened.

◆　　◆　　◆

The Iron Shield's black caravel dropped anchor off the coast of Sessalay near the city of Eastport. The fast ship had made the run from Roma to Sessalay in two days. Normally this wouldn't have been possible, but the Iron Shield had trained his crew to do what other sailors feared: to leave sight of shore and strike out across the ocean. Lacking good navigational skills, most seamen wanted to stay close to their own harbors. A few long-distance merchants were willing to hop up and down the coast to ports spaced a day apart. But everyone, even the pirates, feared the open seas. Yet the Iron Shield did not. The indwelling gods gave his men courage that mere mortals did not possess.

A rowboat was lowered, and the Iron Shield was ferried into Eastport's harbor. The customs officials waved him past, for his deal with the Clan Boss meant that all the right people had been paid their bribes.

As the Iron Shield walked to the warehouse he had rented, he considered the recent raid on the Christiani convents. Everything had gone according to plan. The scouts had done their reconnaissance well. Except for one unfortunate incident, they had prowled the convents by night without being discovered. The women had been taken completely by surprise. The Iron Shield scowled as he recalled the insolent Anastasia with her haughty eyes and proud chin, boldly cursing him in the name of the enemy god. *How I would like to break her spirit!* Yet he did not dare. The woman now belonged to Mulciber, or Vulkain as he was known in Chiveis. The Iron Shield smiled at that thought. *We shall see if Anastasia remains so spirited when faced with molten fire!*

The dark warrior reached the warehouse's rear door and rapped three times. A panel opened. When the supervisor saw his master, he opened the door immediately.

"Welcome, my lord," he said, ushering the Iron Shield inside. Large crates and wooden casks were piled around the room. The odor of rotten eggs hung in the air.

The Iron Shield frowned. "There should be more by now."

"We are doing our best, master. The boys are working as fast as humanly possible."

Turning toward the supervisor, the Iron Shield gave him a cold stare. "You might be surprised to learn what is humanly possible when the right incentives are applied. Perhaps I should show you what I mean."

"N-n-no need for that," the supervisor said, waving his palms. "I believe you."

"What seems to be the holdup then?"

"The boys keep dying."

The Iron Shield tsked and flicked his hand. "There are always more."

"Yes, my lord, so it would seem. And for a time that was the case. But eventually we used up our supply in the nearby villages. Now there is a shortage."

Clasping his hands behind his back, the Iron Shield stared into the distance as he considered the arrangements he had made last fall to mine the brimstone of Sessalay. The triangle-shaped island was ruled from the city of Westport near the Clan Boss's estate. The eastern side of the island had a harbor too, known as Eastport. Yet the dominant feature of Sessalay's east was not its harbor but the massive volcano that raised its head into the clouds. In wintertime the peak became rimmed with snow that clung to it well into spring. For more than a year now, Fire Mountain had been putting on a dreadful spectacle. An immense column of steam and ash rose from the summit, while lava flowed down the mountain's flanks in torpid rivers that turned the night sky orange. *Mulciber is angry*, the Iron Shield mused. *He must be placated . . . very soon.*

Sessalay's turbulent geology meant brimstone was available for mining in the interior. Yet little attention had been paid to the mines in recent years because the work was dangerous and the payoff small. Clothing bleachers had some use for brimstone, and it prevented fungus on crops, so the yellow rock was traded on a small scale. But when the Iron Shield arrived in Sessalay last fall everything changed. He had recruited boys from rural villages to work the mines, since only persons of small stature could crawl into the tortuous tunnels. Once the boys were at the mines they learned the true meaning of toil. Seven days a week they crept deep below the earth to dig, haul, and dig some more. When the boys finally died from overwork or poisonous fumes, their parents were paid enough hush money to keep them quiet. And if that didn't work, the Exterminati knew how to make the more vocal complainers disappear.

The Iron Shield's thoughts drifted to Chiveis. In his mind's eye he pictured barges loaded with precious brimstone floating down the Farm River and across the Tooner Sea to arrive at the town of Entrelac. The High Priestess would ride out from her Citadel, robed in splendor, a delighted smile on her sensuous black lips. "Well done, my faithful servant," she would say. "You have pleased me." Saliva gathered in the Iron Shield's mouth as he considered how the priestess might display her pleasure. He turned to the warehouse supervisor. "Production must double over the next four weeks," he said.

"But . . . my lord, without more workers that is impossible!"

"Is it?" With deliberate steps the Iron Shield approached the trembling supervisor. "I find your lack of faith disturbing."

The supervisor bowed his head and stared at his feet, afraid to say a word. The Iron Shield drew his knife from its sheath. The metallic scraping was the only sound in the quiet warehouse. He touched the man's chin with the flat of the blade. Lifting his servant's face, the Iron Shield examined him with his one good eye. A bead of sweat trickled down the man's forehead. The Iron Shield leaned close so that his mouth was almost in the supervisor's ear.

"Get a wagon," he whispered.

"Wh . . . wh . . . what?"

"I said, get a wagon. A big one."

"From where?"

"*Just do it!*" the Iron Shield roared as he shoved the supervisor across the room. The man stumbled to the ground, then scrambled up and dashed through the door. The Iron Shield waited with his hands on his hips until his rage had cooled.

At last the dark warrior walked outside and surveyed the docks.

Barrel-chested stevedores went about their work, but they were of no interest to him. Then his eyes fell upon what he desired.

He turned into an alley. A lone boy was playing knucklebones. The Iron Shield curled his finger, beckoning him closer.

Tentatively, the boy stood up and approached. The Iron Shield smiled at him. "Hello, son," he said. "I come to you as your savior."

The timid boy did not answer, so the Iron Shield reached into his pocket and produced a one-scudi coin. It was a week's wages for a working man. The boy's eyes widened as the Iron Shield held it in his palm.

"Take it," he said.

"Me, sir?"

"Yes, go on. It's for you. Take it."

The boy snatched the coin, then glanced up at his benefactor. The dark warrior gave him another smile.

"Now listen to me, son," he said. "I want you to spread the word among all your friends. I have some job openings in the countryside for hard-working boys like you. Nothing too difficult, of course. Just light farm labor—but it pays very well. I'll even provide your transportation."

"Oh, thank you, sir," the boy said breathlessly. "My father will be pleased."

"I am your father now," replied the Iron Shield.

✦　✦　✦

The island of Sessalay always awakened from its winter sleep in the third month of the year. That was when the heavy rains started to slacken. The chilly temperatures became more moderate. Days of sunshine began to replace the winter squalls. Even so, the Clan Boss took his drinks hot until after the spring equinox.

The villa's butler arrived from the kitchen and served his master a glass of mulled wine flavored with spices and lemon zest. While the boss sipped the warming drink, the butler unrolled a map of eastern Sessalay. He placed four paperweights on the map's corners as he spread it on the desk.

The boss leaned close. "How recent are these?" He pointed to the red lines inked onto the map.

"Up-to-date as of yesterday," the butler answered.

The Clan Boss considered the red lines. They radiated from certain points on Fire Mountain's flanks, indicating the areas of lava flow. One long tendril extended toward Eastport. Though the lava was unlikely to reach the city, a few peasant villages on the mountainside had already been engulfed.

"Bring me a pen," the boss said.

The butler fetched the quill and ink while the boss hunched over the map. The largest stream of lava flowed through a ravine. At one point a dotted line indicated a trail that ran past the ravine to a high village. Red ink now obscured the village—a place of human habitation no more. The Clan Boss dipped his quill and marked an X where the track came closest to the ravine. Then he removed a piece of parchment from his desk and began to write.

> To Tancred, son of my mother, brother of my own blood, trusted warrior, loyal Clansman—greetings in the name of Mulciber.
>
> Plans proceed apace. Antonio of Roma has secured the brides, and his ships now rendezvous at Napoly for resupply. Arrival on our island is expected shortly. It is time to initiate the matter we discussed.
>
> The woman Anastasia is among the captives. Antonio has left a trail for the other man to follow. As you know, the knowledge these foreigners possess is of the greatest interest to us. I do not believe Mulciber

Lifting his quill, the Clan Boss hesitated. Religious matters always made him nervous. One never knew how the capricious gods would respond to a particular human action. The gods became offended at any supposed slight—even things a human might consider trivial. To complicate matters, the ancient Pact of Beaumont bound the Clan and the Exterminati in inscrutable ways. It was hard to predict how the gods might react to a perceived betrayal of that centuries-old blood oath.

The boss turned to his butler. "You're a religious man, aren't you?"

The butler nodded. "I try to be."

"Let us suppose a man threw a feast for an honored guest. At this feast was every sort of delicacy. The table overflowed with veal marsala, sword-fish, cassata, and marzipan fruits."

"It would be a feast worthy of a king," the butler said.

"Indeed. And let us imagine that at this feast the host spotted a fig that pleased him. Two figs, as a matter of fact. So he reached out and took them and ate them. Do you suppose the guest of honor would be offended?"

"On the contrary, the recipient of such a bounteous feast would want his host to enjoy himself as well."

"Are the gods any different?"

The butler narrowed his eyes as he considered his answer. "The gods are like men," he concluded at last, "though far more powerful. Such absolute power makes them fickle. Yet I would guess that if holy Mulciber received a great gift, he would not begrudge the giver a small portion for himself."

"That is what I thought as well. Go get my signet. And bring wax."

Turning his attention to the page again, the Clan Boss picked up where he left off:

will begrudge one of his brides being substituted. In any case, it is a risk we must take. We must possess the magic powder. My sources inside the Christiani basilica tell me the lore-book has been locked away. Now we must obtain the secret of the powder's composition directly from the foreigners' mouths.

My orders are these: Ready the interrogation chamber. We shall torture the woman to break the man. Furthermore, have engineers construct the device we discussed at the spot I have indicated on the accompanying map. Hide your troops among the rocks nearby, out of the Exterminati's sight. Be ready to act upon my signal on the appointed day.

This year's festival shall be like none in recent memory. The all-glorious Mulciber shall once again have the flesh he craves. I bid thee success.

The Clan Boss was inscribing his personal mark at the end of the letter when the butler returned with a wax stick and a lit candle. After folding the parchment into thirds, the boss melted the wax and allowed a dollop to fall on the letter's overlapped edges. Then he pressed his signet into the warm red seal.

As he was about to hand the letter to the butler, he found his heart beating rapidly. *Could this action be construed as a betrayal of the Pact?* The gods took great interest in such agreements among mortals. They handed out their blessings—or their retribution—accordingly.

"My lord?" The butler had reached to take the letter but now dropped his hand to his side as he saw his master's hesitation.

"Surely Mulciber will be happy with sixty-six brides. It does not matter who they are, right? Only Antonio cares about their specific identity."

"I know nothing of such affairs, lord."

"And Mulciber has no concern whatsoever for Teofil of Chiveis," the boss added, trying to convince himself. "That too is Antonio's personal obsession."

"The warrior is evil. He scares me."

The boss glanced up. "Do you believe the Clan is unequal to his power?"

"I believe all mortals are unequal to his power. The underworld strengthens him."

The butler's statement annoyed the Clan Boss, though his anger was directed more at the reputation of the Exterminati than at the butler himself. Rising from his desk, he pounded his fist on its surface. "Antonio might want those foreigners dead," he burst out, "but the last time I checked, it was the Clan that ruled Sessalay!"

The butler blanched and stepped back. "My lord, I intended no offense—"

"Those foreigners are no use to me dead," the boss continued, ignoring his frightened servant. "I want something from them!"

"Of course! And I am certain you will obtain it!"

"Indeed I shall," the boss replied. "The Clan *always* gets what it wants."

❖ ❖ ❖

The Papa stood in the Christiani basilica under an immense altar canopy. Its spiral columns of bronze rested on marble plinths, rising six stories from the floor. Directly beneath the gilded canopy was a plain wooden table. No doubt the Ancients had placed a more ornate altar on the dais, but the Papa was content with something simple. *A table like this is especially fitting now that I know Iesus was a humble carpenter*, he thought.

Out in the nave the faithful had gathered for the weekly service. In times past they were relatively few: just a handful of tradesmen and shopkeepers from the surrounding neighborhoods. But ever since the Christiani's victory over the Exterminati last summer, the laws against proselytizing had been abandoned. Now many people flocked to the basilica to hear the word of Deus.

Today was the first day of the week, the day on which Iesus had risen from his tomb. When the Papa learned this truth from the New Testament preserved in Liber's memory, he decreed that services on this day should always include the Sacred Meal. Only those Christiani who had committed themselves to Deus through the waters of the Washing were allowed to partake of the bread and wine. Several local peasants who believed in Iesus had asked to be washed today. They were now undergoing the holy rite in one of the basilica's side chapels. Next week they too could share in the Sacred Meal.

Standing before the wooden altar, the Papa bowed his head and gave thanks over the cup and the loaf, just as Iesus had done at his last meal with his twelve followers. After breaking the bread, the Papa offered fragments to the penitents who approached. They received the morsels gladly, then sipped the blessed wine. While they ate and drank in communion with Iesus, the Papa sang the triumphant hymn that he remembered from his boyhood. "*Sanctus, Sanctus, Sanctus, O Dominus Deus Sabaoth!*" he proclaimed. "*Hosanna in excelsis!*"

After the service concluded and the faithful began to disperse, papal assistants came to clear the table. The Papa smoothed his white robe and descended from the dais. The hour after the Meal was the time he customarily entertained visitors with various petitions. He walked to the apse of the basilica, where his chair was located beneath a glorious window depicting a dove in flight. For a long time that image had been misunderstood. Everyone had supposed it to be a dove of Israël's sacrifices, or perhaps the dove that brought Noé a branch when the floodwaters began to recede. But the four biographies of Iesus in the New Testament had revealed the actual truth. The dove represented the spiritual presence of Deus—a mysterious concept that often confounded the Papa.

As he settled into his *cathedra*, one of the doorkeepers approached. "The emissaries have returned from the convent," he said.

"Yes, of course, send them to me right away."

Three men proceeded up the nave, though the Papa recognized only two of them. The Overseer was tall, with a snow-white beard and piercing blue eyes. Sol was shorter and had a more wizened appearance. The third man was middle-aged. His build was stocky, and his clothing was unusual. The Papa's curiosity was aroused.

"Greetings, Holy Father," the Overseer said as the group came near. "We bear tragic news this day."

"May Deus bring good from the evil. What has happened?"

"Kidnapping! Murder!" Sol blurted out.

The Papa leaned forward in his chair, shocked at the announcement. "This is tragic news indeed! Quickly now—tell me your story."

The Overseer related the horrific account. He described how he and Sol had arrived at the convent to give the Secunda to Anastasia, only to be confronted by armed men. After determining them to be under the command of Teofil of Chiveis, the emissaries discovered the convent burned to the ground. The housemother had been slain, and all the women were carried away upon the sea. Teofil possessed evidence that the evil deed was the work of the Exterminati.

The Papa's head spun. Too many important facts vied for his attention at once. He wanted to learn about rescue plans for the captured sisters, and the outcome of Teofil's mission to Marsay, and the housemother's burial arrangements, and the identity of the strange visitor who stood quietly at the Overseer's side. *First things first*, he reminded himself.

"Is Teofil going after the women?"

"Yes, Holy Father. He has located a clue that directs him to Napoly."

"That is a logical destination for whoremongers like the Exterminati. They often dispose of kidnapped women among the pimps of that place."

"Teofil has already set sail for Napoly in Captain Marco's fast ship," the Overseer reported.

"If anyone can rescue those women, Teofil can," Sol added.

The Papa sighed heavily. "Deus will be those women's shield—but perhaps Teofil will be the instrument of his hand. It is a matter for urgent prayer."

"We have already made it so."

"I knew you would, Brother Ambrosius. Let your prayers continue to ascend." The Papa turned his attention toward the third visitor. "And now it appears you have a guest who has not been properly introduced."

Before the Overseer could speak, the stranger stepped forward. In the light shining from the dome far above, the Papa noticed the cross tattoo on his forehead for the first time. "I am Brother Thomas," the stout man said. "I bring you greetings from the Order of the Cross at Marsay."

"Marsay!" The Papa smiled agreeably. "So that place does exist—and with Christiani knights there! I had heard rumors of this but did not know for sure."

A shadow crossed Brother Thomas's face. "Yes, there are knights at Marsay. The order is ancient, and it commands a powerful militia. Our fortress is known as Castle d'If. The abbot Odo is a man who—how shall I describe it? To borrow the words of the Apocalypse, he has lost his first love."

"Yet some at Marsay are still zealous for the faith?" the Papa asked, arching his eyebrows.

"There are friars among the knights who have sworn an oath of higher commitment."

"And are you one of those?"

Brother Thomas grinned and nodded. "The first of them, as a matter of fact. Ten more good men came with me from Marsay. They have sailed with Teofil and Marco."

"Warrior monks, eh?"

"At Marsay warfare was a necessity for many years. We had no alliances with surrounding empires or kingdoms. When enemies attacked, we either fought or we died. Today the knights can marshal a strong force at a moment's notice."

The Papa folded his hands in his lap. "Peace on earth will be achieved when the Promised King ushers in his reign. Until then, peace is bought by the blood of brave men who stand up to oppression."

At these words Brother Thomas rushed forward unexpectedly. He knelt before the Papa's chair, his head bowed low. "I am very glad to hear you say this, Holy Father!" he exclaimed.

"Rise, knight."

Brother Thomas obeyed.

The Papa studied his face. The man's features were plain. Nothing would make him stand out except for the Latin cross etched upon his brow. "Why this earnestness?" the Papa asked.

"Evil rises. Events are converging. A time of reckoning draws near."

"In Marsay or elsewhere?"

"In all lands."

"Yes," the Papa said slowly. "I feel it too."

"Do you know about the Pact?"

"The Pact? What is it?"

Brother Thomas glanced at Sol and the Overseer, then looked back at the Papa. From the expressions on the other men's faces, the Papa deduced they didn't know about the Pact either.

"It is an ancient agreement between the rulers of the nations," Brother Thomas said, withdrawing several sheets of stained parchment from inside his jerkin. "Teofil discovered this secret record of it in our archives."

"Summarize it for me," the Papa said as the friar handed him the evidence.

"Long ago in the age of the Great Destruction a man named Jonluc Beaumont came to Marsay from Chiveis. There he summoned many great kings to himself. They swore an oath to leave each other alone. Each kingdom would command its own destiny without interference from the others. Only in one task did they bind themselves to each other—and this damnable vow they sealed by intermingling their own blood."

"What was that task?"

"The task for which the Exterminati were originally founded."

"Ah. To eradicate Christianism from the face of the earth."

"Yes, Holy Father. And as you well know, their efforts have been vigorous."

"Yet they have tasted defeat."

"A setback, not a total defeat. Their power comes from the 'rulers and principalities of this present darkness,' as the holy writings put it. They will not easily be defeated. One queen in particular orchestrates all these affairs. She is undergirded by the prince of the demons. Teofil has confronted her."

"Who?"

"The High Priestess of Chiveis. She is making a move against a kingdom called Jineve. It is upriver from Marsay. Teofil has journeyed there with me."

The friar's rapid-fire assertions were swirling past the Papa almost too fast for him to comprehend. Each announcement boded dire consequences and demanded an immediate response. The Papa held up his hands. "Brother Thomas, let us distill this matter to its essence. Why did you bow before me just now?"

"You spoke of war. And war is upon us, whether we wish it or not. The High Priestess will come to Jineve in alliance with forest barbarians. That kingdom will fall, and she will secure its resources. New weapons will become available to her. New wealth will enrich her coffers. New armies will be at her command. She will spread darkness over the face of the earth . . . the darkness of a god whose name I will not utter in this sacred place."

For a long moment no one spoke. Then the Papa said, "What would you have me do?"

"Command the Knights at Marsay to fight on behalf of Jineve. Send me back there with a bull from your own hand. Odo may be recalcitrant, but the knights will not disobey a direct order from the Holy Father at Roma. Their war machine is ponderous and reluctant to move. Yet he who has the power to snap its chains of lethargy will find a powerful force for good at his disposal. Use this army to defend Jineve against the High Priestess. In this way you might turn back her evil designs."

The Papa inhaled deeply, then let out his breath. The three men stood circled before his chair, their faces expectant.

"Do you know the words of the second Hymn?" he asked them.

When he did not receive an answer, he quoted a verse from memory:

" 'The kings of the earth rose up together, and the princes plotted against the Lord and his Christ.' " He paused. "Do you know what that hymn says next?"

Still there was silence. The Papa rose from his chair. "Come with me," he said.

The three visitors followed him to the side chapel where the ritual of Washing had reached its climax. Several peasants stood in soaking wet robes, while other men in loincloths waited their turn to go down into the font. As the Papa watched, the priest plunged one of the new Christiani into the healing waters of life. Jubilation was etched on the man's face as he rose up, climbed the steps of the font, and received the new garment of Iesus.

" 'He that sits in heaven shall laugh,' " the Papa said. "That is the response of Deus when earthly kings try to thwart his purposes. No one can stop the rebirth of the Christiani."

"Holy Father," Brother Thomas said breathlessly, "is this the ritual known as the Washing?"

The Papa's head swung around. "You don't know it?"

"The Knights of Marsay do not practice this observance. Teofil spoke of it with me, but it hasn't been a custom among us."

"Are you saying the Knights of the Cross are *unwashed?*"

"Yes, Holy Father. Odo described it as an ancient rite best left forgotten."

For a moment the leader of the Christiani could not speak as his eyes searched the bright recesses of the basilica's dome. At last he turned back to Brother Thomas.

"I will grant you a bull commanding your brothers to defend Jineve against the High Priestess," he declared, then caught the friar's eye with a stern gaze. "Yet I fear more than a piece of paper is needed at Castle d'If."

8

Two sailors picked up the cauldron of barley gruel and turned to climb the steps of the ship's hold.

"More! Give us more!" the sisters cried. It was their third day in captivity, and everyone was hungry.

The men ignored the request and went topside, then returned for the water barrel. As they were about to haul it up, a sister who had been running a fever since boarding the ship vomited across the decking.

"Ew! That's disgusting!" one of the sailors cried, wincing and scrunching his nose.

"You women smell bad enough already without adding that!" the other man put in.

The sailors left the hold. A moment later a mop rattled down the steps. "Clean it up!" yelled a rough voice.

"With what?" Vanita demanded.

"Your drinking water—and make it quick!" The sailors' arrogant guffaws were cut short by the hatch slamming shut.

"I'll do it," Ana said, picking up the mop. "Sister Deidre, please help Sister Miriam find a place to rest."

Ana grasped the lid of the water barrel and tugged it until it popped off. The thirsty sisters crowded around, desperate to make the most of this chance for an extra drink. Ana let them dip their clay bowls as long as they wanted. When they were satisfied, she scooped out water to wash the vomit into the cracks between the deck planks. The filth went down into the bilge, which reeked already. Finally Ana set the mop aside. She was about to wedge the barrel's lid in place again when an idea struck her.

The drinking water level had dropped—a lot. The barrel would feel much lighter now.

Unless . . .

"Vanita! Come here!" Ana waved her friend close.

She walked over. "What is it?"

Ana pointed inside the barrel. "It's almost empty now."

"So? They told us to clean up. We were supposed to use the water."

"Right. But now one of us could hide in there."

Vanita's eyes grew wide. "You should do it!" she whispered.

"Me? Why me? Maybe it should be you."

"No, you're much better at this sort of thing. You have more experience."

"I do?"

"Of course! You've snuck around secret places with Teofil. You've killed men before. You could do it again if you had to."

Ana frowned but didn't reply, knowing her friend was right. At various points in her life Ana had done what was needed. She had put arrows into mortal enemies. She had crushed a man's skull with a stone. She had fought off armed assailants. She had killed a wolf and a bear. Though she didn't relish it, Ana wasn't afraid to draw blood.

"I guess I could hide in there until nightfall," she said at last.

"Right! Then push off the lid when no one's looking, jump overboard, and get away."

"I'd swim straight to the dock and alert the authorities." Though Ana had no idea where she was, she knew from the sounds outside that the Exterminati ship was anchored in a port. Surely the local law enforcement would want to know the ship was full of kidnapped women.

Vanita took the lid from Ana. "Quick! Get in before those bullies come back. They're too dumb to expect a trick."

"Let's hope so."

Ana hiked up her skirt and swung one leg into the barrel, then the other. The little water that was left immediately soaked her leather slippers and the hem of her woolen kirtle. As she was about to crouch down, a fear born out of a horrific memory began to claw at her soul. "Ohh," she groaned. "Don't put that lid on tight. I can't stand the feeling of being trapped in a closed place."

Vanita's face took on a sorrowful expression. Unexpectedly she grabbed Ana's hand and brought it to her lips to kiss it. "I'm so sorry," she whispered.

"It's okay."

"Anastasia, listen to me! I want you to know you're my best friend! You've given me so much. I love you like a sister—like my own flesh and blood."

"Oh, Vanita, me too!"

"Thank you for taking this risk for me. For all of us."

Ana was too choked up to speak. She felt she was saying good-bye to Vanita forever . . . and perhaps she was.

"Girls, gather 'round!" Vanita beckoned the other sisters to draw near. She briefly explained the plan, then asked each woman to lay hands on Ana. After everyone had done so, Vanita led them in a heartfelt prayer for divine protection.

When the prayer was finished, Ana nodded resolutely and bent her knees. The barrel was tight, and the sides seemed to press her, yet there was enough room to move a little as long as she kept her elbows drawn against her chest. She glanced up. Vanita was there with the lid. A worried look was on her face.

"Go with Deu, sister of my soul," she said.

Then everything went dark.

The men came not long after that. They took the barrel up on deck, grunting and heaving, yet oblivious to the secret within. Ana sat in the cold darkness, her ankles and bottom immersed in water, trying to make no sound as she was jostled. Claustrophobia threatened to engulf her several times, but she closed her eyes and slowed her breathing. It helped to touch the barrel's lid and feel it give under her fingers. Ana told herself she could burst free at any moment if she had to.

As time wore on, the circle of light where the lid met the barrel's rim began to grow brighter. Ana realized the sun was catching the barrel in its final rays as it made its way toward the horizon. Now the oak began to grow hot. A musty smell emanated from the moist wood. Sweat broke out on Ana's forehead, and her breathing became labored. *There's not enough air in here! I have to get out!* She felt she couldn't take any more of the confinement, yet to leap from the barrel would ruin her one chance at escape. *Iesus, Iesus, Iesus,* she chanted in her mind, trying to calm the rising panic. *Help me, help me, help me, help me . . .*

The two sailors finally drew Ana's attention away from her cramped quarters. Though the men were ostensibly engaged in some shipboard chore, they seemed to spend most of their time exchanging crude remarks about their plans for the bordellos later that night. Back and forth they bickered, trading insults.

"Hey, that's mine!" one of them shouted.

"But I'm thirsty," whined the other.

"I don't care—get your own!"

"We're out of grog! The chief steward is fetching more tomorrow."

"Then drink water, you tosspot, but you ain't gettin' mine."

"What water?"

"I don't know, whatever you can find. Look there! Take some from the brides."

"I don't want that water. It's dirty."

"If that ain't good enough for ya, then just shut up."

Ana held her breath and listened as footsteps approached. The thirsty sailor grumbled under his breath about wanting grog. He came near the barrel.

Deu, make him go away! Ana's heart raced. Her whole body was prepared for action. The lid moved as someone grasped the handle. Ana tensed the muscles in her legs, ready to spring. Surprise was her best defense now.

"Stupid dirty water," the sailor muttered.

"Hey! Quit loafin' and get back here," shouted a distant voice.

"Alright! I'm comin'!"

The footsteps receded. Relieved, Ana let out the breath she was holding.

"Where's that godforsaken dipper?" the thirsty sailor bellowed, stomping around.

"Just use your hands, you woman!"

"Fine!" the nearby man replied, then yanked off the lid.

No one moved. The man stared down at Ana, his mouth agape. She stared back.

Now!

Ana exploded from the barrel, tipping it over as she scrambled free. "Hey!" the man yelled, grabbing her dress. "Come here, you!" She knocked his arm loose and wrenched herself from his grasp. "Where do you think you're going?" he snarled, his lip curling in his chin stubble. He started forward with his hands held out like eagle's talons. There was nothing else to do. Ana took a running start and dived over the ship's rail.

The water was colder than she expected, its icy chill snatching her breath away. Ana surfaced quickly to grab a lungful of air, then ducked under again and swam as far as she could. She was wearing the type of garment that all the sisters wore, a woolen kirtle over a cotton chemise. The skirt billowed out, obstructing her kicks, weighing her down. She came up for another breath. Though the sun had set already, an evening twilight still illumined the sky. Ana glanced around. The ship was anchored in the open harbor instead of a berth. The nearest dock looked impossibly far away. Ana had grown up on the Farm River and considered herself a strong swimmer, yet now she was half-starved and encumbered by thick clothing. The distance to the pier was intimidating.

"There she is!" a voice called from the ship. "Put a shaft in 'er!"

Something smacked the water near Ana's head. *They're shooting arrows at me!* She went under again, praying an arrowhead wouldn't pierce her between the shoulder blades.

Ana swam hard, remaining submerged as much as possible until she thought she was out of her enemies' range. Every time she surfaced her breath came in ragged gasps. She wished she could kick off her shoes and skirt, but that was impossible. All she could do was struggle through the murky waters. Her destination was a small dock that floated at the base of a pier.

"We're gaining on her! Pull harder!"

Ana turned. The men had lowered a rowboat and were rapidly closing the distance. One of them stood in the bow with a lantern while his comrade tugged the oars. The boat was moving faster than Ana could swim.

Only her head start gave her a fighting chance against her pursuers. The race to the floating dock would be close.

Ana reached it first, but the rowboat was right behind her. She grasped the lip of the dock, trying to heave herself out of the water, but she couldn't find any purchase and slipped back again.

"Gotcha!"

A hand snatched Ana's dress. Though she resisted, the man got a firm grip on her shoulders and hauled her partway into the boat. She hung over the gunwale, her feet in the water and her torso dripping onto the floorboards.

The two sailors towered over her. One of them kicked her in the ribs. "Thought you could get away, did ya?"

Ana winced at the blow, then turned her head and glowered at the arrogant men. "I still do," she said.

Holding the gunwale in both hands, Ana gave it a hard shove, wobbling the boat in the water. Her position on the edge of the craft afforded her a level of stability the standing men didn't have. They uttered a shout of surprise, then toppled into the sea with their arms flailing.

Ana slithered into the boat and stood up. She leaped onto the floating dock and dashed to the ladder that ran to the harbor's main pier above. The wood was slick, and the rungs were slippery beneath her feet as she climbed. Ana's waterlogged garment weighed her down. She forced herself to concentrate on her precarious ascent.

Curses reached her ears. Ana glanced down. The men had managed to climb onto the floating dock and were following her up the ladder. She groaned and struggled higher, though she could feel her stamina giving out.

Her foot slipped off one of the rungs. Ana squealed as she banged her shin against the rough ladder. The nearest pursuer grabbed her ankle. "No!" she screamed, shaking herself free so she could keep climbing.

At last she reached the top and flopped onto the pier. But when she rolled over onto her back, Ana saw the sailor's head clear the edge of the decking. "Come here, little pretty," he leered, grabbing her leg. His fingernails dug into the flesh of her thigh.

"Don't touch me!"

Ana kicked her assailant hard in the face. The man's nose shattered under her heel with an audible crunch. "Arrgh!" he cried as his head whipped back. He clung to the ladder in a daze. Blood was smeared around his mouth like a predator at a fresh kill.

Yet there was nowhere to run. Ana was too exhausted to flee anymore. The man would recover his wits any second, and his vengeance would be swift and violent.

Gathering her final strength, Ana bent her knees up to her body. With a desperate yell she shot both feet straight out. Her soles contacted the two vertical stringers of the ladder where it protruded above the decking. The nails that fastened the ladder to the pier screeched as they came loose. Now the weight of two men on the rungs created forces beyond what the weather-beaten wood could bear. As the ladder broke apart Ana heard two screams, followed by the sickening thud of bodies striking the dock below. Then everything was still.

Ana's side ached from the kick she had taken. Breathing hard, she rose unsteadily to her feet. The alleys around the harbor were dark and forbidding. She was soaking wet, with no money, no friends, and no shelter. She didn't even know what city she was in.

But she had escaped.

✦　✦　✦

"There it is. That's one of theirs." Marco's tone was confident.

Teo stared across the moonlit harbor from the deck of Marco's ship. "How do you know?"

"The Exterminati are the only ones who rig their caravels like that. Square sails on the fore and mainmast, with a lateen on the mizzen. Makes them very fast."

"As fast as the *Glider*?"

Marco glanced at Teo, one eyebrow cocked. "Maybe someday we'll find out."

Impatience threatened to overwhelm Teo, but he forced himself to remain calm. Situations like this required careful planning or everything would come to ruin.

The *Midnight Glider* had made the run to Napoly in good time, reaching the port just after sunset. As Teo had expected, a newly arrived Exterminati ship was anchored there. Since no one along the docks had seen a shipment of whores being unloaded, Teo could only assume the sisters were still imprisoned in the caravel's hold. He intended to get them out.

"What if we just alerted the authorities and let them take care of it?" Teo suggested. "The harbor police have the right to board and inspect. The women are clearly being held against their will." Although Teo didn't like the idea of putting Ana's fate into someone else's hands, he thought it might be the smartest move.

Marco, however, disagreed. "Just about every woman brought to this harbor is being held against her will," he pointed out. "Napoly is a major hub for the flesh trade. All the port officials have been bought off. They have no reason to help us. In fact, they'd probably lock us up just to keep us from making trouble."

"True." Teo frowned. "Alright then, I say we make a head-on attack."

"What, right here in the harbor?"

"Why not? We have your crew of pirates plus the knights. We're more than a match for them. We could overpower the Exterminati."

"You can't just pull alongside a ship and attack like that. It's not that simple. For one thing, the port officials would stop us before we could accomplish anything. But even beyond that, you need maneuverability. Take it from one who knows—you have to be out in the open sea to capture a ship."

Teo let out an exasperated sigh. "Come on, Marco, we have to do something! Ana and Vanita are chained up in that ship, suffering who knows what, while we're standing here doing nothing!"

Marco held up two palms to calm Teo's anxiety. "Listen, *amico*, I understand what you're going through. But we have to be careful or we're going to make things worse for the women. We only have one chance to do this right."

"Yeah, okay," Teo said, putting his hand on Marco's shoulder. "You're right. Thanks for reminding me." He paused. "You have any ideas then?"

"It's a lot easier for one man to infiltrate an enemy ship than for an army to capture it. You'd be surprised how easy it is for a stowaway to sneak on board. Happens all the time. It wouldn't be difficult to get a man on the ship"—Marco flashed Teo a mischievous grin—"if we could find someone willing to try."

"Now I like how you're thinking." Teo motioned for Marco to continue.

"I could have a boat waiting in the water nearby. There are only . . . what? Twenty-five women? If somebody let them out of wherever they're locked up, they could be over the bulwarks in no time. Once they're scattered in the water there'd be nothing the Exterminati could do. We could pick them up and be off in the *Glider* before they even got their sailors out of the brothels."

Excited, Teo realized the plan could work, yet he immediately discerned its one tactical flaw. "The getaway boat would draw suspicion if it lingered by the ship," he noted. "This has to be a precise extraction. Get in, get out, lightning-quick."

"Hmm. I didn't think of that."

"Here's how we should do it. I'll go aboard and get the layout of the ship. Then I'll alert the women to the plan. When it's safe to move, I'll signal you with the ship's lantern. You shoot in with your boat at the exact moment the women jump in the sea. If we time it right, it'll go like clockwork."

Marco nodded resolutely. "Alright. I'm in."

"Good. And may Deu go with us."

"Your God has gotten you out of a lot of tight places," Marco answered. "Let's see if he can do it again."

The *Glider*'s crew lowered the ladder. Teo removed his leather jerkin but decided to wear his boots for better footing if combat became necessary. Slipping into the water in his trousers and shirt, he began to swim toward the Exterminati caravel. A fat half-moon hung on the horizon, casting a splintered yellow sheen across the sea.

Teo stayed underwater for most of the swim, surfacing only to breathe. He drew near the bow of the enemy ship. One of its two anchors hung aweigh, unneeded in the calm harbor. The hawsehole into which the anchor line ran was close enough to the rail that Teo thought he could climb over it.

He swam to the other anchor, the one in the water, then reached up to where the taut rope was dry. Clamping it in his hands and feet, he began to scale the line. The only sound was the drip of water from his wet clothing. Teo hoped no one was watching him from the shadows.

At the hawsehole Teo stretched to the rail and pulled himself onto the weather deck. He panted for a few seconds to catch his wind after his exertion. The deck featured a pair of small capstans—vertical axles with notches into which beams could be inserted. A team of men would push the beams in a circle, winding a line around drums below deck as they hauled up the anchors from the sea floor. Most of the beams were now laid aside for later use.

Without warning a black shadow darted at Teo, moving with incredible speed. As something passed over his head he instinctively threw his hand to his neck. A wire tightened, digging into the flesh of his palm.

Teo wrestled with the shaman at his back. The garrote pressed Teo's hand against his larynx, cutting off his respiration. Only the intervention of his hand kept him from passing out.

Thrashing in his assailant's grasp, Teo reached for the knife in his boot. He fumbled for several precious seconds before finally getting a grip on the hilt. As he struggled to stab the blade behind him, the shaman was forced to release the garrote to deflect the attack. Teo inhaled a lungful of air, but his head still swam, and his movements were weak. The shaman knocked the knife away with a hard chop, then resumed his choke hold with fingers like a vise.

Dizzy and lightheaded, Teo tumbled to the deck. The shaman knelt on his chest. Teo fought to pry his enemy's talonlike grip from his throat, but couldn't. The man was a professional assassin, and strangulation was his specialty. Teo's vision blurred. The masts overhead wobbled. The stars spun in circles.

Deu! It can't end like this! Help me!

His hand closed on a piece of wood. *What is it?* Teo's mind cleared just enough to realize it was the lever that controlled the ratchet on the capstan. *Pull it!* He yanked the lever and released the tension. The capstan spun on its axis as the heavy anchor plunged into the sea—and the lone beam left in the capstan whirled around with ferocious speed.

Crack!

Something warm and sticky hit Teo's face. His lungs heaved as the murderous fingers released their hold. The weight of the shaman's knee slipped from his chest. Teo rolled away, sucking in huge gasps of air. It took a long time for his respiration to return to normal.

At last he sat up. The shaman lay motionless on the deck. His blank eyes stared at the sky, and the pool of blood around his head was glossy black in the moonlight.

Teo struggled to his feet and retrieved his knife. The shaman's spattered blood had obscured his vision, so he wiped it away with a rag from a swab bucket. Then he surveyed the quiet ship.

Nothing moved. If anyone was aware of him they would have sounded an alarm, so Teo assumed the sailors must be reveling onshore. He crossed the deck to the stern and put his ear against a barred hatch.

At first he heard nothing. Then, straining to hear, he discerned the soft sound of female crying.

He lifted the bar. Steps led down into the hold. Teo descended. All was quiet—until a sharp voice broke the silence.

"What do you want with us?"

The voice was Vanita's.

"It's me—Teofil."

"Teofil!" Vanita rushed over, stepping into the shaft of moonlight from the hatch. "What are you doing here?"

"Getting you out. Where's Ana?"

"You won't believe this, but she escaped about an hour ago."

"What! How?"

"In a water barrel. There was a commotion on deck, and she jumped overboard."

Teo sighed and shook his head. He was both frustrated and impressed at the same time. "That woman never ceases to amaze me," he muttered.

"She learned from the best, Teofil."

Most of the sisters had awakened now. They began to gather around.

"Listen up, everyone," Teo said. "Be ready to move as soon as I give the signal."

"You will do no such thing!"

Teo froze. The sisters cried out. Turning, Teo saw men standing at the top of the steps—but not Exterminati. With their wide-shouldered physiques and close-cropped hair they looked like . . . *Clansmen?*

"Alright, I won't," Teo agreed calmly. He gazed up at the men. "However, I might do *this!*"

He charged up the steps, knocking the lead man aside. Hands clawed at him, but the footing was precarious in the close quarters, and everyone hit the deck as Teo barreled into them. He scrambled up, ducking under a punch and countering with a jab to his attacker's jaw. After high-kicking a second man, he turned and dashed for the bulwarks. Without slowing his stride he leaped over the rail in an arcing dive.

Teo hit the water cleanly and surfaced near the rowboat that had brought the Clansmen to the ship. Two unfortunate fellows sat huddled in it, their faces contorted in pain. One had his knee bandaged, and the other clutched a bloody forearm with a pale shard of bone protruding from it.

"Get out," Teo ordered.

The two injured men were in no condition to resist. Moaning at the effort, they tumbled over the side. Teo hauled himself into the rowboat and grasped the oars.

A Clansman had descended a rope ladder on the caravel's hull. Teo gave the oars a hard pull, creating instant separation from the ship. The pursuer looked over his shoulder, then made a desperate leap as the boat pulled away. He fell short, causing a big splash, yet he managed to catch the gunwale in his hands. The boat rocked and nearly capsized.

"Hang on!" shouted one of his comrades from the deck above. "Don't let him go!"

Teo drew his boot knife and displayed the glittering blade. The man's eyes went wide.

"Your choice," Teo said.

The Clansman raised both palms and slipped into the water. Teo began to row in earnest.

"After him!" the man on the deck yelled, but his command was useless. No one could swim as fast as Teo's powerful shoulders could propel the boat.

Something hissed through the air before impacting the hull with a solid *thwock!* Twice more, arrows struck the wood, while other shots landed in the water nearby. Teo kept pulling the oars until he was out of range.

He rowed to the nearest dock but saw that its ladder had come loose from the pier. Continuing to the next dock, he drew alongside it and climbed onto the floating platform. The ladder brought him up to the main pier in Napoly's harbor.

His mind raced. Somewhere in the dark maze of streets Ana was alone and afraid. The Exterminati were after her—and apparently so was the Clan. Though Teo didn't know why those two groups were cooperating, he knew they both posed a mortal danger to Ana.

But he would find her first.

He had to.

He had promised.

◆　◆　◆

"Easy there, boy." Ana touched the horse's muzzle, quieting the skittish animal. The stable was dark and, except for the horse and the woman, empty.

In one of the stalls Ana found a grooming towel. Since the hay was clean, she took off her shoes and dried her feet. Next she removed her woolen kirtle and wrung it out, then did the same with her chemise. After toweling off, she got dressed again. Her hair was all mussed, so she smoothed it down and tied it back with a leather thong. It wasn't fashionable, but it would have to do.

The tavern next to the stable was filled with customers. Ana fished a few pennies from her pocket and clutched them in her fist as she entered the common room. The place was rough. She almost turned around and left, but hunger prevailed. All the tables were taken, so Ana found a stool near the kitchen. A plain-faced barmaid scurried around serving the patrons, who ignored her in favor of the painted girls on their laps. Ana caught the barmaid's attention.

"Please . . . some broth?"

The barmaid eyed her warily. Ana brushed a lock of hair from her forehead, suddenly self-conscious under the disapproving stare.

"You're no streetwalker," the barmaid said.

Ana shook her head.

"Face like that could make you a lot of money in Napoly."

"I just want some soup." Ana opened her hand and displayed her pennies.

"We got minestrone. I'll fetch some."

Ana nodded agreeably. At this point she was hungry enough to eat shoe leather.

The maid returned with a steaming earthenware bowl. Ana wolfed down the soup and was about to beg for more when a man approached. He wasn't the gentlemanly type.

"How much?" he demanded.

Ana held up both hands and waved him off, but the man didn't relent. "Come on," he said. "I don't care what you ask. Follow me." He headed for the stairs, then turned to look over his shoulder.

"I said let's go!" he bellowed.

A few people around the room stopped what they were doing to watch the exchange. Ana stood up, drawing hoots and whistles from the male spectators. She set the bowl on the counter.

"I was just on my way out," she said, starting toward the door.

"I don't think so. I'm buyin' what you're sellin'." The ruffian moved to block her path. He was a foul man with a scrawny body and a beak for a nose. If Teo had been there, the fellow would have crawled into a dark hole like a rat.

Ana swallowed. She knew she could outmatch this runt if everyone else in the place would leave her alone. *What would divert their attention?*

Facing Beak-Nose directly, Ana gave him a brazen smile. "I'm expensive," she declared. "Too much for the likes of you."

"You don't know me," the man snarled. "I'm a big deal around here."

"I doubt it."

The man's expression turned mean, though with a hint of desperation. "I got whatever it takes!"

"Show me."

The man dug into a pouch at his waist. He produced a handful of small silver coins.

Ana scoffed. "You'll need a lot more than that, little man."

The ruffian's face reddened. He pulled out more coins and displayed them.

"I'll take it all up front." Ana held out her palm. The man dutifully paid her.

Ana turned to face the crowded barroom. "Hey, everyone—catch!" She hurled the coins into the air. The tavern exploded with activity as the patrons scrambled to grab the flashing silver.

"You lousy whore!" the ruffian bawled. "What do you think you're doing?"

"As I said—leaving."

Ana shoved the man hard, sending him sprawling across a gaming table. Before anyone could react, she escaped into the night.

The cool air felt good as Ana left the sweaty tavern. She hurried through the alleyways in case anyone followed her, but no one did. Though she was glad to have something in her stomach, she knew her predicament was dire. This city the barmaid had called Napoly was no place for an ingénue. Its streets were mean, and Ana was vulnerable—a lamb among wolves.

Oh, Teo! Where are you? Ana missed him desperately. He always protected her, spread his wing over her, whisked her away from dangers like this. Teo had a way of making good things happen. But now he was across an ocean somewhere. Maybe even dead, if the Iron Shield's words were to be believed. Ana pushed that thought away. Teo was no doubt alive, but far away. He wouldn't come riding to her rescue. Deu alone was her protector, and that was more than enough. *Guide my feet to safety*, she prayed as she stumbled aimlessly through the streets.

Prostitutes were on every corner. Ana passed them without speaking, and most of them left her alone. A few, however, seemed threatened by her presence. "Get off my corner," one snapped as Ana walked past. Another mocked her clothing. "Nice dress! Your nonna give it to ya?"

At last exhaustion began to set in. Ana realized she needed to get off the rough streets and grab some sleep. Though she had no money to pay for a room, that didn't bother her. Finding another clean stable was the best option. She would rise at first light and ask a respectable policeman to help her.

The scent of horses reached her nose. Turning into an alley, Ana tried to find the stable but realized it was a dead end. As she was walking back to the main street a figure materialized from the shadows.

Ana stopped. The man kept coming. She wanted to run, but there was nowhere to go. Ana glanced around for a weapon. An empty bottle lay on the ground. She started to move toward it.

"You shouldn't be out here alone," the man said in a thick Napolese accent.

"I'm fine."

"No, you're not."

The man stepped into a shaft of light from a window above. He was middle-aged, with a stocky build. Something glinted at his throat. Ana looked more closely at the man's necklace. When she recognized it, she gasped.

It was a pendant of the Pierced One.

❖　❖　❖

"Hey, come over here, honey," the girl called. Other alluring shouts followed, many of them more explicit than the first. Teo only felt sickened. This wasn't what humanity was meant for.

Even so, he approached the prostitutes. He was willing to pay for one thing they had to offer—information.

"I'm looking for a woman," he said.

"Aren't they all," replied a scantily clad streetwalker. She could have been pretty except for the hardness etched into her face. It pained Teo to think what her life was like.

He shook his head. "This woman wasn't for sale. She's twenty-six, blonde, slender. She would have been wearing . . . " Teo tried to picture the drab outfits the nuns wore. "A chemise with sleeves, and a thing over it. Plain wool."

The women laughed. Six or seven had gathered around now, like she-wolves scenting fresh meat. "You mean a kirtle?"

"I guess so."

The idea drew more laughter. "Who would wear a kirtle on these streets?" giggled one of the girls.

"Anyone who doesn't want to get paid," said another.

"Just tell me if you've seen her. She's a friend."

"Ain't no such things as friends out here. Only the users and the used." The comment drew nods of agreement from the crowd.

"No!" Teo countered. "There's a third type in the world: those who help. I'm one of those." He glanced around at the women. "Listen, I can see you ladies don't have any information right now. I'll come back later. If you have anything to report, there's a coin in it for you."

Teo left the women on the corner. He was several paces away when he heard footsteps behind him. He turned. A prostitute had followed him—a girl much too young to be in a place like this. Her face was still unsullied, her skin still clear. She had a delicate chin, an upturned nose, and big, wary eyes.

"How old are you?" Teo asked.

"Nineteen."

"I don't think so."

The girl dropped her head. "Fifteen," she admitted.

"What's your name?"

"Sugar."

Sugar. Teo's heart broke. *Deu have mercy on this poor soul!* "What do you want with me, Sugar?"

"I think I saw your friend."

"Where? Tell me—quick!"

"There was a pretty lady wandering around. She was dressed like you said. I wanted to speak to her. She seemed kind."

"She is. Where did she go?"

"I saw her go into an alley. A man followed her."

Teo grimaced and set his jaw. His fists clenched involuntarily.

"Not like that," Sugar said. "He was the religious man."

"The what?"

"There's a religious man who hangs around the streets. Never uses the women, just brings them food. Home-cooked stuff. Sometimes pastries and cakes."

"Where can I find him?"

The girl shrugged. "I have no idea. He's from a group called the Lighthouse." Sugar lowered her voice and leaned close. "The other harlots say if you want to get out, he'll help you. That's why he keeps his place secret. The pimps hate him."

"So no one knows where he lives?"

"No, but if you ask to go with him, he'll take you."

"I have to see this man as soon as possible."

Sugar put her finger on her chin and thought about it. "This time of year he brings a bag of zeppole every morning." She paused, then added brightly, "With jelly!"

The innocent way Sugar spoke made Teo take a second look at her. She was so young, just a teenager. How did she get trapped in a life like this? Teo felt an ache in his gut, not only for Sugar but for all the women who knew nothing better than a stream of dirty men, day after day. That was not what Deu intended.

"Where does the religious man come with the pastries?"

"Over there," Sugar said, pointing. "In the piazza."

"What time?"

"At dawn, when the girls are coming off their shifts. He always treats us real nice. He says we're loved by the great god Deus."

Teo nodded thoughtfully. *So the man is Christiani–and Ana is with him!* He glanced at Sugar. Though he was worried about Ana, apparently she was safe for the moment. But the girl standing before him was in desperate need.

"Is your name really Sugar?"

"Yeah. What else?"

"I bet you had another name before"—Teo waved his hand at the dark surroundings—"all this."

Sugar nodded.

"Will you tell me?"

The girl fidgeted and looked at her feet. Finally she said in a barely audible voice, "My mother named me Gemma."

"Precious jewel."

"No . . . not anymore," Sugar said wistfully.

"You know what? I think we need something from one another, you and I."

"I can give you everything you need, mister."

Teo drew back, appalled. Sugar's demeanor had become sensual in an instant. It was as if she had donned a costume and become a different person.

"Don't do that!" Teo cried. "All I need is a room for a few hours."

"You can come into my room," Sugar teased.

"Stop it!" Teo gave the teenaged girl a disapproving stare, then removed a one-scudi coin from his pocket and held it up. "Just give me your key."

Sugar handed Teo a numbered room key from a tavern around the corner. "That much money would buy you the best girl at the top brothel," she said.

"No, it's going to buy you a journey." He put the coin in Sugar's hand.

"What do you mean?" she asked suspiciously.

"When the man of Deus comes by, talk to him. Let him help you get out of this city."

"And do what? Go where?"

"Just get out of here! Start over in a country village. You deserve a better life. Do you have any skills?"

"I was always a good weaver. But looms cost more money than I could ever earn. The madam keeps most of what I make."

Teo sighed, frustrated at the way evil entrenched itself and refused to budge. He considered how to break its hold on Sugar.

Reaching to his neck, Teo unfastened the crucifix that Ana had tossed to him at their parting. "See this man?"

Sugar nodded.

"He's more than a man. His name is Iesus, and he's the son of Deus—the one true God. Iesus came from heaven to forgive the sins of everyone who believes in him."

"Not the sins of a woman like me."

"Yes, especially a woman like you. If you believe in him you won't be condemned. Evildoers killed Iesus, but he came back to life. He's alive right now, and he offers you new life. Take it, Sugar."

"Take Iesus?"

"Yes, take him." Teo hesitated, then added, "And take this pendant."

Sugar's eyes widened. "It's so expensive!"

"I know. You could sell it. There would be enough to buy a loom and some raw wool to get you started."

Hope flooded Sugar's countenance. "Would that really work?"

"People do it all the time. You could too. This is your chance at something more."

"But that's so . . . scary!"

"Iesus would go with you."

"He would? With *me*?"

"Every step of the way. Just ask him. He won't say no. He loves you."

Sugar closed her eyes. "I ask you, Iesus. Go with me."

Teo saw tears dribble down Sugar's pale cheeks. He put a gentle hand on her shoulder. "Go now, child. Hide until morning. Then see the man of Deus and break free of this place."

Sugar tucked the pendant and coin inside her dress. "Thank you," she whispered as she hurried off.

Teo watched her go. She moved quickly, then paused and turned around.

"What's your name, mister?"

"Teofil."

Sugar's face brightened. She waved with her fingers. "Good-bye, Teofil," she said.

"Good-bye, Gemma," Teo replied.

◆　◆　◆

The mysterious man from the alley called himself a shepherd. The girls of the street were his flock. He thought of them as pure white lambs, even though he knew they were sullied. Shepherd Nicklas didn't mind those stains. He had been washed from that sort of life himself.

Ana sat in his small apartment, a dingy place made lovely by Nicklas's wife, Margherita. The kitchen served as the main gathering area, for every other room had been partitioned off with curtains to form small bedrooms. Ana knew the place was a refuge for girls who needed to disappear for a while.

A delectable aroma emanated from the wood-burning brick oven. Even though it was after midnight, Ana found herself ravenous. The soup she ate earlier hadn't filled her.

"What's that great smell?" she asked.

Margherita smiled mischievously. "You'll find out in a moment."

Ana had been surprised to see the pendant around Shepherd Nicklas's neck when she met him in the alley. He had greeted her with kindness, and Ana immediately sensed the spirit of Deu upon the man. When she heard he gave shelter to women in need, Ana knew he was sent in answer to her prayers.

"Would you like to freshen up?" Nicklas asked. He pointed to one of the makeshift bedrooms. "There's a bowl and a bar of soap. I'll pump some water for you."

"Oh, that would be wonderful," Ana agreed. She felt dirty from her days in the Exterminati ship, and her dip in Napoly's harbor only added to the grime.

After scrubbing her hands and face, then brushing through her hair, Ana returned to the kitchen. The dish that had been making her mouth water for the past several minutes was already cooling on the counter. The golden-brown flatbread was smothered with a red sauce made from the fruits called *pomodores* or apples of gold. White cheese had been melted on top, garnished with fresh basil, then the crust was brushed with olive oil. Ana's stomach growled as she smelled the heavenly aroma.

"What's it called?" she asked.

"It's a Napolese specialty," Margherita said. "We call it *pitsa*." After pouring a glass of pale lager, she instructed Ana to sit down. "No talking now, my lovely. Just eat."

Ana didn't argue.

Instead she ate three *pitsas*.

At last she dropped her napkin on the table. "I couldn't eat another bite," she said as she finished the last of her beer.

Shepherd Nicklas looked at his guest with a twinkle in his eye. He crossed the room to a cabinet, the kind that stored mountain ice in a block to keep the things inside cool. Removing a tub, he spooned out a creamy substance that was pink, green, and brown.

"I think you'll find room for spumoni," he suggested. And somehow Ana did.

After the meal, the threesome sat around the kitchen table sipping chicory coffee. Shepherd Nicklas began to tell his life story.

"I was a young man when the Papa sent a missionary down from Roma," he said. "I understood right away that Christianism was true. Of course there's only one God! It makes perfect sense. All the rest of the deities are wicked. I could see that plainly enough."

"I remember feeling the same way the first time I met Deus," Ana said. "But you didn't know about Iesus back then, right?"

"No one did in those days. Margherita and I gave our lives to the good God even though a lot of our questions were still unanswered. We took the Washing to mark our commitment. Then we devoted ourselves to serving our little lambs on the streets of Napoly. Others pledged themselves to that task too. We have called our community the Lighthouse. For many years this simple life of service and worship was all we knew. We believed there must be more, but we didn't know when we'd learn it. Then, just a few months ago, a priest from the Papa brought us this."

Shepherd Nicklas laid a booklet on the table. It was inexpensively printed and bound.

"The New Testament," Ana breathed, awed by the book's presence here. She glanced at her host. "So now you know the rest of the story."

The married couple joined hands and gazed at one another. "Yes. Now we know Iesus."

A powerful emotion swept over Ana. *This is what it's all about,* she realized. *This is why I've faced all the danger . . . all the hardship . . . all the worry and suffering! This is why Teo and I came over the mountains from Chiveis—for people like Nicklas and Margherita, who waited so patiently for the word of Deu to arise!* Ana trembled at the role she had played in the mighty plans of her God.

A clock on the wall chimed. "You're exhausted, Anastasia. I can see it." Margherita patted her hand. "Why don't you go to bed now?"

She nodded. "I think I will."

"And tonight no one will bother you," Shepherd Nicklas added.

"Thank you. I could use a night like that."

◆　　◆　　◆

Teo was awake and out of Sugar's room before first light. He waited for the man of Deus in the piazza, though not for baked treats and jelly doughnuts. The man knew where Ana was. Teo felt hopeful at last.

Dawn arrived, and many of the weary streetwalkers shuffled past on their way to sleep. No one came to bring them pastries. Teo's optimistic mood began to sour.

The sound of horses' hooves on the pavement came to his ears—a strange thing at so early an hour. Teo crossed the piazza and peeked around the corner. In the distance a prostitute was speaking to a group of seven or eight riders. All the men were young, well-dressed, short-haired, and armed. After the girl in the skimpy outfit finished pointing, the leader tossed her a coin and led his men into a side street. A sinking feeling gathered in Teo's gut. These riders were Clansmen, and Ana was their prey. *Did the prostitute see Ana go with the man of Deus? Has the Clan discovered where he lives?* Teo decided he had better follow and find out.

By the time he arrived at the side street it was empty. Teo was inspecting the packed earth for tracks when a commotion broke out several blocks away. He heard male shouting, the prancing of hooves, the jangle of horse tack. A woman screamed. Teo broke into a run.

Following his ears, he made his way through the narrow lanes and alleys. With all the echoes off the stone buildings it was hard to discern where the sounds were coming from. Finally he spotted the riders as they flashed past a gap and disappeared. Teo noted they were headed in the direction of the harbor.

He sprinted down an avenue he hoped would intersect with his enemies' path. His knife was in his boot—not much of a weapon against fighters on horseback. *I'll think of something,* he told himself and kept running.

Teo reached the docks just behind the Clansmen. His heart lurched as he noticed a woman on horseback in their midst: Anastasia of Edgeton, unmistakable in her beauty. She was barefoot and wore only her white chemise. Though her hands were bound, she rode with her back straight and her chin lifted high. The morning sunlight caught her tousled hair, giving it a golden sheen.

Teo cupped his hands. "Ana!" he shouted. She didn't hear. He tried again, and she began to look around, but the riders blocked her view and hustled her toward the pier.

Suddenly one of the men broke from the group and turned his horse toward Teo. Drawing his sword, he spurred his mount into a gallop. Teo reached down for his knife. The Clansman barreled straight at him, his eyes fixed in a bellicose stare.

As the rider drew near, Teo recognized him as the man who had leaped onto his rowboat from the Exterminati ship. His face was contorted into an angry snarl. Although Teo gripped his knife, he wished he had a longer blade. A good sword could make the difference between life and death, but a knife wasn't much use in a situation like this—except for one thing.

Teo flipped the knife up and caught it by the tip. He had spent many hours tossing knives into tree trunks with his buddies from the Fifth Regiment. Usually he could best them in any game of accuracy. Now he drew upon that skill in a much more deadly contest.

Cocking his arm behind his head, Teo waited for the right moment. He would have only one chance. To wait long enough to make an accurate throw was to remain within the sword's reach if he missed.

But Teo rarely missed.

The knife took the rider in the heart, exactly where Teo intended. The man's face twisted into a look of surprise. His sword slipped from his hand as he swept by, though Teo still had to dive out of the way to avoid the charging horse. When he scrambled from the ground he saw the man lying flat on the pavement. The hilt of the knife protruded from the center of his chest. He twitched but did not stand up.

Teo collected the dropped sword, then approached his enemy and knelt. The man panted between gritted teeth. Beads of sweat lined his forehead.

"What do you want with her?" Teo demanded. "Speak up!"

The man's determined silence made Teo desperate. All these mysterious activities had gone on long enough. Teo wanted to know what the Exterminati and Clansmen were up to—and he wanted to know *now*.

"Tell me what you're doing with those women!" he shouted.

When the man didn't reply, Teo's eyes fell to the knife's hilt. He grasped it. One agonizing twist would wrench the information from his enemy by force. As the Clansman's gaze followed Teo's hand, his body stiffened. He began to breathe faster in anticipation of even more pain.

Teo couldn't do it. He took a flask from the man's belt and unscrewed the lid. After dribbling whisky into the dying man's mouth, he put the flask in his hand, then stood up and turned to pursue the other riders.

"Hey," the man grunted.

Teo swiveled his head and looked down.

"The women . . . they're brides . . . for the fire god."

Brides for the fire god? Was that some local euphemism for prostitution?

"Quick!" Teo urged. "Tell me where they're being taken!"

The Clansman had just opened his mouth to speak when a crossbow bolt hissed through the air and impaled him. His body flinched, and his eyes fluttered shut. Another hiss was followed by the clatter of a bolt striking brick. Teo ducked behind an empty fish stall. Three crossbowmen pinned him down, one firing while the others cranked their weapons. A nearby alley led to a maze of narrow streets.

Teo stared past the crossbowmen at the Bay of Napoly. The Exterminati caravel floated in the harbor. Two similar ships rested beside it now. Down in the water, Teo could see the little rowboat whose evil occupants held Ana in their grip. He was considering how to set up a combined attack on the three caravels when his eyes noticed an unexpected detail.

The ships' anchors had been raised.

CHAPTER

9

The putrid bilge of the caravel made the hold seem like a paradise. Ana had been taken deep within the bowels of the ship. Hand pumps and bailing buckets lay scattered about. Her captors opened a hatch. "No! Please!" she cried, but the men pushed her into the hole anyway. The hatch slammed shut above her.

At first she had been too terrified to cry. The cold darkness and the tight confines stirred up memories Ana wished she could forget. Bilge water clung to her ankles, sludgy with tar and algae and excrement. The stench was noxious. Ana's stomach lurched. She gagged twice, then added to the filth all around her.

Tears finally came to her eyes, though she dared not touch her face to wipe them away. Ana let them drop from her cheeks, the pure water mingling with the foul, until she could cry no more. At last she stumbled forward to where the keel curved up and the nauseating brew was shallower. Sitting out of the muck as much as possible, Ana resigned herself to a long, torturous journey.

Everything had been so peaceful at Shepherd Nicklas's house. Ana had slept soundly there, with a clean body and a full belly, confident that in the morning the port authorities would free the imprisoned sisters. But things didn't work out like that. Somehow the Exterminati had learned her whereabouts. They were being helped by the beefy thugs who belonged to the Clan. Ana had been wakened in her bed by a predawn raid. Poor Nicklas had been roughed up, but he was a strong man and would survive the mistreatment. Ana didn't even have time to don her outer garment before she was hauled outside in her chemise and set on a horse.

"Oh, Deu! How long?" she cried to the darkness. Though Ana's question was prompted by fear of the arduous journey ahead, she let her plaintive cry become more than that. *How long will wickedness reign? How long will the nations set themselves against the Eternal One? How long before good men finally triumph and righteousness prevails?* Ana had no answers to those questions. None at all.

Time slipped by unmarked. The smell was horrendous, making Ana retch and gag. She longed for fresh air. Weary, she reclined against the sloping hull of the ship. By bracing her feet against one of the transverse ribs, she found she could keep herself out of the dirty water. Soon the rocking motion of the ship lulled her into an uneasy sleep.

A hard jolt awakened her. Ana had no way to know how long she had slept. The ship had entered rougher seas now, making it pitch more than before. Ana slid against the slick wood of the bilge, tossed back and forth by the merciless waves.

An unexpected memory pricked her mind. When she was being taken on horseback to the ship, she thought she had heard someone shout her name. But the voice hadn't said "Anastasia." The word—if it was real—was *Ana*. Only one person called her that.

Could it be? Is Teo following me? Is he on the way?

Ana struggled to believe it. Her thoughts went back to the moment in the ship's hold when, through the sisters' hymn, Deu had reminded her of Jérémie 29. "Mighty Deu," Ana prayed, "help my unbelief! I know you have plans to give me a future and a hope. Please, Iesus, speak to my soul and let me know you're with me."

The ship crested a wave, then dipped hard into a trough. The impact was even more forceful than the one that had awakened her. Above her head, a piece of the hull planking broke loose. A tiny ray of light pierced the darkness.

Rolling onto her belly, Ana wriggled up to the hole. Caravels like this one didn't have much of a draft, so the hole was above the waterline. Ana cleared away more of the rotten plank with the heel of her hand until the opening was the size of a saucer. The horizon rose and fell as the ship heaved, and seawater splashed her face, but Ana didn't mind. She had what she wanted: clear sunlight and fresh, sweet air. Closing her eyes, she let the breeze caress her cheeks. And then she knew.

Help was on the way.

◆　　◆　　◆

The *Midnight Glider* was in its berth. Teo ran up the gangplank. "Marco!" he yelled, but there was no answer.

He tried again, checking the captain's cabin and the head. Still there was no sign of Marco or anyone else.

Teo went up on deck. He heard a heavy snore reverberating in the ship's boat. One of the crewmen was inside, snuggled up with an empty bottle.

"Hey, sailor!"

The man didn't move.

Teo reached in and shook him, awakening the man with a start. "Where is everybody?"

The pirate squinted at Teo through bleary eyes. "The brothel, I guess."

"Which one?"

"Right there. The Comfort House."

Shaking his head, Teo walked down the gangplank to the pier. He entered the bordello, which was silent at this early hour.

"Marco!" Teo yelled, shattering the stillness.

Heads peeked from the doors, mostly female. Teo frowned. "Marco, if you're in here, get up now!"

"Take it easy. I'm right here." Marco appeared in the bordello's fancy lobby, shrugging into his navy blue jacket. After running his fingers through his hair he looked debonair enough to go out on the town.

"Why aren't you on the ship?" Teo demanded.

"I stayed there a long time, but you never gave the lantern signal like we agreed, then you rowed away without the women. I had no idea when you'd return or what your new plan was. All I could do was wait for you to show up again."

"At a house of prostitution?"

Marco's face reddened. "What am I supposed to do? A man has needs, you know."

"But what about Vanita?"

"Hey, come on! It's not like she and I—"

Teo cut him off, turning toward the door. "Just get your sailors aboard the *Glider*. I'll round up the knights. It's time to go."

"Why? What happened?"

"The caravels left, and I have no idea where they went."

"All three? Just like that?"

"Yes, right after dawn, which you would have known if you had been watching."

"I told you, I did watch for a long time. But then it grew late, and I needed some sleep."

"Well, I hope you got some good 'sleep' in here."

Disgusted, Teo made his way to the inn where the ten Knights of the Cross were housed. Unlike Marco's pirates, they didn't carouse with women—though Teo wouldn't have put it past some of those who remained at Marsay with Odo.

After rousing the knights, Teo walked to the Port Authority building and barged through the front door. His sudden entrance startled the dozing watchman, who was finishing the night shift.

"I need to know where those three caravels are headed," Teo snapped.

"That information is restricted. Get out."

Teo was in no mood for an argument. He brushed past the bleary-eyed watchman and picked up a register book with the word *Itineraries* engraved on the spine.

"Hey, leave that alone! You're not allowed to—" The watchman caught himself, looking at Teo more closely. "What's your name, stranger?"

"Teofil of Chiveis."

"Is that so? Alright, listen up, Teofil. Just give me a little consideration and I'll let you take a look."

Teo gladly emptied his pockets of all the coins he had. The watchman counted the silver in his palm and seemed satisfied. He turned away and stared out the window while Teo flipped through the itinerary book to its most recent entry. Large bold letters identified the caravels' destination as

Eastport, Sessalay. Teo felt the claws of tension release some of their fierce grip. At least now he knew where to go.

"That's all I need," he said.

"I don't know what you're talking about," the watchman replied without turning around.

All hands were aboard the *Glider* when Teo returned. The crew set some canvas on the mainmast and shoved off. After clearing the bay and entering the open ocean, Marco ordered his men aloft to make more sail on the yards. He was rigging his ship for speed. Teo grabbed one of the passing sailors. "Tell the captain to head for Eastport," he said.

The trip to Sessalay was a three-day journey. At first Teo avoided Marco because his irritation still simmered beneath the surface of his emotions. But on the second day, after the evening mess was over, a whispering in his head told him he ought to seek restoration. Though Teo resisted for a while, he finally approached Marco's cabin and knocked on the door.

"Who is it?" came the gruff voice.

"A friend."

There was silence for a long moment, then the door opened. Marco's face was unreadable. "Come in."

Teo entered the great cabin and settled into a padded seat by the window. Normally Marco would offer him an after-dinner drink, but he didn't do so now. Teo's mind flashed back to a time when he was grieving deeply and Marco's friendship in this very stateroom had meant more to him than a glass of gin ever could.

"You here to scold me again?" Marco asked.

"I'm here to apologize. I shouldn't have lectured you in front of your men."

"And in front of a bunch of two-bit whores. You made me look like a fool."

"I'm sorry. I mishandled that. I let my anger get the best of me." Teo hesitated. "But you *were* a fool."

Marco walked to a liquor cabinet and retrieved a bottle. Teo couldn't see if he was preparing one drink or two. Finally he turned around again, holding two glasses. He offered one to Teo. "You're right. I was."

"I'll drink to that," Teo said with a grin. Marco broke into a broad smile as well. The two men clinked glasses and knocked back their shots.

"You have to remember, I'm a pirate," Marco said, pulling up a chair. "I don't command my crew like an admiral. I don't have naval law to back me up. My men are attached to me only by personal allegiance. I have to give them a long leash."

"I understand that. But what about your own decisions?"

"You mean to go to the bordello?"

"Yes, and at the worst possible time."

"What can I say? I'm a man. I have needs."

"Are those needs stronger than your loyalty to Vanita?"

Marco studied Teo's face. "Sometimes," he admitted at last.

Teo didn't say anything.

"How do you do it?" Marco asked. "Anastasia is a beautiful woman. You're clearly in love with her. How come . . . ?"

"It's simple. My love is based on respect. That makes all the difference."

"I guess you're a stronger man than me."

"Look, don't put me on a pedestal. I'm not without temptations. I have the same urges as every other man. I adore Ana so much, it's impossible not to desire her. But my respect has always been stronger than my desire. I'm grateful to Deu for that."

"If I converted to Christianism, would I get that kind of self-control too?"

Teo chuckled. "Well, it's not like a magic charm you hang around your neck. But it does say in the Sacred Writing that the followers of Iesus are a temple for Deu's spirit. Just like you wouldn't desecrate a holy place, so you wouldn't act in ways that are unfitting toward a Christiani sister—even one you're madly in love with."

"*Especially* not the one you love," Marco added thoughtfully.

"Right. I think you get it."

"I'm going to give this some serious thought, *amico*. You never cease to surprise me."

"I try to keep things interesting," Teo said with a little laugh.

The conversation died down as the two men were lost in their thoughts for a while. Eventually Teo decided to broach a subject he had been wanting to discuss with Marco ever since they left Napoly. "I heard something strange, and I'd like to get your take on it," he said.

Marco arched his eyebrows and waited, so Teo continued. "One of the Clansmen told me the women were supposed to become 'brides for the fire god.'"

No sooner had Teo uttered the words than Marco leaped from his chair. "No! Not that!" he exclaimed.

Teo hunched his shoulders and held up his palms. "What?"

"This rescue is going to be a lot more complicated than we thought," Marco said with a grimace.

Although Teo had assumed his worry for Ana couldn't get any worse, it now shot up to a new level. With a nervous swallow he asked Marco to explain.

"It's an old pagan ritual on Sessalay," the pirate captain said. "I don't think it's been done for years, maybe centuries. But back in the old days the Sessalayans used to placate Mulciber by giving him virgin brides."

"Mulciber is the underworld god, right?"

"Yes. The god of fire and brimstone, the god of the forge."

"In Chiveis we call him Vulkain, but I'm sure it's the same spirit who's receiving the worship under different names."

"He's a voracious god," Marco went on. "He hungers for his brides. Swallows them whole."

Teo felt his heartbeat accelerate. "You mean . . . "

"Yes." Marco's voice took on an ominous chill. "Human sacrifice."

Though Teo dreaded the answer, he couldn't help but whisper, "How?"

Instead of replying, Marco approached Teo slowly, then pointed past him out the window. Teo turned and followed Marco's gaze. Neither man broke the absolute silence in the ship's cabin. As Teo stared into the blackness, horror began to seize his soul.

The sky above the distant horizon smoldered with an angry red glow.

✦   ✦   ✦

The Clan Boss wiped sweat from his brow with his sleeve and leaned on his staff. The trudge up the jagged trail on Fire Mountain was hard enough, but the blistering heat made it nearly unbearable. Yet such were the sacrifices that had to be made for the glory of almighty Mulciber.

Though it was nighttime now, it wasn't dark. The plume of lava jetting from the summit turned Fire Mountain into a giant torch. Molten rock burst from a vent, leaping out of the ground in great pulses like the vomit of Mulciber himself. The sight was spellbinding, and the Clan Boss kept stopping to watch it as he rested on his staff. Lava cascaded down the cone, blanketing the mountain in incandescent rivulets of living rock. Steam billowed up wherever the probing lava fingers touched the snow. Ash swirled about, and dark smoke, and sulfurous fumes. The place was hell on earth—a fitting home for the nether god.

The Clan Boss's map had failed to reveal how arduous the hike actually was. *Perhaps that's because I'm old and out of shape,* he thought, reminding himself to order extra water for the actual event. He gazed up the trail at his brother Tancred. The warrior's face was swarthy and unshaven, yet the filial resemblance was unmistakable. The Clan Boss relied on Tancred to provide the muscle behind the family enterprise.

"How are you holding up, sir?" a Clansman asked, breathing hard as he passed.

"By the strength of the god, I'm fine."

"Good. It's just a little farther now. Right over that rise." The man trudged on.

The Clan Boss was glad he only had to make this journey twice. Today was merely a scouting trip. He wanted to survey the apparatus that had been erected on the mountainside, and also note the hiding places for Tancred's soldiers. Tomorrow was the day that mattered—the spring equinox, when light and darkness hung in perfect balance. Then the hungry Mulciber would receive his virgin brides.

At last the boss reached a place where the ground rose to form a low mound. The lava flowed around it, thick and torpid, its gray skin concealing its red-hot heart. Only a narrow aperture in the lava's flow gave access to the mound. As the Clan Boss went through the gap and topped the rise, a wave of radiant heat struck him like a fist. The far side of the mound plunged into a ravine filled with a blazing stream of lava. The Clan Boss shielded his face and squinted against the intense glare. It was like staring straight at the sun. The air above the ravine shimmered and roiled in the turbulent heat.

Tancred walked over, smiling with the same jocular self-confidence he'd had since he was a boy. "Quite a location you picked here," he quipped as he took his older brother's arm.

"Have your men found places to hide?"

"Right over there," Tancred replied, pointing. "The ground is craggy on the back side of the mound. It's a little farther away than I'd like, but close enough."

"Good. Now lead me—"

A sudden tremor shook the earth. Volcanic thunder rumbled as lava exploded from the summit in a violent display of aggression. For several seconds the mountain shivered and quaked. Only Tancred's support kept the boss from taking a spill. The brothers clung to each other until the fit of rage was spent.

"You were saying?" Tancred asked when the eruption had settled.

The Clan Boss steadied himself with his staff. "I started to say, take me to the crane."

Tancred helped his brother walk to the precipice where the mound dropped into the ravine. Perched at its lip was a wooden contraption erected by a Clan engineer. It consisted of a windlass whose rope ran along a boom and over a pulley. The whole crane was mounted on a swiveling base. A man on the far side of the ravine could tug a cable to swing the boom out over the river of flame.

"I believe you'll find the device to your liking, master," said the obsequious engineer who had constructed the crane. He was a shifty-eyed fellow with ratlike features. The man repulsed the Clan Boss, though he was undoubtedly good at his work.

"I see that you've geared it," the boss remarked.

A smirk lit up the engineer's face. "Yes, my lord. Look here." He bent to the windlass and gave it a few turns. "The gears allow for a gradual descent. Such an immersion will prolong the . . . " Pausing, the engineer searched for the right word. He licked sweat from his upper lip. "Ecstasy," he finished.

"Ecstasy, is it?"

"Oh yes—ecstasy! Death will not come right away. The lava will gradually consume the brides. Their dainty toes . . . their calves . . . their supple thighs . . . "

"Enough!" Revulsion mingled with the Clan Boss's righteous anger. He despised how the perverted engineer was using the holy ceremony to fulfill his twisted needs. The boss turned toward his brother. "Bind him!" he ordered.

Tancred seized the engineer, whose eyes went wide. The man's mouth fell open with a look of bewildered terror. "My lord! What's wrong? Is my device not to your satisfaction?"

"I don't know yet," the Clan Boss replied. "I have to test it first."

✦　✦　✦

The three Exterminati caravels put in at the Sessalayan city of Eastport. Though it wasn't a large settlement, its harbor bustled with a lively energy. Ana was taken straight to a country villa for the night, kept in isolation from the other women. She assumed that was part of her punishment for trying to escape.

The villa was lavish—a stark contrast to the filth of the caravel's bilge. Ana had endured a three-day stint in that dark hole, though she was let out a few times to take food and water. Evidently her captors were walking a fine line between harsh punishment and fatal abuse that would deprive their god of a bride.

The next morning Ana was allowed to wash. The experience was surreal. Ornate fixtures and marble vanities decked out the villa's expensive bathroom. The servants had prepared a hot bath scented with rosewater as if Ana were an honored guest. At no time did anyone accost her while she rinsed the slime from her body. Her cotton chemise, now a filthy rag, was replaced by an ivory-colored gown. All this would have provided a measure of comfort—except Ana had been down this road before.

Strangely, though, she was at peace. Ana knew from the shamans' cruel taunts that something hideous was in the works. There had been much talk of ceremonial nuptials with the local god, a feature common to many pagan religions. Such unions supposedly produced demigods. Ana didn't know what kind of horrific sacrament was being planned for her and the other Christiani women, but she did know what the one true God had impressed on her heart: help was on the way.

She examined herself in the mirror. Her face was thin from her meager diet, but considering all she had been through, she thought she was faring rather well. A basket of cosmetics and hairstyling tools lay on the vanity. The idea of primping for some crude pagan ritual disgusted her. Ana touched the basket with the back of her hand and was about to sweep it aside when a different thought occurred to her.

Do I truly believe Teo is coming?

She paused and considered it. Though she didn't know how, Ana believed Deu would protect her, and she had a strong intuition he would do it through Teo. *And if I were going to see him after all these months—the man I love, the only man whose affections I desire—how would I act?* Ana realized she would dress up for such a momentous reunion. Gazing down at the basket of cosmetics, Ana decided to look her best today, not to please an unclean spirit, but as a symbol of her unwavering faith in Deu's deliverance.

When her beauty regimen was finished, Ana returned to the little bedroom down the hall. The servants watched her at all times, though they kept their eyes down and never spoke. Ana knew the raid on the convent had been carried out by the Exterminati, yet the villa seemed to belong to the Clan. Those two groups were cooperating toward some nefarious purpose that Ana didn't understand.

The rest of the day passed idly. Ana ate some fruit and cheese for an evening meal. The shadows were long, and the travertine walls bore a salmon-colored tint when a Clansman arrived at Ana's room. His foreboding presence stood in marked contrast to the peaceful surroundings.

"Come with me," he said.

Ana followed the man to a courtyard. A wagon was there, hitched to a team of mules. It had wooden sides and a roof. Ana climbed in. As she sat down she realized her heart was beating faster than normal. "Help is on the way," she reminded herself, though her heart continued to race.

The wagon joined others on a narrow road heading north from the countryside villa. Ana couldn't tell if the Christiani sisters were riding in the vehicles, though she assumed they were. The journey continued for what seemed like hours, the road growing ever rougher and steeper. Ana peeked between the wagon's slats and saw she was high on the side of a mountain. Eastport lay in the distance. Beyond it, the sea receded to the horizon.

"Soon," she whispered, scanning the roadside to see if any warriors were waiting to ambush the caravan. But the wagon rolled on undisturbed.

The sky grew dark. Yet something wasn't right. Ana peered through a crack, trying to discern why the light was so strange. A bonfire seemed to be raging nearby, perhaps part of the bizarre ritual planned for the night. Then the wagon rounded a corner, and Ana realized how wrong she was.

The road ahead climbed into a blazing inferno. High on the summit, the mountain belched forth its guts and let the regurgitation ooze down its slopes. The ground seethed with glowing lava, while the sky danced with an eerie orange light. Ana had never seen anything like it. Fear stole into her heart. She swallowed hard and reached out to steady herself.

The wagon stopped, and a Clansman ordered her out. When she stepped onto the road the first thing she noticed was the heat. The air was much warmer than it should have been this time of year. Ana knew things were about to grow even hotter.

A rough hand shoved her toward a trail. Ana began to ascend while looking for a way to escape, but the path dropped off sharply, and the Clan guards were everywhere. Looking back over her shoulder, she saw many other young women being unloaded from the wagons. There was no sign of Vanita in the crowd.

The path switchbacked up the flaming mountain. Soon Ana was sweating in the oppressive heat. The guards didn't let her rest, so she kept trudging upward, her terror increasing with each step. No easy prayers were escaping her lips now.

Without warning, the earth began to convulse as the vent on the summit disgorged its lava with new fury. Ana fell to the ground, the sharp volcanic rocks abrasive against her hands. A sound like thunder rolled down from above. After several more shakes the tremors ceased.

"Get up," snarled a Clansman, yanking her by the elbow. "And don't soil yourself!" He swatted Ana's hip where dirt had smudged her ivory gown.

Ana wrenched her arm from the man's grasp and felt a surge of defiance. "I am not yours to command," she said evenly. Though the guard's expression was belligerent, he said nothing more. Ana turned away and continued up the trail.

The heat began to grow unbearable. Ana longed for a drink to replace the fluids she had lost. Perspiration ran down her cheeks and neck. She put her hand to her chest and wiped sweat from her collarbones. There was nothing she could do about the rivulets that trickled down her belly.

At last the trail arrived at a craggy hillock. The lava approached very close here. Ana stared at it, mesmerized by the sight of rock so hot it would melt. When the lava wasn't part of a fast-moving flow, it assumed a dull gray color. Like steel in a blacksmith's shop, its redness dimmed where it was cooler. Yet a term like *cool* was meaningless in this context. Ana knew there was nothing cool about the thick sludge with the bubbling, steaming skin.

"Keep going, bride," the guard muttered, shoving her along. Ana saw that the lava's flow nearly encircled the hillock. Only one narrow opening led onto the mound ahead. She had no choice but to ascend.

As she crested the rise the heat intensified even more, like an oven door thrown wide open. A river of liquid rock cast a bright glow that illumined the whole area. Perched above the river was a strange construction, the purpose of which Ana couldn't immediately discern.

Then she realized what it was.

Deu! No!

Ana now understood her captors didn't intend some arcane ritual of pagan religion. Not even an orgy of violation and violence was planned, as horrible as that would be. There could be only one purpose for a crane whose boom would swing over the fiery ravine.

So this is how Mulciber's appetite is satisfied!

Ana shivered and closed her eyes, overcome by the horrific scene before her.

The rest of the Christiani women were forced onto the hillock. Some of their faces were unfamiliar, which meant convents besides the one at Lido di Ostia had been raided. Ana estimated their number at more than fifty. The sisters clung to each other in a huddled mass. Many of them whimpered, and some even wailed. If Vanita was there, Ana couldn't see her.

A new group of Clansmen arrived. Their leader was a middle-aged man, balding and potbellied. He leaned on a staff, sweating profusely in the intense heat. After guzzling a drink from a water barrel, he set aside the dipper and raised his staff high. A hush fell on all the watchers. Even the terrified sisters quieted to hear their fate.

"Holy Mulciber, I invoke thy aid tonight," he intoned. "Behold the great gift we bring thee! We have gathered here tonight—"

A deep, authoritative voice interrupted the proceedings. The words echoed with an evil power that could not be denied. "All kneel," the voice urged. Then the Iron Shield stepped from the shadows and made himself manifest.

A horde of shamans dropped to their knees, followed by several of the Clansmen. Many of the sisters did too. The Iron Shield stared hard at the Clan leader, willing him into subjection with his dreadful gaze. For a long moment the man refused to yield. Slowly the Iron Shield raised his arm, extending his palm toward his rival. His hand began to vibrate, and as it did, the Clan leader's resistance broke. His knees buckled, and he knelt with his head bowed.

One by one each of the spectators crouched to the earth. Ana clenched her jaw. *I will die before I bow to him!* Glancing around, she saw one other person had remained standing. The woman wore an elegant gown of green satin. Her hands were on her hips, and she thrust out her chin in defiance. A gust of wind ruffled the woman's short blonde hair. Ana nodded to her, and Vanita Labella nodded back with a look of unshakable resolve.

A low growling caused Ana to look away from her friend. The Iron Shield stared at her with the malevolent expression of a demon from hell. His great height made the warrior seem more like a giant than a man. He stalked over, and Ana tasted fear at his approach, for he brought destruction in his steps. She thought he intended to strike her, yet at the last minute he merely offered his palm in a kind of invitation. An irresistible force compelled Ana to touch the man's outstretched hand. The Iron Shield smiled at this, then seized her wrist and dragged her toward the crane.

A pack of shamans surrounded Ana and bound her hands to the rope that dangled from the crane's boom. One of the shamans grasped the crank to the windlass, but the Iron Shield waved him aside. "This one belongs to me," he declared.

Terrified, Ana watched as her enemy turned the great wheel. The slack in the rope began to tighten. Ana's arms were drawn above her head, then the rope went taut, and her feet rose from the ground. Despair overwhelmed her as she swayed at the end of the boom. She struggled and kicked, but that accomplished nothing.

The Iron Shield gave a sharp whistle. Across the ravine a Clansman signaled that he had heard. He began to haul on a cable. As he drew in the line, the crane's jib began to swivel over the ravine.

A dull roar assailed Ana's ears as the scorching heat engulfed her. She gasped. Such air seemed impossible to breathe. Beneath her feet, the seething river of lava flowed by. It burned with murderous intensity, a viscous orange brew covered with black scabs.

"Anastasia! Look at me!"

The Iron Shield stood on the lip of the ravine, sneering, waving good-bye.

"Beast!" Ana shouted.

The warrior's reply was ominous: "There is no God in heaven. This is your end."

No!

Ana thrashed as the rope began to lower her into Mulciber's gaping maw. Her billowing skirt filled with hot air that seemed to roast her skin. She drew up her legs, desperate to escape the holocaust below. Sweat drenched her body in a losing battle to ward off the relentless heat. The stench of brimstone was all around. Smoke tumbled and swirled, wafting bits of ash in its updrafts. The river of lava glowed like the mouth of a blast furnace. Ana closed her eyes, unable to stand the glare.

Shouts broke out on the hillock, followed by the clash of arms. "Help me!" Ana cried. Her voice was pitiful and weak.

The boom began to swing back toward the edge of the ravine. The torrid heat diminished. Ana spun in circles at the end of the rope.

Her feet touched solid ground.

Strong arms embraced her.

Teo had come.

✦　　✦　　✦

Teo caught Ana as she collapsed into his arms. Her body was hot to the touch and dripping with sweat.

"Ana, I'm here! I have you!"

"Oh, Teo . . ." She clung to him for support.

Across the rocky mound, Marco's pirates and the Knights of the Cross attacked the shamans. The Clan guards appeared to have fled the scene. Teo spotted the Iron Shield doing ferocious battle with two knights at once. His crushing mace split the shield of one man, sending him flying backward. A kick to the chest of the second knight knocked him to the ground. He turned, saw Teo, and smiled.

Teo drew the sword of Armand from its sheath, then his battle-ax. "Hide here," he said to Ana after cutting her loose. She crouched behind the struts of the crane as Teo turned to face his opponent.

The Iron Shield's face glistened. Though he wore a chain-mail hauberk, no helmet was on his head. His long hair was drawn tight against the nape of his neck. A flickering light reflected from his glass eye. "At last my great enemy has come," he said, giving his mace a mighty swing. A long, curved dagger was in his other hand. "It will be a deep pleasure to kill you."

Teo eyed his opponent warily. "You think you have what it takes?"

"I am filled with a legion of spirits!" the Iron Shield roared.

"And I am filled with the spirit of the living God," Teo answered, and the battle commenced.

The mortal enemies fought two-handed, swinging and parrying like men who had everything on the line. The Iron Shield's mace was a fearsome weapon. To be struck by its blunt head lined with sharp flanges would mean certain death, but Teo parried the blows with his war-ax and forced his opponent to dodge the thrusts of his sword. Yet the Iron Shield's dagger was razor-sharp, and his reflexes were superhuman. It was all Teo could do to avoid the deadly blade.

Stepping back, the Iron Shield rose to his full height and panted for breath in the brassy heat. "You fight well, Teofil! I never cease to be impressed. We could have been great allies, you and I."

Teo wiped sweat from his eyes. "I would never join you."

"That is why you must die."

"So you have said—yet here I stand."

Teo's rejoinder infuriated the Iron Shield. He bared his teeth and shrieked as he started forward. The two men leaped into battle again, their combat even more fierce than before. Teo grunted and strained as he fought his opponent, but the dark warrior's ferocity began to force him back. Teo could feel his own attack growing weaker.

"Not . . . long . . . now!" the Iron Shield said through gritted teeth. He pressed his advantage all the harder.

"Arrgh!" Teo's battle-ax was knocked from his grasp by a massive blow from the mace. His left arm went numb. Now that he couldn't parry or counterattack, he had to give ground to his foe. His field of vision narrowed. The rest of the warriors on the hillock disappeared from his awareness; all other sounds were blotted out. Teo focused his full attention on the cat-eyed adversary before him.

The Iron Shield charged fast, raising his mace above his head. He stepped onto a boulder that propelled him high in the air, almost as if he were flying. His mace seemed poised to crash down from heaven itself. Yet bold courage seized Teo as his enemy hurtled toward him. Instead of pulling back, he gripped the sword of Armand in two hands and thrust it up at the oncoming maelstrom of death.

The Iron Shield did not expect it. Pirouetting in midair to avoid the thrust, he twisted in a full revolution. As Teo's blade sliced through empty air, the dark warrior's forearm came whipping out of his spin. His fist crashed into Teo with an impact like a blacksmith's hammer. Teo hit the ground hard, his blade flying from his grasp. His head swam, and the world tilted on end. Though the Iron Shield's mace was knocked from his hand by the tremendous collision, he managed to land on his feet with his dagger still in his grip. Helpless, Teo lay flat on his back, staring up at his enemy.

The warrior drew back his knife. "Now die!" he snarled.

His hand started forward—and then he was gone.

What?

Teo scrambled up.

The Iron Shield staggered backward across the uneven ground, clawing at his throat. A rope was there. A white-clad figure tugged on it.

Ana!

She had looped the rope from the crane around the Iron Shield's neck, crisscrossing it like one of the Exterminati's own garrotes. Now she yanked on the rope in her fierce determination to bring the giant down.

But the Iron Shield was too strong. With a savage pivot he knocked Ana sprawling. Throwing aside the rope, he towered over her with his dagger. She raised her arm in defense.

Teo exploded into a run. He had no weapon but his two hands. At full speed he crashed into the Iron Shield, shoving him as hard as he could. The violent impact lifted the man off his feet. He tumbled across the hillock to the rim of a dark crevasse, then plunged over its edge and disappeared into the steaming earth.

Teo ran to the crack. Though it wasn't lava-filled, the fissure was narrow and steep. If there was a way out of it, the exit wouldn't be anywhere nearby. And no man could climb back up those serrated walls.

Ana stumbled to Teo's side, panting hard. She touched his shoulder. "Teo, look!" He turned.

A party of Clan soldiers had arrived, equipped with crossbows and short swords. Their leader was a tall, swarthy warrior with a square chin. Beside him was the middle-aged man who seemed to be in charge.

"Lay down your arms!" the swarthy man shouted. The crossbowmen fanned out and leveled their weapons. To resist would be suicide. Marco's pirates complied with the order, and the knights begrudgingly followed. Teo's own weapons were already on the ground.

The Clan leader stormed over to one of the shamans. "Where is your master?" he demanded. The shaman looked around and shrugged.

"Tancred, do you see him anywhere?"

"He's gone, brother."

"This is my island," the boss spat, "and we do things my way! I won't have anyone trying to take over!" He stared at the shamans, whose black attire and secretive hoods gave them a mysterious aura. "I ought to have you all hanged," he muttered, though his expression appeared conflicted. He pursed his lips in a frown. "But who knows what that would unleash? Just get out of my sight!"

In a matter of seconds the shamans melted away.

"Tancred, are all the women here?"

The strongman curled two fingers to some of his troops, who held several of the Christiani girls in a tight grip. The men pushed the girls toward the rest of the captives. "A few tried to slip away," Tancred said, "but we rounded 'em all up."

The boss nodded. "Good. Mulciber shall receive his full due." He pointed to Teo and Ana. "Now bring those two to me."

Though Teo tried to resist, four soldiers converged on him with drawn swords and escorted him to the boss. Ana was brought as well. Meanwhile the other Clansmen collected the dropped weapons and put them all in an empty water barrel. Teo watched his own sword and ax get wedged in with the rest.

"So you're the man Antonio hates so much," the Clan Boss said.

"That's not even his real name."

"I assumed as much, but no matter. He's gone now, and you belong to me."

"What do you want with us?" Teo asked defiantly.

The Clan Boss leaned on his staff. He seemed to be sweating more than everyone else, if such were possible. "Certainly not the same thing as Antonio," he said. "He wanted to kill you, so he left a trail for you to follow. Lots of hints and secret messages. He knew you'd come. And sure enough you did—all for this pretty little thing." The boss gripped Ana's chin in his hand and examined her face before releasing her abruptly. It angered Teo, but he held himself still.

"Why are you in league with those shamans?" Ana asked.

"Ha! I have no choice in the matter, little one. That decision was made long ago in the presence of gods more powerful than you could ever imagine." The Clan Boss waved his hands. "But enough of this! There are some things I wish to know from you before we proceed with the wedding."

When the Clan Boss snapped his fingers, Tancred and his men sprang into action. Some of them forced a Sessalayan slave girl to stand with the Christiani sisters. Other soldiers held Teo's arms behind his back.

"Teo?" Ana whispered. "What's happening?" Her eyes were wide as she watched him be led away.

He knew Ana was seeking encouragement from him, so he gave her a confident nod, though inside he was afraid. His enemies owned every advantage, and he didn't see any way out. He glanced toward his men under guard. Marco stood at the front of them, and Teo met his gaze. Though no words were exchanged, their eyes communicated the message: *Be ready.*

The Clansmen lashed Teo's wrists to the base of the crane. It was a strange thing to do, but at least it meant they didn't plan to swing him over the lava. Even the heat at the lip of the ravine was overpowering.

A hush fell on the hillock. Every eye held on the Clan Boss. He began to walk to the place where the lava parted to give access to the mound. As he reached the steaming gray sludge, he turned and looked at the crane. Smiling, he dipped the end of his staff into the molten rock, revealing its red-hot heart.

"*No!*" Ana screamed, thrashing in her captor's grip. The man cuffed her. She fell silent, though her face bore a look of sheer horror.

Teo clenched his jaw. Now he understood.

The Clan Boss's staff blazed into a bright flame where it touched the lava. He lifted out a clump of the glowing orange goo, which bubbled and dribbled from the end of his staff. As he returned to the crane, little blobs fell to the ground, but most of the lava congealed into a black mass on the staff's tip.

Teo peered over his shoulder as the Clan Boss approached. His heart raced wildly, and his breath came in gulping pants. He steeled himself for what was coming.

"Now then," the Clan Boss said, "we have some vital matters to discuss."

"Perhaps there is an arrangement we could negotiate," Teo said.

"This is not a negotiation. I will ask the questions. You will give the answers."

"If I can," Teo said. His knees felt weak. *Deu, help me endure!*

"Teofil of Chiveis," the Clan Boss shouted, "what are the ingredients of the explosive powder?"

The powder! I can't put Astrebril's fire in the hands of the Clan! They'll murder countless people with it!

Teo shook his head; and so the pain began.

For the briefest moment it felt like nothing more than being touched with a piece of ice. Then, like a volcanic eruption, agony exploded in the center of Teo's back. The torment was beyond his worst imagination. It was the sort of burning pain from which one normally recoils with a cry of distress—except in this case the contact remained, so the pain multiplied with every passing second. Teo threw back his head and howled as the Clan Boss ground the superhot mass of fiery stone into his back. It burned through his jerkin and shirt to sear his flesh. Teo had never felt anything so terrible.

At last the Clan Boss retracted his staff. Teo struggled to remain upright as the pain pulsed from the fresh burn. He inhaled and exhaled in quick bursts, trying to cope with his suffering.

"It seems you are somewhat resolute," the Clan Boss said. "Your courage is admirable. Yet I doubt it is unbreakable." He turned to his henchmen. "Take him down."

Teo's wrists were untied, and he was forced to lay prone on the ground. A soldier put the tip of a sword against the back of his neck. By turning his head just a little, Teo could see the Clan Boss return to the lava with his staff.

No! Not again!

He grimaced and squeezed his eyes shut. *Please, Deu! Not again!*

"Hold still," the soldier said, pressing the point of his blade firmly against Teo's neck.

He heard a commotion as he waited, then footsteps approached. The Clan Boss uttered an evil laugh. Teo gritted his teeth.

"I have thought of a way to increase your pain, Teofil," said the boss.

There was a long pause—then something happened that Teo would never forget.

Ana's agonized scream shattered the unholy stillness on Fire Mountain.

◆ ◆ ◆

It hurt so much.

Ana stood with her hands tied to the crane, weeping at the pain in her back. It burrowed into every fiber of her body and wouldn't relent. "Ahhh," she moaned, unable to remain silent in the face of such affliction.

"Do it again," Tancred said. "Make her hurt."

Ana wriggled in her bonds. "Teo, help me! Don't let them!"

But the boss came near with his stick. "Maybe a little longer this time?" he suggested.

"Deu!" Ana screamed at the top of her lungs. "Stop them!"

And he did.

The earth heaved underfoot, throwing everyone off balance. Ana would have tumbled to the ground except for her bonds. High above, a thunderous boom shattered the sky. The vent that had been spewing lava all night now sent up a gigantic plume that reached for the stars. Chunks of molten rock rooster-tailed from the summit, swathing the mountain's head in a corona of flame. The tremors intensified as ash and pebbles rained down on the terrified spectators. Everyone cowered beneath the assault. Some of the soldiers fled. The mighty conflagration no longer inspired awe; it foretold judgment.

Ana saw Teo leap to his feet. He was at his best in moments like this, as if he were carrying out a prearranged plan instead of improvising on the run. He dashed to the barrel that held the collected armaments and kicked it over. Before any of the Clansmen could react, Teo had pitched weapons to a dozen of his men. Others snatched them from the quaking ground.

But the soldiers didn't hesitate forever. Tancred was a warrior who knew how to fight. "Engage!" he shouted. "Cut off their escape!" The clash of arms rang out across the mountainside.

The thongs on Ana's wrists weren't well tied, so she pulled them loose with her teeth. Though the throbbing pain in her back was relentless, her urge to survive was even stronger. Ana crouched down next to the crane and glanced around. On the far side of the mound, Vanita was leading the women toward the opening in the lava's flow. Meanwhile, Marco had gotten some of his men with their shortbows behind a jumble of rocks.

Ana could see right away that if the women could get through the narrow opening, the archers could hold the gap and prevent any enemies from following.

Tancred, his face livid, saw it too. "Crossbows! Crossbows! The brides must not escape! Dead or alive, men! Take them down!"

"Teo!" Ana screamed. His head swung around, and she pointed desperately at Tancred's soldiers as they cranked their weapons. "Stop them!"

Teo reacted swiftly. He ran to a barrel of drinking water and slammed the lid on it, pounding it down with his fist. Then he tipped the barrel on its side and shoved it with his foot. It careened down the slope toward the bowmen, whose focus on their quarry prevented them from seeing the approaching danger. The barrel smashed into them from the side, toppling them like dominos. After hitting a bump, the barrel caught air as it went over a drop-off. It landed in the lava and exploded in a hissing cloud of steam. The vapor billowed across the women's escape route, blocking them from view. A few crossbow bolts chased them through the mist, but the shots were random.

With the women gone, the knights who were fighting hand to hand with the Clansmen began to retreat. Ana realized she needed to move too or she'd be left behind. Though every motion was like a knife stab in the back, she set her jaw and started to go. Then a cruel hand wrenched her arm.

"Where do you think you're headed?" said a menacing voice.

The Clan Boss began to shove Ana toward the lip of the ravine. Though he was middle-aged and overweight, his sheer bulk gave him the advantage. Ana struggled but was inexorably pushed back. The heat from the river of lava grasped at her like voracious hands trying to pull her down. She wrestled with her opponent but couldn't prevent him from pushing her to the brink of death. One more step backward would send her plunging into the deadly orange flow.

"Tell me the formula," the Clan Boss demanded, "or I'll throw you in!"

"Let go of me!"

The boss gripped Ana's dress in his fist and shook her hard. A chunk of rock broke away beneath her foot. She arched backward, her hair dangling over the flaming abyss. The shimmering air distorted her enemy's sweat-drenched face. His lip curled up, and his teeth were bared.

"Tell . . . me . . . that . . . formula!" he snarled.

"I'll never tell you anything! Never!"

"Then you belong to Mulciber!" the Clan Boss screamed.

Suddenly the man's head tumbled from his shoulders in a fine red mist. He released his savage grip. His decapitated body collapsed to the ground, and Teo stepped into his place with the sword of Armand in his hand. He caught Ana around the waist and drew her close. His gaze met hers.

"You belong to Deu," he declared.

Grabbing Ana's hand, he turned toward the narrow exit from the mound. Battle was raging there as the knights retreated into the shadows. Several of the Clansmen who weren't part of that fight turned and saw Teo and Ana standing by the crane. They began to advance with their swords drawn.

Teo snatched the rope that dangled from the end of the boom. "Hold this," he said, then bent to the crane's base and heaved it around. The effort was intense, and his face showed it. Ana couldn't look at the raw red wound in the center of his back.

When the boom was out over the lava, Teo stood up and took the end of the rope from her. He cupped her cheek in his hand. "Can you trust me one more time?"

Ana flung her arms around Teo in the tightest embrace she could manage. "I trust you completely," she said. Then she was lifted from the ground.

The ovenlike heat engulfed her again. Ana screamed as she swung over the inferno, clinging to Teo with her arms and legs. Red-hot death flowed beneath her, but only for a moment, and then it was gone. Teo let go of the rope and landed on the far side of the ravine. He released Ana from his grasp and drew his battle-ax in the same motion.

The man who had been given the job of pulling the cable on the crane charged at Teo with a thick quarterstaff, but before he could close the distance Teo sent him reeling. The Chiveisian battle-ax had a secret weapon in its haft. Made by the clever metalsmith Shaphan, the ax could dislodge steel balls into a cup at its tip by pressing a button. When the ax was flicked with a strong whip of the arm, it would send the balls flying. Teo's practiced hand put the missile on the point of the Clansman's chin. The man's head whipped back, and he dropped to the ground, moaning and clutching his jaw.

Ana felt something whiz past her. She glanced up to the far side of the ravine, which was slightly higher than her current position. Men were standing by the crane with their crossbows aimed at the fugitives. Bolts ricocheted from the volcanic rock at Ana's feet.

"Teo!" she shouted. "Up there!"

He saw the danger, then beckoned her with his hand. She ran to him. Side by side they dashed to the horse of the man with the broken jaw. Teo swung into the saddle and helped Ana up behind him. Though she clasped him around the chest and was pressed against his injured back, he didn't flinch. Dark fumes swirled across the mountainside. Angry shouts and hissing bolts filled the air as Teo and Ana disappeared into the night on the back of a single horse.

10

Stratetix and Helena made their way up the trail from the ferryboat on the river. The headquarters and barracks of the Fifth Regiment sat on a low hill called the Belpberg. The name was ancient, predating the founding of Chiveis, though the buildings of those days had long since disappeared. Today the Royal Guard used the forested prominence to guard the Farm River and spy out the surrounding land. The view of Chiveis's snowcapped peaks was magnificent on a clear day.

As the married couple walked uphill, Helena admired the way her husband moved so effortlessly despite being encumbered by a bolt of thick woolen cloth. It was early spring, which meant no grain or vegetables were available for sale to the guardsmen. However, the dark winter months were perfect for spinning and weaving at home, so Helena had some excellent fabric to offer. That was the genius of the Chiveisi. Though the kingdom's natural resources were few, its clever and industrious citizens excelled at processing raw materials into something worth having.

"Hail, farmer!" the quartermaster called as the couple passed. The man knew Stratetix by name, but *farmer* was his friendly term for all the villagers of Edgeton, whether they tilled the soil or not. Stratetix returned the favor by calling the quartermaster *soldier*, though his slim build suggested he might not fare too well in an actual fight.

"Cloth to sell today," Helena said, pointing to Stratetix's bundle. "There must be some men who could use new blankets."

"Aye. The boys will be happy to see you. Set up on the bench outside the barracks and you'll be sold out in an hour."

True to the quartermaster's prediction, Stratetix and Helena had no problem disposing of the cloth in measured lengths. The soldiers crowded around, eager to purchase something better than the standard-issue blankets supplied by the army. The nights atop the Belpberg were cold.

One young corporal with a smooth face wrapped his piece of cloth around his shoulders. "By Astrebril's beard, that feels good! Wish I'd had it back in the dead of winter."

"Astrebril might not have wanted you to have it," Stratetix suggested.

Helena glanced up from her scissors. Her heartbeat quickened. *Here we go. Easy now.*

The baby-faced corporal looked surprised. "I ain't done nothing to offend him," he said.

"Who?" Stratetix asked mildly.

"Astrebril. What have I done to make a god take notice of a man and his blanket?"

Stratetix held up his palms in a soothing gesture. "Nothing, I'm sure. No doubt you keep all the rules required of you."

"What did you mean then?" demanded another soldier. He had a thin mustache on his upper lip, and his expression was sour. "Why wouldn't Astrebril want him to have a blanket?"

"Oh, you know . . . " Stratetix smiled and waved his hand around. "Rules, rules, rules. That's how it is with the gods. Always the rules."

"For our own good," said Mustache-Lip.

"Or the priests' pockets," a third man chimed in. He scoffed as he spoke.

"The temple coffers certainly are overflowing these days," Stratetix observed.

"How do you know?"

"They have to be, with all the taxes we're paying. The gods are said to dwell in golden halls, but they sure seem to like the steel coins of us men."

"That's for sure," said the third man. "And you're right about the rules. I'm sick of it all."

The soldier with the thin mustache spun toward his comrade. "Sick of it all? You better watch what you say or the fire of heaven will get you."

"And that's another thing! What kind of god smashes the homes of harmless peasants?"

"A cruel one," Helena put in. She couldn't help herself.

All three soldiers turned and looked at her.

Helena offered an innocent smile, trying to charm the lads with sweetness. "What did I say?"

"You said Astrebril is cruel," Mustache-Lip accused.

"If a man did such things, we'd call it cruel, wouldn't we?"

"Astrebril is not a man! He can do whatever he wants!"

"That doesn't make it right."

Stratetix laid his hand on his wife's arm. "Look, men, we're not here to offend anyone. It's obvious things are different now than in the old days. We're just making an observation about facts anyone can see."

"I agree with this guy," said the smooth-cheeked corporal to his friends. "The laws of Chiveis are piling on too thick. I didn't become a third-generation soldier to enforce a bunch of religious rules. My old man says it's ridiculous. We're supposed to be a free kingdom, but life under Astrebril is turning into . . . "

He faltered, unsure he wanted to go further. Mustache-Lip gave him the evil eye. "Go on," he egged. "What were you going to say?"

Tyranny, Helena thought.

"Tyranny," Stratetix said.

Helena sucked in her breath.

Everyone turned to look at Stratetix, but he didn't back down. "Admit it. He's a god of tyranny. There, I said it."

"It's true," agreed the third man. "The heavy taxes. The religious laws. The bowing and scraping before the priests. Chiveis didn't used to be like that."

"No, it didn't." Helena paused, then decided to follow her husband's lead. "In the days of Armand things were different. Back then Chiveis stood for something noble and good."

The man with the mustache jabbed his finger toward her. "What does a farmer's wench know about war heroes?"

"More than you do," Helena shot back.

The reply infuriated the cocky guardsman. "Don't you lecture me about the old days, lady! I know what Armand would think. He would support the current regime."

Helena tried to calm her emotions, but they were running hot. "No, he wouldn't!" she insisted.

"You shut up! I'm a soldier of the Fifth Regiment. Armand of Edgeton was the commander of my unit!"

Rising from her seat, Helena met the guardsman's gaze. "Armand of Edgeton was my father," she declared, "and I say he would never have sided with cruelty and oppression."

The other soldiers' eyes widened at this announcement, but Mustache-Lip didn't want to lose face. He waved his finger under Helena's nose. "Armand would not have blasphemed Astrebril!"

Helena swatted the man's hand away. "Armand would have served Deu!"

An awkward silence descended on the group. Helena felt her face redden. The guardsmen stared at her with slack-jawed expressions. Several other men standing around the barracks craned their necks to see what was going on. Some of them were whispering.

Stratetix stood up and defused the situation. "Gentlemen, it seems our business here is concluded." He gathered his things and nodded politely before escorting Helena away. She turned her back and did not speak as they left the regimental headquarters.

Back at the dock on the Farm River, Stratetix and Helena waited for the ferryboat to arrive. Neither of them felt like talking; they needed time to process what had just occurred.

Someone coughed nearby. Helena turned. An old man gazed over the water, his eyes bloodshot, his face unnaturally pale. Though he looked as if he was once physically fit, the wasting disease now had a grip on him. His short haircut and scarred cheek suggested a military background.

The man noticed Helena looking at him. "I knew your father," he said.

Helena glanced around. No one else was at the waterfront, so she stepped closer. Stratetix followed.

"You served in the Fifth?" Helena asked.

"I was your father's camp doctor." The man touched his cheek. "Got this scar at the Battle of Toon."

"That means you were there when he died."

The old-timer nodded. "Yeah, and I know some secrets about that." Before he could speak further, he broke into a violent coughing fit that seemed it would never end. At last the hacking ceased, and the man composed himself. "Curse this consumption," he muttered, dabbing his bloody lips with a handkerchief. "But old men can't live forever, right? And they shouldn't keep secrets all the way to the grave."

"Will you tell us your secrets?"

"I will, but I'll have to speak of some things you may not wish to recall." The army physician glanced first at Helena, then at her husband.

"You can speak freely," Stratetix said. "My wife and I have no secrets between us."

"Alright then. My story begins with a young man named Hanson. Cocky young fella, but what a warrior! He could beat any man in the Guard in hand-to-hand combat. Everyone in the Second Regiment adored him."

Stratetix shifted his feet. Helena nodded without speaking.

"As you know, he started courtin' you." The old-timer looked at Helena. "You must've been what—eighteen?"

"Seventeen."

"Right. Too young, whatever it was. But this guy Hanson thought he could win the heart of the Warlord's daughter."

"He didn't," Helena said flatly.

"We all knew that. But when your father punished him so severely, the men of the Second took it hard. They had pinned their hopes on Hanson. There were public complaints, even some riots. But truth be told, things were much worse than that."

"How so?"

The old-timer glanced around the dock, then beckoned the couple closer. "Nobody knows this, but there was an outright rebellion. I'm talking about sedition—a planned coup. Hanson had connections to an aristocrat with royal blood that he wanted to install on the throne."

"By overthrowing King Piair?" Stratetix's face was incredulous.

"No, by *killing* him. The outsiders' invasion at the Battle of Toon wasn't a complete coincidence. The top brass in the Second Regiment set it up. They let the enemy get close to the king, then drew back."

"That's despicable!" Helena exclaimed.

The old-timer coughed up a wad of bloody mucus and spat it into the river. "I know. Only the heroism of your father kept the king alive. That sword of his saved Chiveis. But then the mighty Armand took an arrow. Some say it came from our own ranks."

Helena closed her eyes and covered her mouth, shaking her head at such a senseless waste of a great man's life. "What happened next?" she whispered.

"Your father died, and the conspirators were tried before a secret tribunal. Every one of them was executed for treason at the king's command."

"How do you know all this?"

"I testified at the trial. Then the whole thing was hushed up. I was sworn to absolute silence on pain of death." The old-timer smiled ruefully. "But why should I fear death now?"

In the distance the ferryboat came into view. The old-timer began to edge away.

"Wait!" Helena said. "Why did you tell us these things?"

Unexpectedly the grizzled army veteran hurried back and knelt before Helena on the dock. "For the memory of Armand, my lady," he murmured with his head bowed. "The men of the Fifth love your father. And someday they'll find their courage again."

✦   ✦   ✦

Teo's back hurt like hell. The god of the fiery underworld had reached up and branded him with a grievous wound. The only thing worse than the knife-edged pain between his shoulder blades was knowing that Ana suffered too. He rode into the dark night with the woman he loved clinging to him from behind. She didn't speak, though sometimes she moaned softly as the horse plodded across the barren mountain slopes. Teo regretted that he hadn't been able to prevent Ana's burn.

But it was shelter, not pain relief, that concerned Teo most at the moment. Away from the volcanic lava, the warmth had been replaced by the high-elevation chill of a spring night. This was no place to be caught in the open, sweat-soaked and without a cloak. He and Ana had been riding for an hour to establish some distance from their enemies, but now she was reaching her limits, and Teo could feel exhaustion sapping his strength as well.

The tired horse meandered off the mountain toward lower ground. Teo let the animal have its head, and it soon found its way to water. The terrain dropped into a vale carved by a tumbling stream. After following a game trail down to the water's edge, Teo dismounted, then helped Ana from the saddle.

"How are you feeling?" he asked.

"It hurts."

"Let me look at it."

Teo made Ana sit on the ground beside the stream. Striking a match from the saddlebag, he inspected the wound on her back. She flinched as his fingers gently pulled back the seared fabric of her dress. The actual burn was the size of a large coin, though the skin all around it was red and inflamed. Most of the lava had dripped off the Clan Boss's staff while he walked, so the injury wasn't much wider than the staff's tip. Yet the superheated rock had made a deep burn where it contacted Ana's flesh. Teo winced as he looked at it. He knew from his own wound how much pain she was in.

"I don't know if I can go any farther," Ana said.

"We have to find someplace to get out of the elements and make a fire."

She nodded wearily. "Okay. Let me just get a drink first. I'm so thirsty."

Ana started to move toward the stream, but Teo stopped her. "Stay still. I'll get it for you." He turned and scooped up the ice-cold water. Ana bent her head to sip from his cupped hands. After she had enough to drink, he used a piece of wet moss to cool her burn. It seemed to soothe her. Teo helped her lay back in the grass, then stood up.

"You rest here while I look for a place to camp," he said. "The vale narrows into a canyon ahead. There might be a cave or something."

"Oh, Teo, don't leave me alone."

"I don't want to, but we need shelter. Just relax for a little bit. I'll come right back."

"No . . . please . . . I'm scared."

Teo was torn. Ana was in no shape to go exploring, yet they had to find refuge immediately. He scanned the area, hoping to spot a nook or overhang that would provide a dry place to make a fire. Nothing presented itself.

Kneeling next to Ana, he took her hand and bent to kiss her forehead. "I'll only be gone a moment. Deu will watch over you."

Ana relented with a nod. "I know," she acknowledged, then clutched Teo's sleeve. "But even so, hurry back."

Teo stood up. A breeze had begun to waft down the vale. He glanced at the sky. Clouds were rolling in, scudding across the moon. It was going to be a cold, rainy night. "Just what we need," Teo muttered.

That was when the dogs started barking—not little yappers, but big creatures with deep-throated barks. Ana's head swung around. "Oh! Are those wolves?"

"No, wolves don't bark like that. They sound more like some kind of mastiff."

"Way out here in the wilderness?"

Teo drew his sword. "Apparently we're not alone. Someone lives nearby with guard dogs. I'm going to check it out."

"Be careful, Teo."

He nodded and moved downstream. Moonlight gleamed on the water. The walls of the vale steepened on either side. As Teo caught the sound of the barking dogs, he realized he had gone past them. Somehow he had missed the place they were guarding. Doubling back, he peered through the dense vegetation but couldn't see any sign of human habitation.

A sharp female voice startled him. "Who are you and what do you want? Speak quickly, or I'll let Scylla and Charybdis do the talking!" The rumble in the dogs' throats added an ominous punctuation to the woman's words.

"I mean no harm," Teo said. "I seek shelter."

The woman stepped from the shadows, holding her two massive dogs on chains. Though the light was dim, Teo could see she was a tall, willowy woman whose dark hair draped over her shoulders in thick ringlets. She appeared to be young, perhaps around Ana's age. Her black dogs were powerfully muscled, with cropped ears and tails. "These are Cane Corsos," the woman said, "and they don't like strangers who approach by night."

"I'm sorry to give you a scare." Teo sheathed his sword. "I'm wounded and need a place to stay."

"You look fine. What's wrong?"

"A deep burn to my back. I'm in a lot of pain, and so is"—Teo hesitated, then decided to take a risk—"the woman I'm with. Can you help us?"

The mention of a female companion changed the dynamic. "Is it just the two of you?"

"Yes."

"My name is Jané." The woman indicated a faint trail that appeared to lead nowhere. "My cottage is up there. Bring your friend, and let's see what can be done."

Teo hurried back to Ana and helped her into the saddle, then led the horse toward Jané's home. The cottage was nestled against a cliff in a dense copse of trees. Only by turning onto the trail did it come into view.

"I'm not sure we can trust her," Teo warned as they approached.

"We can," Ana replied, pointing to a row of herbs drying on a string. "Those are the plants of a healer."

"She's expecting you, so just knock on the door. I have to see to the horse first."

After caring for his mount in the stable, Teo returned to the cottage. He found its interior warm and welcoming. A stone hearth bristled with kettles, roasting spits, and cast-iron pots. Two pallets had been laid in front of the fireplace. Ana sat on a low stool, smiling and chatting with Jané. A steaming mug was in her hand.

"Come on in," Jané said, filling a mug for Teo. "I've brewed up a strong tea from poppy pods. You'll want a little honey with it to cut the bitterness, but it will deaden your pain in no time."

Jané set aside Ana's empty mug and took up a position behind her. Frowning, the healer began to investigate her wound. After dabbing a poultice on a bandage she reached for the buttons of Ana's gown, then caught Teo's eye.

"Unless she's your lover, this is the moment when you should look away," she said.

"Oh, right! Of course." Teo felt his face redden. He suddenly found the logs in the fireplace altogether fascinating.

"To tell the truth, Teofil is the love of my life," Ana announced with a hint of mischief in her voice. Teo stole a sideways glance in her direction. Ana's gown hung loose over her shoulders, though Jané hadn't taken it all the way down yet. Ana gave Teo a playful stare and pointed her finger at him. "But you should still look away, Captain."

"I will for now—but not forever," Teo teased in return. Ana said nothing at first, then her eyes widened and her mouth popped open. Laughing to himself, Teo returned his gaze to the fire and propped his feet on the hearth. *She's going to be okay*, he realized. Relief washed over him as he settled into the plush chair.

Once Ana was bandaged, Jané turned her attention to Teo. The horrible-tasting tea had decreased his pain dramatically. Teo held still as the healer's capable fingers probed his wound. "Yours is even worse," she remarked. "The Clan?"

Teo peeked over his shoulder and gave Jané a nod. "How did you know?"

"Two identical wounds. Obviously the torture of evildoers. What did you do to offend them?"

"It's a long story, but the heart of the matter is, we're worshipers of the one true God."

"As am I," Jané said.

Ana sat up on her pallet. "Really? You know him?"

"Not his name, but I believe in a bountiful God who created our world."

"His name is Deus," Ana said, using the local term. Though she had been speaking Chiveisian with Teo, they had switched to Talyano upon entering the cottage.

"Deus," Jané said thoughtfully. "It's a good name. You shall have to tell me more of him."

Ana started to speak but Jané held up her hand, palm out. "Not tonight, Anastasia. Soon you'll be sleepy from that tea, and you need your rest. We can talk of divine things later."

Ana nodded and sank back to her pallet. When Jané finished bandaging Teo's wound, she made him lie down on an adjacent mat. The woolen blankets were thick and soft. Jané banked the fire, then bid Teo and Ana good night and retired to the back room.

Teo could feel the somniferous effects of the tea setting in. The fire's orange glow had dimmed, through a few flickering shadows still danced on the ceiling. Ana breathed steadily beside him. Teo glanced over and was surprised to see she wasn't asleep. She pursed her pink lips, smiling tenderly at him. Moving a little closer, she reached for his hand beneath the quilts.

"You came," she whispered.

"I did, though you didn't make it very easy."

"And you didn't come very quickly!" Ana shot back with a laugh.

"I tried, but you were always out of reach."

Ana closed her eyes and exhaled a deep breath. "Well, you have me now, Teo." Her fingers interlaced with his. "I always knew you'd come."

"Listen to this. You're never going to believe where I came *from*."

Opening one eye, Ana gave Teo a curious glance. "Marsay?"

"Farther."

"That other kingdom upstream?"

"Yes, Jineve. But I went even farther than that."

"I don't know what's beyond Jineve."

Teo sat up on one elbow and leaned over Ana. She gazed back at him with a surprised expression.

"You do know," he said.

Ana shook her head, amused.

"Chiveis."

The cottage held absolutely still. Ana's mouth was a tiny circle. Her eyebrows arched, and her eyes grew wide. She seemed unable to speak. A log popped in the fireplace, sending up sparks.

Teo grinned. "It's true. I found a new way to Chiveis. I even saw your parents."

The statement snapped Ana out of her stunned silence. "You went to *Chiveis?*"

"Shh, you'll wake Jané."

Ana ignored the warning. "Teo, I can't believe it! Chiveis! How are Father and Mother?" Moisture glistened in the corners of her eyes, and a tremor was in her voice.

"They're still living in Edgeton. They've been grief-stricken these past . . . what? Almost two years now."

"What did you tell them about me?"

"That you're alive and that one day—"

Teo paused. Ana stared at him as she reclined, waiting for him to speak.

"—we'll return," he finished.

At those words Ana burst into tears.

Teo lay back on his pallet, though he didn't let go of Ana's hand. He briefly considered saying something but decided to hold his tongue. Although crying wasn't the response he had anticipated when he imagined this moment, he understood Ana's tears represented powerful emotions welling up from her soul.

At last Ana collected herself. She looked over at Teo with a radiant smile that told him the crying was joyful.

"Thank you for all you've given me, Teofil," she said.

He shrugged. "I haven't given you that much."

Ana pulled Teo's hand close and kissed it with tear-moistened lips. "That's not true. You came to me in the Beyond, and on Hahnerat, and now on Fire Mountain. You've given me life itself."

Teo marveled at the intensity of Ana's love. He could feel its warmth erupting from her, offering healing instead of harm. A lump gathered in his throat as he lay beside the beautiful Chiveisian farm girl who had so completely captured his heart. *I want to take her home with me*, he thought. *That's the only thing I still need to do to make her truly happy.*

Teo smiled as another idea occurred to him.

Okay, maybe there's one more thing.

◆　◆　◆

The crevice was hot and narrow and deep. It wound through Fire Mountain for more than a league, but eventually the Iron Shield emerged from it like a night creature crawling from its den. His hands were abraded by the sharp volcanic rock, though his body had taken no serious harm thanks to the chain-mail hauberk he always wore. He arched his back and swore. Teofil of Chiveis had escaped him again.

The dark warrior made the long trek back to the hillock where the sacrifice had been planned. No one was there now. Several dead bodies lay on the ground, most of them Clansmen, though a few were Christiani. If any shamans had died, their brethren would have retrieved their corpses to ensure proper cremation according to the rites of the Exterminati.

Stalking to the lip of the ravine, the Iron Shield peered into the raging lava. He didn't expect to see anything, and indeed he did not, for the molten rock consumed anything it touched. He glanced at the crane. The jib hung over the ravine, its rope dangling. The Iron Shield doubted it had been used for sacrifice. Mulciber hungered on.

A dark mass on the other side of the crane caught the Iron Shield's eye. He walked over and saw it was the Clan Boss's decapitated corpse. The Iron Shield recognized the clean sword stroke as the work of a powerful warrior. *Teofil!* He put the toe of his boot under the boss's body and tumbled it into the lava. A bright flame blazed up, then the infernal fires of Sessalay swallowed the crime lord's mortal remains.

Since nothing more could be accomplished at the hillock, the Iron Shield tightened the laces of his boots and prepared to leave. He might have a long walk before he could steal a horse and head for the mines. Thirsty, he licked his cracked lips. Though the water barrel was missing, one of the dead Clansmen carried a flask. The Iron Shield took a long swig of the liquor, then wiped his mouth with the back of his hand and tucked the flask in his belt.

As the warrior began to march across the barren slopes under a ghostly gibbous moon, his mind turned to the frustrating dilemma that faced him. He had devised an ingenious plan that would bring together his mistress's two goals. The High Priestess wanted Teofil and Anastasia dead, and she also wanted brimstone. The Iron Shield's deal with the Clan Boss should have accomplished both purposes, but now one of them was thwarted. Teofil and his woman had disappeared with no way to pick up their trail. To find them again would be time-consuming, if not impossible.

Impossible? The legion of voices in the Iron Shield's head rebuked his unworthy thought. *Nothing is impossible for us! Though a mere man could not find Teofil, the god of this world can do all things!*

"I do not have time to chase my enemy across land and sea," the Iron Shield argued. "You know what my mistress desires most. She is Astrebril's queen and must not be denied."

Yessss, hissed the spirits, *but the Morning Star might grant both your prayers.*

The Iron Shield knelt. "What do you want from me? You already have my soul."

Worrrrship us . . .

"I exalt you, gods of the bottomless pit."

Give us a pledge . . .

"Tell me what to give and I shall."

Lavish upon us what you dearly love . . .

The Iron Shield rose and walked to a steaming vent. Sulfurous fumes belched from it, irritating his lungs. He gazed down into the crack, a portal to the subterranean world.

"Behold!" he cried. "I offer to Astrebril a token of my bondage and obedience. Hear now my request. Bring me safely to my mistress with the brimstone of Sessalay, and give me the chance to slay the man of Chiveis!"

Hot smoke wafted from the hole in the ground. The dark warrior curled his finger behind his glass eye and plucked it out. Sweat stung the empty socket, now formless and void. He held out his hand. "With this votive I bind thee to my desire, Astrebril of the Dawn!"

The Iron Shield dropped the lump of glass into the foul mouth of the abyss.

◆ ◆ ◆

A golden droplet of honey dangled from Ana's slice of bread. She tipped back her head and caught it on her tongue before it could fall. Anything that tasted as good as Jané's honey shouldn't be wasted.

"Isn't that your fourth piece?" Teo asked as he reclined on the riverbank. The day was cool but pleasantly warm in the sunshine.

"My fifth," Ana replied as she licked the stickiness from her fingers. Teo's only response was a chuckle and a shake of his head.

The pair had devoured a fine picnic lunch of smoked fish, dried fruit, and coarse brown bread. A wineskin of sweet marsala had added a welcome finish to the convivial meal. Jané's hospitality seemed to know no limits. Her cottage had become a haven for Teo and Ana over the past two weeks.

Ana eased back into the grass next to Teo and sighed. "Now I'm officially stuffed."

"Good. Keep it up. Your ordeal took a lot out of you."

The sun felt good on Ana's face as she relaxed by the stream. Blades of new grass tickled her bare feet. She smoothed her homespun tunic, then glanced over at Teo, whose shirt and trousers were made of a similar fabric. "We look like a couple of Sessalayan peasants," she said.

"Yeah. Laundry service is yet another comfort provided by our generous hostess. As if food and shelter weren't enough already."

"We have to find a way to thank her."

Teo shrugged. "You heard what she said. Her needs are more than met by her other patients. The best way to thank her is to tell her more about Deu and Iesus."

"That I am happy to do."

"Me too. I just wish we could get her a copy of the Sacred Writing."

Ana nodded but said no more. The heavy meal and fortified wine had brought on a comfortable drowsiness. Though the burn on her back still hurt from time to time, it was healing well. Pleasant moments like this almost made her forget it ever happened.

At last Ana dozed with her ankles crossed and her hands clasped across her stomach. Periodically she awoke, but each time, she noticed Teo's reassuring presence next to her and slipped back into her catnap.

The sun had lowered to a midafternoon angle when Ana finally roused from her sleep. Teo was awake too, chewing on a stem of grass as he watched the clouds drift by.

"I think this is what they refer to around here as the sweet life," Ana said.

"'A desire accomplished is sweet to the soul.'"

Ana glanced at Teo. "The Maxims?"

"Uh-huh. Chapter 13, I think."

"What does it mean?"

"The sweetest thing in life is to attain your heart's desire."

Ana rolled over next to Teo, resting on her elbows. His dark hair was thick and messy from lack of a barber, though he had a razor at the cottage, so his chin was shaven. Ana looked into Teo's gray eyes. "What's your heart's desire, Captain?" Though her tone was playful, the question was actually quite serious.

"The same as yours, I guess."

"That's not much of an answer."

"I know, but men don't talk about their feelings."

Ana tsked at Teo's excuse and pressed on. "You know how much I want to return to Chiveis. Are you saying you want that too?"

"Yes," Teo admitted. "I want to take you back there and see everything restored. And I wouldn't mind seeing some major changes at Marsay and Jineve along the way. My mission was a complete failure."

Ana offered a sympathetic nod. Teo had explained that although he had made contact with the people the Papa sent him to see, few had responded favorably to the message of Deu. "I'm sorry," she said, stroking his arm with her fingernails.

"It's not your fault."

"I suppose not. But when we parted on bad terms, I felt like maybe I burdened you. I didn't want that. I wanted to be a support. I hope you know how much I prayed for you."

"I do know. And I definitely felt your support. I often remembered how you ran to me on the dock and threw me the pendant of Iesus."

"That's why I threw it to you—to be a reminder." Ana glanced at the collar of Teo's shirt. "Where is that pendant anyway?"

A strange expression crossed Teo's face, almost as if he was embarrassed.

"What's wrong?"

Teo ran his fingers through his hair. "Well, to put it in the most shocking terms possible, I gave that necklace to a pretty, blue-eyed, fifteen-year-old prostitute."

What?

Ana pushed herself up to a sitting position while Teo continued to relax on the riverbank. Apparently there was a reasonable explanation for his action. Even so, Ana couldn't suppress the jealousy that rose within her.

"It wasn't like that, of course," Teo said. "She was a girl in desperate need, dragged into a horror you and I can't comprehend. I told her about Deu's love, and she believed. The pendant was a practical way to get her out of that life."

"But you gave that necklace to me! It symbolized our quest to find the New Testament together!"

"And Deu fulfilled that quest, didn't he? What can I say? I felt an unmistakable prompting to help that girl."

"Girls are always trying to get their claws into you."

Now Teo sat up as well. "What are you talking about? What girls?"

Ana wanted to raise the name *Sucula*, but she knew that would cross a line, so she went in a different direction. "Girls like Bianca," she said with a hint of accusation.

"Who?"

"That flirty scullery maid at Vanita's estate in Ulmbartia."

"Bianca? I can barely remember who she is."

"Vanita once told me—"

Teo's hand shot up. "Stop right there, Ana. All these hints and suspicions are wrong. You're not in the spirit of Deu."

Ana frowned but said nothing.

"I've never given you any reason to be jealous, have I? I was just trying to help a human being in need."

"You're right," Ana said, shaking her head with a heavy sigh. "You released that girl from slavery when you gave her the pendant. I guess that's the perfect use for it."

"I hoped you'd see it that way." Teo gently touched Ana's shoulder. "I only have eyes for one woman, you know."

"I do know that, Teo." Ana fiddled with a blade of grass. "So how do I overcome a jealous feeling like that when it arises?"

"It's just like any temptation. We have to ask Deu for strength every day, then make some hard choices when it counts."

"So is victory based on Deu's strength or our choice?"

"Both, I think."

Ana fell silent, lost in her thoughts, until finally Teo scrambled to his feet. "Come on. We've rested here long enough. Are you ready to go find the springs?"

Lighthearted once more, Ana stood up with a smile. "Yes! Show me the way and I'll be right behind you."

The pair went to the river's edge. Its flow was turbulent, for as warmer weather approached, the snow on Fire Mountain was melting. On the riverbank lay two coracles—tiny boats made of wicker, each small enough to be carried by a single person. Teo and Ana got into the boats and pushed off with their paddles. The swift current carried them along at a pace Ana found exhilarating.

"Watch out now," Teo called. "We're about to enter the gorge."

"Hey, don't forget I'm a farm girl from Edgeton. I grew up on a river!" Ana laughed as she dug in with her paddle to stay close to Teo.

The river valley in which Jané lived now closed down to form a narrow canyon. Teo entered first, but Ana followed close after. The river rushed through the gorge, twisting and turning as it careened off the white stone walls. In some places the cliffs cast deep shadows, but elsewhere golden sunbeams shone on the stream like waterfalls of light. Side eddies formed crystal-clear pools whose rocky beds looked impossibly close to the surface. The swirling river bore an aquamarine tint that took Ana's breath away.

Teo looked over his shoulder, pointing ahead. "There's the fallen tree! The springs are just beyond! Be ready to turn!"

"Here we go!" Ana cried.

As she swept under the tree behind Teo, a grotto opened on her right. Ana thrust her paddle into the stream and twisted it hard. Her coracle made an abrupt turn a moment before Teo shouted, "Now!"

Ana shot forward, gliding into the grotto a split second ahead of Teo. Her boat ground to a halt on a pebbly beach. She turned and gave Teo a cocky grin as he slid up next to her.

"Nice move, farm girl," he said.

Ana threw back her head and laughed.

The pair stepped out of their little boats and pulled them from the water. Glancing around, Ana surveyed the secret grotto. A waterfall cascaded over a rock lip, trickling down the cliff before hitting a plunge pool. A shaft of sunlight scattered glittering diamonds across the ruffled water. But most intriguing of all, wisps of steam rose from the pool's surface.

Kicking off her sandals, Ana walked to the water's edge and dipped her toes. The pool was the temperature of a very hot bath.

"Just like Jané described," she said. "Therapy straight from the Creator."

Ana waded in slowly, trying to acclimate to the warmth. Teo followed her, shirtless, then plunged deeper.

"Ooh! How can you stand it?"

"You have to go all at once," Teo said.

Suddenly he lunged at Ana and dragged her squealing into the pool. The heat was intense, creating an instant sting in the middle of her back. She winced, but Teo was right. The sting disappeared as the healing waters enveloped her.

Ana sank down until all but her face was submerged. Teo did the same. For a long time the pair soaked in the hot spring without speaking. A sense of deep relaxation descended on them. Somewhere nearby a bird warbled, but no other sound broke the stillness. Then, unexpectedly, Teo rose from the pool to stand in the waterfall's cooling flow with his head down.

As Ana looked at Teo standing in the trickle of water, a wave of aching desire caught her by surprise. It wasn't the superficial infatuation of a girl with a crush, but the full-bodied yearning of an adult woman, ripe for love with the man in her life. Teo's powerful arms were spread as he braced himself between the grotto's walls and let the water roll down his back.

The corded ripples of his shoulders, the square-cut shape of his chest, the leanness of his muscular stomach—these things aroused a breathtaking ardor in Ana.

So she swam to him.

Teo glanced up as she rose from the water, her dress clingy against her skin. Ana's heart fluttered in her chest, and her limbs felt shaky. Something was about to happen, and she was entirely willing.

"Ana . . ." Teo's tone was uncertain. He had seen the look in her eyes and didn't know what to make of it.

She approached very close. "I remember when you got this," she said, tracing her finger along one of the three scars that crisscrossed his chest. "You were looking out for me."

Teo lowered his hands to his sides. Though he did not embrace Ana, he leaned toward her. She tipped back her head and lifted her chin until she was cheek-to-cheek with him. Her lips were close to his ear.

"Why are you so good to me, Teo?" she whispered.

"Because I love you. I've loved you since the day you stepped out of the forest with your courage and your bow."

Ana could resist no longer. She slipped her arms around Teo. Though his hands didn't move, she felt him trembling against her.

"Kiss me," she said.

Teo exhaled against her neck but did nothing else.

"Quick," she urged. "Don't wait anymore. I'm ready."

"Here? Now? Is this how you want it to be?"

For a long moment Ana could not speak. Warring desires battled in her mind, her body, her soul. The shouts of her sexual craving demanded satisfaction, yet another voice spoke too. It was faint at first, and she tried to shove it away, but it persisted. *Not like this,* it said. *No, daughter . . . not like this.*

But I've waited so long! I love this man with all my heart! You know it's a holy love! Why not? Why not?

The voice didn't answer, but Teo did.

"Hard choices," he said through clenched teeth. His words came out more like a groan.

The spell broke. Ana shook her head, covering her eyes with her hand. "Oh, Teo, I'm sorry."

She backed away, but he refused to let her go. Following her, he took her hand in his. Now he did kiss her, though on the cheek; then he put his hand under her chin and lifted her face. She looked up into Teo's eyes. His warm smile was a solid anchor in an unsteady moment.

"Ana?"

She waited.

"Let's take our steps one at a time, okay?"

"Alright, Teo." She nodded demurely. "As long as you keep walking them with me."

◆　　◆　　◆

Nestled among the bluffs that rose above the sea, the village of Tara Mena spread out before Teo and Ana. Though it was little more than a tiny hamlet of houses and shops surrounding a harbor, Teo thought it looked like a metropolis after four and a half weeks of isolation. The respite in the wilderness had been refreshing, but now he was looking forward to being among people again.

"There's a little water left in here. You want it?" Teo offered his canteen to Ana.

"Only if you promise my next drink will be sparkly." Ana winked at him, then put the canteen to her lips and finished it off.

Teo laughed. "I can probably find you something in the village." He examined Ana more closely. "How are you holding up?"

"It was a long walk, but I'm fine."

"Jané said it was twenty-five leagues. Is your back feeling okay?"

"It doesn't hurt anymore, though I'll be scarred for life."

"If it's any comfort to you, so will I."

Ana slid her arm into Teo's. "Then I guess we match, Captain. Now take this girl into town for that drink you promised."

The pair continued walking until they reached the outskirts of Tara Mena. Most of its buildings clustered around the harbor, though a few spread uphill before giving way to the countryside. It was late in the fourth month, so the orange trees were in blossom. Afternoon sunshine warmed the road, and puffy clouds dotted the sky.

The country lane became a village street that meandered past shops and homes and markets. Teo didn't see a tavern, but a man with a cart had unrolled an awning and appeared to be selling refreshments.

"Something cold to drink, sir?" the merchant asked as Teo approached.

"Cold and sparkly, my friend."

"Aha! I have just the thing." The man reached into his cart and produced a bottle of chilled rosé champagne, which he poured into two flutes. Teo paid the man with some of the money left over from the Papa's mission. A nearby bench in the shade of a palm tree served as the seating area of the merchant's makeshift restaurant. Teo and Ana sat down with their drinks.

"Did you see the harbor as we turned the corner?" Teo asked.

"I saw it. No sign of the *Midnight Glider*." Ana glanced at Teo. "You sure Marco is coming?"

"I told him to meet me here on the next full moon if we got separated. Escorting the captives to safety was his first priority. The other convents are a lot farther away than Lido di Ostia."

Ana sighed. "That place was a haven for me. Now it's burned down. Nothing is left for me there."

"We'll regroup in Roma and figure out what to do next. The Papa will have insight."

"Assuming Marco shows up."

"He will. The moon will be full tonight. I expect to see him tomorrow."

"What do we do until then?"

"Would you like to visit the ruins?" Teo pointed to some crumbling structures poking from the forest.

"Oh, yes! I'd love to see the old theater Jané mentioned."

Teo stood up. "Alright. Hand me your glass and we'll go."

He approached the merchant with the cart. After returning the empty champagne flutes, he asked for directions to the ancient site.

"The Teatro Greko!" cried the merchant. "According to legend it was built by people who lived long before the Great War."

"You know how to get there from here?"

"Easy. Follow that lane. It will become a footpath. Keep going—you can't miss it."

"Thanks."

Teo turned to go, but the merchant stopped him. "Sir! You need something special if you're going up to the theater."

"What?"

The clever merchant smiled as he reached into his ice-packed cart. He rummaged around for a moment, then produced an inexpensive clay bowl. Two seashells protruded from the red substance heaped inside it. A triumphant smile was on the man's face.

"What is it?" Teo asked.

"It's called *jilatto*. A frozen cream. Raspberry flavor."

Teo turned to Ana. "You want it?"

She looked at him like he was crazy. "What girl would turn that down?"

Chuckling, Teo paid the man, who covered the bowl and put it in a small sack. The walk uphill was pleasant. Prickly pear lined the way, and the orange blossoms gave the air a fragrant scent. At last the trail came to an end. As Teo and Ana emerged from the undergrowth, they were confronted with a breathtaking spectacle.

"Wow, look at that!" Teo exclaimed. He glanced at Ana. Her mouth hung open.

"What a magnificent view," she breathed.

The theater was semicircular, carved from the hillside in a series of tiers. Its stage was backed by a screen decorated with columns, though it was broken in the middle so Tara Mena's sheltered bay was visible below. The azure sea stretched to the distant horizon. Off to the side, Fire Mountain's snowcapped summit sent a column of smoke into the sky.

Sitting down on one of the risers, Teo and Ana dipped their shell spoons into the raspberry *jilatto*. Its cool sweetness made the perfect treat under the warm Sessalayan sun. When the bowl was empty, Teo and Ana leaned back on their elbows against the tier behind them. Teo removed his outer jerkin, and Ana hiked her gown's skirt above her knees. Jané had done a marvelous job of patching the burn holes in both garments.

"Ah, the sweet life," Ana said.

Suddenly Teo sat up, staring past the theater's stage. A malevolent presence had appeared in the bay, like a stain upon the clear blue sea.

Ana sat up too. "What's the matter? What's wrong?"

Teo pointed. Ana followed his gaze, then uttered a little cry as she put her hand to her chest. A ship had arrived in the harbor.

A black caravel.

◆　◆　◆

Ana tugged Teo's sleeve. "I think that's close enough."

"Just a little more. It's dusk. They can't tell who we are."

Let's hope not, Ana thought.

She stood with Teo in the shadow of a warehouse along Tara Mena's waterfront. The Iron Shield's caravel had docked alongside the wharf, as ships often did before tackling the dangerous Strait of Mezzine. Legend said the strait was guarded by a whirlpool on one side and a sea monster on the other. Ana thought the real monster was lodged aboard the ship itself.

Teo inched closer, craning his neck. Though a few Exterminati moved around on deck, their dark lord was nowhere to be seen. A full moon hung low on the horizon, bathing the ship in its pale glow. A rat scurried across the wharf and was enveloped by the shadows.

"The ship is sitting low in the water," Teo remarked. "That means its hold is full of cargo."

"Human cargo wouldn't weigh it down like that."

"Right. So no slaves. I wonder what it is?"

Ana peered over Teo's shoulder as he examined the caravel. "Do we really need to know? Isn't it enough that we escaped?"

Teo turned around, resting his hand on the pommel of his sword. "He's our enemy, Ana. He stands opposed to everything we believe. I can't back down out of fear. If I don't confront him, who will?" Teo glanced down at his waist. "This is the sword of Armand. Your grandfather believed in fighting injustice with courage and honor. I'm a soldier of his regiment. Those are the principles I live by as well."

Ana stared at the sword for a moment, then lifted her eyes to Teo's. "Alright. Whatever you face, I'll stand at your side."

Teo was about to reply when he noticed movement on the ship. "Look! There he is!"

The pair retreated into the shadows as the Iron Shield appeared at the top of the gangplank. His impressive height and wide-shouldered physique were unmistakable even in the evening gloom. He descended to the wharf and began to walk away.

"Come on, let's follow him," Teo said.

Ana took a deep breath and nodded her assent. Though the Iron Shield had profoundly traumatized her, she decided Teo was right: she couldn't give in to fear.

They followed the dark warrior at a distance. He turned into an alley, but when Teo and Ana reached it, their enemy was gone. Cautiously they advanced. Teo's hand was on his sword. Ana's heart was pounding.

A door opened, spilling a shaft of light from inside. Teo yanked Ana into a dark corner. They crouched behind a crate, not daring to breathe.

Several shamans exited the building, a tavern of some sort. A moment later the Iron Shield followed them, engaged in sharp debate with another man. Each held the edge of a large parchment. They jabbed their fingers at it as they argued.

"It *is* possible!" the Iron Shield insisted. "This chart proves it. Strike out across the open sea and maintain a northwesterly course. If we don't stop at night we'll reach land within a matter of days!"

"My lord, such things are not done!"

"What do you mean, 'not done'? We did it when we came to Sessalay from Napoly!"

"That is not the same," the other man pleaded.

"You are my navigator! You will do as I say."

"The sea is vast. We could get lost in that great expanse."

"We will not get lost! My mistress has ordered me to bring her the brimstone of Sessalay. The god of this world shall ensure its safe delivery."

"Straight . . . across the ocean?"

"Yes, and even beyond. At Marsay we shall transfer the cargo to riverboats and proceed up the Rone. We have a long and arduous journey ahead of us. It is a good thing we have divine protection."

"But, my lord, what god can rule over so vast a domain?"

The Iron Shield released his hold on the chart and raised his finger to the sky. "The god of my mistress can! He is the Beautiful One, the Star of the Morning, the sovereign of land and sea! He is Astrebril the Great, and every knee shall one day bow at his name."

Ana gasped in her hiding place. *Astrebril!*

Suddenly a barrel of refuse toppled over with a crash. The shamans' heads swung around at the commotion.

"What was that?" The Iron Shield stalked over. Ana remained frozen like a statue, her eyes wide, her muscles tensed. Teo gripped her arm in the shadows.

The Iron Shield picked up a rock. Ana could see his gaping eye socket where he had once worn a lump of yellow glass. He hurled the rock down the alley, and a cat yowled in the distance. "Join me next time, little one!" the Iron Shield called, then turned back to his men. "Come! We must return to the ship." The shamans departed with their master, and the alley fell silent. Teo blew out a breath as he released his grip on Ana's arm.

She turned toward him. "Teo! Did you hear what he said?"

"I did. It changes everything." He rose to his feet. Ana stood up too.

"The ship is loaded with brimstone," she said. "With an amount like that he could make huge quantities of the explosive powder."

"Yes, if he knew how. But he doesn't."

"Then what does he want with the brimstone?"

"You heard him. He said it's a delivery."

"To whom?"

"His mistress. Don't you see, Ana? He's taking it to Marsay to put on riverboats."

"Right . . ."

"And he believes Astrebril will protect him. Where would he have learned about Astrebril? The same place a shipment of brimstone would become the world's most deadly weapon."

Ana felt her knees go slack as the implications dawned on her. "He's going straight to Chiveis," she said, "and that means . . ."

Teo nodded. "So are we."

PART THREE

CATHOLICITY

The rabbit's eyes were swollen shut, and its breath came in raspy pants. It lay on its side, twitching spasmodically. From time to time it mewed, though the creature's pitiful cries did it no good.

"You have served your purpose well," the High Priestess said as she plunged a knife into the rabbit's flank. "Return now to the bosom of Astrebril."

Laying aside the bloodstained dagger, the High Priestess left the rabbit's hutch and walked to the window of her lofty spire. Her temple was located above the treeline, nestled against the north face of one of Chiveis's highest summits. From this vantage point, the queen of Astrebril could survey all the lands her god had given her.

But she wanted more.

"Where are you now?" the High Priestess whispered to the wind. Somewhere beyond the jagged peaks that receded to the horizon, her servant, the Iron Shield, was obtaining the sacred brimstone so necessary to her sulfurous yellow gas. Soon armies would flee and kingdoms would fall before the deadly fumes. The new weapon was a glorious provision of Astrebril—a way to extend his worship across the face of the earth. Every inch of territory reclaimed from the Creator and the Criminal was a victory for the Beautiful One.

"Where are you right now, vassal of my heart?" the priestess wondered again. She knew she could find out if she wished, but that information wouldn't be worth the toll the spirits would take on her body. She would wait. Spinning away from the window, she shouted to the doorkeeper who stood outside. "Send in the scientist!"

Moments later the door creaked open and a humpbacked old man entered. His eyes were fearful, yet the priestess discerned intelligence in his visage as well. The man was both gifted and afraid, useful qualities in a servant.

"You brought one of the canisters?" she inquired.

"Yes, Your Eminence." The scientist held up a metal cylinder.

"It is empty?"

"Of course."

The High Priestess pointed to the window. "Prove it to me before we continue." She backed away.

Obediently the scientist walked to the spire's window and opened the can. Though he aimed it outside, no sickly fumes emerged from it. "See?"

"Bring it here then."

The bent scientist shuffled over. "It can be pressurized," he said. "This gasket seals the opening."

The High Priestess licked her lips as she leaned close to the old man. Though he started to recoil, she ordered him to be still. Trembling, he waited until she had brought her mouth close to his ear. "I have a secret to share with you," she breathed.

"Y-y-yes, m-m'lady?"

"The substance needs further testing."

The scientist did not answer, so the High Priestess turned away and slinked to the rabbit's hutch. "Come here," she commanded.

The old man went to her side.

"See what this gas has done?"

The dead rabbit lay in the cage. Blisters covered its carcass. Blood and serum oozed from the knife wound.

Swallowing hard, the scientist nodded.

"Now we must see what it can do to a man." The priestess paused, then caught the scientist's eyes and stared directly at him. "I was thinking of testing it upon you."

"No!" The scientist's face paled, and he began to wave his hands. "Your Eminence, what have I done—"

"Someone else then?" the High Priestess asked sweetly.

"Yes! Please! Someone else!"

"Hand me the canister."

The terrified scientist obliged. After examining the smooth cylinder, the priestess removed the gasket. "What would happen if this seal were missing?"

"My lady, the can would become unstable."

"And what if you also doubled the normal pressure inside?"

"Then it would explode on the first person who handled it!"

The High Priestess waited while the old man stared back at her. Suddenly she lunged at him and grabbed his coat, drawing him near. Her other hand snatched the dead rabbit by the ears.

"Do it," she snarled, dangling the carcass in the scientist's face, "or this will be your fate!"

❖   ❖   ❖

"Vanita! Over here!"

Teo watched Ana wave to her aristocratic friend on the deck of the *Midnight Glider*. Before the ship was fully moored to the quay, Ana bounded up the gangplank. Teo followed. The two women embraced like long-lost sisters.

"Anastasia, it's so good to see you safe!" Vanita exclaimed. "I haven't talked to you since you got into that water barrel."

"Oh, let's not bring up that horrible memory."

"Can I at least ask how your burn is? That was so awful! I still have nightmares about it."

"Don't worry. I'm all healed now, but no backless gowns for me anymore."

"Then it's a good thing you've already snagged your man," Vanita said with a playful smile. She paused for a moment, then grew more serious as she clasped Ana on the shoulder. "You were . . . you were great up there on the mountain."

"So were you, Vanita."

"Tch! You think I was gonna bow down to a one-eyed giant with an oversized ego?" The two women burst into a fit of laughter.

Finally Vanita turned toward Teo. "Thanks for watching out for my friend," she said.

"And thank you for making sure Marco returned to pick us up. We have a lot to talk about. Where is that rogue anyway?"

"He's in his stateroom. He said we all need to meet. There are some things we need to tell you as well."

"Come on then. Let's go find him."

Teo and the two women dodged busy sailors and piles of ropes as they crossed the deck toward the stern. The *Glider* had arrived in Tara Mena at noon, a few hours after the Iron Shield departed. Teo wanted to leave as soon as possible to intercept the shipment of brimstone. He felt certain Marco's fast clipper could overtake the black caravel. Yet he knew Marco would need to resupply his ship before heading out in pursuit—if indeed he could be persuaded to do so.

The dashing pirate captain rose from a chair as Teo and the women arrived at the stateroom. Brother Thomas was there too, along with Teo's old friend Sol. Their presence told Teo things had gotten interesting in Roma.

After greetings were exchanged, everyone gathered around a small table. Sol set out a platter of cured ham, dried fruit, and soft cheese, then distributed mugs of ale.

"We have a lot to be grateful for—each one of us," Teo said as the friends took their seats. He motioned toward Brother Thomas. "Would you offer a prayer of thanksgiving?"

After the stout monk prayed, the food was shared around the table. The conversation grew animated as the friends caught up on all that had happened since they had last seen each other. Nevertheless a serious mood permeated the cabin. Everyone understood that weighty matters were at stake.

"Good news, Teofil," Sol said. "The Papa has issued a bull commanding the Knights of Marsay to defend Jineve."

"Even that rascal Odo won't be able to dodge a direct order from the Papa," Brother Thomas added.

"Excellent. We can't let Jineve fall to an invasion from the High Priestess. She'll become too powerful."

"Didn't you say she intends to give all the Jinevan women as slaves to those horrible outsiders?" Ana winced and shuddered. "We have to prevent that." Teo knew her loathing was born from her own terrifying experience at the hands of the forest barbarians.

"For my part, I'm afraid I have bad news," he announced when there was a lull in the conversation. "Anastasia and I saw the Iron Shield here in Tara Mena. He left this morning with a shipment of brimstone that the High Priestess could make into explosive powder."

Marco wagged his head at the implications. "I can't even begin to imagine how much destruction she could wreak with an entire shipload of that stuff." He frowned, catching Teo's eye. "But stopping him isn't going to be as easy as you might think."

"We can take him, Marco. I'll put your pirates up against those shamans any day. We'll scuttle that black ship of his and send the Iron Shield to the bottom of the sea with all his evil cargo."

Marco shook his head. "Wait until you hear what we saw in the Strait of Mezzine."

"Clansmen!" Sol interjected. "A whole flotilla of ships, bristling with fighters and rigged for speed. The black caravel met up with them, and they all set off on a northwestward course."

Teo's heart sank. "That can only be an assault force. The Iron Shield must be planning to use the Clan as part of the priestess's invasion strategy."

"Is Jineve strong enough to resist?"

"I doubt it. The Chiveisian army is in league with the outsiders. They'll close in from the east while the Clansmen and Exterminati advance from the south. Jineve will be caught between two armies, and they'll be facing the High Priestess's new weapon. It doesn't look good."

"The nations are rising," Ana said. "The High Priestess's move against Jineve is only the beginning."

Sol nodded. "Anastasia is right. If Jineve falls, Marsay will be next. Then what? Likuria would be easy prey. Even Roma is vulnerable. The

High Priestess would love to see the basilica of the Universal Communion going up in flames. The age of isolation is over. Astrebril is on the move."

Everyone sat quietly for a moment, numbed by the dire prediction. At last Teo reached into his pocket and laid his copy of the New Testament on the table. It was one of the inexpensive little versions being produced at Roma for mass distribution. "It's time for a pact of our own," he declared. "We can't let this fate come about."

Ana rested her hand on the Sacred Writing. "I swear to stand against the schemes of the evil one," she said. "I dedicate my life to the victory of Deus."

Teo covered Ana's hand with his. "I swear it too. My sword will fight on behalf of the God of heaven."

One by one the friends around the table reached out and affirmed the sacred vow. Only Marco remained uncommitted, until finally he placed his hand upon those of the others. "I don't yet have faith like all of you," he said, "but I freely join your good cause."

"Then it's decided," Teo said. "We will journey to Marsay—and to wherever else the Lord God might take us."

❖　❖　❖

A week slipped by on the open ocean, a week during which Marco's normally fearless pirates were nervous and edgy. They weren't used to sailing through uncharted waters. Only their love for their captain made them do it—and even that almost wasn't enough.

The *Midnight Glider* caught sight of the Clan flotilla on the first day out of Tara Mena. Marco kept the enemy sails on the far northwestern horizon, hanging back like a lone wolf shadowing a herd of deer. Sometimes one of the warships would slow down to investigate the pursuer, but Marco would respond by ordering a halt until the ship resumed its place in the fleet. For six days this game of cat and mouse continued. On the seventh, land was sighted: the coastline of Marsay.

Marco stood next to his helmsman at the wheel, assessing the movements of the enemy ships through a spyglass. A low gray sky was spitting rain.

"How many can you see out there?" Teo asked his friend.

"I'd estimate twenty ships. If they're all packed with fighters, that would have to represent the bulk of the Clan's manpower. They're really putting everything into this endeavor."

"The Clan is very superstitious. After the disaster on Fire Mountain, I'm sure they're willing to do whatever the Iron Shield orders. They're desperate to appease their gods."

"Ships coming about, sir!" the helmsman barked.

Marco's head snapped around. "Where?"

The helmsman pointed, and Marco ran to the rail with his spyglass. Teo could see the maneuver even with the naked eye. The enemy ships had divided to the right and left, and now two had peeled off to attack the *Glider*. They approached across the choppy sea with ominous intent.

"All hands to battle stations!" Marco shouted. "Prepare to engage!"

A thunderclap boomed in the distance, accompanied by a flash of lightning. Marco's sailors scurried around the deck while Brother Thomas and eight friar knights strapped on their weapons. Evasion was the primary goal, but everyone knew that might not be possible.

"Teo, there you are!"

He turned to see Ana arrive, carrying a bow and wearing a quiver of arrows on her hip. She was a fine archer—in fact, Teo owed his life to her skill—but he didn't like the idea of Ana being on deck when the fighting began. He started to say so, but she put her hand on his arm and gave him a firm look.

"We've come this far, Captain," she said, "and I should stand at your side now."

Teo relented, recognizing the truth of her claim. "Alright, Ana. Then may Deu protect us both."

The seas grew rougher as the enemy ships neared. Both were large and intimidating. Since they approached from either side of the *Glider*, Marco couldn't turn and run. Instead he barreled straight ahead in a desperate attempt to get clear of the attackers before they hemmed him in.

"Faster!" Teo yelled to no one in particular. He knew the sailors were doing everything they could to evade the enemy's pincer move. The *Glider*'s raked prow rose and fell as it clipped through the waves, but the two attacking ships kept closing in. Everyone was racing to a single point: the juncture of a Y. Whichever ship reached it first would be the victor.

A fierce rain started to fall, blowing in sheets from the leaden skies. Teo looked back through the downpour to see Marco at the helm, holding his course with intense concentration as he tried to thread the needle between the two ships.

The wind howled, and the rain stung Teo's cheeks. Now the massive Clan warships loomed off the port and starboard bow. Ravenous warriors lined the enemy's rails, their swords raised high. At any moment Teo expected to feel a violent concussion or hear the crunch of splintering wood as the ships slammed together. A grappling hook soared through the air and snagged the *Glider's* bulwark. Teo drew his weapon with a wild yell, preparing himself for battle.

"Hang on!" Ana screamed as the deadly impact neared. "They're going to hit us!" The three ships were on a collision course and no one was backing down. The smashup was going to be tremendous.

At that moment a great swell lifted the *Midnight Glider* like a toy in a child's bathtub. Ana leaned far over the rail, her left arm extending her bow stave and her right hand drawing the string to her chin. The ship rose high above its attackers as it rode the crest of the wave. Ana loosed her arrow, sending the man holding the end of the grappling rope tumbling into the sea.

As the breaker crashed down, the *Glider* hit the trough hard. Teo flailed wildly in an attempt to steady Ana but missed her as he toppled to the deck. Seawater cascaded over him, and he was dimly aware of a massive reverberation behind him.

He scrambled up, wiping brine from his eyes, to see the two enemy ships in the *Glider's* wake. Their wrecked prows were entangled in a colossal head-on collision. Ahead of the *Glider* lay only the open sea.

"We made it!" Teo exclaimed. He turned toward Ana with an exuberant cheer.

But she was gone.

✦   ✦   ✦

Vanita Labella sat in Marco's stateroom below deck, keeping company with the old teacher named Sol. Vanita was neither a fighter nor a sailor, so she knew the best thing she could do was to stay out of the way. For an hour she and Sol had endured the vessel's constant pitching and heaving while the storm raged. The near miss with the Clan ships had sent them both to their knees in grateful prayer. Now the *Glider* was speeding toward the port of Marsay. Nothing could be seen in the terrible maelstrom outside, until Vanita noticed a bright beam piercing the evening darkness.

"Sol, look at this!"

Vanita pointed out the window at the welcoming beacon. The old teacher who had taught her to read and write now came to her side as a friend, smiling as he recognized the lighthouse that marked Marsay's harbor.

"Praise Deus, we're almost to safety, child! This storm would have broken us to bits if we had stayed out any longer!"

Vanita decided she could now risk a foray above deck. "I'm going to find Marco," she declared, exiting the cabin despite Sol's protests.

Arriving topside, Vanita realized the storm was even more fierce than she had imagined. The merciless rain drenched her immediately, plastering her hair to her forehead and dribbling down her face. A roaring wind whipped at her cloak even though it was buttoned up tight. Vanita fought her way to the stern where the ship's great wheel was located. Marco saw her approach, though he couldn't leave his position at the helm.

"Get below!" he shouted. "We're not out of this yet!"

Before Vanita could answer, something whooshed through the air and sent up a gigantic plume in front of the ship.

"What was that?" Vanita cried.

"The knights at the castle have us in range of their catapults. They don't know who we are, so they're bombarding everyone!"

Vanita turned around and gazed from the stern of the ship. Marco's incredible sailing had put the nimble *Midnight Glider* in reach of Marsay's harbor ahead of the Clan's cumbersome troop transports. Yet the enemy was close behind.

"Will there be a battle?" Vanita asked as she reached Marco's side.

"Hard to say. At this point everyone's just heading for the harbor to survive. Anyone who doesn't make it in soon is going to see the ocean floor up close."

The ship pitched suddenly, and Vanita started to fall until Marco reached out and caught her in a surprisingly strong grip.

"You're okay with me, Vanita Labella," the pirate captain said, smiling at her through his dark goatee. He kissed her lightly on the lips before setting her back on her feet. It was the first time he had ever done anything like that. Vanita struggled to catch her breath as Marco turned back to the wheel.

The rain continued to fall, and lightning rent the sky, but the lighthouse beacon was close now. Vanita could see that if the ship could round the jetty and dart through the harbor's narrow entrance, the winds would die down and the crew would be safe. She looked again at all the Clan ships converging on the harbor—and that was when a terrible yet wondrous idea popped into her mind.

No . . . I can't ask that . . .

But I have to! It would mean everything! Everything!

She turned to Marco, gripping the sleeve of his oilskin coat. He glanced at her from the corner of his eye as he held the great wheel.

"What is it?" he asked.

Vanita steeled her resolve, though her voice felt shaky. "The Clan ships are all headed this way, you said?"

"Every one of them. They're doomed if they don't make it into port."

"Marco, look at me."

Surprised, he turned to face her.

"You are not a rogue. You are not a scoundrel. I've known it since the day I met you." Tears welled up in Vanita's eyes, mingling with the rainwater that dripped from her lashes. "I know exactly who you are! I can see it! You are a good man. You are a *hero*."

The pirate captain looked at her with an expression she couldn't read. "Vanita . . . why did you say that?" he asked in a voice barely audible over the howling wind.

"Because I want you to do something. Right here. Right now. I want you to do something that will change the course of history. Something that will deal a mighty blow to the powers of evil."

Marco stared at Vanita's face, searching for answers. Desperate now, she grasped his coat in both hands.

"Drop the anchors at the mouth of the harbor," she said. "Lower the boats for the crew to escape, and leave the ship behind."

"*What?* I can't do that! The *Glider* would be smashed into a million pieces! I would lose everything I have!"

Vanita lifted her hands and cradled Marco's cheeks, pleading for understanding. "I know!" she cried. "I know! But Marco . . . my love . . . think of what else it would do!"

Marco's eyes widened as Vanita's intent dawned on him. He clasped his forehead and leaned back, overwhelmed by what he was being asked to do. At last he looked up and met Vanita's gaze.

"It would block the harbor's entrance," he said, "and utterly destroy the Clan."

✦ ✦ ✦

Teo hit the water as close as possible to the flash of white he had glimpsed among the billowing waves. Instantly he was fighting for his life. The cold sea sucked his breath away, and its churning waters assaulted him from every direction. Yet Ana was out there somewhere. He had to find her.

The white flash appeared again but was quickly engulfed by the turbulence. Ana had been wearing an ivory-colored gown since Sessalay, so Teo knew it must be her. Nothing else that color would be bobbing in the ocean. He called her name, but there was no reply. The ferocious wind and pounding rain stifled his pitiful shouts.

Lightning slashed across the sky, and in its brilliant glare Teo finally caught a glimpse of Ana. Her head was barely above water as she flailed around, trying to snatch a breath. Distress was written on her face. Then everything went dark again.

"Over here!" Teo screamed with all the volume he could muster. "I'm coming!"

Proper swimming was impossible in the heaving ocean, but Teo fought his way to where he thought Ana was. He swiveled his head, completely disoriented. The *Midnight Glider* was long gone now. Teo saw no sign of Ana. *Deu! Where is she? Help us!*

At last she surfaced a short distance away, clawing up from the black sea in a desperate attempt to stay afloat. No doubt her gown was weighing her down, dragging her into the deep like a lead weight. "Ana!" Teo shouted, but she didn't hear. He swam to her, determined not to let her go this time. But the sea had other plans. Just as he was about to seize her, she went under the surface again.

Teo plunged into the inky blackness, waving his arms in every direction as he tried to find Ana. Horror filled him at the thought that she had run out of strength and was now sinking into the abyss forever. He thrashed wildly, urgently, ferociously. His breath was running out, but he paid it no mind. *Ana! Where are you?*

Something bumped him.

He spun in the water . . . grasping . . . reaching . . .

And then Ana was in his arms.

Teo shot to the surface, clinging to his beloved with fierce determination. They surged from the ocean with their lungs heaving, gasping for air in a world that seemed to offer only water. Ana made desperate whimpering sounds as she tried to breathe.

"Hang on to me!" Teo yelled. "I have you!" Though she grabbed him, Teo knew he couldn't support her for long.

Something smashed Teo in the back of the head, making stars blaze before his eyes. He shook away the dizziness and saw that a large chunk of wood had struck him from behind. Looking around, he realized he had floated into the debris field from the two Clan ships that had collided.

"This way, Ana! Come on!" Teo held her with one hand and paddled with the other as he struggled through the roiling sea. The swell lifted them high, then plunged them down again. Teo kicked with all his strength, dragging Ana toward a large hatch door that had come loose from one of the ships.

After heaving Ana onto the hatch, Teo flopped next to her on his belly. The hatch was big enough for the two of them to lay side by side. Teo's legs remained in the water, enabling him to steer. He quickly discerned he didn't have to propel the makeshift raft, for the relentless waves drove it along.

The cold rain continued to fall as Teo and Ana drifted at the ocean's mercy. In the distance a dark shadow indicated what Teo assumed was a headland. Ana clung to the raft, coughing periodically but mostly lying still. Teo let the rolling swells carry them both toward shore as nightfall set in.

The dull roar of breaking waves finally snapped Teo out of his lethargy. The cliffs were close now, and Teo knew that to be caught in the toothy rocks at their base would mean certain death. Summoning his final reserves, he kicked his legs to guide the raft toward an opening in the wall. Apparently some kind of inlet pierced the seaside bluffs here.

The winds subsided as soon as Teo entered the inlet. Compared to the high seas outside, the narrow cove seemed like a tranquil paradise. Towering walls on either side sheltered the exhausted castaways from the brunt of the gale. Even the rain started to lighten up.

Teo ran the raft aground on a little beach at the back of the cove. Ana gagged, retched, and vomited up a bellyful of water. Groaning, she lay prone in the sand. Teo collapsed next to her, and for several minutes they lay together unmoving. At last Ana rolled onto her back and found the strength to speak.

"I hit him," she said.

"You what?"

"I hit him. The guy with the hook."

Incredulous, Teo struggled to a sitting position and looked down at Ana. She regarded him with the steely gaze of a victorious warrior. Both of them knew that if the man had been able to tie off the grappling rope, the *Midnight Glider* would have been tethered to the other two wrecks. All three ships would probably be on the sea floor right now—with their occupants.

Teo shook his head. "You amaze me, Anastasia of Edgeton."

"I *am* a pretty good archer," she agreed with a grin, then rolled over and coughed up more seawater.

◆　　◆　　◆

When Scylla and Charybdis began barking, Jané knew she had a visitor. Normally it wasn't anyone threatening, just patients in need of healing. But out here in the Sessalayan wilderness, Jané was glad to have her two fierce dogs just in case. Their watchful presence helped to even the odds.

The visitor this time, however, was no one to be afraid of. He was a peasant boy whose style of clothing and clean hands suggested he was from a village instead of a farm. The boy carried a small parcel wrapped in paper. Jané realized she would have to call off her dogs if she wanted to find out what it was.

"Down, boys!" she called, swatting Scylla on the muzzle to make her point clear. The dogs quieted as soon as their mistress showed no alarm at the unknown intruder.

"What can I do for you?" Jané asked the wide-eyed boy. "Come to swap something for a bottle of medicine? If so, you've come to the right place."

"No, ma'am," the boy said. "I have a delivery."

"A delivery? Well, come inside and let's open it up!"

The boy shook his head, eyeing the dogs warily.

Jané laughed. "Alright then, have it your way." She crossed her cottage yard to meet the boy at the gate. "We'll do it out here."

"A man paid me to bring this to you," the boy said, holding out the parcel.

"A man? What kind of man?"

"A handsome man."

Jané scoffed. "Since when do handsome men give gifts to wilderness-dwellers like me?"

"But you're pretty," said the boy.

"Aha! You're gonna be good with the ladies someday, little fella." Jané grinned at her visitor, then began to tear open the wrapping on her delivery.

Inside was a book. It was small and inexpensively bound, yet it had a look of substance to it. Flipping it over, Jané's heart skipped a beat as she read the title: *The New Testament of Deus, and His Son, Iesus Christus.*

"Oh my!" she exclaimed, delighted by the gift she now held in her hand. Opening to the title page, she saw a note scrawled there: *To Jané, with friendship and deepest gratitude, from Teofil and Anastasia.*

"What is it?" the boy asked.

Jané glanced at her visitor's curious face. "A storybook full of amazing things."

"About what?"

"About a great teacher named Iesus, who came down from heaven because he loved us." Jané paused, then asked, "Have you ever heard of him?"

The boy shook his head.

"Go sit under that shady tree," the healer instructed. "I'll get a couple of cold lemonades, and then Miss Jané is going to open up a window in your soul."

❖ ❖ ❖

"There's a light up there," Teo said.

Ana craned her neck from her seat on the beach. "I see it."

"Probably a fisherman's cottage. Think you can make it?"

"As long as I'm on solid ground, I can go anywhere." She gathered her legs under herself and stood up. Her gown was soaked, but the rain had stopped, and the moon was already peeking out from behind tattered clouds. All things considered, Ana was feeling okay.

"I don't know how you swam in that heavy thing," Teo said.

Ana smiled ruefully. "I didn't."

The pair trudged up the trail from the beach toward the cottage on the inlet's clifftop rim. Now that there was a little light, Ana could see what a stunning place they had found. The moon's pale glow reflected off a dramatic landscape of sheer limestone cliffs that enclosed a narrow arm of the sea. It was a deep, hidden cove of incredible beauty.

As the cottage came into view, Teo shouted a friendly greeting. The light streaming from the window changed as someone picked up a lantern and opened the front door.

"Who goes there?" called the tentative voice of an old man.

"Two strangers in need of help," Teo answered. "We fell from our ship and washed up here."

"A woman and a man," Ana added. She knew the presence of a woman often put people at ease in situations like this.

"Oh dear, how dreadful for you both," the old man said in a kindly voice. "Tell you what. My cottage stinks of fish, and it's a mess, but the barn is warm, and the loft is filled with clean hay. Make yourselves comfortable there, and I'll bring you something to eat."

"Thank you, sir," Teo replied.

Ana found the barn to be just as the old man described. Wearily she and Teo climbed up to the loft and collapsed in the sweet-smelling hay. Before long the hospitable fisherman arrived with two thick blankets and a picnic basket. Ana pulled out a large jug and guzzled the cool water. It occurred to her that her mother would have frowned on that, but the salty seawater had made her thirsty, and she knew Teo wouldn't mind her bad manners. Passing the jug to him, she found smoked tuna and pickled olives, along with a couple of dried pears.

"What's this place called?" Teo asked the fisherman after taking a drink from the jug.

"It's known as En Vau Calank. There are several of these narrow calanks along the coast here." The old man smiled. "Well now, I guess I should leave you to your rest. Sleep late, you two, and in the morning you can join me for a hot breakfast."

"You are far too kind, sir," Ana mumbled past her mouthful of olives.

With her belly full and her thirst quenched, Ana felt the heavy weight of exhaustion settle onto her shoulders. Teo gave her the privacy to wring out her gown and chemise and hang them up to dry before wrapping herself in one of the blankets. After she found a dark corner in the hay, Teo also hung up his damp clothes, then lay down on the far side of the loft.

As Ana examined her thoughts, she realized she felt a little rejected by Teo's obvious physical distance. Though the two of them were not sexually intimate, their unique circumstances had often caused them to sleep in close proximity. After the day's harrowing events, she especially craved his comforting presence.

"You could . . . come over here," she offered.

Teo was silent for so long Ana thought he might have fallen asleep. At last he said, "You're just a little too much for me to handle in that blanket."

Ana suddenly felt shy and embarrassed. "Oh, I see . . . okay."

"You stay on that side and I'll stay on this. That'll be our rule tonight."

"Alright . . . so, um . . . good night, Teofil."

"Good night, Ana," he answered with a little laugh. In a matter of minutes he was breathing steadily in the hay.

Ana stared at the barn's roof, thinking about the tall, rugged man with whom she shared her life. She often experienced a deep longing to give herself to him in body and soul. From what she understood, those desires were even more urgent in men. Yet in all the time she had known Teo, despite all the intimate experiences they had shared, he had never tried to prevail upon her. Tender kisses were their only form of physical affection. Ana's last waking thought was a grateful prayer. *Thank you for sending this man to spread his wing over me*, she said to her God as she drifted off to sleep.

✦ ✦ ✦

The sound of horses' hooves clip-clopping against hard stone awoke Teo at dawn. Instantly alert, he leaped from the hay and threw on his clothes. Though he had left his sword and ax on the ship, he made sure his knife was still in his boot.

Ana sat up in her blanket, clutching it around her. "Teo, what's wrong?"

"Strangers. Six or seven of them. I doubt they're having an early breakfast with the old fisherman. Get dressed—quick."

Peeking out the hayloft door, Teo spotted the riders in single file along the rim of the calank. All of them wore black hoods. They had paused to converse with someone. *The fisherman!* He was pointing toward the barn.

"We've been betrayed to the Exterminati," Teo barked. "Hurry! Down the ladder."

"But what about my dress?" Ana had donned her chemise, which was essentially a tunic that all peasant women wore as their outer garment. Upper-class women, however, wore it as a shift under their gowns.

"Leave it. We're in trouble. Let's go!"

Teo and Ana hurried down the ladder and exited the barn into the cottage's yard. One path descended to the beach, but Teo preferred to take the upper trail. They hurried along it, ducking low to keep the shamans from seeing them. Teo thought it might be possible to disappear among the limestone pinnacles and escape.

"Let's hide here and watch," he said, indicating a clump of boulders. Ana crouched next to Teo. The Exterminati rode to the barn and dismounted. After a brief search, they saddled up again.

A high-pitched whistle pierced the air nearby. Teo looked up to see the old fisherman pointing down the trail toward the fugitives.

"But he was so nice!" Ana cried.

"Looks can be deceiving." Teo took Ana's hand. "Come on! We have to make a run for it!"

They dashed down the trail as the shamans scrambled in pursuit. Teo realized they had one advantage—being on foot. He and Ana could take rocky paths that a mounted enemy could not navigate. He left the main path and clambered along the rim of the calank. The water far below was a beautiful emerald green as it shimmered in the morning sun.

"This way," Teo said, leading Ana down a narrow track with a sheer drop-off on one side.

"Oh, I don't like this!" Ana's fear of heights made her clutch Teo's jerkin as she followed him.

They wound their way downward, sometimes sliding, sometimes climbing with hands and feet. Shouts and hoofbeats resounded from the calank's rim, but Teo knew the shamans couldn't follow unless they dismounted.

He rounded a corner and pulled up sharp.

"Oh no," Ana groaned as she held Teo from behind.

The little trail had terminated at a ledge that dropped straight to the sea.

"We'll have to backtrack."

Teo started to turn, but a loud *crack!* stopped him. Something ricocheted from the cliff wall. Ana gasped.

"Get back!" Teo cried, pulling Ana behind a limestone protuberance. Up above, the shamans had found a vantage point and were shooting arrows at the trapped fugitives. Several others started easing down the narrow path, daggers in their hands.

Teo drew his boot knife. "Stay down," he instructed. "This is going to be—*ach!*" He stumbled backward as something slammed into his leg.

Looking down, he saw an arrow protruding from his calf. The narrow bodkin point was bloody where it had passed through the muscle below his knee. Though the wound wasn't deep, it would certainly hinder him in battle. Teo reached down to the arrow and snapped off the fletching, then slid the shaft free with a grimace. Blood seeped from the two holes.

"Here, take this!" Ana handed him a piece of moss, which he stuffed into the wound. Another arrow careened off the cliff. The approaching shamans were very close now.

Teo slid his arms around Ana's slender waist. She clung to him, though her face bore an uncertain expression. He stared into her eyes.

"I love you *so much*," he said.

"Oh, Teo! Me t—"

The affectionate words became a high-pitched scream as Teo leaped off the cliff with Ana in his arms.

They fell for what seemed like forever. Teo's stomach churned as he plummeted, and Ana's terrified squeal rang in his ears. They hit the turquoise water at the same moment, plunging deep beneath the surface in a cloud of bubbles. Teo's feet touched bottom, and he used the contact to propel himself upward. He shot into the brilliant sunlight, exhilarated to be alive. Ana popped up a moment later, blinking and gasping. The high walls of the calank surrounded them.

"Teo, look out!"

He spun to see a lone shaman approaching in the fisherman's sailboat. The hooded figure held a fishing harpoon above his head.

"Dive!" Teo said, ducking underwater again. Ana followed his lead, but Teo immediately realized it would provide no cover. The water was so clear, the shaman would have them in view at all times.

The harpoon whizzed pass Teo's side, leaving a frothy trail as it planted itself in the sandy bottom. Teo lunged to retrieve it. Rising to the surface, he saw the shaman in the boat had gained on him. Another harpoon was in the man's hand. Although Teo had nothing to push against, he rose up as high as he could and hurled his own spear at his enemy. Seawater splashed him as he threw, so he couldn't tell if he hit or missed.

Wiping his eyes, Teo saw his enemy still poised in the prow with the harpoon raised high. Cold fear gripped him. The shaman couldn't miss at such close range. Teo crossed his arms over his body, hoping to protect his vital organs.

Suddenly the hooded figure went limp like a rag doll dropped by a child. His eyes closed, and he toppled into the sea. Teo gazed at the grisly corpse floating facedown in the water. A bloody exit wound was visible in the middle of his back. Teo pushed the body away and climbed into the sailboat.

The wind had picked up as the morning wore on. Teo trimmed the sail and took a seat at the rudder, heading for the inlet's mouth. His calf injury ached, and a trickle of blood ran down his leg, but he ignored it.

He came alongside Ana, who was swimming through the crystal-clear water. Her hair streamed out behind her, and her long, muscular legs propelled her forward. When she surfaced for a breath Teo called her name. She stopped and turned, smiling when she saw him in the boat. Her bright eyes perfectly matched the blue-green sea. Droplets glittered on her forehead like a diadem.

"Now I believe in mermaids," Teo joked as he reached out his hand.

Ana clasped his arm and let him pull her aboard. She tumbled onto the floor of the boat, then sat up on one elbow, dripping wet, panting for breath. Her hair was a tangled mess, and her outfit was that of a peasant, but Teo thought she was the most beautiful woman he had ever seen.

"How would you like to go to Marsay?" he asked.

She glanced up at him. "I'm going wherever you are, Captain."

Teo met Ana's eyes, and they burst into laughter as the sailboat left the calank under the warm Mediterranean sun.

✦　✦　✦

The Bay of Marsay was a disaster. Wrecked ships were strewn everywhere, upended, rolled on their sides, or partially submerged. Debris bobbed in the water and washed up on shore. The worst was near the entrance to the harbor. The jumble there was so bad, Teo couldn't tell where one ship ended and the next began.

"What *happened?*" Ana wondered.

"I guess they got tangled while making a run from the storm. I doubt many people survived." He glanced at Ana, who bit her lip. Teo grimaced and said nothing.

The little sailboat was able to slip past the deadly tangle through water too shallow for an oceangoing ship. Teo lowered the sail as he neared the dock, and Ana looped a hemp mooring line around a bollard. Stevedores and sailors gawked at the strange pair clambering onto the pier.

"I don't see the *Midnight Glider*," Ana said disconsolately.

Teo was reminding himself not to offer her any cheap assurances when a familiar voice hailed him. "So the sea threw you back, eh, *amico?*"

A wide smile spread on Teo's face as he turned and saw Marco and Vanita approaching down the wharf. Ana uttered a cry of relief and ran to greet her friend. Vanita was equally relieved to see Ana alive.

"Quite a day yesterday!" Teo said as he shook hands with Marco and clapped him on the back. "Looks like you made it in safe though."

Marco dropped his head, and Vanita quickly intervened. "Our friend made a grievous sacrifice for a noble cause. He gave up his ship in order to destroy the Clan."

The foursome was quiet for a moment, until Marco finally broke the awkward silence with a laugh. "What can I say? I was looking for a new direction in life. This was my best chance to find it."

"He's a hero," Vanita said, entwining her arm in his.

"Well done," Teo agreed.

Although he wanted to head straight to Castle d'If, Teo realized his first priority had to be medical care for his leg. The arrow had entered his calf just below the knee, but fortunately it had angled out instead of penetrating deep into the muscle. Marco's ship doctor irrigated the wound with a syringe, then applied an ointment of honey and garlic before affix-ing clean bandages. A bitter concoction of willow bark helped with the pain. The wound had already started closing, and Teo found he could lean on a stick and limp around enough to get by.

An afternoon ferryboat took the two couples from the harbor to the island in the bay. Marco explained that Sol and Brother Thomas had been awaiting news of Teo and Ana before deciding how to proceed. "Now that you've shown up," Marco said, "they're going to want to confront Odo head-on."

The stocky friar was standing next to Sol on the dock when the ferryboat arrived. "I thought that was you on the boat! Praise Deus, you're alive!"

"*Je suis difficile de tuer,*" Teo said in Brother Thomas's native tongue. The remark made the knight break into laughter.

"*Fêtons ta survie avec un cadeau,*" he replied, then brought his hands from behind his back.

"My weapons! You saved them! Thank you, my friend!"

Brother Thomas leaned close and spoke in Teo's ear as he handed over the sword and ax. "I got the Secunda too," he said, "but I thought I'd better bring the weapons now. Belt them on. You might find you'll be needing them."

The six friends turned to walk—or hobble—uphill to the castle. The island was busy. Militiamen skirmished and drilled on the parade grounds or navigated the obstacle course. Teo could detect a heightened sense of urgency around Castle d'If.

A young page met the visitors at the castle gate and escorted them upstairs to Odo's chambers. Teo took Ana's elbow and drew her aside. "This guy doesn't allow women in his immediate presence," he whispered. "Maybe you and Vanita should wait in the guest rooms."

"Okay. I'm not really dressed for a meeting like this anyway."

"We'll go find the castle steward," Vanita agreed. The two women moved off down the hall.

The page opened the door to Odo's private chambers. Luxurious tapestries draped the walls, and a thick Likurian carpet lay spread on the floor. Odo emerged from his bedroom as his visitors entered, wearing an impeccable military uniform with chevrons on the shoulders. His demeanor was cordial. "My, my, Teofil! It seems you have quite a knack for trouble! I heard you were thrown overboard in the storm. It is good to see you alive."

"It's nice to see you as well, Commander Odo," Teo replied diplomatically.

"Please, take a seat." Odo gestured to some chairs, then snapped his fingers at the page, who pushed a wine cart forward and began to fill the glasses.

At that moment the bedroom door creaked open, and a long-haired young woman peeked out. Her makeup was as heavy as her clothing was scanty. Odo's face flushed. He frowned at the girl and shooed her away with the back of his hand. She hurried to the door and dashed out.

Odo turned back to his visitors as if he had done no more than brush lint from his sleeve. "Now then, gentlemen, perhaps one of you can tell me why I have the pleasure of your company today."

"Commander, it's time to marshal your forces for war," Teo said.

"To defend Jineve," Brother Thomas added. "There is no time to waste."

Odo sighed and leaned back in his chair. "Haven't we been down this road before?"

"We have," said Brother Thomas. "You advised us to obtain the counsel of the Holy Father."

"Indeed I did. I fear it is most unwise for the knights to move without his advice. Unfortunately, our great leader is far from us."

Teo nodded toward Sol, who drew a leather wallet from his tunic and removed the parchment inside. "Not as far as you might think," Teo said.

Odo snatched the parchment from Sol. His brow furrowed, and his cheeks grew red as he scanned the papal bull ordering the Knights of Marsay to march to Jineve's defense. He rose from his chair, his face livid. "It's a forgery!" he cried.

Sol shook his head. "It has the Holy Father's seal impressed into the wax."

"This is insane! Why should we interfere in the affairs of that foreign kingdom?"

Teo finally snapped. He rose to face Odo, though Marco's hand on his arm restrained him from taking a step forward. "You want to know why?" Teo barked. "I'll tell you why! Because the Iron Shield is on his way to Chiveis with a cargo of deadly chemicals! If the High Priestess gets ahold of it, she'll turn it into a weapon that will cover the whole earth in evil!"

Odo gave Teo an icy stare. "I am well aware of that man's movements,

Teofil. He sailed into the Rone delta just before the storm hit. My toll inspectors collected a hefty tax from him."

"Toll inspectors!" Teo couldn't believe his ears. *"You let him pass?"*

"Of course I let him pass. He has committed no crime that I know of. And the money we obtained can be used for holy purposes."

Teo darted forward and grabbed a handful of Odo's shirt. "Like what? More courtesans?"

"Get your hands off me!" Odo shrieked.

The commander spun hard out of Teo's grasp, but as he whirled, his foot snagged on the wine cart and he stumbled toward the fireplace. Though he caught himself on the hearth, the slip of parchment in his hand was hurled into the flames. In a matter of seconds the papal bull went up in smoke. Everyone stared at it, dumbfounded.

Odo was the first to speak. "Well, gentlemen," he said with forced composure, "so much for the will of the Holy Father."

Before anyone could reply, the page reappeared at the door, ringing a little bell. "Commander Odo, I have urgent news. A ship has just arrived."

"Where from?" Odo snapped.

"From Roma."

CHAPTER

12

The great eagle gazed across the jagged peaks, its wings folded, its visage impassive. For more than four centuries the hulking sculpture had been guarding the mountain pass, a stern-faced sentinel carved from blocks of stone. Though the Ancients had erected the monument to mark their Simplon Pass, the place was now called Eagle Pass in honor of its long-time resident.

Count Federco Borromo stood beneath the eagle statue as he stared toward the far northern horizon. Everything behind him belonged to the Kingdom of Ulmbartia, while everything that lay ahead was untamed wilderness.

The count had been skirmishing with the Rovers on the civilized side of the pass for the last two months. Ever since the great victory at the avalanche, things had been going his way. The kidnapped prisoners had been rescued, and the Ulmbartian hinterland had been cleared of the Rovers' presence. Now Federco intended to station a garrison on the pass until the winter snows closed it next fall. No longer would the vicious barbarians be able to raid the shepherds and villagers trying to eke out a living on their hardscrabble farms. That was a fine accomplishment, but Count Federco had his eyes on more.

The young lieutenant who served as the expedition's second-in-command approached Federco from behind. "The mule train has arrived with the tents," he said. "Where would you like us to set them up?"

The count pointed to the remains of a hospice building along the road. "The Ancients picked a good spot. Erect the tents in the lee of that old ruin."

"Very good, sir."

The lieutenant turned to go, but Federco stopped him with another command. "And send me the tracker right away," he added.

It wasn't long before the fair-haired pathfinder came to Federco's side. He saluted crisply. "You asked for me, Commander?"

"I did. You're one of the few men who's been down the far side of this pass. What's out there?"

"A wide river valley runs through the mountains. It's flat and fertile in places. Grapevines will grow on the south-facing slopes. Not a bad land, actually. The Ancients had many settlements there."

"But it's all returned to forest now."

"Yes, sir."

"And the river flows westward, if I'm not mistaken?"

"That's right. You follow it downstream about eighty-five leagues, then turn south to reach the pass discovered by Teofil of Chiveis."

Federco glanced at his chief tracker. The slender man had an effeminate way about him, yet his intuitive knowledge of wilderness paths was uncanny. "What's upstream?"

The tracker looked startled. "I don't know, sir. We've never explored that direction. There are some animal trails that follow the river up to a high glacier. I don't know whether there's a way through the mountains or not. There might be another pass, or it might be a dead end."

Count Federco pointed toward the ancient roadbed that descended from Eagle Pass into the unknown. "Well, Bard, don't you think it's time we found out?"

◆　◆　◆

Teo limped out the front gate of Castle d'If and looked at the island's dock. His heart leaped when he saw the ship that had just arrived, for he recognized its make as Roman. It was an archaic type of vessel propelled by oars in addition to sails. Such galleys had been used by the Exterminati, who enslaved people with physical deformities to work as rowers. When these "defectives" rebelled against their masters and threw off their yoke of oppression, they sailed to Roma and helped turn the tide of the battle at the basilica. In recognition of their contribution, the Papa had renamed them the Beloved. He had even appointed some of them to row his personal ship, a well-paying job with honor and prestige.

The galley maneuvered close to the dock and lowered a gangplank. Men and women in the brown robes of the Universal Communion started coming ashore. Teo watched until he saw what he hoped for: one of the visitors was dressed in white. Even from a distance, Teo recognized the aristocratic bearing and aquiline features of the Papa. Though he wasn't tall or imposing, his demeanor was naturally authoritative. The Papa was in his midforties, a trim, energetic man with close-cropped dark hair. An aura of godliness surrounded him, an intangible quality that came from his habit of constant prayer.

Things are about to change at Castle d'If, Teo thought.

"Out of my way," Odo grumped as he brushed past. "I must greet my esteemed guest."

The commander of the Order of the Cross met the Papa a short distance from the dock. Teo winced as he watched the obsequious Odo put on a pretense of civility, leading the Papa toward the castle with a stiff grin plastered on his face. Around the island, the knights and Marsayan militiamen set down their practice weapons and began to edge toward the keep. The distinguished visitor had created quite a stir, and everyone wanted to hear what he would have to say.

Soon a large crowd had gathered in the dim light of Castle d'If's courtyard. Torches burned in wall sconces, their smoke seeping past the awning above. Although the spectators were packed shoulder to shoulder, more kept pressing in. Teo spotted Marco across the way, and he also noticed the arrival of Liber, whose physical strength made him an obvious choice to be one of the Papa's rowers. Brother Thomas was there too, but Teo saw no sign of Ana or Vanita.

"Quiet, everyone," Odo said from the walkway that encircled the courtyard like a balcony. "As you can see, we have a visitor from afar. I am pleased to introduce the Papa of our religion, who has come all the way from Roma. He wishes to address a matter of supreme urgency." Odo glanced at the Papa, then looked back to the upturned faces. "Let us pray all his words will be in accord with the holy scriptures of Deus."

A hush settled on the crowd as the Papa climbed the stairs to the gallery. For years the Holy Father of the Universal Communion had been little more than a symbol, a distant figurehead who might not even exist. But now here he was, in the flesh and ready to speak. His words would be nothing short of momentous.

"I bring you greetings, brothers and sisters, in the name of Almighty Deus and his son Iesus Christus!" A translator relayed the Papa's saluta-tion from Talyano into Fransais, and the people nodded their approval. "As you well know," he continued, "times have been hard at Roma for the past four decades. Evildoers have prevented me from contacting you. But things have begun to change! Deus has done a mighty work, defeating our most hostile opponent. I now have the freedom to travel for the first time in many years. Long has my heart desired to establish a friendship with the Christiani of Marsay, and today I do so! I welcome you with open arms as fellow believers in Deus." The Papa paused, his face growing troubled. "Unfortunately, my meeting with you is bittersweet, for it comes with bad news."

At this last statement the crowd let out a collective groan. No one knew what the bad news would be, but coming from such an august visitor it must be grievous indeed. Everyone leaned forward to hear the dreaded announcement.

Resting his hands on the gallery's wrought-iron railing, the Papa pressed his point. "My friends, the forces of wickedness are stirring in the world. No longer will the nations isolate themselves from one another. War is coming—war that is undergirded by dark powers of the demonic realm. But do not fear! It is for times like this that you have prepared yourselves. This is why you have trained so diligently under the knights' watchful eyes. Now it is time to act! The kingdom of Jineve lies a few days' journey up the Rone River. That land stands in great peril, for a pagan priestess from another kingdom seeks to invade it. If she achieves this goal, empowered by unclean spirits, she will spread a blight not only upon Marsay but all the known world. Therefore I call upon you now, men of valor! I call upon you to stand firm against this atrocity and turn back the tide of evil."

For a long moment, absolute silence hung over the courtyard as everyone grappled with the Papa's bold challenge. Then, before anyone else could speak, a single voice broke the stillness.

"Heresy!" Odo cried. "The Holy Father speaks heresy!"

Teo's head snapped around. He bristled at Odo's outrageous allegation. Angered, he began to force his way through the crowd toward the stairs.

"Heresy!" Odo accused again as he approached the Papa with a book in his hand. The onlookers shrank back as the ominous word echoed around the courtyard. Opening his leather-bound volume, Odo stabbed a page with his forefinger and read aloud: "Hear the book of Departure, chapter 16, verse 29: 'Let each man remain in his place, and let no one depart from his place.'" Flipping the pages with a triumphant expression, Odo found another passage. "Now listen to the words of the Maxims, chapter 20, verse 3: 'It is an honor for a man to abstain from quarrels, but every fool indulges in passion.'" Odo lowered his book and pointed a finger at the Papa. "This man is filled with turbulent passions! That is why he tells you to act contrary to the will of Almighty Deus! He urges you into fights and quarrels, when the holy writings tell us to remain in our place."

"I agree!" called a voice from the crowd. "The Holy Father is a heretic!" Teo recognized the speaker as one of Odo's ever-present toadies.

The Papa had been meditating with his head bowed during the outburst, but now he looked up at Odo. His eyes blazed, and his jaw was set firm. "Stand aside, Commander," he said. "Your interpretation of scripture is poor, and your motives are even worse. You shall not prevail today. Again I say to you: stand aside or be judged."

"What? You want me to stand aside? You're the heretic here!"

Odo nodded toward several of his guards, who began to climb the stairs to the gallery. When the leader drew his sword, Teo burst into action as well. Dashing up the steps behind the men, he ran the opposite way around the gallery and arrived at the Papa's side just as the knights reached Odo. Pain throbbed in Teo's calf, but that was irrelevant. He drew the sword of Armand and stepped in front of the Papa, creating a stalemate on the narrow walkway.

"Now what are you going to do?" Teo challenged.

The Papa intervened. Gently touching Teo's wrist, he said, "Teofil of Chiveis, please put away your weapon."

Teo glanced at the Papa for clarification and received a confirming nod. Reluctantly he sheathed his sword, though he kept his hand on the hilt.

Odo assumed an aggressive posture. "Now then, heretic, you stand condemned! I hereby place you under arrest so that an inquisition can be made into your false doctrines."

The guards moved forward. Teo began to draw his sword once more. And then a brilliant light flooded the courtyard from above.

Everyone gasped and craned their necks as the sailcloth awning that had blocked the sky's light was cast off. Late-afternoon sunshine gleamed against stone walls that hadn't seen the sun's rays for years. A breeze swirled into the courtyard of Castle d'If. The torches sputtered and went out. All the onlookers blinked and stammered in the blinding glare. Confusion reigned, until the Papa's clear voice rang out like a bell.

"Let the light shine down and expel the darkness!" he exclaimed with his arms raised. "Odo of Marsay, by the power vested in me as the Holy Father of the Universal Communion, I strip you of your rank! Many good knights have shed their blood for the cause of Deus, and you are not worthy to be numbered among them. You are dismissed from the Order—you and all who will follow you!" The Papa gestured to the onlookers. "Will any of you stand with him?"

"Why should we?" someone shouted. "Good riddance!"

"He's a wastrel!" another voice accused.

Soon the clamor was raised to such a pitch that the Papa had to quiet the crowd. Odo's guards abandoned him. The Papa faced the stricken commander and took the leather book from his hand. Then, ripping the chevron epaulettes from Odo's shoulders, he said, "Be gone, and do not come back." Odo hung his head and fled through a doorway.

Turning toward the crowd, the Papa offered a blessing with his hands outstretched. "And now, brothers and sisters, peace be with you!"

"And with your spirit!" came the jubilant reply.

Teo stood on the gallery behind the Papa, stunned by what had just occurred. The situation had turned in an instant. Good had triumphed over evil, yet without violence. Teo grimaced as he realized how quick he'd been to draw his weapon. Now he felt relieved the affair hadn't come down to swordplay. *But what did happen here?*

A flicker of movement above caught his attention. He looked up. Someone was standing at the rim of the courtyard's opening, backlit by the bright sun. Teo squinted and raised his hand to shield his eyes.

Anastasia waved down at him, a broad smile on her face.

✦　　✦　　✦

The temple precincts were dark and still as the rebel monk Lewth approached a low building. Though the scientific laboratory was locked for the night, he had stolen a key to the outer door and was able to dart inside. Not daring to strike a match, he crossed the shadowy room by the light of the moon. The lab's inner chamber interested him most. Although the key to that door was unobtainable, Lewth had noticed a security breach above the doorframe: the transom window that let out deadly vapors was often left unlatched.

Lewth did not like the fact that everyone in Chiveis thought he was a faithful monk of Astrebril, but there was nothing he could do about it. Though he had formerly been devoted to that god, fasting and mortifying his flesh in obedience to the Beautiful One, he came to realize Astrebril's thin veneer of beauty disguised a corrupted heart of death and destruction. Nevertheless, the god had immense power; that was his allure.

When the wise university professor Maurice began to suggest there might be a good God, Lewth had been all ears. As a monk at the High Priestess's temple, Lewth could research lost religions in the secret archives. There he discovered the outlawed faith of Christianism. He even pilfered a cross-shaped necklace from a chest of relics. Yet Lewth had longed to know more about the Creator God. That was when Teofil and Anastasia had returned from the Beyond, chosen by Deu to recover the first testament of the Sacred Writing. A community of truth-seekers formed, and for a brief time life was good. But then the High Priestess laid down her ultimatum. Lewth had denied his faith on pain of death, and

Teofil and Anastasia fled Chiveis. Perhaps they would return one day, just as Teofil promised.

Lewth now considered himself a spy for Deu within the ranks of the enemy. Viewing himself that way helped take away the sting of his moral failure. Though he wished he could have found the courage to die as a martyr, or at least go into exile like Teofil and Anastasia, fear had gotten the best of him. His stealthy activities around the High Priestess's temple eased his sense of shame. Now Lewth was determined to learn the secrets of her deadly new weapon.

After dragging a stool near the lab's interior door, Lewth climbed up and tugged on the transom. It resisted momentarily, then popped open with a screech. Lewth winced, but nothing stirred outside, so he grabbed the bars of a grate in the ceiling and lifted his feet to the transom. The move required some dexterity, but Lewth was slim and agile. He dropped to the floor of the inner room, his heart pounding.

The arcane laboratory had a large table at the center. A bench along the wall was littered with mortars, pestles, vials, ampoules, and other types of alchemy equipment. Since the room had no windows, Lewth took the risk of lighting a candle. He tiptoed around the lab, examining the strange paraphernalia. What he desired most was an instruction manual that would explain the mysterious project. His eyes fell on a small wooden chest. Lewth thought a book might be hidden inside.

He set down his candle and lifted the lid. The chest did not contain a book, only a small metal canister. Lewth lifted it out, cradling the device in both hands. The canister had a nozzle but no label of any sort. Turning it over, he noticed a single word incised into the metal. He brought the canister close to the candle's flame, squinting to make out the word.

DANGER.

A black shadow darted across the table. Though it was only a rat, Lewth gasped and jumped back by instinct. The canister slipped from his fingers and banged hard against the floor. Instantly it began to hiss as a gas cloud billowed from it. Lewth fumbled to find the can beneath the workbench. A pungent mustardy smell filled his nostrils, but he ignored the stench until he finally grasped the can. He hurled it into the chest, still smoking, then slammed the lid shut and blew out the candle. The vapor was thick now, making his eyes water. Lewth coughed and waved his hands before his face as he stumbled to the door. He could open it from the inside, so he exited the chamber and hurried from the laboratory building. A sulfurous smell clung to his monk's habit.

The night was pleasantly cool. Lewth inhaled deeply, filling his lungs with fresh, sweet air. He coughed a few times to expel the last remnants of the stifling gas. Soon he was breathing normally again. A smile came to his face.

So that's the priestess's great weapon? A choking gas that makes it hard to breathe? Lewth acknowledged it would be difficult to battle a foe while swathed in a thick cloud of the stuff. But the gas would hinder both sides alike. Any combatants who encountered the fog would fight their way clear of it and resume the contest elsewhere. Lewth could not see how the secret weapon would give an advantage to one side over the other.

The monk pulled his cowl over his head and folded his arms into his sleeves. *If Teofil ever comes back to Chiveis, he'll be relieved to hear what I've discovered!* Coughing one last time, Lewth turned away from the laboratory and slipped into the shadows beneath the lofty spire of Astrebril.

◆　◆　◆

Castle d'If was a hive of activity. While some of the knights made preparations for the expedition to pursue the Iron Shield, other workers were busy giving the castle's courtyard a thorough cleansing. The walls gleamed, the floors were scrubbed, and the well at its center had been reopened. The sailcloth awning that Ana and Vanita had rolled back during the confrontation with Odo was discarded. Sunshine now illumined the courtyard with the light of heaven itself.

Purifying the well had been a top priority for the Papa, who was in charge of the castle now that Odo was gone. Bucket after bucket had been hauled up from the shaft until clear water replaced the brackish. The Papa had tasted the water several times before finally acknowledging its purity. Only when a papal assistant arrived at Ana's room to deliver a white robe did she learn why. The Order of the Cross at Marsay was being rededicated to holy purposes, and the ceremony was going to include the ritual of Washing for all who had not yet received it.

Ana arrived at the sun-drenched courtyard as the noon bell began to ring. She wore her plain robe and no shoes, just as she had been instructed. Many other white-robed figures had gathered in the plaza as well. Most were Knights of the Cross, but Ana smiled when she saw that Teo and Vanita also wore the special tunics. Marco, however, did not.

On the Papa's signal, a small choir of men and women began to sing the Sanctus. "Holy, holy, holy!" they repeated over and over, until the stones of the castle itself seemed to cry out in praise to the Eternal One. Ana bowed her head and crossed her arms over her breast, seeking to become small. To make much of herself at a moment like this could only be sacrilegious.

When the last echoes of the angelic canticle had died away, the Papa rose from a chair and went to a lector's stand. He was dressed in a full-length white cassock with a pallium of red and gold around his neck. Opening his ornate copy of the Sacred Writing, he delivered a homily on the Washing to the gathered faithful. His explanation of its meaning was both learned and devout.

"In this ancient observance," the Papa said, "we make an appeal to Deus for a good conscience through the resurrection of Iesus Christus. He came to us by water and by blood. The spirit testifies with the water and blood, for the three are in agreement. All who are washed by the savior are washed indeed, but if he does not wash us, we have no part in him. Today I call upon you to repent and be washed in the name of Iesus Christus for the forgiveness of your sins. He who has ears to hear, let him hear."

"Amen," the people replied in unison.

A space was cleared in front of the Papa so that the candidates in their white robes could step forward and kneel. Though Ana wanted to be next to Teo for such a momentous event, she was unable to reach him. The Papa drew an olivewood pail from the well. With a delicate silver ladle he poured water over the head of each candidate, offering the simple invocation, "I wash you in the name of the Father, and the Son, and the Holy Spirit."

As Ana waited her turn, she glanced up from her kneeling position and met the eyes of Liber. He stared back at her with a look of desperation. Ana immediately realized he wanted to join the others in the ceremony of holy Washing. Liber's childlike heart was open to Iesus, and his soul was sensitive to the promptings of Deu. Yet somehow he had been overlooked.

When the Papa arrived to stand before Ana, she looked up at him as he withdrew the ladle from the pail. "Please, Holy Father," she said, pointing, "what about our beloved brother Liber? Can he not receive the Washing as well?"

The Papa turned and saw Liber hiding under the stairwell. He beckoned the bearded giant with his hand. "Come forth, friend," he said. "Come forth and be free, as befits your name."

Timidly Liber came and knelt next to Ana. She intertwined her fingers with his. He smiled back.

"Thank you, Stasia," he whispered.

Ana bowed her head. Liber did the same. They closed their eyes, and together they received the water of life.

✦ ✦ ✦

King Piair II felt breathless and jittery. He always felt like that when the High Priestess came to his rooms for her rituals of union. Piair wished he could be in control of himself like a man should be, but somehow the sensual woman reduced him to a lusty he-goat. She was in charge, and he was led along as if by a ring in his nose. Even so, he looked forward to her visits every time.

When the knock came, Piair felt his knees go weak. *Not long now . . .* He swallowed the lump in his throat and squeaked, "Come in!" but there was no response. Only when he tried again in a firmer voice did the door swing open.

And there she was.

By all the gods, I want her!

The dark-haired priestess swept into the room in her gauzy robe. An iron slave collar was around her neck. Though black makeup lined her eyes and glossed her lips, the rest of her face was pale and delicate like fine porcelain. Only one flaw marred it—a thin scar along her cheek.

"W-welcome, lady," Piair said. "You look . . . lovely." *Ach! Stupid!*

The High Priestess narrowed her green eyes as she floated toward him. "Are you ready for the union, my young prince?" she whispered in his ear.

"Of course," Piair answered, his heart skittering wildly.

The High Priestess spun away. "Unfortunately, the gods will no longer allow it."

What?

No!

For a moment the king stood in dumbfounded silence as the priestess walked away, but at last he found his voice. "My lady, why not?" he cried. "What's the matter?"

"The gods are not pleased with you anymore. They have ordered the cessation of our rituals. I came to tell you."

The priestess moved toward the door. Piair ran and caught her sleeve. "Wait!"

She turned, a tiny smile on her lips.

"What can I do to . . . regain the gods' favor?"

The High Priestess shrugged. "Nothing, I fear."

"There must be something! Just tell me and I'll do it."

"The gods are angry. Only a major offering would appease them."

Piair shifted uncomfortably, still inflamed by his randy desires. "Please," he begged. "Don't go. I need you."

The queen of Astrebril raised her eyebrows in a way that Piair found charming. "You need me?"

"Yes! I need you to intercede with the gods. What gift could I give them?"

Taking Piair by the hand, the High Priestess led him to a plush divan and sat down next to him. "There is perhaps one thing that would placate the Beautiful One," she said.

Piair nodded for her to continue.

"You know your history books, so I don't have to tell you how Jonluc Beaumont conquered the kingdom of Jineve long ago. Over time we lost contact with that land. But lately the great Astrebril has been speaking to me. He believes his glory should be appreciated by everyone."

"All my subjects worship Astrebril, my lady. Chiveis belongs to him. I have made sure of it."

"Yes. But now Astrebril wishes the Jinevans to come under his dominion as well."

Piair drew back. "You mean he wants an invasion? Like Beaumont's?"

"Like Piair's."

Like . . . Piair's.

Piair the Conqueror!

The High Priestess stroked his hand with her black fingernails. "Are you the man for this heroic task, my prince?"

Piair wanted to say yes, but he didn't want to commit himself to a course of action that would shame him later. "What about the Jinevan army? Is it formidable?"

"The underworld spirits tell me the Jinevans are strong enough that we would need an alliance to defeat them."

"An alliance? What does that mean?"

"It means we must follow in the footsteps of Beaumont. He made a Pact with the outsiders. They fought alongside him and divided the spoils of war. So must we."

"The outsiders? They're barbarians!"

"Indeed! But they're barbarians who know how to wield a sword. They would be useful confederates, nothing more. After the war they would disappear." The High Priestess smiled, her face bright with anticipation. "Think of it, my prince! Think of the splendor that would crown your head! I find that so . . . *alluring*."

"R-really?"

"Of course! There is nothing more attractive to a woman than a man with the will to power."

I could be that man, Piair thought. His mind raced as he considered the details. "Arrangements would have to be made. Supplies and arms would be needed. The outsiders would have to be contacted about this."

"My priests have been in contact with them already. In fact, the outsiders are massing just beyond our borders. Your Highness, you must grant them access to Chiveis! Let their army encamp in the fields in front of the

Citadel's wall. A levy must be instituted so that provisions can be gathered from all the towns and villages. Then we will march forth and make war."

"*Make war*," Piair repeated, liking the sound of it.

"Yes! A war like that of Beaumont—and like your father before you."

Piair's attention snapped back to the High Priestess. "But my father fought against the outsiders! He didn't ally with them!"

"Times change. We must adjust."

The young king hung his head, conflicted by the choice before him. "I just don't know what to do," he muttered, clutching his forehead in his hand. "It's all so radical."

The High Priestess rose from the divan. "You disappoint me, Piair."

She turned away, but Piair grabbed her hips, spinning her around. He clenched the priestess's robe in his fists as he stared up at her from his seat. She regarded him with a steady gaze. Piair thought he could detect desire in her eyes.

"If I do this, my lady, will Astrebril be pleased?"

"Yes, my prince." She paused, smiling a little. "And so will I."

Piair pulled the High Priestess to himself. "Then so be it."

◆ ◆ ◆

Ana reclined in a canvas chair on the roof of Castle d'If, awed by the beauty of the stars that dotted the nighttime sky. Liber was there too, but he had little interest in the stars. He was busy munching sweet biscuits and guzzling a mug of apple cider.

"Want some, Stasia?" he asked.

Ana took a biscuit from the tin and thanked her friend. She nibbled it as she stared at the milky band that stretched across the heavens.

"Does the Father in the Sky see me?" Liber asked.

"Yes."

"Even at night?"

"Mm-hm. All the time."

Liber reclined in his chair. "I like that."

For a while the pair was silent, then Ana turned to Liber with a question. "Why did you seek the Washing today?" she asked.

"You told me the story of how Iesus was washed. I wanted to be like him." Liber took a long draught from his mug, then wiped his mouth with the back of his hand. "I didn't see the little bird though."

"What little bird?"

"When Iesus was washed, a little bird sat on his head. I wanted it to land on me too."

"Oh," Ana said. "The dove."

"I guess so. Why didn't it come?"

"Well, Liber . . . the dove is a symbol." Ana quickly realized her friend's mind didn't comprehend abstractions, so she added, "It's the spirit of Deu."

"What's a spirit?"

Ana bit her lip and thought for a moment, then said, "The spirit of Deu is his presence in our midst that we can feel but not see."

"Oh. Like the wind."

Glancing at Liber, Ana nodded with a grin. "Exactly!"

"Why is he left out then?"

Ana tried to follow Liber's line of thinking. "What do you mean, left out? Who's left out?"

"The little dove—the spirit who blows like the wind. The Papa gave us the Washing in the name of the Deu and Iesus and the spirit. But the spirit is left out."

"Where is he left out?"

"In the Twelve Words."

Startled, Ana mentally rehearsed the eleven words that had been chosen at the Council of Roma. *Creation, sin, sacrifice, Iesus Christus, faith, washing, holiness, remembrance, love, proclamation, hope.* These terms were supposed to encapsulate the message of Christianism. They told a story of creation's destruction and Deu's restoration of it. Yet somehow the role of his spirit had been omitted.

Ana bolted from her chair. "Come with me, Liber. There's someone we need to see right away."

Liber obligingly followed Ana to the chambers that had belonged to Odo. Although it was dark outside, the hour wasn't so late that Ana was afraid to knock. A papal assistant opened the door.

"We were wondering if we could speak with the Papa," Ana said. "We have an urgent matter that only he can address."

"The Holy Father is meditating. I will see if he can be disturbed. Wait here."

The assistant walked away, then returned momentarily. He beckoned with his hand. "This way please."

Ana entered the outer chamber, now refitted as sleeping quarters for the Papa's aides. She and Liber were led to a back room that was divided by a curtain. Ana assumed the area behind the curtain included a bed, while the front area had been converted into a study and reception room. The Papa sat at his desk, his beautiful book open before him. A lantern on a hook provided a bright yellow glow.

"Good evening to you both," the Papa said, rising to his feet. His tunic was simple, and he wore plain leather sandals. A wooden cross hung from a thong around his neck. He gestured to two chairs. "Will you have a seat?"

Ana sat down next to Liber as the Papa resumed his place at his desk. "I'm sorry to disturb you, Holy Father," she began.

The Papa looked at her with a twinkle in his eye. "The last time you came to my chambers like this, you had a secret code to reveal. What will it be this time?"

"Something so obvious we should have seen it long ago."

"Is that so? Well then, Anastasia of Chiveis, you must tell us what we are missing."

"I think I may have found the twelfth word. I don't mean to be presumptuous. I'm not trying to circumvent the council. It's just that . . . well, Liber brought to my attention something we left out."

"The little bird," Liber said. "The spirit who blows like the wind."

The Papa leaned on his desk, regarding his two visitors in grave silence. Unexpectedly he lowered his gaze to his book and began to read: "*In novissimis diebus, dicit Dominus, effundam de spiritu meo super omnem carnem . . .*"

Closing his eyes, Liber picked up the chant in a sonorous tone: "*Et prophetabunt filii vestri et filiae vestrae, et iuvenes vestri visiones videbunt, et seniores vestri somnia somniabunt, et quidem super servos meos et super ancillas meas in diebus illis effundam de spiritu meo.*"

The Papa caught Ana's eye. "These scriptures say that in the last days, the Lord will pour out his spirit on all flesh," he explained. "Young and old, men and women—they will all see visions and dream dreams. The Lord will pour out his spirit on male and female servants alike. This is the passage that came to my eyes tonight. Do you know it?"

Ana nodded. "The book of Deeds, chapter two. The sermon of Petrus."

"You are correct in your suggestion, daughter."

"I remember the chapter because I read it not long ago."

The Papa waved his hand. "I did not mean you are correct about the chapter, though you are. But what I meant was, you have indeed found the twelfth word."

Ana inhaled sharply. "You think so?"

"I know so, for it was on my mind as well. Deus led me to this passage tonight after I sensed a profound gap in our faith. He disturbed my soul so much that I prayed for resolution. Then he placed an idea in Liber's mind, and you listened to the divine whisper that came through our brother. Now you have arrived at my door to discuss the precise matter that was already stirring my soul, the matter I asked Deus to resolve for me! Such things are not a coincidence. Do not believe those who assign them to random chance. This is the nature of Deus's work. He binds his people and his book together in the revelation of his truth."

"I do not doubt that. I have seen him do it before."

"Your faith is worthy of praise, daughter." The Papa rose from his chair and came around his desk to stand in front of his visitors. "Two great tasks now lie before us. Mine is to go to Jineve with the message of salvation. The Knights of the Cross will accompany me, and the armies of Marsay will defend that land as best we are able."

Ana accepted the statement but did not respond, for it seemed better to wait and hear what the godly man would say next.

Placing his hand on Ana's head, the Papa spoke in a gentle voice. "You, Anastasia, must go even farther. You must return to your land with the truths you have discovered. Just as I sent Teofil on a mission, so I now send you. This day I name you *Anastasia Apostola Domini Chiveisorum*—the apostle of the Lord to the people of Chiveis. Do you accept this call?"

"I will go," Ana whispered. "It is my heart's greatest desire."

Liber's loud voice broke the reverent stillness in the room. "No! I don't want her to leave!"

"Hush, Liber," the Papa said. "Such yelling is unbecoming at a moment like this. Listen to what I have to say."

"But—"

Ana squeezed Liber's arm. "Be still. Listen to the Holy Father."

The Papa placed his hand on the bald top of Liber's head. "Your mind is innocent like a child, my son, but your body is strong like a bear. I have a mission for you as well. You must go with Anastasia, facing whatever dangers she faces, and serving as her strong defender."

Liber's face brightened. "You mean I get to go to Chiveis too?"

Ana smiled at him and nodded.

"I knew it!" he exclaimed. "The Father in the Sky does see me!"

◆   ◆   ◆

On the first day of the fifth month, only three days after their arrival at Castle d'If, Teo's expedition embarked from Marsay's harbor and crossed the bay to the mouth of the Rone. Though the weather could often be sunny this time of year, the skies on the day of departure had decided not to cooperate. A heavy overcast dropped intermittent rain on the four longboats that entered the marshy delta known as the Camarg. Strange pink birds with elongated necks populated the swamps, along with the elusive white ponies called camargs after their habitat. Unfortunately, the wildlife Teo encountered most often wasn't quite as endearing. Fierce mosquitoes swarmed him, and only an ointment of eucalyptus oil kept them at bay.

The four boats navigated their way up the Rone channel through a landscape of briny lagoons and low, reedy wetlands. Although Teo was in command of the expedition to overtake the Iron Shield and his load of brimstone, he let Brother Thomas lead the way while the arrow wound in his calf finished healing. Sixty good knights rowed the boats north, aided by Liber, who made pulling the oar look effortless. Ana and Vanita were assigned cooking duties each evening because the men would be tired from rowing, and Marco joined the expedition as a night watchman. Now that the *Midnight Glider* lay in pieces on the bottom of the ocean, the former pirate had decided to cast his lot with his friends.

On the second day out of Marsay, the boats left the Camarg and entered a more attractive region. Teo recalled seeing numerous lavender fields here on his previous journey to Jineve, but now the purple flowers weren't in bloom. Instead Teo occupied himself by studying the Ancients' crumbling architecture. He tapped Ana's shoulder and pointed to a stone bridge whose four remaining arches thrust out from one bank but no longer spanned the river. "Those are the kinds of structures that were old even for the Ancients," he said. "They were built hundreds of years before the Great War of Destruction."

"It must have been lovely in its day," Ana mused. "I can imagine people dancing and singing on it. Now they're all gone. How did so much beauty come to be lost?"

"Man's lust for power."

Ana nodded wordlessly, a frown on her lips.

Around noon on the third day Teo spotted one of the Iron Shield's camps. He ordered a halt so he could inspect the site for clues about his enemy. The cargo of brimstone had been transferred from the black caravel to riverboats, some of which had been pulled close to the shore, where their keels left gouges in the mud. Based on the size of the camp and the number of cooking fires, Teo estimated the force to number about five hundred men—far more than he had expected.

Marco gave a low whistle and shook his head. "Who are they? Mercenaries?"

Teo held up a black thread he had pulled from a thornbush. "Worse. Shamans."

"This is really bad," Brother Thomas said. "Where did the Iron Shield get so many men? There aren't that many Exterminati around Marsay."

"He must have summoned them to the area. They could easily hide in the Camarg and no one would know."

"Is this an invasion army? Is he going to attack Jineve right away?"

Teo rubbed his chin as he tried to think through the Iron Shield's strategy. "It could have been an invasion army if he had the Clan fighters too. But Marco's sacrifice at the harbor took care of that." Teo clasped his friend's shoulder in gratitude, and Brother Thomas also offered an affirming nod. "So now," Teo continued, "I think his first goal will be to deliver the brimstone to the High Priestess. She's creating some kind of fearsome weapon. They'll want it before they invade Jineve. We may still have some time."

"How far behind him do you think we are?" Marco asked.

"I estimate three days. But we can make it up. We have the advantage of traveling as a much smaller party."

"That will cease to be an advantage once we catch him," Marco said drily.

"We'll worry about that later. Until then we press hard. Let's get moving again."

Several more enemy camps were discovered as the expedition's four boats rowed north up the Rone. After almost a week on the river, the travelers watched the landscape change dramatically. Lofty alpine peaks loomed in the east, including one Brother Thomas called White Mountain. "It's the highest summit anywhere around," the friar knight said. "It's massive and always covered in snow."

Teo called for another halt at a juncture where a tributary river ran down from the high mountains. Marks on the shore indicated that the Iron Shield's army had started to sail up the branch instead of remaining on the Rone. Yet the move was confusing. Was the Iron Shield going to lurk in the wilds and pounce on Jineve later? What about the brimstone? Although men could travel overland on horses, it wouldn't be possible to transport a large cargo to Chiveis by any means except riverboats, and that would require staying in the main channel.

Teo had just decided to establish a camp and send scouts up the tributary when the arrival of a Jinevan patrol boat changed things. The boat was small, yet it bristled with crossbowmen whose weapons were cocked and aimed.

"Who are you?" shouted the boat's captain, using the local dialect that was similar to Teo's own native tongue. "These borderlands belong to the Kingdom of Jineve!"

"I'm a friend," Teo yelled back from the riverbank. "I've been through here before, and I dined with Mayor Calixte!"

The knowledge of the Jinevan leader's name seemed to mollify the patrol boat captain. "What's your business now?" he inquired.

"I'm seeking an acquaintance of mine. A big man with one eye. He goes by the name of Antonio."

"We've seen him," the captain replied. "Three days prior. We gave clearance to four ships and three-score men. They were headed to the capital on unknown business."

His business is to destroy you, Teo thought, but instead of voicing that dire prediction he asked, "What about the others with him? There would have been several hundred men in dark clothing."

"We saw no others."

Of course you didn't. They're masters of stealth.

Brother Thomas came to Teo's side and leaned close. "Looks like they've split up," he said. "That evil cargo was allowed to pass through Jineve like a viper slithering across the bedroom floor. The Iron Shield is taking it straight to Chiveis like we thought. Meanwhile the shaman army has melted into the mountains to await their call."

Teo tsked. "He probably played the role of charming businessman to Mayor Calixte again. By now he's left the city and crossed Leman Sea. We have to hurry."

He turned to the patrol boat captain. "We're headed the same direction as Antonio. We seek permission to pass through your kingdom as friends."

"Gather your rowers," the captain said. "I'll escort you to the city."

Jineve, the Jewel of Leman Sea, hadn't changed much since Teo had been there six months earlier. The waterfront still sparkled with elegant stores and the mayor's luxurious palace. The fountain on the jetty still spewed its waters into a graceful arc that landed on the lake as a mist. Even the people of Jineve seemed especially beautiful and exotic. Teo thought he could have enjoyed spending a few days here with Ana if he wasn't on such an urgent mission.

The palace steward met Teo's expedition at the dock. "I see you have returned to us, Teofil of Chiveis," he said in a tone that was barely civil.

"At least you have brought more attractive companions this time." He nodded at Ana and Vanita, then turned back to Teo. "Are you still spreading rumors of imminent invasion, or have you finally given up that fairy tale?"

"The threat has only grown since I saw you last."

The steward threw his hands into the air with an exasperated scoff. "What is it with you? Why do you come here to plague us with groundless worries about foreign enemies?"

Teo was about to answer when Ana interrupted. "Don't talk to him like that!" she burst out, jabbing her finger at the steward. "Teofil has risked his life to protect your kingdom! You have no idea what kind of storm is brewing over the horizon right now! All hell is about to be unleashed while you sit around doing nothing! You ought to—"

"It's okay, Ana," Teo said, putting his hand on her arm. "I've already tried that. We just need to pass through here and catch up with . . . Antonio."

Ana fell silent, though her look of suppressed anger remained. Her brow was knit, her jaw was clenched, and her lips were puckered in fierce defiance. Teo couldn't help but smile at the feisty Chiveisian farm girl he had come to love so much.

"You may pass through our lands," said the haughty steward, "but I advise you to leave as quickly as possible. The commissary at the far end of the harbor will supply whatever items you may need, if you have the means to pay."

"We do," Teo said. "We will be on our way very soon."

Despite Teo's confident assertion, the expedition wasn't able to leave until late the next day. A strategic decision had been made that the Marsayan longboats would be exchanged for horses during the final leg of the journey. Because Teo knew where the Iron Shield was headed and had already scouted the way to Chiveis, he felt he could make up more ground by taking an overland route that would avoid time-consuming river portages. Several of the more experienced knights concurred that in this situation, horses could travel a direct course that would quickly gain on the riverboats' convoluted path.

Brother Thomas, however, raised a concern. The Knights of the Cross were mustering the militia at Marsay to bring an army up the Rone River at the Papa's command. They were expected to arrive at Jineve's borders within a week. No one knew what Mayor Calixte would have to say about that surprising development, yet everything hinged on his response. Brother Thomas pointed out that the knights would need the most up-to-date intelligence about the status of the High Priestess's invasion plans, which meant a trustworthy figure would have to remain at Jineve to receive messages from Chiveis and relay the news to the arriving army. Reluctantly the friar knight volunteered to be that person.

"Can't someone else stay instead?" Teo asked. "I want you with me when I face those shamans in battle."

Brother Thomas shook his head. "This is a job only I can do. I know this city already. I can keep a low profile here and meet the knights when they arrive. They trust me, so they'll believe whatever I have to say. I need to be the link between you and them."

Teo wanted to argue further, but he could see the force of Brother Thomas's logic. "Alright," he agreed, "then here's what I'll do. Over by the commissary there's a pigeon post. I'll take some birds with me. Once I know the situation in Chiveis I'll dispatch them back to you. In about a week, start checking for my messages."

"I'll do it."

Brother Thomas reached out for a handshake, but Teo grasped his hand and pulled his friend into an embrace. "Deus be with you," he said, clapping the stocky friar on the back.

"And with you, my brother."

The two men met each other's gaze for a moment. Then, having said all there was to say, they turned away and did not look back.

✦　✦　✦

A week passed, riding by day, camping by night. Now Ana stood near the edge of the expedition's encampment, staring down at the little game trail at her feet. The sixty knights were caring for their horses or starting campfires, but Ana couldn't think about such things. The narrow path held her complete attention.

"Go up," Vanita said gently. "I'll take care of things here."

Ana nodded, yet still she hesitated to move.

Teo came to her side. "Come on. We'll go together." And so she went.

The sun sat low on the horizon as Ana climbed toward the top of the bluff. She walked in silence, holding hands with Teo, taking her time. A thick carpet of forest debris muffled their footsteps. The only sound was the warbling of a robin that flitted from branch to branch as if it enjoyed their company.

At last the game trail topped out. The bluff wasn't particularly high or dramatic. Its views weren't all that spectacular. Yet to Ana it was the most beautiful place she could imagine.

"There it is," Teo said, breaking the contemplative silence. "The great bend in the Farm River." He pointed to a ribbon of water that curved around in a tight arc. The bluff lay inside the bend like a peninsula. It was the official boundary between the Kingdom of Chiveis and the Beyond.

"Where's the clearing?" Ana asked. "Can you tell? I think it's this way." She pulled Teo's hand toward an opening in the trees.

"You're right," he said, glancing around. "It's more overgrown now, but I can still see the ruts left by the wild boars."

"Look!" Ana ran to a whitish object buried in the brush. She bent down and turned it over—the skull of a large bear. A hole pierced the skull beneath the eye socket.

Teo knelt next to Ana, searching the soil. At last he found what he sought. He held out a muddy arrowhead in his palm. "One of the three greatest shots I've ever seen you make," he said with a grin.

Ana cocked her head and looked at Teo. "Three? You probably think the second was the guy with the grappling hook, right?"

"Yeah. That was unbelievable."

"So what's the third?"

Teo mimicked the motion of an archer drawing a bow. He released the imaginary string, then intoned, "You picked the wrong woman, Rothgar!" Ana burst into laughter at Teo's imitation, yet she could tell that behind his playfulness lay deep admiration. All three of those shots had saved Teo's life.

For a while the pair fell silent, each lost in thought as they meandered around the clearing. A gentle breeze stirred the high, cathedral-like trees. Rosy light filtered through the branches, dappling the forest floor. At last Teo approached Ana.

"What are you thinking right now?" he asked.

She turned to face him, slipping her arms around his body and laying her head on his chest. "Oh, Teo, what can I say? When I met you here almost three years ago, how could I have imagined all the things we'd experience? The mountains of Ulmbartia, the seas of Likuria, the basilica of Roma, the wild beauty of Sessalay. We made great friends in the Beyond, and horrible enemies too. I faced trials I thought I'd never survive. But Deu was faithful to us in everything." Ana sighed deeply as she rested in Teo's embrace. "You and I have shared an amazing adventure, Captain."

At those words Teo pulled back from Ana so he could look into her eyes. She tilted her chin to gaze up at him. His handsome face held a tender expression. "Do you think our adventure is over?" he asked.

A broad smile came to Ana's lips. "With all my heart, Teo, I hope it's just begun."

CHAPTER
13

Queen Mother Katerina stood on the highest balcony of the royal palace, her hands resting on the balustrade as she gazed across the great Kingdom of Chiveis. The Citadel's wall stretched below her, spanning the cleft in the mountains and overlooking the rugged frontlands beyond. All the buildings of the Citadel, including the palace, relied on the wall for protection. Some lay in the flat area directly behind the imposing granite face, while others rose in tiers on the adjacent mountainsides, culminating with the royal palace at the highest point. The only other building to stretch so high was the spire-adorned Capital Temple of Astrebril—a nest of shifty eunuch priests and seductive cult prostitutes.

Yanking her eyes from the temple, Katerina looked beyond the Citadel's wall to the thriving town of Entrelac. Flanked on either side by two large lakes, Entrelac was the connection point between the valleys protected by the Citadel and the wider environs of Chiveis. The fishermen who lived on the lakeshores and the farmers along the Farm River could flee to the Citadel if times grew perilous. The Beyond was infested with deadly threats, and only Astrebril held them back.

Or so it was said.

A knock on the door inside the palace signaled the arrival of a steward. Katerina was in her son's chambers, waiting for the impetuous king to return from whatever political duty occupied him at the moment. Katerina recalled how busy her husband Piair I had been when he ruled as king. Their son had yet to prove himself capable of carrying such a load.

Hurrying to the door, she pulled it open but found the steward had already walked away. The man spun in the hallway when he heard the door open behind him. "Oh, my lady! I thought no one was in."

"Piair is busy, and I was out on the balcony. What did you need?"

The steward held up an envelope. "A message for the king. A dispatch from the army."

"You can give it to me. I'll pass it on."

The steward chewed his lip as he sought a diplomatic reply. "Well . . . my lady . . . it's an important military matter. I'd prefer to deliver it to His Highness personally. You understand, I'm sure."

"What I understand is that the king does not wish you to be rude to his mother," Katerina said pointedly. She held out her hand. "Leave it with me. I will take responsibility and absolve you of all blame."

The steward placed the letter in Katerina's palm. "As you wish, Queen Mother." He bowed at the waist, turned, and left.

Katerina took the letter back to the balcony and laid it on the table. Pouring herself a mug of cold juniper tea, she sipped it as she enjoyed the warm sun on her shoulders. Puffy white clouds dotted the sky, casting shadows on the jagged Chiveisian frontlands. The queen mother glanced again at the envelope. On impulse, she snatched it up and opened it.

Her eyes grew wide as she scanned the note. It was from the commander of the Royal Guard's Second Regiment. Katerina set down her mug and stared at the message in her hand:

TO HIS ROYAL MAJESTY, PIAIR II

I regret to report a problem has arisen among the peasants—a religious matter about which you asked us to warn you. Four weeks ago a farmer and his wife from Edgeton visited the headquarters of the Fifth Regiment. The woman spoke favorably about the god Deu in the presence of several witnesses. Both were heard to blaspheme Astrebril and criticize your most glorious and beneficial reign. The aforesaid peasants are called Stratetix of Edgeton and Helena d'Armand. (No doubt your quick mind will recognize that surname.) Since I did not know your royal will in this matter, I have refrained from action. I await your instructions and stand ready to carry them out immediately.

Rexilius of Toon
Commander, Second Regiment

Katerina rose from the table. Her heart was beating fast as she leaned against the balcony railing for support. Glancing around, she ascertained that no one could see her, then reached to a jeweled locket at her neck. By pressing on the silver filigree in just the right way, the case could be made to pop open. A tiny painting was hidden inside: a youthful face with a dark goatee, a man of science and learning. The queen mother stared at it for a long time before snapping the pendant shut.

A cloud covered the sun, bringing welcome shade. The wind stirred a tendril of Katerina's hair, and she brushed it from her forehead.

"What are you up to, Helena d'Armand?" she whispered to the hills.

✦　　✦　　✦

Teo crouched behind a rocky crag, staring down at the Farm River. In the distance, four heavily laden boats approached from the Beyond, longships rowed by fourteen or sixteen shamans. A tall man was visible in the prow of the lead ship—clad in dark mail, carrying a mace, and searching the river ahead with his one good eye. The Iron Shield had come to Chiveis.

Rising from his hiding place, Teo turned toward the trail. Though it was rough, he made good time as he hurried downhill to the river. The last time he came this way, he was limping badly, for he had sprained his knee while stumbling before an onrushing bear. But that was nearly three years ago, and his body bore no such harm now. He was lean and fit from his weeks of wilderness travel. His calf wound had fully healed. Teo was ready to do battle against his greatest foe.

The sixty Knights of the Cross were stationed along the riverbank under deep cover. They were armed with enough arrows to keep shooting at the longships if they tried to escape, though Teo didn't think that would happen. After the first volley, the boats would turn and engage or they'd be decimated from behind. And besides, running from danger was not the way of the Iron Shield.

"You ready?" Teo asked Marco as they knelt in the brush. The handsome ex-pirate grinned and nodded with the kind of panache few men could muster in the moments before a skirmish. Teo clasped Marco's shoulder and drew strength from his brother-in-arms.

"I just hope the women will be safe," Marco said.

"They're saddled and waiting at the rendezvous point. It was all I could do to convince Ana to stay out of the battle. I had to appeal to her father's unbearable grief if his daughter died just as she reached the border of her homeland."

Marco gave a little laugh as his eyes scanned the river. "She's a fighter, that girl of yours."

She's had to be, Teo thought.

The men waited in silence as the sun rose higher. Occasionally a knight coughed or rustled the bushes, but otherwise everything was still. Teo tightened the strap on the helmet he had borrowed from the brotherhood. It was a finely wrought piece of armor with eyeholes and a nose guard, though not a full visor. A bead of sweat rolled down his cheek and dropped from his chin.

"They're here," Marco whispered.

And they were.

The four vessels eased upstream, slinking ever closer to Chiveis with their deadly cargo. Barrels and crates were piled amidships. Though the shamans' attitude was not carefree as they rowed, they seemed oblivious to the imminent attack.

Teo stood up and drew his longbow, its yew heartwood creaking under the strain. Down the shoreline, he knew the sixty Christiani archers were doing the same.

"Do me a favor," Marco said as he looked up at Teo from a crouch. "Put a few shafts in the tall guy before he hits land." Teo threw his friend a smile but made no promises.

The longships drew even with the archers, their oars sweeping and catching in unison. Teo waited until the last boat had reached him, then took a deep breath and shouted, "Now!" At the same moment he released the bowstring and sent a shaman to his eternal destiny.

The whispering sound of the barrage of arrows was followed by yells of alarm. The Farm River wasn't a broad watercourse, and the longships were close to the near bank. Though some of the black-clad shamans slumped in their seats, many more still manned the oars. They turned hard at the shouted commands, maneuvering surprisingly well in the mayhem. Two more volleys whistled toward the ships before the enemy reached the shore. Now the time for bows was over. Blade against blade would determine the final outcome.

The Exterminati swarmed over the gunwales like hornets from a nest. Their war cries reverberated among the trees as they rushed to engage their unknown attackers. Teo dropped his bow and slid the sword of Armand from its sheath. One warrior in the distance held his attention, but Teo knew he would have to fight his way to the Iron Shield.

A shaman rushed at Teo in a whirlwind of black robes and flashing steel. Teo parried the attacker's curved dagger with his ax and countered with a thrust of his own. The sword's razor-sharp tip slid through the man's sternum like a knife in hot butter. Teo let the wide-eyed man fall off the slick red blade, then stepped over the corpse and leaped into the melee.

Battle raged along the bank of the Farm River. Teo weaved among the combatants, swinging his ax and sword with deadly effect. Cries of anguish filled the air as blood-smeared warriors fell to the ground. A snarling shaman reared in front of Teo, whirling a heavy flail over his head. Teo ducked under the ball as it whizzed past on its chain. He was about to counterattack when a blow rang hard against the back of his helmet. Dizziness engulfed him, and he stumbled to his knees. His vision dimmed as he tried to shake off the effects of the impact. The shaman with the flail threw back his arm, readying the spiked ball for a crushing blow. Suddenly a blade sliced down from the periphery of Teo's view. Gore spattered his face as the enemy shaman's arm was severed from his shoulder by a pirate cutlass. Teo scrambled to his feet and kicked the one-armed attacker aside, but there was no time to stop and thank Marco for his lifesaving intervention. The fighting was heavy, and Teo quickly lost contact with his friend.

Not far away, the Iron Shield fought his way across a sandy beach, cleaving a path through the knights with his giant mace. Three arrows protruded from his chain mail, but the points hadn't gone deep. Teo ran to the powerful warrior just as he crushed a knight to the ground in a heap of pulp and bone.

The Iron Shield stared at Teo's helmet for a moment, then smiled as recognition came to him. "So you found me," he said, spreading his arms wide. "Very good. Come and get what you seek."

Teo gestured at the raging battle. "You've lost. Look around. Your men have fallen. You're outnumbered now."

The Iron Shield threw back his head and laughed. Teo flinched at the otherworldly rumble that emanated from his enemy's chest. The dark warrior took a step forward, hefting his mace. "No, Teofil. It is you who should look around."

From the river a trumpet sounded. Teo felt the icy grip of fear as he glanced over the Iron Shield's shoulder. Armed men on the opposite bank were shoving boats into the water, probably a hundred or more. It wouldn't take them long to cross. All were hungry for a brawl.

Outsiders!

Stunned, Teo drew back. His knights couldn't resist both the shamans and the new arrivals. Even a strategic withdrawal seemed impossible now. Utter defeat was at hand.

"I'll have your woman tonight," the Iron Shield vowed. "Perhaps I shall let you live long enough to see it." The sadistic warrior spat out his threat like venom, then raised his mace and charged.

Teo reacted by instinct. He clicked the gemstone on his war ax, which advanced a steel ball into a cup at the end of the weapon's haft. With a strong flick of his arm Teo whipped the ball at the Iron Shield, striking him on the forehead. The warrior stopped in his tracks and cursed, clutching his face. Though he wasn't disabled, he was stunned, and for a split second Teo considered attacking him. Yet he knew that even if he managed to kill his enemy, the horde of outsiders would do the same to him. Escape must be his sole objective now, and only one thing would keep the shamans from pursuing.

Teo ran to the lead ship, which contained the expedition's supplies. He snatched a large cask and held it above his head in two hands as he dashed to the next ship. Without stopping, he hurled the cask against the crates stacked between the thwarts. The barrel broke open in a cascade of lantern oil, dousing the wooden boxes.

An arrow from the river slammed into the gunwale near Teo's hand. Another whizzed past his ear. He ducked behind the longship, hunching against its hull as he fumbled for the matches in his pocket.

"Stop him!" roared the Iron Shield, who knelt on the beach with a hand to his bloody forehead. "Kill that man!" Two shamans swiveled their heads and spotted Teo. They barreled at him with their daggers drawn.

Help me, Deu, Teo prayed as he struck the match against the side of the box. The flame flared up. He tossed it over his shoulder. It spun through the air.

And the wind blew it out.

No!

What happened next was a blur. High above, something yellow and bright lifted from the trees and curved through the sky in a graceful arc. At the same moment the charging shamans reached Teo in a maelstrom of murderous fury. Just as they were about to plunge their daggers into him, he sprang onto the gunwale of the ship and dived over their heads. Their blades stabbed the ship's planks where Teo had just been crouching. He hit the ground behind them and rolled to his feet to see the fire arrow plant itself in the stack of brimstone crates. The lantern oil exploded into a leaping blaze.

"Nooo!" came an anguished cry from the beach. "*Get water! Hurry!*"

While all the shamans scurried toward the burning boat, Teo joined the other knights escaping into the trees. Horses had been stationed nearby in case a retreat became necessary. The surviving knights would have to withdraw into the wilderness to fight again another day.

Teo reached the rendezvous point and swung into the saddle. As he kicked his heels and urged his horse into the dense forest, the full weight of the rout settled onto his shoulders. Many good warriors had fallen. Although some of the Iron Shield's infernal rock might have been destroyed, not all of it was. The dark warrior would have a large shipment to give to his queen.

Yet even as Teo considered this disaster, a positive thought crept into his mind, lifting his spirits amid the gloom of defeat. He couldn't help but shake his head in wonder.

That was a fourth great shot, he decided as he was enveloped by the Beyond.

◆　◆　◆

Helena d'Armand gripped her husband's hand when the carriage door opened. Guardsmen stood at attention outside the royal palace at the Citadel, their faces impassive.

"Follow me," the military escort said brusquely.

"Be brave," Stratetix whispered as he alit from the carriage.

"And may Deu be with us," Helena answered even more quietly.

The soldier led the husband and wife through a back door of the palace. Though they had been arrested on charges of illegal activities, they were not in chains and had not been treated cruelly. Yet Helena knew how serious the situation was. She had already been threatened with death once because of her association with Deu, and she had no reason to expect otherwise this time.

A series of winding staircases brought the couple to a plain wooden door. Helena sensed she was being escorted through lesser-used corridors instead of the main hallways. She didn't know what to make of that.

"Enter," the soldier ordered.

"What's in there?" Stratetix asked.

"Don't ask questions. Just go."

Stratetix slid his arm protectively around his wife, and she nestled close to him. "Whatever is inside, let's face it together," he said to her.

The room was small and sparsely furnished, though the decorations it did have were elegant. A plush carpet was on the floor, and three chairs were arranged around an oaken table. A window in one wall looked out over the city.

Stratetix held Helena's chair, then sat down beside her at the table. No one else was in the room. Helena nervously tapped her fingernails on the polished wood while Stratetix stroked his beard.

At last the door opened, and when Helena saw who entered she scrambled up along with Stratetix. "My lady!" she exclaimed, bowing at the waist.

"You may rise."

The queen mother's face was stern as she walked across the room. She was an attractive older woman with a proud chin, gray eyes, and silver hair streaked with dark strands. Though her figure had become more rounded since Helena had seen her last, she was still a striking beauty.

"Sit down with me and we shall talk of important matters," Katerina said, taking her place at the head of the table across from her guests. She drilled Helena with a hard stare. "I would not have expected treason from you, Helena d'Armand."

"Your Majesty, I am guilty of no such thing."

"Traitors never think so. They always justify their illegal actions by claiming to serve the higher good."

Helena remained silent, but Stratetix spoke up. "May I ask why we've been brought here today? The accusations leveled against us were vague and preposterous."

The queen mother turned to regard Stratetix. "You are the type of man upon which our kingdom is founded," she said. "Sturdy. Hard-working. Patriotic. By the sweat of your brow the people are fed. Why do you have to stir up so much trouble?"

"I do not seek trouble, only the well-being of Chiveis."

"As *you* define it."

"No, my lady. As heaven defines it."

"And who speaks for heaven? Astrebril?"

Stratetix was about to answer when Helena laid her hand on his arm. "Queen Mother Katerina, I remember you as a religious seeker. Many years ago we used to debate divine things. How would you answer that question today? Do you believe Astrebril reigns on high?"

The queen mother sighed. "Perhaps not. Yet it is agreed by all that your God caused my husband and daughter to be snatched from this world."

"That was the work of evildoers, not Deu."

"Aha! So you do not deny your loyalty to Deu?"

"I have only known my God a short time," Helena replied, "yet he has done me no wrong. Should I now blaspheme the one who saved me?"

"It would be in your interest to do so. According to my son, your faith is a capital offense. Piair hates your God."

"He shouldn't. Deu didn't kill your husband, or Princess Habiloho. That was arranged by—"

"I know what you think," Katerina interrupted bitterly. "And even if it's true, that too is a crime to suggest."

"Should we not prefer the truth over the laws of men?"

"Crime cannot be allowed to stand in Chiveis, Helena d'Armand."

Stratetix leaped to his feet. "Crime? This kingdom is infested with crime! The Royal Guard has been turned into a band of marauding thugs! Cultic religion is crammed down our throats! Freedoms have been taken away from the good people of this land!"

Helena tugged on her husband's tunic. "Sit down, love. Remember we are in the presence of royalty." The queen mother's outraged expression softened at Helena's soothing words.

"Forgive me, Your Highness," Stratetix muttered as he took his seat again.

Katerina acknowledged the apology, then looked closely at Helena. "Do all the people of Chiveis feel this way?"

"Many do. Times have changed."

"When did they start to change?"

"In recent years," Helena answered evasively.

"The daughter of Armand may speak her mind in my presence. Do you think my son is unworthy of his father's rule?"

"I would not go so far as to say that, Your Highness. Yet I do not believe the younger Piair has found his footing yet as king."

"We loved and admired your husband," Stratetix put in. "That cannot be said of all who lived during his reign."

The queen mother shot him a sharp look. "What does that mean?"

Helena and Stratetix exchanged glances, then Stratetix said, "Some say the events surrounding the Battle of Toon were suspicious."

"Explain yourself, Stratetix of Edgeton."

"Well . . . we have learned on good authority there was a conspiracy against King Piair."

"A conspiracy during which my father was killed," Helena added, "and not by outsiders."

"By whom then?"

"Rebels within the Second Regiment."

"Pfft! Those men are tools of the High Priestess," Katerina scoffed.

"Yet greatness is still to be found within the Royal Guard."

"Let me tell you about greatness, Helena d'Armand. Your father defended my husband's life with his own. He stood over him with his mighty sword while the enemies raged and the arrows flew. Piair loved Armand like an older brother. Well do I remember the day he brought home that sword after your father died. Piair held it in great honor. He said it must become an heirloom of Chiveis, to be awarded only to a warrior of supreme skill."

"That warrior is now in exile," Helena said.

"Yes. Because he chose Deu. As have you."

"I have only chosen to seek the truth wherever it may be found. I have chosen to reject corrupted deities and to seek the good Creator. And I remember when you longed to do the same."

Katerina frowned. "Be that as it may, you have defied my son's orders. You have spoken of Deu. He is a forbidden divinity."

"But what if he is the one true God?"

"I am not the regent. I cannot change my son's commands."

"But you have other kinds of power," Stratetix suggested.

Helena leaned forward, resting her elbows on the table. "My lady, I know you recall what Chiveis used to be. You remember the ideals upon which our kingdom was founded. Use your influence to restore those ideals! The people don't support the oppression of our land. Nor do the troops. Give them cause, give them hope, give them a reason to fight and they'll resist! Don't let our kingdom be enslaved to the High Priestess."

Katerina lowered her chin and covered her eyes with her hand. She sat in that posture for a long time, kneading her forehead with her fingers. "Oh, Chiveis," she whispered.

Stratetix and Helena waited silently.

At last the queen mother raised her gaze to the couple. Her authoritative demeanor had returned. "Very well," she said. "I think it is time for the Royal Guard to hear your story, Helena d'Armand."

She nodded obediently. "As you wish, Your Majesty. But should I speak of . . . everything?"

"No! Not everything! Just what is asked about the Battle of Toon."

The queen mother pulled a string on the wall to ring a bell outside. "A hearing before the Warlord will be arranged in a few days. Until then you must remain locked in my guest chamber. I will tell no one you are here, not even Piair. You must testify to what happened at the battle. Now more than ever, Chiveis needs to be reminded of its past."

"Are we under arrest?" Stratetix asked. "Is this going to be some kind of trial?"

"It is a military hearing, not a trial."

"Are we to be charged with a crime?"

"Not formally, though I cannot guarantee you will remain unharmed. There are those who do not wish the truth to be heard."

"I will accept the risk and speak of what I have learned," Helena said, "though my knowledge of the conspiracy is secondhand. Shouldn't we summon eyewitnesses?"

The queen mother uttered a little laugh and waved her hand. "Perhaps we can do that. But corroboration of the facts is not my main concern."

"Then what is, Your Majesty?"

Helena stared at Katerina's face until she looked up. The two women locked eyes.

"I do not merely want your testimony," the queen mother said. "I want *you*."

"Why me?"

"Because in times like these, only the daughter of Armand can help the soldiers of the Fifth remember who they are."

✦ ✦ ✦

When the Papa arrived in Jineve at the head of an army, Mayor Calixte could no longer hide in Montblanc Palace. Brother Thomas smiled to himself as he saw the consternation on the mayor's face. Even the haughty palace steward looked worried. *Maybe now they'll start taking action!*

The Papa's arrival had coincided with Teofil's urgent message from Chiveis. The slip of paper on the pigeon's leg had carried dire news: an army of three thousand barbarian warriors had gathered at Chiveis's borders and was preparing to move out. Combined with the kingdom's Royal Guard and the elite force of shock troops called Vulkainians, Teofil estimated the invasion army to number five thousand men. The only thing preventing an immediate march on Jineve was the need to gather sufficient supplies and mounts.

Mayor Calixte welcomed the Papa to Jineve with hastily arranged fanfare suitable to the visitor's high station. Although the Jinevans didn't know much about the Universal Communion, they still had a memory of distant Roma. Everyone could see the Papa represented a powerful faction from that legendary city. Of course, the presence of three thousand knights and Marsayan militiamen only served to reinforce the Papa's standing.

A translator who spoke Talyano was summoned to assist Mayor Calixte and the palace steward on the dock at Jineve's harbor. "Forgive me for not offering a more elegant welcome," Calixte said through his translator. "I would certainly have gathered the surrounding nobility had I known you were on your way."

"That is not necessary," the Papa replied. "It is to the average citizens of Jineve that I wish to speak."

"It can be arranged," the palace steward said. "In a few days we can erect an appropriate podium, with a lectern and risers and a canopy over the platform."

The Papa waved his hands. "There is no time for such things. War is upon you whether you wish it or not. You must decide today how to respond."

"The Holy Father can speak from his ship if the people will congregate along the waterfront," Brother Thomas said. "I am sure they are more interested in what he will say than in the trappings of rhetoric."

In a matter of hours the city of Jineve was abuzz. The curious and the concerned gathered on the lakeshore, waiting for the big announcement from the foreign visitor. Rumors spread like a disease—rumors that portended an imminent invasion by dark forces. Yet Brother Thomas wasn't too worried about the rampant gossip. A measure of anxiety was needed right now. He knew today's hearsay would become tomorrow's reality unless something was done to stop it.

By midafternoon the crowd had swelled until it thronged the entire shoreline. The official translator was joined by heralds with amplifying horns so that everyone could hear the Papa's address. Brother Thomas piled some empty crates on one of the Christiani riverboats, which was moored lengthwise a short distance from the bank. The Papa ascended this makeshift podium while the translator was stationed at his feet. Several heralds stood nearby, up to their waists in water, ready to repeat the translator's words to the masses.

The crowd quieted as the Papa offered greetings on behalf of Marsay and Roma. He told the people he did not come to make war against Jineve but to defend it from aggressors. "Even now an army is gathering in the east," he said. "A message has just been received from our spy in the Kingdom of Chiveis. The wicked High Priestess of that land is preparing to invade Jineve. She will force your men to fight her battles. She will give the bodies of your women as prizes to the lascivious barbarians. She will plunder the resources of the realm to make horrific weapons. These are not empty threats—no, indeed! Terrible events are about to occur unless you take action."

The Papa paused to allow the translator to catch up, but before he could begin again the stunned crowd exploded into panic. The men gaped at each other, and many women broke into wailing. Even the soldiers looked frightened. Desperate pleas were addressed to Mayor Calixte in his open-top carriage, yet the Jinevan ruler had no comfort to offer.

In all the commotion Brother Thomas slipped over the riverboat's gunwale and waded halfway to shore. He had picked up some of the local language during his time in the city, so he yelled, "Listen!" in the language of Jineve. Repeating this word again and again, he flapped his arms like wings in an attempt to hush the crowd. Finally some of the people noticed him. Brother Thomas pointed to the Papa. "Listen!" he cried once more— and they did.

"History is trying to repeat itself, my friends," the Papa continued. "Centuries ago Jonluc Beaumont came here from Chiveis. He had departed Jineve an exile but returned as a conqueror. When your kingdom was defeated he went on to Marsay, and there he initiated a binding Pact. The rulers of the earth swore an oath in their own blood, and the heavenly powers took notice. I ask you: What human goal would make the demonic pantheon pay attention? What could possibly be so important to the unclean spirits that they would set aside their usual bickering and unite behind a common cause? Do you have any idea?"

The Jinevan citizens turned and muttered among themselves, but no one knew the answer. "Money!" someone shouted. The Papa shook his head. Cries of "Sacrifices!" and "Power!" were closer to the mark, yet the Papa let the debating continue. At last he raised his hands to call for quiet again.

"What the spirits desire most is to exterminate what they fear. Good people of Jineve, listen to me now! There is one true God in the heavens! His name is Deus—Deu in your speech. He is the good and loving Creator of our world. The demons hold men in bondage, using the chains of our lusts against us. Indeed, the entire cosmos is enslaved to sin! To free us, the Creator sent his son Iesus from his right hand. Iesus became a man to teach us the truth, but evil men put him to death. Yet that was not the end of the story. Deu raised his son to life again, and in that moment the bondage of sin and death and the demons was broken. *Shattered*, I tell you! Only Deu is strong enough to vanquish the evil powers. That is what they fear. Do you want to be free? Do you want to be free this very day? Then come . . . come to the faith of the Christiani! Come into the shelter of Deu's holy communion. Only there will you find refuge from the powers that assail you."

The Papa stepped back and stood still. Time hung suspended. The awestruck crowd was silent—until a voice broke the otherworldly hush.

"I will come!"

The speaker was a dark-haired boy. Brother Thomas beckoned him into the water. "Come, lad," he said. "Come and be washed by Deu."

"Me too!" said a woman with a baby on her hip. She waded out beside the boy.

"And me," cried a burly man in a blacksmith's apron. "The gods scare me!"

Then, as if an invisible wall had crumbled, the crowd surged off the shore and into Leman Sea. Up and down the Jinevan waterfront the citizenry left the bank in a mass exodus. The waters teemed with an innumerable host. Humble peasants mingled with wealthy aristocrats in the frothy waves. Some of the taller citizens waded out to chest level to make room for the others. Even Mayor Calixte joined the throng. Men, women, and children alike stood in the cold lake and stared expectantly at the Papa.

Brother Thomas swam back to the longship and climbed aboard. The Papa had been conferring with the translator, but now he resumed his stance on the crates. He lifted his face to the crowd and spoke in the local tongue.

"Jineve! Do you take Deu and Iesus as your own?"

"Yes!" came the resounding reply.

"Then be washed!" the Papa cried, and the people of Jineve plunged beneath the cleansing flood.

◆ ◆ ◆

A lump settled in King Piair II's gut as he stared at the horde that had massed before the walls of the Citadel. The warriors milled about, churning up the soil, dropping trash, defecating wherever the urge took them. They weren't guardsmen. They weren't even soldiers at all. They were outsiders. And he, the sovereign monarch of Chiveis, had invited them into the heart of the realm.

By Astrebril's beard, what have I done?

The chieftain's tent was visible in the distance, reminding King Piair of his recent meeting with Vlad the Nine-Fingered. The man was a buffoon, yet he knew how to wage war and take booty, which made his retainers adore him. A week earlier Piair had signed the treaty of cooperation with Vlad under the High Priestess's watchful eye. The illiterate barbarian could only sign the agreement with an X. Two glass vials had sat on the table, encrusted inside with the scabs of an ancient oath. Now, as before, the Chiveisi had joined themselves to the outsiders.

Piair grimaced as he stood on the balcony. The thought of a such an unlikely confederation made him sick to his stomach. *What do the people think of all this? Do they hold me up to scorn? Do they judge me unequal to my father?*

Whirling away from the railing, Piair left the balcony and went inside the palace. It was time to take the pulse of the streets. He was about to call for a royal litter when an idea hit him. *What if I mingled in the crowd anonymously? Wouldn't that be the best way to learn what my subjects truly think?* Piair was contemplating how to accomplish this when one of the servants solved his dilemma. The youth had just left the bedroom with a porcelain chamber pot in his hands. Piair stopped him.

"Give me your tunic," the king ordered.

After changing into the peasant garment, then rubbing his face and hands with dirt from a potted plant, Piair went downstairs and exited the palace through the stables. A hostler's cap and an old horse blanket around his shoulders gave him an even greater degree of anonymity.

The streets of the Citadel were alive with activity, but not of the sort that might be expected in Chiveis. Instead of fishmongers and food vendors haggling over their wares with their customers, Royal Guardsmen moved through the markets with their weapons drawn. The shops were closed and the stalls were empty, yet that didn't keep the soldiers from their pillaging. Army wagons were being loaded with salt pork, flour, beans, and cheese, along with many other items that didn't look like military provisions but were valuable nonetheless.

A scuffle nearby caught Piair's attention. A fat innkeeper and his alewife wrestled with a guardsman for control of an old nag. The horse was skittish, rearing back on its hind legs as the innkeeper and soldier fought for the lead line.

"You can't have it," the alewife insisted. "How will we draw our cart?"

"That's your problem," the guardsman retorted. He snatched the halter in a firm grip.

Piair approached the antagonists. "Hey, what's the matter here?"

The soldier scowled. "None of your business."

"It's theft!" cried the innkeeper.

"No, it's the king's will!" The guardsman placed his hand on his sword's hilt. "Stand back, all of you, unless you want to taste my steel."

He jerked the horse's head around and began to lead it away, but Piair intervened. "The people need to continue their livelihoods while the kingdom is at war."

"The people need to shut up and provision the Royal Guard! One quarter of their possessions go to the war effort. The surtax was just levied by royal edict."

"Looting and horse stealing were never my intent!"

The guardsman eyed Piair with a cold stare, then approached him in menacing fashion. "*Your* intent doesn't matter here, runt."

Fury erupted in Piair's soul. "Give me that horse!" he screamed, lunging for the rope.

The guardsman's response was quick and violent. He swatted Piair's hand away, then smashed the king's lips with his fist. Piair staggered back and tripped on the curb. He fell into a gutter that reeked of urine. The iron taste of blood filled his mouth.

"By the sword, Chiveis lives," the guardsman declared.

Piair stared at the soldier, then flicked his glance to the frightened innkeeper and his anguished wife. Though Piair wanted to reveal himself as king, to do so would be to admit blame for all that was happening in the realm. Instead he wiped his bloody mouth on his sleeve. Tears of shame burned his eyes.

"By the sword, Chiveis lives," he agreed.

❖   ❖   ❖

It was only a matter of time until the torture would be over. Shaphan had never seen anything so horrible. Death would be a mercy.

Poor Lewth! Just take him, Deu! Make his suffering end!

A few years back, the kindhearted monk had become one of Shaphan's best friends. When the community of seekers formed to study the Sacred Writing, Lewth was one of the first to join. His mind was lively, and his wit was sharp. Now he was a wreck of a man.

"Wat . . . er," he gasped.

Shaphan trickled a spoonful of liquid past Lewth's cracked lips, though he knew easing his friend's thirst would bring agonizing spasms of his ravaged esophagus. The monk's face contorted into a mask of pain as he choked down the drink. He coughed and cried at the same time, thrashing in the sticky sheets. A pustule on his neck burst with the exertion and oozed yellow bile down his chest. At last, gagging and moaning, he collapsed onto his pillow.

"Wat . . . er," he whispered a few moments later.

Shaphan's heart broke. *What is this devilish weapon unleashed upon mankind?*

A few weeks earlier, after his nocturnal visit to the laboratory, Lewth had appeared at Shaphan's door. Both men had rejoiced that the priestess's great weapon appeared to be ineffective. Then the itching had started, and the sneezing, and the flood of mucus and tears. It wasn't long before Lewth's eyes had swollen shut. Bulbous blisters rose in his armpits and groin. Thick fluid clogged his lungs. His airways had been seared by the poisonous vapor, so every breath rasped over a raw wound.

Lina had tried to help with the medical care but gave up when Lewth's nighttime screaming wouldn't stop. Nothing could relieve his internal and external burns. One look at the suffering man made Lina dizzy and nauseated. Shaphan told Lewth it was because the time of her delivery was near, but he knew the real reason for Lina's distress was his friend's ghoulish appearance. The man was burning and thirsting and drowning all at once.

Sighing, Shaphan spooned a little more water into Lewth's mouth. Together they endured another fit of racking coughs. There was nothing else to do.

Sometime that night the wretched monk slipped into Deu's sweet embrace. Lewth had appeared to be dozing, and Shaphan nodded off at his bedside. When Shaphan awoke he immediately noticed the absence of the hoarse death rattle. Lewth's limbs had the inert limpness of a corpse, and his jaw hung slack. Relieved that the ordeal was over, Shaphan tumbled into bed next to Lina and slept like a dead man himself.

The slanting light of early morning woke him the next day. He rolled over and yawned, though he wasn't yet ready to get up.

"Is he gone?" Lina whispered.

"Gone from this world, but living forever in the next."

"How do you know?"

"Remember what Teofil said? If you believe Iesus died and was raised up, you will dwell in his kingdom forever. Lewth believed that."

"Do you believe it too?"

"Yes. The Sacred Writing is trustworthy."

Lina took Shaphan's hand as they lay side by side in their bed. "Then I believe it with you."

The young couple was silent for a while, until Lina asked, "What are you going to do with . . . ?"

"We have to bury Lewth in secret. You've seen all those signs the Vulkainians have put up. They're scouring Chiveis for someone with his symptoms."

"Maybe we could wait until dark and bury him in the yard."

"No, somewhere else. I have to dig a grave, Lina. The neighbors could see me. It has to be outside of Vingin."

"Where?"

"I was thinking of Teofil's teaching theater. It's overgrown. Nobody goes there anymore. I'll do it tonight."

"I'm coming with you," Lina said. "Lewth deserves an honorable burial."

The day passed uneventfully. Shaphan left the door to the guest bedroom closed and went about his business, though he didn't have much of an appetite. When the sun had set, he slipped into Lewth's room and rolled the corpse onto a plank, then wrapped it in the ruined sheets. The smell was horrendous, and Shaphan had to exit twice to avoid vomiting. At last he got the bundle swaddled in thick burlap and bound with twine. It wasn't much of a death shroud, but Shaphan knew Lewth wouldn't mind. He was rejoicing in the presence of Deu.

A fog settled on the alpine village, diffusing the moon's light into a luminous white glow. Shaphan dragged the awkward bundle to the stable. "Watch your step," he said to his pregnant wife. "The ground is uneven here."

Though Shaphan couldn't afford a decent horse, his mother-in-law had given him an old mare that could still pull a two-wheeled cart. After loading the body and covering it with a tarp, the husband and wife made their way to the outskirts of Vingin. They arrived at a small amphitheater with stone risers arranged around a stage. Not long ago Shaphan had taken classes here from Teofil, a gifted professor at the University of Chiveis. All that now seemed like another world.

Shaphan chose a spot in a copse of trees near the cottage that had served as Teofil's study. He began to dig with a wooden shovel while Lina rested in the grass, softly singing a traditional Chiveisian lament. At last he stood up in the hole and leaned on the ash wood handle.

"I think that's deep enough—"

"Caught ya!" shouted a rough voice.

Shaphan's heart jumped, and Lina screamed as two Vulkainians hemmed them in. The older of the pair hauled Lina to her feet while his companion, a youth with a short crew cut, knelt to examine the burlap bundle. He slit it open with his knife, then turned away with a disgusted groan.

"It's a dead guy, boss. Eyes swole shut. Lots of pustules." He stood up and gripped his stomach, wincing and gagging as he spat out the bile that had risen to his mouth.

The older leader leveled his acid gun at Lina. "Walk ahead of me," he ordered Shaphan, "and don't try anything unless you want to see your wife in pain."

"Hey, wait a minute, boss," the younger Vulkainian said. "I kinda like the way she looks. What if we had some fun first?"

"Gods, man. She's pregnant."

"So what? We can do what we want, then kill the husband. We can say he fought us. We'll still get the reward no matter what shape they're in."

The leader thought about it for a moment, then smirked and nodded. He reached for the knife at his belt—and Shaphan swung the shovel.

The flat blade took the man square in the face. He dropped in a heap as Shaphan spun to face his second opponent. The crew-cut youth was drawing his acid pistol, but Shaphan smashed the shovel against his arm. The gun's reservoir exploded in a burning spray. Screaming, the Vulkainian clawed his eyes and stumbled away. Though Shaphan tried to follow, the fog was too thick, and the man disappeared.

Shaphan hurriedly laid Lewth to rest and backfilled the soil. After gathering the Vulkainians' two horses, he returned to Lina. She stared at him with big eyes. They walked in silence back to their house, leading the new horses behind the cart.

"I'm scared," Lina said as they entered the dark cottage.

"Me too."

"What should we do now?"

"Pack up all the food we have. I'll get blankets and clothing."

Lina gasped as she gripped her husband's sleeve. "Shaphan! Where are we going?"

He put his hand on Lina's shoulder and gave her a grim look.

"I think you know."

✦   ✦   ✦

Ana hiked up her skirt and set her foot in the stirrup. Throwing her other leg over the saddle, she gathered the reins of her dapple gray and urged it forward.

"Are you sure about this?" Vanita asked, walking alongside the horse.

"I can't wait anymore. I just want to take a look."

"Teofil will be worried when he finds out. He'll think it's dangerous."

Ana smiled down at her friend. "Then I guess he'll come for me like he always does."

"Can't you wait?" Vanita pleaded. "He's been scouting the enemy all day. I'm sure he'll return soon to send another message to Jineve."

"The outsiders are on the far side of the river. I won't cross. I just want to take a look at Edgeton. Besides, the outsiders are apparently Chiveis's allies now. The Vulkainians have been escorting them into the kingdom in droves. It's unheard of."

"Teofil would want to go with you," Vanita repeated.

"I know. But I won't go into town. I just want to see it from a distance."

Vanita sighed. "I can understand that. You've been waiting for this day for two years." She placed her hand on Ana's knee. "Hurry back."

"Thank you, Vanita." Ana squeezed her friend's hand, then called for a trot from the gray.

The game trail was familiar to Ana, for she had walked it many times on hunting trips with her father. The ride was easy, and she settled into the saddle as the evening wore on. Her mind drifted to yesterday's battle. Teo had wanted her to be ready to flee on horseback, and she had agreed to that plan, but then the idea of fire arrows occurred to her. Though she had merely hoped to start a fire among the Iron Shield's supplies, Teo's decision to spread lantern oil on the brimstone crates made the strategy even more effective.

Ana laughed to herself as she recalled making the arrows. She had once helped Teo fashion similar missiles with resin-coated strips of fabric from her dress. Teo had shot them at outsiders from the very same bluff. She and Teo were strangers to each other then, having only just met in the woods. Though she had liked him right away, and he liked her too, neither knew what to make of the other. Now the dashing Captain Teofil was the man she hoped to—

What? Marry?

Ana pushed the thought away. Too many daunting obstacles hindered that idyllic dream. She was under a death sentence for treason, and the kingdom itself was in turmoil as the aggressive invasion was being planned. Nothing in Chiveis was how Ana wanted it to be. She longed to feel her father's strong arms around her again, to hear the melodious sound of her mother's voice. She wanted to see the sturdy Chiveisian farmers streaming home at dusk, eager for an ale and a meal. She wanted to sit at her kitchen table and eat goat cheese and pickles like she did as a girl. Ana pictured her little bedroom with its balcony overlooking the town square. It had a dresser, a wardrobe, a fireplace, a sleigh bed—even a bathtub! She had loved to soak there at length, calling for another kettle while her father complained about the cost of firewood. Tears gathered in Ana's eyes as these memories rushed through her mind. She was adrift in a sea of homesickness when she rounded a bend and spotted Edgeton across the Farm River.

The first sign of trouble was the presence of the Royal Guard. Soldiers scurried from the village stockade to the dock, carrying sacks and kegs and crates to be piled onto flatboats. One of those rafts approached now, preparing to pick up its load of supplies. The poleman hailed Ana on the shore. "Need a lift across?"

"Um, no thanks," Ana called.

"Then what are you up to over there?"

"N-nothing," Ana stammered as the boat drew near.

"Are you sure?" the poleman pressed. "It's getting late."

"I . . . I guess I would take a ride after all."

Ana had donned a cloak to hide her identity, so now she pulled up the hood as she led her horse onto the raft. She hoped the outer garment would cover her Marsayan clothing, which had a different look from what Chiveisian girls wore.

A stocky villager stopped her as she reached the village gate. "Who are you and what do you want?" he demanded.

Fynn!

Ana nearly identified herself to her childhood friend but decided the situation was too uncertain for that. "I'm a kitchen girl from the regiment," she mumbled with her head down. "The quartermaster sent me for a couple of items he forgot."

"Well, hurry up. The gate closes at full dark, and I won't reopen it for you." Fynn waved her inside.

The streets of Edgeton were dismal and empty. Shutters covered the windows where lanterns used to cast a friendly glow. Ana recognized each shop, each tavern, each home. The alehouses on the main square should have been overflowing with thirsty farmers but instead were locked up like fortresses. At any other time the villagers would have been outside enjoying the late spring evening. But on this day Royal Guardsmen and Vulkainian thugs owned the streets.

Ana passed a withered old man in a worn-out cloak who noticed her as she walked by. His head swung around, and he craned his neck to get a better look. Even in the gathering darkness Ana could see his face was abnormally pale. An eerie redness lined his mouth like the lipstick of a garish streetwalker. Ana hunched into her hood and hoped the man was only a lecher, not a government informant.

She arrived at her house. It was dark and forbidding like the rest. Though all the shutters were closed, Ana noticed the flowerboxes overflowed with healthy geraniums, evidence that her mother had tended them recently. She knew her father wouldn't leave during planting season unless he had to. Perhaps her parents were home but hiding from the soldiers like everyone else.

She stepped onto the porch and knocked.

No answer.

After trying several times Ana sneaked around to the back. A hole in a gnarled tree held a rusty key. Many times as a teenager she had stayed out too late and let herself in with the hidden key. Now she slipped it into the lock once again. The mechanism was stiff, but it turned.

The chalet was quiet. Ana wandered the rooms, fiddling with the furniture, inhaling the familiar smells. She wanted to jump around in ecstasy, but the mood wasn't right. No one was present to celebrate her return.

She walked upstairs, finding her bedroom just as she left it. Her traditional Chiveisian dirndls hung in the wardrobe. A neat pile of logs had been laid in the fireplace. She sat on the edge of the bed, then kicked off her shoes and flopped back on it.

A tear trickled down her cheek. Unable to contain her grief any longer, Ana curled up on her quilt and wept for a long time. Through burning eyes she stared at the ceiling and cried out to Deu. *What has happened to Chiveis? What sickness has infected even little Edgeton on the frontier? Outsiders swarm in while guardsmen loot the people! Where are my parents, who should have welcomed me home?* She received no answer to those wrenching questions—yet Deu spoke to her nonetheless.

"Ana?"

She bolted from the bed, her heart pounding. *Who . . . ?*

The voice called again. "Ana, are you here?" Footsteps ascended the stairs to her bedroom.

Teo!

He entered, and she embraced him. As his arms enfolded her, Ana realized how truly solid Teo was. He provided reassurance in an ever-shifting world. Ana found she needed his strength now more than ever.

"Why did you come here without me?" he asked.

"I didn't mean to. It just . . . happened." Ana put her hand to her forehead. "Nothing turned out like I imagined."

Teo looked closely at Ana's face. "You've been crying."

"Yeah. Now my eyes are all puffy."

He kissed her cheek. "You're still beautiful though." He smiled warmly. "Remember, we walk together, okay?"

She nodded. "Hand in hand, Teo. I promise."

Downstairs a door creaked open. Ana's head swung around, and she let out a gasp.

"Wait here," Teo said.

He drew his sword.

CHAPTER

14

The ruby-red wine caught the light of the candles as it swirled in the crystal goblet. It was an excellent vintage, the best Chiveis had to offer. The full-bodied wine was heavy in the mouth and dry on the palate, the perfect accompaniment to the meal of roasted venison in garlic sauce. Everything about the dinner was perfect: not only the food and wine but the moonlit view from the terrace, the pleasant coolness of the air, the glittering stars overhead. Pink roses were on the table, their delicate, voluptuous folds heightening the sensual mood. Yet despite these many allures, the most enchanting vision of all was the magnificent woman across the table. No man could tear his gaze from such an exotic beauty—so powerful, so enticing, so bewitching. The High Priestess of Chiveis had arrayed herself in splendor, and the Iron Shield was captivated.

"More wine?" she asked, raising the decanter.

"Gladly. We have much to celebrate. The mission was successful."

The High Priestess refilled her guest's glass. "I am pleased to hear it. Yet my sources tell me you lost some of the brimstone."

"There was an attack," the Iron Shield admitted. He took a bite of meat and chewed it as he calmed himself, then sipped his wine. "Teofil managed to destroy some cargo, but most of it remained unharmed."

"I have seen it. An excellent shipment."

"It pleases you?"

"Indeed. I now have enough for my needs."

The Iron Shield nodded at the beautiful priestess. "It has long been my desire to satisfy your needs, my queen."

A servant approached with the next course, a tossed salad of leafy greens in a vinaigrette dressing. He served the two diners, then disappeared into the shadows.

"What news of the invasion?" the Iron Shield asked.

The High Priestess slipped a fingernail behind a dark wisp of hair and drew it back from her forehead. She wore her hair parted in the middle so that her white cheeks were framed by long, glossy tresses. Her eyes flicked away from the table to the distant horizon. "Our confederates have encamped before the Citadel's walls. Even now my soldiers are gathering supplies. I expect to march on Jineve within a week."

"Count on five hundred of my shamans at your service."

"Not at my service. They serve the Beautiful One."

"That is what I meant. Exalted be the name of Astrebril."

The invocation brought a coy smile to the priestess's lips. "I like a man who understands where power lies," she said.

"Power is an intoxicating drink," the Iron Shield agreed. "My brotherhood has a saying: *Crudelitas vis est.*"

"And that means?"

"Cruelty is strength."

"Ah, yes. Cruelty is indeed a form a strength, though there are others as well." The High Priestess raised her glass to her guest. "May your strength always last."

"It will last long," replied the Iron Shield, and together they drank.

A different servant returned with the cheese plate. Although his movements were smooth and efficient, the Iron Shield immediately detected the man was on edge. He set out a selection of hard, soft, and moldy cheeses, along with freshly sliced fruit in a bowl. After handing the cheese fork wrapped in a linen napkin to the High Priestess, he darted back inside the temple.

The Iron Shield had trained himself to notice the tiniest details, and now he pointed to the fork in the priestess's hand. "A message," he said.

The High Priestess withdrew a slip of paper from the napkin. Her eyes flared as she read it, and a snarl curled up her mouth. She stroked the iron collar at her neck as if it were a talisman.

"There is a problem, my queen?"

The priestess glanced up, her face livid. "The queen mother has decided to probe into matters that should be left in the past. She has summoned the mother of Anastasia to testify at a tribunal before the Royal Guard."

"What does the woman know?"

"I am not certain. But there are secrets about the Battle of Toon that must not come out."

"Can she be silenced?"

The Iron Shield received no reply. Instead the priestess stood up from the table and strode to the terrace railing. The moon's pale glow reflected off the inky blackness of the Tooner Sea, but the warrior paid it no mind. He could only stare at the priestess's shapely form as she gazed across the whitewashed landscape. At last, when he could remain still no longer, he rose and took a step toward her. He did not dare approach any closer. She did not turn around.

"The Exterminati are adept at secret killing," he suggested.

"No," replied the High Priestess, still motionless. "Not with Katerina and the Warlord involved. In such cases death must come as divine judgment. Leave the matter to me."

"If there is another way I might serve you, I am willing."

The priestess whirled, hands on her hips, eyes eager and bright. The Iron Shield saw the hunger on her face. A low, feral growl escaped him, and his heart began to pound.

"As I told you, I like a man who understands where power lies." The High Priestess leaned forward and licked her lips. "Come now, my servant. Come and worship your queen."

✦　✦　✦

Ana held her breath in her bedroom as Teo crept downstairs. She heard his shout of accusation followed by a terrified yelp. Fortunately the commotion wasn't followed by the sound of a struggle.

"Ana, you can come down," Teo yelled. "There's a man here who says he knows your parents."

She descended to the living room and was surprised to see the pale-faced old man she had passed on the street. A thin scar traced down his left cheek. Now Ana could see the reason for his pallor and reddened lips: the man had the consumption disease. He probably didn't have long to live.

"I'm sorry to intrude," the man wheezed, "but when I saw the daughter of Helena had returned, I knew there were some things I had to say."

Teo sheathed his sword, yet his tone was still suspicious. "Have a seat, stranger," he said. "We'll hear you out, but at this point we don't trust anyone in the kingdom."

"You can trust me. I'm a man of the Fifth, and a loyal servant of Armand." The visitor looked at Ana. "My name is Barnabas, and I was your grandfather's personal physician." No sooner had he finished speaking than he broke into a fit of violent coughs.

Ana went to a sideboard and poured a cup of water, handing it to the suffering man. "Welcome to my home, Barnabas," she said.

"Thank you, dear one." Barnabas dabbed his mouth with his blood-stained kerchief. "I apologize for my condition. It seems I'm a walking corpse these days." After a few more hacking barks he gathered himself and tucked his cloth away. Teo and Ana sat on seats opposite their visitor, waiting for him to speak. Barnabas sipped his water, then said, "I will tell you what I told your parents. I believe Armand's death was an act of treachery."

Teo raised his eyebrows. "That is a serious accusation, friend."

"Even more so if I had evidence to back it up."

"Tell us your story," Ana said.

Barnabas leaned back in his chair and took another sip of water. When he had safely swallowed it without coughing, he began to recount a tale of intrigue and betrayal. "Thirty years ago at the Battle of Toon, the Royal Guard was divided over a captain named Hanson. He was a handsome fellow, a powerful warrior from the Second Regiment and a charismatic leader of men. Hanson had fallen in love with a young girl who only partially returned his affections. She was the Warlord's daughter."

Ana inhaled sharply. "My mother."

"Yes. Hanson made a play for her, and things turned physical, until he was caught in the act by your grandfather. The punishment was severe, and Hanson's regiment resented it. The men of the Fifth, however, supported Armand. But there was more to this than regimental rivalry. Political and military careers hung in the balance. Many high-ranking hopefuls had tied their futures to one man or the other. Secret plots were devised. Everything came to a head at the Battle of Toon."

Teo leaned forward with his elbows on his knees. "Are you suggesting the battle was a setup? A coup or something like that?"

"The battle was a real battle, because the outsiders attacked Chiveis. Yet certain covert assurances were given to them. I witnessed with my own eyes how the Second Regiment fell back from the king and left him to die."

"Cowards!" Teo spat.

Barnabas gave a little nod.

"What happened next?"

"Armand stepped in." The old man's expression took on a faraway look as he recalled the fateful day. "Never have I seen a warrior with such skill. Armand cut down the enemy left and right. His blade was like a scythe through grass. The king had been stunned by a slingstone, but Armand stood over him with"—Barnabas lowered his eyes toward Teo's belt—"the sword you now wear."

Teo stood up. Ana watched him withdraw his weapon from its sheath. The hilt was inlaid with silver, and the blade was forged from the finest steel. Ana couldn't help but marvel at the historic sword. Many times she had seen it make the difference between life and death—for herself and for others in need. Admiration swelled in her heart as she saw the man she loved holding such a noble weapon.

"You are worthy to wear that sword," she said.

"Armand would have been proud to see it," Barnabas agreed, "but an arrow took him down."

Teo frowned as he sheathed the blade. "A tragedy."

"You might call it something else when you consider the enemy's archers were nowhere near."

Ana's head snapped around, and so did Teo's. "What are you saying?" she asked.

"I'm saying your grandfather was shot by the Second Regiment. At least, that is how it appeared to me. The arrow came from their direction. Armand fell just as the soldiers of the Fifth arrived to deliver the king. The wound was in his chest. He was taken to a nearby orphanage, where he died."

"I was raised at that orphanage," Teo said. "It was an infamous event. Many of the older children remembered it, though I wasn't born until a few months after the battle."

Barnabas nodded grimly. "I nursed Armand to the best of my ability. The wound turned septic, but I used the most effective herbs to draw out the infection. At last he seemed to improve. Then he took an unexpected turn for the worse, and death claimed him."

Ana hung her head. "I never knew him."

"He was a great man," Barnabas said. "King Piair was deeply saddened. He took Armand's sword as a treasure to be awarded only to a warrior of equal skill. Then he ordered an investigation into the conspiracy. I testified to what I just told you. I even said something I still believe to this day, though I have no evidence to back up my claim."

"And what is that?" Teo asked.

"I believe Armand was poisoned. There is no other explanation for his sudden demise."

Ana recoiled with her hand to her chest. "Who would do such a thing? It seems beyond any guardsman to poison his own Warlord in his sickbed."

"The men of the Second were scattered by then, so an assassination would have been difficult to pull off even if they wanted to."

"Who else, then?"

"Hard to say. The previous High Priestess had no use for Armand because he was outspoken against her religion. No doubt she would have liked to see him dead, but she had no access to him."

"Who did have access? Were you the only caretaker?"

"Yes, it was only me. I cooked all his food myself. A few of the orphan children cleaned the laundry and emptied the bedpans, but they were just little girls who were never alone with him."

"Are you sure?" Teo probed.

Barnabas tipped his head in a shrug. "Who can be absolutely sure about such things? It's not like I could sit at Armand's bedside every second. I do remember one of those girls—Greta, her name was. She was just a child at the time, though she had a precocious way about her. Long, black hair—a pretty little thing. *Too* pretty, if you know what I mean. I caught her in the Warlord's room one day and shooed her out. I remember how she stared at me with her green eyes. Then she just smiled and left."

"You say her name was Greta?"

"As I recall."

Ana exchanged glances with Teo. She knew they were thinking the same thing: *That description sounds awfully familiar. We need to find out more about little Greta.*

Barnabas broke into coughs again but soothed himself with the cool water. At last he stood up from his chair. "It's dark now, and I should be going. Lock the doors tonight unless you want to be disturbed by marauding guardsmen." He shuffled over to Ana. When she reached to shake his hand he waved her off, conscious of his disease. "I'm very sorry about your mother and father," he said. "But perhaps the truth shall prevail."

"What's the matter with Mother and Father?" Ana asked, alarmed. "Where are they?"

Barnabas's eyes grew wide. "Oh! I assumed you knew!" A bleak expression settled onto the old man's pallid face. "They were arrested earlier today by the Royal Guard."

"Arrested? Does the High Priestess have them now?"

"I'm not sure." The army doctor wrapped his cloak around his shoulders. "I'm very sorry, Anastasia. I truly am."

Ana wrestled with the dreadful news while Teo showed Barnabas to the door and locked it behind him. When Teo returned, Ana stared at him with her mouth agape. She felt like crying again, yet she fought back the tears and clung to hope by the thinnest of threads.

"What are we going to do?" she asked Teo.

"Deu will show us the way."

"Deu has abandoned Chiveis! The kingdom is overrun with outsiders.

Our soldiers steal the crops of hard-working men. My parents are jailed while murderers go unpunished. Everything is turned on end!"

"No, Ana."

"Yes! Chiveis has come to ruin."

Teo shook his head. He reached down to Ana's side and curled his hand around hers. "Follow me," he said.

They went upstairs to Ana's bedroom. "Go out on the balcony," Teo instructed. "I'll join you in a moment." He turned toward his rucksack while Ana stepped outside.

The hour was late now, and the moon had risen. The balcony's wooden floor was cold against Ana's bare feet. She waited at the railing until Teo came to her.

"I have something to give you," he said. "I've been waiting for the right moment."

She flashed him a halfhearted smile. "After all this time, haven't you realized I'm not the kind of girl you can buy off with presents?"

Teo grinned. "With this one I can. Close your eyes and hold out your hands."

Ana complied. Teo laid something solid and heavy in her upraised palms.

"Now look."

When Ana's eyes popped open she saw the gift was a book—the beautiful edition prepared at Roma called the *Versio Secunda Chiveisorum*. The book's cover was decorated with silver filigree, and its central panel displayed her embroidery of a pastoral landscape. Snowcapped peaks rose into a blue sky. Milch cows grazed on the lush grass. The mountain-star flowers dotted the meadows. And above it all, a triumphant turtledove soared over Chiveis, its outstretched wings catching the light of the rising sun.

"Oh," Ana breathed, "it's beautiful. Thank you, Teo."

"Thank Deu. The Sacred Writing has come to Chiveis at last."

Ana looked up and met Teo's gaze. "That has long been my dream."

"I know. I'm happy to see it come true."

"Teo, you're so good to me! I don't deserve you . . . but I'm glad you're mine."

"I am yours, Ana. You've conquered me. My whole heart belongs to you."

He smiled at her in the moonlight, and Ana's heartbeat quickened. She arched her back and leaned forward, welcoming Teo with excitement, drawing him to herself. He stepped close and took her cheeks in his hands. Bending his neck, he kissed her with surprising gentleness. Teo lingered for a long time as the two lovers relished the soft caress of their lips. When he finally parted Ana did not want him to go. Her body was alive to the profound connection that united her to the man she loved. Although the bond wasn't new, it felt even more vibrant after the intimacy of their kiss.

Teo took a deep breath as he gestured over the balcony's railing. "It's time, Anastasia. Are you ready?"

She released the Secunda with one hand so she could intertwine her fingers with his. He pulled her close. Ana clasped the book to her chest as she stood beside Teo.

"I'm ready," she said. "Just lead the way, Captain."

◆　　◆　　◆

Deep in the woods of the Beyond, Lina screamed at the sky as she lay on her back. The young woman's face was twisted by pain and exhaustion. Her white-blonde ringlets hung lank against her face. She writhed in the grass as the baby's head finally crowned after twenty hours of labor. Lina bore down hard—pressing, squeezing, pushing the way women have for millennia. Her cheeks were flushed, and her brow was furrowed. Somehow she managed to pant and cry at the same time.

Shaphan gripped his wife's hand. "You can do it, Lina! Just push!"

She gave another great effort, and then it was over. The baby's head slid free, followed soon after by its chubby body. Though Shaphan was no midwife, the basic principles weren't so different from birthing a lamb. He swatted the baby's behind and was rewarded with an energetic cry.

"It's a girl," he told Lina, who burst into tears of joy that mingled with the sweat on her cheeks.

Shaphan cut the cord and gave Lina the infant to nurse. Cool rags from the stream helped soothe his wife. Only three days prior, the little family had left Chiveis over the Great Pass. Now they were all alone.

"What should we name her?" Lina asked as the baby suckled.

"She was born in the Beyond, so she'll need a courageous woman as a namesake."

"I was thinking the same exact thing," Lina said. She exchanged a nod with her husband.

The afternoon wore on. Shaphan foraged for wild greens while Lina and their child rested in the shade. Then the breeze shifted. When Shaphan's two horses whinnied and their heads came up together, he knew it meant trouble. A sick feeling gathered in his belly. He drew the Vulkainian dagger from his belt.

Deu . . . we need you. Guard my family!

The young metalsmith quickly brought the horses under cover along with his gear. He gathered his daughter in his arms and helped Lina scramble into the underbrush. With a frail wife and an hours-old baby to defend, Shaphan couldn't imagine being in a more vulnerable position.

The horsemen entered the clearing a few moments later, nine barbarians clothed in rough garments of leather and fur. Their hair was long, and their eyes were cruel. No women were among them.

Shaphan could sense Lina trembling as she stood next to him. She cradled the baby against herself with one hand and held the horse's nose with the other. Shaphan also held his mount's nostrils, trying to prevent a whinny. The animals seemed to understand the danger and stood still. Everything was completely silent—until little Anastasia belted out the lusty cry of a hungry newborn.

The warriors turned, spurring their horses. They plunged into the bushes as Lina squealed and the baby wailed. Though their dialect was strange, their words were decipherable to Shaphan's ears. He understood enough to realize that for the second time in a matter of days, murder and rape loomed in front of his family.

"Take our food!" Shaphan cried, not even bothering to threaten the warriors with his pitiful dagger. "You can have the horses and supplies! Just leave us alone!"

Lina clutched the baby to her bosom. "Have mercy! Have mercy!" she pleaded. But nothing was going to stop the men from having their way.

The leader of the pack reined up next to Shaphan, his fierce war ax raised above his head. Lina screamed for help. Shaphan lifted his arms in defense. The ax started down. And then a feathered shaft pierced the eye of the murderous barbarian.

Mayhem erupted among the outsiders as more arrows whistled in. The men ducked low and wheeled their horses but didn't know where to turn. Shaphan threw his arm around his wife and collapsed into the underbrush, heedless of the whipping branches and clawing thorns. Other horses crashed into the confusion. Steel blades clanged against each other, but the confrontation didn't last long. In a matter of seconds the nine barbarians lay dead, and the men who had attacked them stared down at their corpses.

A distinguished middle-aged man with a gray mustache rode about issuing commands to the others. All were dressed in what seemed to be military uniforms. The commander spotted Shaphan peeking around a tree. He said something in a melodious tongue, but Shaphan couldn't understand him.

The man snapped his fingers, and a blond subordinate approached. "I will translate," the new arrival said.

The man on horseback asked what the young couple was doing in the woods among the barbarians. "Exile," was Shaphan's reply.

The baby fussed a little, and now the military commander took a closer look at Lina cowering in the bushes. His features softened.

"Your woman?" inquired the translator.

Shaphan nodded.

"That is a new baby. Very new."

Shaphan nodded again.

The commander asked a question in a gentler tone. "Where will you go now?" the blond man translated.

Shaphan shrugged. "To find a new home."

No sooner had he spoken than an idea struck him. These men obviously were civilized. Shaphan couldn't keep living off the land and hiding from outsiders. He needed to set up a shop in an established village and ply his trade of metalwork. Among the limited options facing him, the unexpected soldiers represented the best possible outcome. He gathered his courage and extended his hand to the blond translator.

"My name is Shaphan," he declared with a friendly smile. "This is my wife, Lina. We would like to emigrate to your kingdom."

Although the translator shook Shaphan's hand, he was taken aback. He turned and relayed the message to his boss, who frowned until the baby's cry caught his attention again. Shaphan detected compassion on the man's face. *He's a father too!*

The commander spoke to the translator, then nudged his horse toward Shaphan. When he offered his hand, Shaphan eagerly grasped it.

The translator could only smile and wag his head as he stared at the strange convocation in the woods. He gestured toward the commander. "Shaphan," he said, "this is Count Federco Borromo. He invites you to come live in the Kingdom of Ulmbartia."

◆　　◆　　◆

"Teo, wait for me!" Though Ana tried to keep her voice low, she didn't quite achieve her objective.

"Shh! Quiet!" Teo reached down and clasped her arm. With a quick tug he hauled her up to the tree branch where he was seated. They sat side by side in the darkness, panting to recover their breath.

"I haven't climbed a tree since I was a little girl," Ana whispered.

Teo leaned close and spoke in her ear. "Looks like you're out of practice."

"Maybe you should try climbing up here in a skirt and see how you do," she replied good-naturedly. Ana had changed into the traditional dress of a Chiveisian farm girl—a white blouse under a black lace-up bodice and a flowing red skirt. Teo smiled but had no defense against her argument.

The couple sat on the limb until the moon went behind a cloud, then they dropped onto the thatched roof of Teo's orphanage. Such roofing was less desirable in Chiveis than wood or slate, but it was considered good enough for a bunch of unwanted waifs. Ana crept across the stiff straw next to Teo.

"You sure you know what you're doing?" she asked.

"I've done it many times."

"How long did you live here?"

"Until I was eighteen. Then I was sent to the University. I paid for it with a military scholarship from the Guard."

"And that's how you became the soldier-scholar I met ten years later." Ana glanced at Teo as she lay prone and rested on her elbows beside him in the prickly thatch. "When my mother told me you were a respected professor and not just a cocky guardsman, I couldn't believe it."

"You thought I was cocky?"

"Of course."

"Really? Me?"

"Teofil—you were *very* cocky."

"I still am," he said and leaped off the roof.

Ana blinked, taken aback by Teo's sudden disappearance. She crawled to the eave and peered over. He crouched on a thick haystack in one of the orphanage's inner courtyards, which was being used as a stable. Ana didn't like heights, and she certainly didn't like the idea of leaping from the roof to the haystack. If she missed she would probably break a bone or sprain an ankle on the pavement. But Teo held out his arms and beckoned her silently. *He hasn't let me down yet*, she thought. So she jumped.

The hay was soft underfoot when she landed. Teo arrested her momentum and helped her stand. They clambered to solid ground and hugged the shadows as they darted into the stable. One of its walls adjoined the main orphanage building. Teo jiggled a flimsy door whose lock popped open after a few shakes. He peeked through, then slipped inside the opening with Ana close behind.

"What a gloomy place," Ana remarked as they sneaked down a hallway. The musty smell of stale urine permeated the air.

"Orphans can't be choosy," Teo whispered back.

A flickering orange glow appeared around a corner ahead. Teo snatched Ana's hand and drew her into an alcove occupied by an ill-carved statue of Jonluc Beaumont. They crouched at its base as the night watchman approached. The sour-faced man held a candlestick and a stout hickory cane. The thought of Teo's youth in this dismal orphanage saddened Ana. She silently thanked Deu for the loving home she'd had.

When the hallway was empty again Teo and Ana hurried to the head warden's office. Ana tried the doorknow and found it locked. Glancing at Teo, she wondered how he would open it. His solution was simple: he cracked one of the door's glass panes with the butt of his knife, then flicked away the shards and turned the knob from the inside. "I would *never* have done that as a boy," he said. "It would have earned me ten hard strokes from Ol' Hickory. I'd be unable to walk for a week." Ana tsked but did not reply.

The head warden's office was illumined only by the light of the moon. Teo and Ana circled behind a heavy desk and entered a closet. Teo struck a match and lit the candle lantern that dangled from the ceiling. The space was lined with numerous cubbyholes, each stuffed with scrolls tied with strings. Letters scrawled on the cabinetry provided meager organization to the institutional records.

"Here are the G's," Teo said. "Start looking."

For half an hour the two investigators sifted through the scrolls but discovered nothing of interest. At last Ana unrolled a parchment with a mysterious name across the top: Greta Izébela.

"Teo, I found it! See here? This girl was a direct descendant of Greta the Great, the consort of Jonluc Beaumont."

"That would qualify her as a potential High Priestess. What else does it say?"

The admittance report said Greta Izébela came to the orphanage when her parents died of plague. Her hair color was entered as black and her eyes green. Nothing was recorded about her behavior or academic achievement. Ana flipped to the certificate of discharge. She gripped Teo's sleeve as she read it. "Look at this! When Greta was seven, she was released from the orphanage to become an acolyte under the previous High Priestess!"

"That's a rare privilege for an orphan. She must have done something remarkable to win the favor of the power-brokers in the Order of Astrebril."

"I'd say killing one of their most prominent critics would count." Ana chewed her lip as she analyzed the dates in the report. "This would have been . . . wait a minute . . . yes. Thirty years ago."

"Just after the Battle of Toon. The timing is right."

"Exactly! Combined with Barnabas's testimony, this document implicates the High Priestess in my grandfather's death. She was the little girl named Greta who was alone in his room."

"All the evidence is circumstantial," Teo pointed out.

"Yet it's enough to raise doubts. That's all we need." Ana tucked the papers into her bodice.

"If Greta is the current High Priestess, that would make her thirty-seven now."

"I've seen her up close. That seems about right."

"Uh-huh," Teo said evasively.

"She's very young for someone so powerful." Ana glanced at Teo's face. "And very pretty."

"I suppose in a weird way you could say that."

"So, you do think she's pretty?"

"What are you trying to get at, Ana? Yes, she's a beautiful woman. What about it?"

"Beautiful? I didn't know you thought she was beautiful. That's a strong word."

Teo sighed. "Look, I won't lie and say it isn't true. I'm not proud of it. The wrong part of me finds her seductive, for all the wrong reasons."

"I don't understand that." Ana frowned and shook her head. "I could never be attracted to the Iron Shield, even though in a different context— if he were a different person—he might be considered handsome. But he only repulses me. I can't understand why it wouldn't be the same for you and the High Priestess."

"Male sexuality is a blessing and a curse. It can be a powerful force for good or evil. A force like that is difficult to contain."

"What do you mean?"

"In the context of a marriage and a home, it's fruitful and productive. Outside of that boundary it's destructive. Think of Napoly and all it represents. Nothing but the perversion of men can take an innocent little girl named Gemma and turn her into 'Sugar.'"

"Men have caused that horror," Ana said, disgusted.

"Not all men. Some stand against it. I don't want to partake of that filth in any way. I prefer to be part of the solution."

"Good men like you are scarce in the world." Ana fought off her twinge of jealousy and met Teo's eyes with an affirming nod. "I believe you're the best of the best."

"I know you do, Ana, and I love you for that. You expect the best of me. That makes me want to live up to it. When I lived here at the orphanage, no one thought I would amount to anything, so I didn't bother trying."

"Master Maurice believed in you."

Teo nodded. "He was more than a professor. He was like a father to me. When I came to the University, he took me under his wing right away."

"How did you get accepted there? It's hard to get in."

"*J'ai appris des langues facilement,*" Teo replied. "I learned languages easily."

"No one sponsored you?"

"Not that I know of."

Ana turned toward the cubbyholes. "Let's take a look at the T's before we leave. I want to see your records."

"Okay, but we have to hurry. It'll be dawn soon."

They searched through the scrolls until Ana found a thick packet with Teo's name on it. She thumbed through the parchments, most of which were disciplinary write-ups.

"I was a little rebellious back then," he said sheepishly.

"All that caning! It makes me feel sorry for you." Ana patted Teo's shoulder, but he just shrugged.

She flipped through a few more pages until her eyes fell on the discharge certificate. "Teo, look here. It says Master Maurice personally requested that you be released to the University. Somehow he had heard of you in this orphanage and took an interest in your welfare."

"Hm. I never knew that." Teo considered it for a moment, then dismissed the thought. "Come on. We really need to get out of here."

"Just one more second. Check the hallway and I'll be ready to go."

While Teo stepped out, Ana turned to the admittance report. It stated that Teo had arrived at the orphanage as a newborn baby several months after the Battle of Toon. He had been dropped off by a seventeen-year-old girl. *I wonder who she was?* Curious, Ana continued to read . . . then gasped when she spotted the girl's name.

Helena.

Ana's mind recoiled as a deep sense of dread seized her. Though she didn't want to, she found herself doing mental calculations. *Teo is four years older than me. That makes him thirty. Mother is forty-seven—a seventeen-year difference.*

Could Teo be my . . . ?

No!

His sudden return startled Ana. "The hallway is clear," he said. "It's time to go."

"Yeah . . . um . . . okay."

Ana stuffed the parchments back in the cubbyhole, her heart thudding at the unexpected revelation. *Please, Deu,* she prayed as she followed Teo out the door, *don't let that be true!*

❖　❖　❖

Helena d'Armand approached the performance hall in Entrelac with more peace than she would have thought possible in such circumstances. The last time she was here was three years earlier, when Ana had come for a poetry competition that she deserved to win but did not. Today, however, it would be Helena's words that captured everyone's attention.

The imprisonment she had endured with Stratetix over the past week had been of the mildest sort. Queen Mother Katerina made sure her two captives received plenty of food and drink. Their room was comfortable, with a private balcony to receive fresh air and sunshine. Katerina had even sent books and writing materials to pass the time. Helena thought the greatest hardship was the boredom, but that was about to come to an end.

"Do you remember the recital?" Stratetix whispered to Helena as they alit from the carriage. Evidently his memory had been jogged along the same line as hers.

"I was just thinking about that. Ana was so brave to stand up and sing in front of that snobby crowd."

Stratetix took his wife's hand. "A brave daughter comes from a brave mother. Stand tall and tell the truth today. Perhaps the soldiers will realize what happens when corruption infects their ranks."

And may they have the courage to respond, Helena prayed.

The plaza outside the recital hall basked in the early morning sun. Yet it wasn't only sunshine that warmed Entrelac. Helena could see the cloud wall above the distant mountains that signaled the arrival of the foehn wind. Hot gusts swirled in the streets as the dry air rushed down from the heights into town. According to folklore, the foehn could make a person go mad. Helena suspected the day would hold plenty of madness already without the addition of winds.

"This way," said the soldier escorting the couple to the hearing. He was a young man with the callused hands of a farm boy. Helena knew the type; there were many in Edgeton.

"New recruit?" she asked.

The man glanced at her, then nodded.

"Why did you sign up?"

His answer was the national motto: "By the sword, Chiveis lives."

"Don't be so sure of that," Helena replied as she entered the performance hall.

The building was one of the few in Entrelac made of stone instead of timber. It was built on a grand scale, with heavy columns lining its nave and high clerestory windows admitting shafts of sunlight. Though the hall was designed to seat several hundred spectators for performances and recitals, today it was crowded with Royal Guardsmen. The flags of the five regiments hung from poles at the rear of the stage. The Warlord sat on one side of the dais in an oaken throne, flanked by the commanders of the Second and Fifth Regiments. Two empty chairs faced the three military officials, and a lectern stood in the middle. Helena glanced around but saw no sign of Katerina.

The young soldier brought Stratetix and Helena to the stage. "Sit there," he instructed. They sat down while the Warlord and his two associates watched, their faces stern and unyielding.

A trumpet sounded from the vestibule at the rear of the nave. All eyes turned as the herald blew several clear notes, then signaled for attention with a flourish of his hand. After a call to order in which everyone took their seats, the herald announced the purpose of the military tribunal. "New information has emerged about the Battle of Toon," he said. "By the will of our beloved Queen Mother Katerina, we will hear today from some of the eyewitnesses so that the truth may come to light. Foremost among these witnesses is the woman whose father once defended our realm: Helena of Edgeton, the daughter of the great Armand."

At the mention of that august name a buzz circulated through the crowd. The guardsmen nodded and whispered as they contemplated what the day's events might hold. Finally the herald called for quiet, then pointed to the dais at the front of the hall. "Let us now give our attention to our general," he said.

The Warlord sat erect in his throne. He was an austere man with an authoritarian bearing, yet he was known to be fair. Above all, he was a loyal soldier of Chiveis. Pointing a finger at Helena, he summoned her to stand and bear witness.

Deu . . . give me your strength.

Helena gripped the lectern to hide her trembling hands as she faced the Warlord. To the right she could see the crowd in her peripheral vision, but she kept her attention on the man in front of her.

"Tell us who you are," the Warlord said.

"I can give you my name, but to tell you who I am is a much longer story."

The Warlord frowned behind his bushy mustache. "We have the time, so speak."

"I am Helena d'Armand, wife of an excellent farmer, daughter of an excellent soldier. I am a citizen of Chiveis—a noble land, a beautiful land, a land that has made me what I am today. Its mountain peaks lift my soul toward heaven. Its good earth brings forth the wheat by which we live. The cattle of Chiveis are made fat on the meadow clover, giving us the bounty of their milk. With my own hands I have squeezed the teat and churned the butter and molded the wheels of cheese. I am not an aristocrat, despite my father's high rank. In truth I am just a peasant, a village housewife whose table is never empty and whose flowerboxes are always full. Yet that is not all! I am also a woman who carries some dark secrets."

At this last statement a murmur rippled through the crowd. The Warlord leaned forward in his throne. "Those secrets are why we have summoned you here today, matron of Chiveis. Tell us what you know."

"My story begins with a captain named Hanson. Most of you gathered here today do not recall that name, for he was executed in dishonor, and his name faded from the lips of men. When we met three decades ago, I had just turned seventeen. He was handsome and charming, a very fine warrior in the Second Regiment. I will not deny I was flattered to learn that a dashing older man desired a romantic relationship with me. Captain Hanson pursued me, and as girls will do, I entertained his affections—yet only to a point. Deep down I knew he was not the man for me. At last I told him this. He grew despondent, then angry, then desperate. He came to my chambers and tried to prevail upon me. I was confused, and I resisted as best I could."

As Helena paused to gather her composure, the commander of the Second Regiment spoke up for the first time. "What happened that day in your room? You must tell the court exactly what occurred."

"No," Helena replied emphatically. "I will not give those details in the presence of my husband and this company. Suffice it to say that my father caught us in an embrace. I was humiliated, yet things were much worse for Hanson. A few of you in this hall are old enough to remember Armand. He rarely grew angry, but when he did his rage was terrible. He ordered Hanson to be whipped and demoted to the rank of private. The captain's military career was over, and with it went the careers of those who had tied themselves to his rising star."

The commander of the Second Regiment shifted in his chair. "Perhaps this justifies what my men have believed for years: the 'great Armand' is overrated."

The Warlord silenced the man on his left. "Rexilius! Enough with the regimental rivalries! I wish to hear the conclusion of Lady Helena's story." He motioned for her to continue.

Though Helena had been speaking from the lectern to the Warlord seated across from her, she now turned to address the crowd directly. The hall was so silent she thought she could hear her own heart thumping in her chest. Raising her voice, she said, "You men may recall that my father was killed at the Battle of Toon, which happened a few months after the events I just described. What you do not know, soldiers of the Guard, is the way in which he died."

"He fell in battle! He's a hero!" someone shouted from the audience.

"Indeed he is a hero. Yet there are those who believe he was *murdered*."

At this announcement the performance hall exploded into a frenzy. Shouts of "Liar! Liar!" mingled with other voices that cried, "Quiet!" and "Let her speak!" The uproar forced the Warlord to rise from his throne and bark out a call for silence. The soldiers reluctantly hushed at their general's command. He turned to Helena. "Tell us what you meant by that!" he demanded.

Helena refused to cower. "On the authority of an eyewitness who fought at the Battle of Toon, I declare to you today that the Second Regiment was involved in a rebellion. The conspirators coordinated an attack with the outsiders, then fell back from the king—"

The Second Regiment's commander bolted from his seat. "*Outrageous!*" he roared. "*How dare you say that!*"

"—fell back from the king," Helena repeated firmly to the stupefied crowd, "and left him to die. Only the bravery of the great Armand spared the king's life. Then an arrow struck my father—an arrow from within our own ranks!"

The crowd's agitation could be contained no longer. Once again the soldiers burst into heated arguments over the veracity of Helena's claim. The men of the Fifth pointed fingers at the men of the Second, and tussles broke out across the hall. The Warlord shouted for calm, but this time no one could hear him over the din.

The commander of the Second Regiment approached Helena with hatred in his eyes. He jabbed his finger at her. "*Blasphemy!*" he snarled.

The ominous word caught the attention of the crowd. Heads swung around as the squabbling soldiers forgot what they were saying and focused their attention on the stage at the front of the hall.

"This woman was involved in blasphemy!" the regimental commander screeched with spittle flying from his mouth. He wrinkled his nose and bared his teeth like a wild animal. "Two years ago she was accused of worshiping an evil god! I should know—my soldiers were the ones who tracked her down in the wilderness of Obirhorn Lake! I tell you, she's a heretic!"

Stratetix left his chair and came to his wife's side, slipping his arm around her waist. "That matter has been settled," he said.

"Has it? Or do you continue to harbor blasphemies against holy Astrebril in your heart?"

"I am no heretic," Helena said.

"Yes, you are! You are an infection upon our land! Your own daughter was banished from this realm because of her false beliefs!"

"Leave her out of this," Stratetix growled. "What does she have to do with anything?"

Helena met her adversary's fierce gaze. "You're just trying to deflect attention away from the facts," she accused.

The regimental commander spun toward the spectators. "The facts, she says! Ha! I ask you, comrades, can we believe the so-called facts offered by a heretic?"

"Blasphemer!" yelled an anonymous voice.

"Away with them!" shouted another.

Seizing his advantage, the commander whirled to face Stratetix and Helena. His eyes blazed, and he raised his fist in triumph. "Tell us the truth then! Do you or do you not serve the god Deu?"

Helena glanced at her husband. She did not see fear in his eyes, only resolve. They joined hands.

"I ask you again!" the commander shrieked. "*Tell us whether you serve Deu!*"

"For Ana," Stratetix whispered.

Helena straightened her shoulders and lifted her chin. "We do," she declared.

"And so do I," said a voice from the back of the hall.

Teo had thrown open the double doors for Ana just as her mother made her noble confession. Ana's cry of agreement welled up from her soul—a witness she had wanted to bear since the day she knelt under a blue sky and became the handmaiden of the Eternal One. Her bold words caused her father and mother to turn in unison. Their eyes met hers. Their mouths fell open.

"Ana!" Stratetix exclaimed.

"My love!" Helena echoed.

The overjoyed parents rushed from the stage and dashed down the center aisle. Though the Warlord snatched at their garments to restrain them, their desire for Ana was a tide that could not be held back. Stratetix flung his arms around his daughter, lifting her from her feet as he swirled her in the air.

"Daddy!" she cried, though she hadn't intended to use that nearly forgotten word.

"Little Sweet!" he answered as tears gushed into his beard.

"Oh, Ana, you're home!" Helena offered her arms, and Ana embraced her mother as well. The jubilant family huddled in the vestibule, pouring out their mutual love.

Around the hall the stunned soldiers struggled to comprehend the new turn of events. They were expecting the condemnation of heretics, not the emotional reunion of a daughter and her parents. Ana could see the confusion on the men's faces as they sought direction from a strong leader. Teo provided it.

"General!" he shouted to the Warlord. "I am a loyal captain of the Fifth Regiment of the Royal Guard! I seek your permission to speak!"

From the stage the Warlord peered at the strange commotion at the back of the hall. "Captain Teofil, by royal edict you are a condemned criminal. Yet according to the laws of our land, it is the Warlord, not the High Priestess, who is in charge of military tribunals. I will grant you the opportunity to explain yourself."

Teo grabbed a chair and leaped onto the seat. Everyone in the hall turned around to hear what he would say.

"Brothers-in-arms," Teo began, "I greet you as a fellow soldier of Chiveis. In secret I have listened to your words today, and now I have come to tell you the rest of the story. You have just heard how our kingdom's finest warrior, Armand of Edgeton, was betrayed by conspirators. I will not lay the blame for this deed at the feet of the Second Regiment, but only those who made their devious choice thirty years ago. Yet there is one person alive today who does bear blame for murder."

Teo paused, and Ana could see he had the crowd in the palm of his hand. Every eye held him as he continued. "The High Priestess of Chiveis was once a little girl named Greta Izébela, who assisted in the care of the injured Armand. See here, we have a record from the orphanage." Teo swept his hand toward Ana, who held the papers aloft. "We also have an eyewitness who is prepared to testify that Greta was the only person alone in Armand's room before his recovery took a fatal turn. Everyone knows the Order of Astrebril was often the target of Armand's criticism. How hard would it have been for a little girl to pour a deadly poison down an injured man's throat? That is what his attending physician believes happened. I acknowledge the evidence is circumstantial. But does it not raise questions in your minds?"

"It does, Teofil!" said a man in the audience who wore the uniform of the Fifth. "It's very suspicious!"

"Based on these facts," Teo went on, "I suggest a thorough investigation be made into the High Priestess's involvement in this affair. And surely we must call into question the legality of the edict under which I stand condemned. Anyone can see it comes from the priestess's own urging."

"That is a matter for the law courts to decide," the Warlord called from the dais.

Teo nodded. "Very well. Then let us do that." He turned back to the audience, raising his arms. "My brothers, as you may know, I am not only a soldier but also a professor at the University of Chiveis. Today it is time for a lesson in recent history. Perhaps you are wondering where I have been the past two years."

"Yes!" someone shouted. "Tell us!"

With that invitation Teo began to narrate an epic tale of faraway kingdoms and great societies in the Beyond. After descending from a frozen wasteland with the woman he loved, he joined the army of a land called Ulmbartia, a land filled with marble palaces and glittering aristocracy. Through many trials and intrigues, Teo was separated from Ana, who went to live in the glamorous kingdom of Likuria on the Great Salt Sea. There she encountered horrific danger, and for a time Teo believed he had lost her. Yet he persevered, and after many months the lovers were reunited on a lonely island. Events culminated in a colossal battle at the legendary city of Roma. Good triumphed over evil. Yet that was not the end of the story. Teo was sent on a mission by a holy man, and during those months he found his way to Chiveis again. "But it was not the Chiveis I left," he declared. "It was a land of oppression and fear."

Ana glanced around the hall. Many heads were nodding. *Yes, Deu! Come to Chiveis!*

"What did you do about it?" a voice called out.

"There was nothing I could do at the time, so I went back to Roma. But I returned to find evildoers had Anastasia in their grip." Teo recounted his desperate pursuit of his beloved and her rescue over the blazing chasm of Fire Mountain. His daring deeds and heroic sacrifices had every soldier listening to his story in wide-eyed wonder.

"And so at last we made our way home," Teo concluded. "Anastasia and I have suffered unimaginable hardships. We have been bonded by fiery trials that nearly claimed our lives. Yet our God has been faithful to us, and now we have brought his Sacred Writing to you."

An awed silence hung over the crowd as Teo finished his story. No one knew what to say next—until an accusing voice broke the stillness.

"Lies!" shouted the commander of the Second Regiment. "You have no proof! Who's to say you haven't invented all these fantasies?"

Teo faced his accuser at the opposite end of the hall. "Actually, Commander, I've brought a few eyewitnesses with me."

Ana ran to the double doors at the back of the vestibule and beckoned with her hand. Three figures strode into the hall.

"Let me introduce my friends," Teo said from his perch on the chair. "I give you Lady Vanita Labella, daughter of an Ulmbartian duke! I give you Captain Marco, master of the Great Salt Sea! And last but not least, I give you Liber of Likuria, a mighty warrior of the Beloved!"

The regimental commander swatted his hands. "Bah! These strangers prove nothing!"

"Then just look around, everyone! You will find proof of what I've said today. Chiveis has lost its way. Our leadership has become prideful and arrogant."

At these words, one of the soldiers began to recite a poetic stanza: "'You summit-heights of wide renown, clad ever in your ice; take care lest you come falling down! 'Tis pride, your fatal vice.'"

"I know that poem!" exclaimed another man in the audience. "I was there the day Anastasia sang it."

"Me too," a third man chimed in. "She should have won that competition! The rest of it was nonsense. She was the only poet who truly understood Chiveis."

"Sing it for us now!" someone yelled, and then a general acclamation rose from the crowd. "Yes! Sing it, Anastasia! Sing it!"

Ana didn't know what to make of the boisterous request, but Teo flashed her an encouraging smile. "You can do it," he mouthed.

"Sing it for Deu, Little Sweet," Stratetix whispered in her ear. He pushed a chair into a ray of sunlight from the clerestory window.

Ana mounted the chair and found her pitch. She smoothed her skirt and straightened her fitted bodice. After collecting her thoughts and taking a deep breath, she began to sing:

My kingdom fair and full of light,
What darkness hath crept in?
O how can you escape this plight,
To cleanse away your sin?

The gods, they trample down upon
My beautiful Chiveis!
O who will come deliver us
From pride, our fatal vice?

I wait, alone, with longing heart
My soul begins to pine
For one who reigns o'er all to give
A prophecy divine!

Ana sang the lyrics with such clear tones that the cavernous hall was filled with sweetness. The notes swirled among the stone columns, penetrating to each hidden corner. Everyone crowded close, even the Warlord. As the last echoes of the ballad reverberated in the stillness, the spell that had fallen upon the onlookers lingered for a final, suspended moment. Ana stood alone on the chair, her crystalline song melting away in the recital hall. The soldiers began to rise to their feet in a spontaneous ovation.

And then the world exploded.

CHAPTER

15

Ana tried to push herself from the floor, but dizziness fogged her brain, and she collapsed. A heavy weight pressed her legs. Although cries and moans surrounded her, the dull roar in her ears muffled all sounds, making them seem distant and unreal.

What . . . ? Who . . . ?

Her vision dimmed. Ana succumbed to oblivion for a few moments as she lay sprawled on her belly. Finally she found the strength to open her eyes and blink away the darkness. The air was thick with dust. She could taste its earthy grittiness on her tongue. Through the swirling gloom she saw a mass of bodies littered around a large stone hall. Most of the men writhed on the ground. Some staggered to their feet. Others lay deadly still.

Ana's head throbbed. She reached back and felt warm stickiness there, along with a sharp pain. "Ahh," she groaned as she waited for the ache to subside.

The stone floor was hard against her cheek. She tried pushing herself up again and managed to raise her torso by leaning on her outstretched arms. Looking down, she discovered several soldiers had fallen across her lower body, along with an overturned bench. She shifted her legs but couldn't extricate herself from their combined weight.

Where am I? She concentrated on her surroundings. *The recital hall . . . Entrelac . . . Astrebril's fire!* Ana's heart skipped a beat. *Mother? Father? Teo?*

She glanced around but couldn't identify her loved ones. Though she wanted to stand up and look for them, she didn't have the strength to break free of the weight that pinned her to the floor. Her whole body felt weak and lethargic. All she could do was wait for help.

The explosive powder had devastated the performance hall. Ana noticed the stage area was completely destroyed. A gaping hole revealed the undercroft below, and the bodies strewn in its vicinity did not stir. Yet many of the spectators had moved toward the vestibule at the rear before the explosion hit. The extra distance made all the difference. Several soldiers were already upright, brushing themselves off or helping their comrades to stand. Ana could see most of the men would survive.

An ear-splitting *crack!* drew a collective yelp from the crowd. Ana squealed as the sharp report sounded above. Despite her headache she craned her neck and looked up. A fissure had opened in the stone vaulting. Dust and debris trickled from the cleft, raining pebbles on the horrified spectators. Suddenly the shouts grew urgent as a large piece of masonry broke free from the ceiling. Unable to move, Ana could only hunch her shoulders and hope the stone chunk would miss. But it was directly overhead.

"Look out!" someone screamed.

Ana scrunched her eyes and covered her head with her arms.

Deu! Help me!

For a split second everything was still. Then . . .

A dull thud. A clatter of stone. And silence.

Ana felt no impact, no crushing blow. Heart pounding, she opened her eyes—and shrieked at the top of her lungs.

"Noooo!"

Liber lay on his back, staring blankly at the ceiling. A pool of blood oozed from beneath his thick black hair at the nape of his neck. His respiration came in labored pants, yet his body did not move. Next to him was the broken masonry that had plunged from the ceiling.

Ana grabbed his hand, which was limp like a rag doll's. "Liber!" she cried. "Get up!" But the bearded giant remained still.

A terrible sense of inevitability settled on Ana. She twisted her body until she could lean over Liber. His eyes fixated on her face, then a tiny smile turned up the corners of his mouth. Ana clutched his hand to her chest. "Oh, Liber," she moaned, "thank you! Thank you, my dear friend!"

The injured man's breathing grew even more shallow. Every inhalation required an effort. Hot tears welled from Ana's eyes and cascaded onto the face of her strong defender. She brushed them away from his cheeks with her thumb.

Liber made a raspy sound as his strength began to fail. *Is he trying to speak?* Ana bent low until her ear was just above his mouth. A series of gurgling words escaped Liber's lips, each punctuated by a gasp for air.

"I . . . love . . . you . . . "

Ana wept uncontrollably.

" . . . Stasia," he finished, and exhaled his final breath.

She collapsed on his chest, embracing his wide shoulders, sobbing in her grief and loss. "Why, Deu?" she cried, pounding the floor with her fist. "*Why?*"

A pair of boots appeared in front of Ana's eyes. She rotated her head to see the Warlord looming over her. He stooped and heaved the wooden bench and dead bodies off her legs. Though Ana was grateful to be free, she watched the general closely, uncertain as to his intent.

The austere soldier did not speak as he unfurled a red and yellow cloth—the tattered flag of the Fifth Regiment. Kneeling next to Liber, he closed the big man's eyes with two fingers. Then, covering the body with the military standard, the Warlord said, "That was an act worthy of a man of the Fifth."

Outside in the streets, a bugle blared.

It was the Royal Guard's call to arms.

◆　◆　◆

Everything around Teo was a confusing swirl of lights and sounds. His ears rang, and his head pounded. A nice-looking fellow with a dark goatee knelt in front of him. Though the man uttered some words, Teo had no idea what he was saying.

"Teofil! Can you hear me? Wake up, *amico!*"

"My inkwell is gone," Teo answered. He hoped it was the right response.

A loud splintering noise burst from the ceiling. People screamed, and a commotion broke out. Teo stared around the hall. *The performance hall?* He began to recognize his surroundings as the intense throbbing in his temples abated. After drawing himself up to one knee, he unsteadily regained his feet. The fog was dissipating from his brain at last.

"Are you alright?" Marco asked.

"Yeah," Teo said, gazing at the floor with his hand on his forehead. "I guess so. What happened?"

"Someone set off the black powder. It threw you across the room pretty hard."

Teo's head shot up as full clarity returned to him. He gripped Marco's sleeve. "Where's Ana?"

Marco pointed over his shoulder—and then Teo heard a sound that would chill the blood of every Chiveisian soldier.

The call to arms! Invasion!

The Royal Guard used bugles to signal many of its daily activities, but one fanfare stood out from the rest. The call to arms meant the Guard was being mobilized for its ultimate purpose: to fend off an attack by outsiders while the civilians fled behind the Citadel's protective wall. Until now Teo had heard that particular call only in training situations. Today, however, the notes ringing from the streets were no drill.

Although Teo didn't know what was happening outside, his first priority was Ana. She stood where Marco had indicated, her face buried against her father's chest. Helena was there too, along with Vanita. Teo ran up to them.

"Ana, are you hurt?"

She shook her head but did not turn away from Stratetix's embrace. Everyone else appeared to be uninjured as well. Relief filled Teo as he saw his friends had survived the explosion.

The bugle fanfare sounded again, this time from the direction of the Citadel.

"What's happening out there, son?" Stratetix asked.

"Chiveis has been invaded."

"By whom?"

"I'm about to find out, though I think I already know." Teo clasped Stratetix's shoulder and looked the sturdy farmer in the eye. "Guard her well," he said.

"With my life," Stratetix replied.

Teo ran from the recital hall into the chaotic streets of Entrelac. The hot foehn winds assaulted him as soon as he stepped outside. He saw no soldiers, for the nearby regiments would already have rallied at the Citadel, and the Fifth would be coming in from the frontier. The townsfolk of Entrelac, however, were in an uproar. Dismay was evident on their faces. Though foreigners hadn't invaded from the Beyond in thirty years, their looming menace was a deep-seated fear of every Chiveisian citizen. Now that menace had actually crossed the line.

A neighborhood temple of Astrebril stood nearby. It was just a little shrine, yet it possessed the unifying feature of all such temples: a spire. Teo entered and glanced around. The place was deserted, its eunuch priests having fled. He ran to the spiral staircase and ascended the spire, which lifted higher than the surrounding rooftops. The window at the top revealed exactly what he had expected: the Knights of the Cross and the militia of Marsay had made a preemptive strike into Chiveis. Their army had already penetrated deep into the kingdom and would reach Entrelac in a matter of minutes. Thousands of mounted soldiers rode along the southern shore of the Tooner Sea, while others crossed the white-capped lake in hijacked boats. Either way, they would soon converge on the town, and from there they would march to the Citadel.

Yet as Teo looked more closely, he realized many of the soldiers did not wear the uniforms or armor of Marsay. He stared at the troops in the lead, trying to identify the men. And then his eyes fell on something remarkable: the soldiers' shields and standards had been hastily marked with the sign of the cross. Only one explanation presented itself: *the Jinevans!* Apparently they were newly converted to the religion of Christianism. Now they had joined the Marsayans in coming to Chiveis for war.

Back in the streets, Teo untied a horse from the hitching rail at the recital hall. With the recent mayhem inside there would be plenty of animals to spare. He mounted the excellent warhorse and headed for the outskirts of town, taking a shortcut he hoped would put him ahead of the man he desperately needed to find. At this point only one person could avert a colossal battle: the Warlord.

Teo reached the city limits and left Entrelac's houses and shops behind. Now only a grassy plain lay between him and the Citadel. He stared at the fortress as he galloped toward it, awed by its majestic beauty. It was the beating heart of the kingdom he loved. The great wall stood above a moat that was bridged by a causeway. Towers and spires rose behind the wall, proud banners flying from their pinnacles. The emblem of Chiveis was a white sword against a square field of red. Teo's heart swelled to see that flag waving over the mighty Citadel. For two years he had wondered if he'd ever see it again. Now here he was, a soldier of the realm returning to his homeland—and he was about to go into battle *against* the Royal Guard! Teo never thought such a day would come.

Busy movement was visible in the outsiders' encampment beneath the fortress wall. Though the Germani didn't know the exact meaning of the Chiveisian bugle calls, they understood something was amiss. Men scurried back and forth, strapping on their helmets or mounting their horses. Teo spotted a squad of Vulkainian militiamen riding from the Citadel's gate to the encampment, no doubt to coordinate battle tactics. A threefold army of outsiders, Vulkainians, and Royal Guardsmen would stand against the Marsayan and Jinevan invaders. The winning side would own the future of Chiveis. Yet Teo still hoped the battle could be avoided.

His searching eyes finally spotted the Warlord's gray courser on the main road out of Entrelac. Teo angled across the fields on an intersecting route, then reined up a short distance in front of the Warlord. The gusty foehn winds blew against Teo's back as he blocked the commander of the Royal Guard from entering his capital city. A trumpet fanfare sounded from the Citadel's ramparts once more, calling all loyal warriors to the defense of Chiveis.

"General!" Teo cried, holding up his hand. "You must put an end to the madness that has gripped Chiveis!"

The Warlord's horse pranced on the road, eager to keep running. Its rider's face was implacable as he looked at Teo with a flinty glare. "Get out of my way, Captain," he said.

"Don't do this, sir."

"Don't do what?"

"Look around! Look at what Chiveis has become! It's all the priestess's fault. You know this in your heart. Don't let the Royal Guard become her tool! We're supposed to be the protectors of Chiveis, not its oppressors. Throw off the yoke of Astrebril and become what you were intended to be."

"What I intend to be is a soldier who does his duty."

"General, don't you see? You must rebel against the High Priestess."

"To rebel against her is to rebel against the will of His Highness the king."

"King Piair is corrupted! The High Priestess has twisted his mind like she did his father's. When a ruler becomes a tyrant, the only just action is to resist."

The Warlord pointed over Teo's shoulder. "Look there, Captain."

Teo twisted in the saddle to see that the portcullis had been raised in the Citadel's gate. The double doors had also opened, and now the Royal Guard marched across the causeway in full battle array.

Teo turned back to the Warlord. The commander stared at Teo with all the authority of his rank behind him. "Draw that sword of yours, Captain Teofil," he urged. "Rally with me at the Citadel like a soldier of the realm. Our kingdom has been invaded. You hear the call to arms ringing from our walls. Do your duty as a man of the Fifth Regiment! Use that noble weapon for the defense of Chiveis!"

Teo reached to his waist and slid the sword of Armand from its sheath. He held it high. "That is what I am doing," he said.

The Warlord's eyes narrowed as he drew his own weapon. "Then may your God protect you."

He collected the reins so sharply that his spirited courser reared on its hind legs. Kicking his heels, the Warlord darted ahead with his sword raised. The clangor of blades rang out as he swept past Teo on his way to the Citadel. The blow was easy enough to parry, yet the commander of the Chiveisian army had made his point.

We are enemies.

◆　◆　◆

Ana knelt next to Liber's body, mourning the loss of her beloved friend. Vanita was there too, holding Ana's hand, providing the kind of comfort only another woman can give. Liber's face was covered by the flag of the Fifth Regiment, whose emblem was a bear. Ana thought that was appropriate, for Liber was a bear of a man: big, shaggy, fierce, and strong.

Now he was with Deu.

Though Ana knew this was true, and part of her heart rejoiced in it, another part grieved the appalling waste of life. She turned toward Vanita. "I don't understand," she admitted.

"Me either. But I keep thinking of what Paulus wrote in the Sacred Writing."

"What?"

"That our mortal bodies will be clothed in immortality. The sting of death is swallowed up in victory. I've thought about that passage often."

Ana sighed deeply, wiping tears from her eyes. "I do believe Iesus has given Liber eternal life. But right now I'm feeling the sting."

"I know, sweetie." Vanita squeezed Ana's hand. "It hurts, I know."

The two women lapsed into silence as they knelt in the decimated hall. A shaft of sunlight poured through the hole in the roof, isolating the mourners on a golden island in a gloomy sea. Ana struggled to accept Liber's death. She couldn't make sense of the tragedy. Though the man who was once called defective was now perfect and whole in the arms of Iesus, Ana's soul cried out for answers.

Why did he have to die, Deu?

It was only when she looked up that Ana began to understand. Drawn by an irresistible pull, she raised her head and stared through the jagged hole where the masonry had broken away. As her eyes adjusted to the brightness, she thought she could make out the form of a bird perched on the edge of the opening. It was an alpine chough, a large bird like a crow that often scavenged the village dumps. The black chough was sacred to Astrebril, for it soared in the sky that the god claimed as his own. Yet even as Ana watched—with her outer eye or her inner, she wasn't sure—another bird appeared in the sky. It was brownish-white and much smaller, yet plucky. It dived at the chough, driving it away, then came to rest in its place. Cocking its little head, the turtledove gazed down at the woman kneeling on the floor. At last the vision broke as Ana's eyes could endure the light no longer.

She dropped her gaze, blinking and shaking her head. Vanita glanced at her. "Are you alright?"

"I . . . I think so." Ana paused, then said, "I know why Liber covered me like he did."

"He loved you, Anastasia."

"Yes. But it was more than that."

Vanita was silent.

Ana grasped the battle flag of the Fifth Regiment and clutched the bloodstained standard to her chest.

"Deu is going to do great things today," she said.

◆　◆　◆

The portcullis was up, the gates were open, and the Royal Guard marched out to war. The First, Third, and Fourth Regiments had rallied to defend the Citadel, while the Second was already in the field, and the Fifth was soon to arrive. Glancing toward the tents off to the side, Teo saw that the barbarian warriors had formed into platoons as well, their helmets strapped on, their swords drawn, their pikes bristling like porcupine quills. And if that were not enough, the Vulkainians rode into battle on the wings of the defenders' formation, wielding their evil pistols whose acid could blind a man in seconds. Taken as a whole, it was a formidable array, one the invading Marsayans and Jinevans would not easily overcome.

Teo rode his war horse to the vanguard of the invaders' army. Brother Thomas was at the front of the line, ready to lead his company of knights into battle.

"Hail, warrior," the friar called. "At last we shall fight side by side!" Turning in his saddle, he summoned a squire, then pitched Teo a helmet. After Teo had donned it, Brother Thomas gave his head a swat with the flat of his blade. "It's a good piece. You'll be needing it today."

"Those outsiders will strike a lot harder than that," Teo observed.

"We're about to find out," Brother Thomas replied.

The Marsayan and Jinevan soldiers had split into two divisions.

Across the grassy plain, the Chiveisian troops had lined up with the wall of the Citadel as their backstop. Teo estimated his own army was perhaps three-fourths the size of the opposing force. Yet nothing could be done about that. Numerical advantage or not, it was time to fight or be killed.

The young King Piair rode out of the Citadel's gate on a white destrier. He crossed the moat and pranced around giving orders. A golden crown was upon his brow.

"Is that your king?" Brother Thomas asked.

"I'm afraid so. He has good blood in his veins, but he hasn't lived up to his potential."

"Today his line comes to an end," the friar said. The boast made Teo sad.

A pair of heralds reined up beside King Piair. Instead of bugles they carried long brass trumpets. At the king's signal the heralds put their lips to the mouthpieces and sounded the battle charge. The defending army heaved into motion like a bear waking from its sleep. A raucous shout went up, the horsemen kicked their heels, and the army of Chiveis began to canter across the field.

"To war!" Brother Thomas yelled as he spurred his own horse. "To war! To war!"

The Knights of the Cross were mounted on horseback, so they led the initial attack. Several Jinevan brigades were also mounted, though most were foot soldiers who marched alongside the militiamen of Marsay. As the gap between the two armies narrowed, the riders at the leading edges broke into a full-out gallop. Teo rose in the saddle and leaned forward, urging his steed toward the outsiders' ranks as they barreled toward him across the field. Though the Royal Guard was fighting on behalf of the High Priestess, Teo decided not to cross blades with a fellow guardsman if he could help it. There would be plenty of outsiders to worry about, so he directed his mount toward them.

The thunder grew louder with each passing second. Teo could see the barbarians' fierce eyes staring from their helmets. He could hear their deafening war cries ringing in his ears. He could feel the rumble of innumerable hooves reverberating through the ground. Snatching the sword of Armand from its sheath, he pointed it toward the heavens with a mighty shout. His galloping horse strained at the bit as the frenzy neared. Teo's eyes widened. Clods of earth flew up. And then the maelstrom consumed him.

Teo's world shrank to the immediate space around him—a world marked not by the alleged glory of battle but the horror of death. Screams and gore, shrieks and blood, curses and sweat filled the air. Teo wore no chain mail, so quickness and agility were his only protection. He never stopped moving, never stopped hacking, never stopped dealing out destruction. The outsiders charged him continuously, sometimes two or more at once. Teo parried and thrust, dodged and ducked, stabbed and sliced. His sword pierced many a throat; his ax split many a skull. It wasn't pretty; it wasn't glorious; it wasn't exhilarating. It was the ugly face of war, and Teo did what he had to do.

As the pitched battle wore on, the outsiders began to be pushed back. Teo found a clear space and reined up, wiping blood from his eyes. Across the field he could see that the Marsayan militiamen had disrupted the ranks of the Royal Guard. Meanwhile, the Jinevans had swarmed the Vulkainians, pulling them from their saddles. Now was the time to press the advantage. With the Citadel's moat at the enemies' rear, they would have nowhere to retreat if the assault continued to bear down on them.

"To me, knights!" Teo cried, raising his sword. "Rally to me!"

The knights responded right away, gathering with Teo for a final charge. Though the outsiders fell back and attempted to regroup, fear was in their eyes as they prepared for a last stand. Teo readied his men to attack. He was about to leap into the fray when a black filth oozed onto the field of war.

Teo felt the evil before he saw it. It hit him like a thunderbolt, a raw power that clutched at his soul and melted his heart. He turned to see a horde of Exterminati enter from the side. All were mounted on dark-colored horses as they streaked toward the knights' exposed flank. Their black garments and hooded faces made them look more like specters of death than men—and indeed that is what they were. Though the unclean spirits couldn't be seen or heard, Teo could sense them accompanying the shamans into battle. The Exterminati raved and gnashed with the ferocity of the underworld. The gods bore them along on dark wings. And nowhere was their malevolent presence more strongly felt than upon the diabolical warrior who galloped at the head of the pack.

"Turn, men!" Teo shouted. "Watch your flank!"

He wheeled his horse and bolted toward the Iron Shield. Teo knew this battle was his alone to fight. *Go before me, Deu!* he prayed, and then his enemy was upon him.

The Iron Shield leaned from his saddle as he swept by, his mace a murderous blur, but Teo kept out of reach. At the same time he hurled a steel ball from his ax but missed. Whirling, the two men sized each other up.

"You cannot win, Teofil," the Iron Shield said with a rumbling laugh. He wore no patch over his missing eye. The gaping socket gave his face a skeletal appearance.

"The victory is already won," Teo said.

"Ha! I defy you, little pup! I defy your whelp of a god."

"This is the last day you shall."

"No. This is the day the Morning Star rises!"

The horses lunged forward as the mortal enemies charged each other once more. Teo stood in the stirrups and swung his sword with all his strength. The Iron Shield took the stroke against the haft of his mace. Teo's arm quivered at the impact. The tremendous blow knocked him so far out of the saddle he couldn't maintain his balance. He tumbled from his horse's back and hit the ground hard.

Stunned, Teo rolled over and tried to collect his wits. His weapons had been hurled from his grasp. He felt along the ground until his fingers closed on his sword's hilt. Scrambling to his feet, he saw the Iron Shield running toward him with incredible speed. Teo did not wait for his enemy's arrival. He gripped his weapon in two hands and raced to confront his foe.

The Iron Shield had lost his mace when he was unhorsed, so he drew his longsword from a baldric across his back. He brought the weapon around in a slashing attack that Teo barely managed to block. Now the unmistakable sound of swordplay rang out as the blades clashed and the two men did battle. The Iron Shield was the taller combatant, and his reach was longer; yet Teo's weapon was the lighter of the two, which gave him an advantage in speed. Even so, Teo found himself pressed hard, for the Iron Shield was a master swordsman. His footwork was impeccable, and his movements were impossibly fast. Each attack was ferocious, each parry impenetrable, each riposte immediate. Sweat streamed down Teo's face as he fought to keep his enemy's deadly edge at bay. His pulse pounded in his temples, and his breath came in grunts of intense exertion.

"You grow tired," the Iron Shield observed. "Your strength is failing."

Teo had no boast in return. He knew the words were true.

The Iron Shield renewed his attack with increased vigor. Raising his sword overhead, he brought it down in a chopping move. Teo got his weapon up at the last moment, but the Iron Shield rebounded off the blade and hacked again. This time the overpowering force of the blow drove Teo to his knees. The Iron Shield towered over him. An evil glint burned in his one good eye. Both his arms were raised above his head.

"Now die!" he screamed and chopped down a third time.

Teo ground his teeth and clenched his jaw. He held his blade parallel to the ground as his enemy's weapon sliced through the air like a woodsman's ax. Steel met steel with a resounding crash—and the Iron Shield's blade shattered against the sword of Armand.

Aghast, the dark warrior stared at the hilt in his hand. Instead of a glittering blade it now bore a useless stump. Teo bent his elbow and cocked his arm.

"Meet your maker!" he cried, and thrust his sword into his enemy's heart.

An agonized roar burst from the Iron Shield as he reeled away with the blade in his chest. Even in defeat his face was a twisted mask of malice and scorn. He regained his balance, staggered, and dropped to his knees. His baleful glare was fixed on Teo's face.

"We hate you," snarled an unnatural voice that was not of this world.

"Go to hell," Teo replied.

The Iron Shield closed his lone eye. His body sagged. Tumbling forward, he impaled himself on the full length of the blade. Twice he twitched. Then he lay still.

Teo panted as he knelt on the bloody grass. His muscles ached, and his mind was numb. He struggled upright and surveyed the field. Though the lord of the Exterminati was dead, the battle was far from over. Hand-to-hand combat raged all around. Teo could see the shamans weren't the only recent arrivals to swell the enemy ranks. A new battalion of outsiders had swarmed out of the woods, breaking the knights' formations. In a sudden and unexpected reversal, the odds had tipped in the defenders' favor.

Teo rolled the Iron Shield's body with his toe and extracted his sword. After retrieving his ax as well, he gathered his horse's reins and mounted again. From his vantage point in the saddle he could see many good soldiers lying dead on the field. The men of Marsay and Jineve were going down, and even the knights were falling before the outsiders' reinvigorated onslaught. Teo knew how formidable the Royal Guard alone could be; but with the Guard fighting alongside a horde of fresh barbarians and a legion of shamans, defeat seemed inevitable. The idea of escaping into the Beyond crossed Teo's mind, though he hated the bitter thought of retreat. *Where's Ana?* he wondered. At that moment a surge on the periphery of the battlefield caught his eye.

A new contingent of soldiers now entered the conflict. They wore the uniforms of the Royal Guard, yet they attacked from the invaders' side. Teo blinked, trying to understand what was happening. It made no sense. Then, as the riders crested a low rise and came into full view, Teo recognized them. He gasped.

The galloping warriors followed a resplendent figure bearing the flag of the Fifth Regiment. The rider was no soldier, no general, no famous leader of men. She was a humble farm girl from Edgeton with more courage than all the rest combined.

"For Armand!" the soldiers shouted as they charged. "For Armand! For Armand!"

"And for Chiveis!" Teo cried, prompting his horse into battle once more.

The men of the Fifth thundered across the field between Entrelac and the Citadel in a wedge-shaped formation. Ana's flag rippled as she galloped at the tip of the spear. She sat light in the saddle like the excellent horsewoman she was, leaning forward with her weight on her legs. Her arms moved in rhythm with the horse's neck as it strained for even more speed. Ana's head was bent low so that her hair streamed behind her like a golden banner catching the light of the sun. She was majestic in her traditional Chiveisian garb, magnificent in her boldness, dazzling in her beauty. Teo's mouth fell open. Though he had been amazed by Ana before, he now found himself utterly awed by the woman he loved.

As the wedge of riders drew near, Teo merged into their ranks. The men of the Fifth crashed into the terrified outsiders, who were not expecting such a determined attack. "Brothers!" Teo yelled as he swung his sword. "The outsiders serve the High Priestess! Fight them! Fight the Vulkainians! But do not lift your weapons against the Guard!"

A tumult now raged in the center of the battlefield. The barbarians were harried from every direction. Yet as the fighting continued, it became obvious that the men of the Fifth were avoiding their brothers-in-arms. Whenever a platoon of guardsmen tried to circle around the outsiders, the Fifth Regiment shied away. Teo kept shouting his exhortation: "Not the Guard! Not the Guard!"

At last the dam broke. A platoon from the Third Regiment had edged into position to attack, but the Fifth refused to engage. Confusion and ambivalence were written on the attacking soldiers' faces as they tried to decide what to do. Guardsmen weren't supposed to fight guardsmen; they fought outsiders. Suddenly one of the soldiers in the Third Regiment turned away from the Fifth and leveled his sword at the barbarian horde. With a wild yell he charged into the fray while the rest of the platoon watched him go. The men glanced at each other, then roared in unison and turned to follow their comrade.

Teo cheered from his horse's back as he watched the stunning reversal of allegiance. Victory was near; he could feel it. Though the outsiders still presented a dangerous threat, Teo knew if the entire Guard turned against them, the battle would be over. *And nothing can prevent that now! Thank you, Deu! Nothing can stop—*

Teo's jubilation evaporated as he caught a glimpse of the Citadel's gate. Dark fingers of despair reached inside him and grabbed hold of his soul. It was as if Astrebril himself had seized Teo's flicker of hope and extinguished it between his finger and thumb.

The High Priestess sat astride a black charger at the end of the Citadel's causeway. Her dark hair swirled in the hot winds blowing at her back. She carried a sword in one hand and a serpent-shaped scepter in the other. Yet the unholy queen of the underworld was not the most terrible sight of all. She had unveiled something far worse.

Behind the priestess on the bridge, perched upon four wooden wheels, stood a war machine of fearsome and unknown power.

✦ ✦ ✦

Ana hit the wall of outsiders at full speed and did not stop. She knew her role wasn't to swing a sword or take down any foot soldiers. It was to carry the banner as deep as she could into the enemy ranks—to pierce all the way through if possible. Ana was the razor-sharp tip of a human spearhead that would cleave the outsider army in half.

She stormed through the melee, dodging attackers, even mowing down a few under her horse's churning hooves. Clutching the flagpole to keep it upright, she guided the stallion with her legs as the barbarian warriors seethed around her. *There!* A gap appeared, and Ana headed for daylight. She broke out of the fracas into open space.

Several guardsmen of the Fifth reined up next to her. "Well done!" exclaimed the exultant commander of the regiment. "Your grandfather couldn't have done it better!" Ana held her back straight and nodded graciously to the silver-haired colonel.

The riders' swords were slick with blood. They had swung their blades at enemies as they charged through the ranks while Ana carried the flag. Now the men whirled their horses to reenter the fight. The Fifth Regiment had succeeded in splitting the outsiders' force in two, but the battle was still undecided.

"Your work here is done, Anastasia d'Armand," the commander said. "Today you've proven you are brave beyond measure! Leave the field in honor, and let us finish this fight."

Ana considered protesting, but she knew nothing about close-quarters combat from horseback or even how to wield a sword. It wasn't exactly a skill taught to the village girls of Chiveis. "Very well," she agreed, then smiled at the commander and added, "I'm proud of you, sir. Today you remembered who you are."

The remark surprised the old soldier. He raised his eyebrows and flushed at the compliment. Looking away in embarrassment, he barked to one of his men, "Take the flag." Ana removed the pole's tip from the carrier attached to her stirrup and pitched it to the captain.

The soldiers returned to the action and left Ana alone in the field. She gazed at the jumble of men spread across the plain. Teo was out there somewhere. *Deu, protect him!*

As she turned to go, Ana glanced toward the gate of the Citadel. What she saw there made her suck in her breath and rein her horse to a halt. The High Priestess was near the end of the moat's causeway, robed in white, bearing a double-edged sword. She rode about on a black charger, thrusting her blade into any man who dared attack. Yet her Vulkainian guards had surged forward, leaving the priestess's flank unprotected.

Ana looked down at her mount. She had grabbed a standard-bearer's horse after issuing a call to the Fifth Regiment at the recital hall. Her ultimatum fell like a spark on a dry forest that was primed to ignite. Teo's eloquent speech had already prepared the way, and Liber's noble sacrifice steeled the soldiers' resolve. When Ana challenged the men, they decided they'd had enough of tyranny. The regimental flag served to rally them behind the granddaughter of Armand. Ana had chosen the horse because it was trained to lead a charge, but now she remembered a standard-bearer wasn't a ceremonial position. In war, an ensign sometimes had to bear arms. For that reason a scabbard rested against the bay stallion's ribs, carrying a recurve shortbow, some arrows, and a cavalry saber.

Ana removed the bow stave from the scabbard along with the sinew string. Dismounting, she strung the bow, then climbed into the saddle again. *The reign of terror ends today*, she vowed. Ana set her jaw and began to trot toward the Citadel.

The High Priestess's head swung around as soon as Ana neared the causeway. With a confident sneer she turned her black horse and walked it forward. A moment later she moved up to a canter. Ana squeezed her own mount, and the animal picked up its pace.

Dropping the reins, Ana nocked an arrow on the string. This would be the most important shot of her life. Her field of vision narrowed as everything else became an irrelevant blur. Ana focused all her attention on her approaching adversary.

The High Priestess raised her sword as her horse transitioned to a gallop. Ana's hand drew back to the anchor point on her chin. Though the bow's draw weight was heavy, her muscles were used to holding the tension. The stallion heaved between her thighs as it sped across the grass. Ana rolled with the motion, merging with her mount to become a swift messenger of death.

The gap narrowed. Ana's heart raced. An enormous collision was inevitable now. The stallion arched its neck, straining ahead, churning the earth. The priestess's face blazed white-hot in triumph. She held out her brass scepter like a weapon, shouting a profane curse. Salty sweat stung Ana's eyes.

Deu! Help me!

Ana released the string.

A bloodcurdling scream erupted from the priestess's black lips. Yet she kept coming, standing tall in the stirrups, holding her sword aloft. Its bright edge sliced around. Ana snatched the saber from her scabbard to parry the vicious blow.

Clang! The two blades rang out across the battlefield. Their massive impact hurled Ana backward over her horse's rump. Her world spun. Blue and green swirled together as everything turned upside down. The ground rushed up to meet her, then smashed her body like a sledgehammer. She gasped as her wind was pounded from her lungs. Her head blazed with the agony of a thousand firebrands. Darkness claimed her as its own.

Somehow Ana managed to open her eyes. Her shoulders lay on the ground, but her foot was elevated. She yanked and twisted her ankle but couldn't free it from her horse's stirrup. Every muscle hurt. She moaned softly, struggling to breathe amid the intense pain.

A shadow darkened the sun. Ana squinted into the glare. The High Priestess stared down at her from the saddle. Reaching out, she gathered the stallion's reins in her hand.

"You missed," she spat and began to drag Ana away.

✦ ✦ ✦

Teo deflected a pike thrust, then dispatched the attacker with a back-handed slash. Another blow banged off his helmet, but the steel held firm, and Teo whirled in the saddle to club his assailant with the head of his ax. The pikeman fell to his knees, and Teo rode him down.

At last he broke free of the melee. He had been striving to reach the High Priestess, but the battle was raging in the middle of the field, so Teo had to fight his way through. Now, having cleared the last of the enemy's ranks, he had a straight run to the Citadel's gate. Perhaps the priestess could be defeated before she could use her war machine.

Teo examined the strange device as he approached. The biggest part of it was a copper cylinder like a vat used in a brewery, with hoses and conduits snaking across its surface. The machine rested near a little guard post at the end of the causeway that spanned the Citadel's moat. A snout-like nozzle protruded from the cylinder, pointing toward the battlefield. The whole contraption rested in a transport wagon.

The foehn winds blew down the Maiden's Valley into Teo's face as he neared the High Priestess. She did not see him, for she was leading a bay stallion by the reins. Something bright-colored dragged from the captured horse. Teo looked more closely.

A blonde woman . . .

With a white blouse . . . a black bodice . . . a scarlet skirt!

Teo urged his horse into a run once more as he saw his beloved Anastasia in the High Priestess's grip. "Hang on, Ana! I'm coming!" he yelled, though he knew she couldn't hear him. Her inert body dangled from the stirrup as she was towed along the ground.

The High Priestess slipped past her war machine and reached the wood-and-earth bridge that led to the Citadel's barbican. Though the portcullis was up, the double doors were closed, so apparently the priestess did not intend to enter the fortress. Instead she dismounted and released the stallion's reins. Ana dangled precariously over the moat on the lip of the causeway.

Approaching the machine from behind, the High Priestess grasped a giant lever and heaved it with two hands. A yellow gas began to spew from the nozzle onto the grassy plain in front of the Citadel. Teo swore under his breath. He didn't know what the substance was, but there was no doubt it was deadly. Perhaps it was poisonous, or suffocating, or maybe a spark would ignite the stuff and consume all the combatants in a scorching conflagration. Whatever the case, one thing was certain: the gas was going to envelop everyone on the battlefield. The High Priestess intended to use the weapon on her own troops as well as her enemies.

Teo galloped toward the end of the causeway at an angle. Though he couldn't approach head-on because of the lethal fog, he believed his horse could make the jump from the rim of the moat onto the low bridge, putting him behind the machine once he landed. It would be close—but it was his only chance to turn off the gas before it consumed the soldiers.

The High Priestess stood on the causeway, gazing at Teo with her hands on her hips. He gave her a fierce glare and pointed his finger at her as if to say, "Here I come!" She stared back at him, daring him to approach.

Teo's horse surged toward the edge of the moat. The poisonous gas billowed from the terrible machine. Teo prepared to make the leap, like a steeplechase competition with everything on the line.

The priestess turned away. She unfastened the girth on Ana's stallion. The saddle slipped off its back. Entangled in horse tack, Ana tumbled into the moat.

No!

Teo jumped.

◆　◆　◆

The heavy weight of the saddle dragged Ana into the murky depths. Leather and pondweed ensnared her. She fought to free herself, but in the dark waters she couldn't tell which way was up. The feeling of being trapped underwater terrified her, yet thrashing only disoriented her more. The oxygen in her lungs began to run out. She couldn't hold her breath much longer. Ana stretched out her hands . . . grasping, sinking, dying. *Help me! Help me!*

A nightmarish creature of the deep grabbed her. Though she fought against the monster, it seized her leg and yanked her ankle, painfully scraping her skin. The creature enfolded Ana in its arms, then pressed her body against itself in a loathsome embrace. Suddenly it shot upward with a powerful burst from its legs. *Perhaps it's making for the surface!* Ana kicked her legs too, yearning to break free of the water. Yet the surface refused to come.

Her lungs cried out for relief. Her lips opened involuntarily. Filthy water flooded her mouth, but her throat did not let it pass. Dizziness clouded Ana's mind as she went limp in the monster's arms. A bright light sparkled high above. It drew closer . . . closer . . . and then . . .

Air!

Anastasia burst from her watery grave and sucked in the sweet oxygen that banished the suffocating pain. Her chest heaved as she floated like a doll—head thrown back, face to the sky, arms dangling at her sides. She sputtered and coughed, greedily gulping down lungfuls of air. The monster had finally released her.

But where am I?

Her body ached, and her skull throbbed. Ana's vision gradually came into focus. The wall of the Citadel loomed above her. She spat out a piece of algae and turned her head.

Someone's there!

The stranger's gaze was fixed upon her. She yelped and drew back, fearful of his intent—until suddenly, with a soaring spirit, Ana recognized him as the man who had promised he would always come.

"Teo!" she cried, reaching out for him.

He met her as they tread water in the moat, yet his face was grim. "What's the matter?" she asked. Teo pointed over her shoulder. Swiveling her head, Ana saw the High Priestess had turned on her war machine. The cloud of gas that belched from it had grown thick on the battlefield. Toxic tendrils wafted toward the soldiers, borne along by the winds.

Ana's jaw dropped. "What *is* that stuff?"

"I don't know, but I have to stop it."

Teo swam to one of the wooden piers of the bridge and hauled himself up. The High Priestess turned and watched him clamber from the moat. She curled her black-nailed finger, beckoning Teo close, and he needed no further encouragement. With his sword in his hand he charged down the causeway toward Astrebril's favorite queen.

Just before he reached her, the High Priestess rolled a small grenade in his direction. It exploded under Teo's feet, knocking him off balance at the exact moment the Priestess launched her attack. Ana could see she was skilled with a blade. Though ordinarily she wouldn't have been a match for Teo, he was stunned by the concussion. The proficient swordswoman pressed him hard.

Yet Teo recovered his composure quickly. His strokes grew strong again as his sword clashed against his adversary's. He locked blades with her, staring into her eyes, then gave her a hard shove that forced her back. As the priestess staggered away, the tip of Teo's sword caught her across the chest. She screamed as a red streak appeared on her white gown. Before she could recover, Teo high-kicked her and sent her sprawling. She flew against her heinous machine, knocking its lever into the off position. The hissing of the gas abruptly ceased.

Nevertheless, as the High Priestess regained her footing, triumph gleamed in her eyes. A Vulkainian guard had led the black horse to her. The priestess could mount it and escape the sickly yellow nebula that had already spewed from the machine.

"Look into the face of death, Teofil!" she snarled. "In a moment every soldier in Chiveis will be mortally wounded. They will all die in agony and leave the kingdom to me!"

Ana's eyes went to the battlefield. What the priestess said was true. The fog was drifting across the plain now. The soldiers had stopped fighting as they saw the poison approach. Though they covered their mouths and backed away, Ana could see they had no chance of escape. While the men fought, the gas had crept close. Now it was almost upon them.

Teo stared at the High Priestess on the bridge. He sought some preventative action he could take, but there was nothing to do. The machine was already turned off, yet the cloud kept advancing, driven along by the wind.

The Vulkainian released an arrow in Teo's direction. "Look out!" Ana cried. Though the arrow missed, the man fumbled to nock another. His mistress was in the saddle now. Teo drew back, helpless to prevent the impending disaster.

Down in the moat, Ana stared at the malignant vapor that rolled toward the soldiers. Good men were out there, men like Marco and

Brother Thomas and the Royal Guard. "Mighty Deu!" Ana shouted to the heavens. "Help those men! *Save them!*"

At that moment the double doors of the Citadel's gate burst open. Horsemen erupted from inside the fortress. Teo whirled, startled by the commotion behind him. Ana craned her neck, trying to identify the new arrivals.

The man at the front was a distinguished gentleman. Yet he was no Chiveisian, for he wore the garments of an Ulmbartian aristocrat. Ana gasped as she recognized him. Somehow Count Federco Borromo had found his way to Chiveis—and at his side was Shaphan!

The count pulled up short as he saw the fearsome cloud. Teo stood between the Ulmbartians at one end of the causeway and the High Priestess at the other. And then, as Ana watched, a strange thing happened.

Perhaps it was the different air currents created by the opened gate, or perhaps it was the very breath of Deu himself. Whatever the cause, the foehn winds rushing down the valley began to spiral upward at the end of the causeway. The poisonous fumes were sucked into the updraft, swirling toward the sky instead of across the plain. An eddying gust captured an arm of the gas and wafted it backward. The dense mustard-colored smoke enveloped the war machine and began to drift down the bridge.

"Get back, Teo!" Ana shrieked. "Dive! Dive!"

Teo turned and arced into the moat, disappearing into its inky waters.

The whirlwind collapsed, and the cloud receded from the causeway. For a long, agonized moment, nothing moved. Then, slowly, the High Priestess emerged from the yellow fog. A look of sheer horror was on her face. Tears had created black streaks down her white-painted face. Ana instantly perceived what the priestess understood as well. *She has received a lethal dose. Nothing is left for her now but torment and certain death.*

Stumbling to the edge of the causeway, the High Priestess lifted a dagger above her head and plunged it into her breast. She toppled into the moat just as another gust came hurtling down from the mountains. As the air streamed through the portal of the Citadel's gate, its passage made a piercing whistle that forced Ana to cover her ears. The great wind blasted across the causeway and formed another updraft on the battlefield.

The noxious gas was borne into the sky by the furious gale. A black vapor curled up with it, climbing higher and higher in the whirlwind until it was almost out of sight. Then, like a mist at dawn, the cloud disappeared as if it had never existed.

"My God," Ana whispered as she stared at the sky, "you did it."

◆   ◆   ◆

Teo held his breath as long as he could, swimming underwater with powerful strokes that propelled him away from the bridge. He surfaced to find he had gone past the place where Ana was treading water. She gazed up at the clear blue sky, and so did all the men on the battlefield. The fight was over. The outsiders began dropping their weapons as the Royal Guard surrounded them.

Paddling up behind Ana, Teo touched her shoulder. She jumped and spun around, then smiled when she saw it was him.

"Which way did the High Priestess go?" Teo asked.

"She succumbed to the gas."

"She's dead?"

Ana nodded. "Gone forever."

Teo contemplated the news for a moment. "Come on then," he said. "Let's get out of this muck."

They swam to the edge of the moat and crawled onto the bank. Teo thought he had never felt so exhausted. He collapsed next to Ana, who reclined on her back and breathed hard to recover her wind. An overwhelming sense of relief descended on them as they lay side by side under the afternoon sun.

At last Teo glanced over at Ana. She was soaking wet. Her hair was a tangled mess. Muddy water dribbled down her cheeks, and pond scum flecked her face. Her white blouse was torn and dirty. Yet despite these things, Teo couldn't help but stare at the woman lying in the grass beside him. She was beautiful in every way—the fairest flower in all of Chiveis.

"Well, Ana—we're home," he said.

She gave an emphatic nod as a broad smile lit her face.

"And we brought the Sacred Writing to Chiveis," he added.

Again she nodded blissfully.

"The High Priestess is gone too. I can only think of one thing left to do."

Teo rolled over and rested on his elbow above Ana. He curled his free arm around her waist, drawing her close. Her lips were slightly parted, and her blue-green eyes were bright. As Teo gazed at the adorable, indomitable, unpredictable farm girl from Edgeton, he knew she was the woman for him. He wanted to cherish her and care for her and tenderly love her . . . always.

Softly he caressed Ana's cheek. His heartbeat quickened at the gravity of what he was about to say. He swallowed the lump in his throat.

"I love you, Anastasia," he said in a solemn voice. "I want to spend the rest of my life with you. Will you . . . will you be my wife?"

"Oh, Teo," she replied earnestly, "I can't."

CHAPTER

16

When King Piair II heard the knock at his door, he didn't even bother to respond. He knew who it was. The visitors would enter whether he welcomed them or not. Chiveis was under martial law, and the Warlord was in charge for now.

The young king slumped on the plush divan in his chambers, his shoulders sagging, his chin resting on his chest. He fiddled with a tassel on a cushion. *How did it come to this? I tried to do everything the gods demanded of me! But now . . .*

The knock came again, followed by a loud inquiry: "Are you in there?" Not, "Are you in there, Your Highness?" or "Your Majesty" or even "King Piair." Just a crude shout, like one commoner speaking to another. Normally such an address would be unthinkable, but today it didn't matter. In fact, it was as it should be. *I don't deserve the titles of a king.*

The door opened, and Piair turned to see the Warlord come in. His stride was purposeful, and his bushy mustache couldn't conceal his frown. He was accompanied by a colonel whose insignia identified him as the commander of the Fifth Regiment. Both men were armed, though their weapons were sheathed. The third arrival was the chief magistrate of the High Council, whose black robe and white wig signaled his business was official.

"Do you know the reason for our visit?" the Warlord asked.

Instead of answering, Piair rose from the divan and walked out to the balcony. Beyond the Citadel's wall, the battlefield lay spread before him.

Though it was now bathed in the orange light of sunset, Piair could still see how its grass had been churned into mud by thousands of boots and hooves. Many bodies lay strewn on the field, while the injured were being carried away on stretchers. The outsider warriors were returning to their encampment under the close supervision of the Guard—whether as confederates or captives, neither side knew for sure. Meanwhile, the invaders from Marsay and Jineve had pulled back under a fragile truce until the situation played itself out and the next steps could be determined.

The Warlord came and stood by Piair at the railing. He pointed to the copper machine at the end of the causeway. "You knew about that thing?"

"I knew of its existence. I didn't know how it would be used."

"Hmph," the Warlord grumped, folding his arms across his chest. "So in effect you were letting the religious authorities dictate your will as king."

"No! The High Priestess and I made our strategy together. I was just as much in charge as she."

"Ah, I see. Then you take responsibility for the unprecedented alliance with the barbarians? The war levy that turned into looting? The policy of aggression that forced a neighboring kingdom to invade us? The near outbreak of civil war in the Royal Guard? The attempted murder of our entire army? All of this you planned with the High Priestess—is that it?"

"It wasn't supposed to turn out like that," Piair said, hanging his head.

The Warlord refused to let the beleaguered king off the hook. "What did you know about that machine?" he pressed.

"N-nothing! I swear it."

"You said you knew of it."

"I knew it would spew poison. That's all."

"And how did you imagine such a weapon could injure our enemies yet not harm our own troops?"

"That never occurred to me," Piair insisted, though the creeping weight of guilt began to oppress his soul. He glanced nervously at the Warlord to gauge whether the savvy general could sense the lie. King Piair had heard the High Priestess mention the idea of an attack on the Royal Guard. It had almost seemed like a joke, just a frivolous whisper in the dark of night, a whisper shared in the warm afterglow, a whisper to suggest a horrific idea and test whether it might come true. Piair had told himself he would never agree to such a thing. Yet the idea of absolute rule over an armyless kingdom with the priestess at his side was intoxicating. The young king had lusted for such a reality, though he had feared it too.

Recovering his composure, Piair examined his fingernails and tried to assume a nonchalant air. "So, General, speaking of the High Priestess . . . what does she have to say about all this? I'm sure she and I could provide you a reasonable explanation of recent events."

"The priestess is dead," the Warlord said flatly.

No! It can't be true! She can't be gone!

"What do you mean, *dead?*" Piair burst out. "Speak plainly, General!"

"I did speak plainly. She's dead. She was enveloped by the gas, and its torments drove her to take her own life. Now the carp shall have her flesh, and her name shall be forgotten in the annals of Chiveis."

Piair gripped the balustrade to control his trembling hands. "I, um . . . I had not heard that."

"The news seems to trouble you far too much, Piair." The Warlord glanced over his shoulder at the chief magistrate. "Have you seen enough?"

"Yes. The king shall stand trial for treason against the homeland and dereliction of his duty to the realm. If found guilty, he shall forfeit his reign."

Piair whirled to confront his three visitors. The commander of the Fifth Regiment put his hand on his sword's hilt, but Piair waved him off. "There is no need for that," he said. Reaching to his forehead, he removed his crown and held it out to the silent men.

"This is the symbol of my royal authority, is it not?"

The Warlord nodded.

"I am unworthy to wear it."

Piair hurled the crown to the floor and crushed it underfoot. The startled men recoiled at the violent desecration. After four or five hard stomps, the young king lifted his head and faced his accusers.

"Gentlemen," he said, "I hereby abdicate the throne of Chiveis."

❖   ❖   ❖

For the first time in many months, Ana awoke on a soft mattress under a warm duvet. She could have enjoyed luxuriating in the bed's exquisite comfort, except her body was so sore she could hardly move. But she was content to lie still, staring at the ceiling, glad to be alive.

A rumbling snore reverberated from the hotel room's other bed. Ana smiled at the sound, which was familiar and not bothersome. She had grown up hearing that noise every night. It always reminded her that her daddy was close by.

Ana's thoughts turned to the events of the day before. After the battle ended, the Warlord instructed her to take lodging at one of the Citadel's upscale hotels at the government's expense. The general said her testimony might be needed, so she should clean up, purchase suitable clothing, and stay put until she was summoned. Though the political situation in Chiveis was uncertain, it was clear that egregious misjudgments, if not crimes, had been committed at the highest levels. The Royal Guard's dramatic switch of allegiance amounted to a vote of no confidence in the king. The Warlord said it would take time to sort things out. In the meantime, Ana and Teo and everyone associated with them should wait.

Teo . . .

Ana's heart ached as she recalled the look on his face when she rebuffed his marriage proposal at the Citadel's moat. Shocked and hurt, he had rolled away from her and stood up. Ana quickly explained her discovery of his admittance report at the orphanage. Teo recoiled at the idea he was Helena's son, conceived out of wedlock by her lover Hanson. Ana was in agony about it too. Yet they could both see its likelihood—and the implications for their future. "Just ask your mother for the truth," Teo said. "I'll wait for you to find out. We'll go from there."

But where will we go if you're my half brother? Ana had wondered. She had been dreading the conversation with her mother ever since.

A rooster crowed outside, adding to the din of Stratetix's snore. Gingerly, and with several grunts of her own, Ana sat up in bed and pushed back the duvet. Her body hurt, yet it was nothing compared to her pain at the prospect of losing Teo. She swung her bare feet to the floor. *I will find out today, one way or the other,* she vowed. Yet even as she made the decision, her resolve melted away and anxiety took its place. *Please,*

Deu, she begged, *don't let it be true! Please don't ask me to walk one more road of sacrifice!*

"Good morning, honey. How did you sleep?"

Her mother's cheerful greeting startled Ana. She glanced over to her parents' bed to find Helena leaning on one elbow in her nightshift, her ash-blonde hair rumpled from sleep. Ana knew she would grow to look even more like her mother over the years, and that notion was perfectly agreeable to her. Helena was a lovely middle-aged woman. *And no doubt she was a beautiful teenager too*, whispered a shadowy voice of fear. Ana pushed the thought away as she stood up. She rolled out a kink in her neck and arched her back, then said, "I guess I slept pretty well for somebody who fell off a galloping horse." She went to the stove to stir up the coals and get the kettle going again. "This white willow tea really helped."

"Keep taking it," Helena advised. "And make sure you put more salve on that lump on your head."

Ana nodded but said nothing further. A little while later a hot breakfast was brought up from the kitchen, and Stratetix awoke to a hearty meal. He gathered his family at the table and started to give thanks to Deu but choked up halfway through the prayer. Covering Ana's hand with his, he finished the blessing, then smiled at her as he dug into his eggs. She smiled back, delighted to be reunited with her family. Yet the burden of her impending conversation weighed on her mind. She picked at her food but could hardly eat.

After breakfast Stratetix announced he would go to Teo's room for a mug of cider. The men had been telling some rousing yarns, and Stratetix enjoyed meeting the exotic foreigners Marco, Brother Thomas, and Bard. The women, too, had been regaled with amazing stories as Ana and Vanita recounted their adventures. Even timid Lina had a tale to contribute: she had fled into the Beyond with Shaphan, given birth in the wilderness, nearly died at the hands of the Rovers, met an Ulmbartian military expedition, and guided the soldiers back to Chiveis. The intrepid Count Federco hadn't realized how close he was to the homeland of his friend Teofil. When he learned it from Shaphan, nothing could prevent him from pressing on. The establishment of a route between Chiveis and

Ulmbartia—even one that traversed a vast wilderness—was an important discovery for both kingdoms.

Stratetix exited the room, leaving his wife and daughter alone. Ana's stomach grew queasy, and her heart began to pound. She knew the moment of reckoning had arrived. The answer to a simple yes or no question was going to determine her future.

"Are you alright, my love?" Helena asked. "You didn't eat your breakfast, and your face is as pale as a bedsheet."

Just do it. Get it over with. Ana took a deep breath. "What happened when you were seventeen?" she blurted out.

"Um . . . I'm not sure what you mean."

"We heard about the Battle of Toon at the hearing. But you wouldn't tell the whole story."

"Oh, Ana. Do we need to dredge up that again?"

"You're hiding something!" Ana accused.

Helena's expression grew wary. "What makes you say that?"

"I snooped in the records at the orphanage. I found a report that said a seventeen-year-old girl named Helena dropped off a baby."

"That . . . doesn't prove anything."

"Mother! It was the same year you were seventeen! A few months after the battle, a baby shows up at an orphanage!"

Ana clenched her skirt in her fists. The terrible truth was poised to come out, and she couldn't hold it back anymore. If Teo was her half brother, she needed to know—even though it would mean they could never be together as husband and wife. Taking a step forward, she seized her mother's arm. "Tell me the truth! The girl who came to the orphanage was *you*, wasn't it? You bore that child! You!"

Helena stared at the floor, wrestling with her emotions. At last she met Ana's eyes and nodded.

Ana burst into tears as her nightmare became a reality. She collapsed against her mother's shoulder, sobbing at the loss of the future she had been dreaming of, on some level, since the day she met Teo. Yet even as she wept, prayers of resignation swirled through her mind. *I'll let him go, Deu! I'll step into the future you have for me! I'll walk whatever road you ask! But please help me! I'm in anguish!*

Helena held Ana close, soothing her with gentle words. Finally she separated from her daughter and brushed a crumpled lock from her forehead. "Honey, as far as I'm concerned this is all in the past. When I handed that baby to the warders I put him out of my mind forever. You should too. Let's never speak about this again, okay?"

"Mother, you don't understand!"

"You're right, I don't. Why are you so upset about this?"

"Because the record at the orphanage was Teofil's! That baby was *him*!"

Now it was Helena's turn to be staggered. Her jaw dropped, and her eyes grew wide. "No!" she said in a trembling whisper. "It can't be! *Teofil?* Then that means . . . "

Abruptly Helena turned and rushed to the door. She flung it open as Ana followed her into the hallway. They burst into Teo's room as the men were enjoying a hearty laugh. At the sudden intrusion their faces turned toward the two agitated women.

"Is something the matter?" Teo asked.

Helena knelt beside his chair. "Take off your boot."

"My boot?"

"Yes. The left one."

Bewildered, Teo complied. Helena seized his foot and examined it. Teo glanced up at Ana with a perplexed expression, but she could only shrug in response. She had no answers to give him.

Helena stood up, dumbstruck.

"I have to go somewhere," she muttered.

Stratetix came to her side and took her by the arm. "Helena, what's going on? Is everything okay?"

"I . . . I'm not sure." She began to edge toward the door.

"Whatever it is, I'll go with you."

The husband and wife hurried out, leaving everyone in the hotel room agape. Ana ran to the doorway behind her parents. "Wait!" she called. "Where are you going?"

"To see the Queen Mother," Helena replied as she disappeared around a corner.

◆　　◆　　◆

A steward led Teo and Ana through a maze of corridors at the royal palace of Chiveis. Though Teo had visited quite a few impressive residences in the Beyond, he had never actually been inside the palace at the Citadel. He thought it stacked up well against the others he had seen, being suitably august yet not overbearing. Heavy draperies lined the bay windows, and potted plants stood on columns at intervals. The artwork on the walls portrayed heroic scenes from Chiveisian history, many of them depicting the life of Jonluc Beaumont and his consort, Greta the Great. The woman's long dark hair and sensual eyes reminded Teo of her descendant and namesake. He frowned and looked away.

A palace messenger had arrived at the hotel room several hours after Ana's parents left, bearing an invitation to a private audience with the Queen Mother. Teo had hurriedly changed into a new tunic while Ana donned the light-blue gown she had purchased at the Warlord's request. Though she looked nice in the form-fitting dress, Teo forced himself not to pay attention. Ana had reported to him what she learned from her mother, and now Teo was grieving the awful truth that the only woman he could ever love would never become his wife. Numbed, he followed the steward through the palace halls like a criminal being led to his formal sentencing.

At last they arrived at a courtyard with a fountain at its center. Red roses climbed the walls, and an ornamental cherry tree provided shade for a seating area. Two stone benches faced a wicker chair with a cushioned seat. Stratetix and Helena occupied one of the benches.

Teo sat down next to Ana after briefly greeting her parents. Distracted and upset, he waited in silence until the steward returned. The man in the long tailcoat gestured to the door with a flourish. "Her Majesty, the Queen Mother," he announced. Everyone rose as Katerina entered the courtyard.

After the appropriate introductions were made, the four visitors took their seats opposite their hostess. She was an attractive woman with elegant gray hair gathered into a spiral bun. Though her gracious manner was intended to put her guests at ease, Teo could only dread the momentous news that had caused the noble lady to call this meeting.

Katerina turned to Ana's mother and addressed her with aristocratic courtliness. "It has been a long time since we sat in this courtyard discussing divine things, Helena d'Armand," she said. "You were only a girl, and I myself was still in my twenties."

"I remember those days fondly," Helena replied with equal grace. "The three of us had many stimulating conversations."

"Ah, yes . . . the *three* of us." Katerina's eyes took on a faraway glaze as she stared into the distance for a moment before turning back to her guests. "That brings me to the reason I have summoned you here. I have an interesting story to tell."

"Don't hold anything back, Your Highness," Teo said firmly. "Be forthright. Tell us everything so we can deal with the facts as they are."

"Indeed I shall, Captain Teofil. And you may hear some very surprising things." A strange inflection was in Katerina's voice as she spoke.

The Queen Mother leaned back in her wicker chair and began to recall her youth. She was born into a noble Chiveisian family whose lineage included kings. Her overbearing father, eager to make the perfect match for his daughter, refused to give her hand in marriage until she reached the age of twenty-seven. That was when Piair, who was soon to inherit the royal throne, began to romance her. Katerina was flattered by his attention, and of course her father was overjoyed—but another man had already won her heart.

She turned to Helena. "Do you remember how handsome he was? Handsome and intelligent too."

Helena nodded. "I remember. He retained those qualities into his old age."

"Who was it?" Ana asked.

Katerina brightened as she supplied the answer. "You knew him as Professor Maurice."

Teo sat up straight in his seat. *Master Maurice!* His wise mentor at the University had never had a family. In fact, he didn't like to speak of the subject. Now Teo knew why. Intrigued by this disclosure, Teo asked Katerina to continue her tale.

"I loved Maurice," she went on, "so we decided to elope. I realize now how foolish that was, but at the time we were young and naive. We disguised ourselves and found a village judge who would join us. The night we spent together in a country inn was one of the happiest of my life."

The Queen Mother let out a heavy sigh. "Unfortunately, it was only one night."

Katerina described how her father arrived the next day, furious at her impetuous deed. He summoned the terrified judge and demanded an immediate annulment. By the time the sun went down, Katerina was no longer the wife of a dashing university professor but of Chiveis's future king. A few months later Piair was crowned as the regent. That was when things grew complicated: the newlywed queen discovered she was pregnant.

"Piair was insanely jealous," Katerina said. "He knew about my brief marriage, and it gnawed at him. He was tormented by the thought the child would be Maurice's. I feared for the baby's life. Finally my term was completed, and I delivered a beautiful little girl. She was tiny and delicate. Her skin was so pale it was almost translucent. Even as a baby her hair was bright red."

"The Flame of Chiveis," Teo said. "Princess Habiloho."

Katerina nodded and closed her eyes. Her visitors remained quiet until she found her composure. "I loved her very much," she said at last.

"All of Chiveis did, my lady." Helena touched the grieving mother's hand. Katerina glanced up to meet her gaze, smiling at the kind remark.

"King Piair was redheaded too," Stratetix observed. "Habiloho was clearly his daughter."

"Yes, she was, and I was so relieved the child was his. But then something strange happened. As I lay in the delivery room, my pains came upon me again. At first I thought it was the birth sac, but when I looked, it was a little boy. He was dark-haired and swarthy. I could see Maurice's features in his face. Even his little ears were attached to his jaw like his father's. Then I understood: two men had brought forth life in me, and Piair would never let this boy live. He would be a rival to the throne. In desperation I summoned Maurice. 'Take the child!' I cried. 'The king will kill him!' But Maurice knew he couldn't raise the baby. Everyone would know whose it was. So that very night we made a sacred vow. We decided to hide the boy to save his life, and never speak of him again."

As Katerina paused her tale, Teo sat back on the stone bench, grappling with what he had just heard. His mind spun as the revelation's significance began to sink in. He was about to speak when Ana broke in.

"You and Maurice both knew my mother!" she exclaimed to Katerina. "You asked her to take the baby to the orphanage!"

"That's right," Helena confirmed. "But Maurice did something important that night. Before he handed the boy over to me, he identified him with a secret mark: a tattoo of three dots on the sole of his foot."

Absolute silence hung in the courtyard. Teo could feel his heart pounding. "I . . . I have a birthmark like that on my foot," he said, "but it's not . . . " He looked at Ana. She spun toward him on the bench, clutching his sleeve.

"I noticed it! Remember? By the lake on the pass in Ulmbartia. You said it was a birthmark, but I thought it was a tattoo."

"It *is* a tattoo," the Queen Mother said. "I saw it made."

"So did I." Helena turned toward Teo. "But I never knew it was you, Teofil. Not until Ana told me earlier today."

Teo gripped his forehead in his hands. "Maurice was my father! It makes sense—he always called me his son. He must have known who I was! Yet he could never tell me."

"Maurice loved you very much, Teofil. And think of what else this means." The Queen Mother stood up and approached Teo as he sat on the bench. She reached out and touched his earlobe. "Just like your father's," she observed, "and mine. Look! My hair was once dark like yours. Our eyes are gray. We have the same chin." Katerina gave Teo an affectionate smile as she gazed down at him. "Do you see? You are my long-lost son."

Teo scrambled to his feet. "I, uh . . . I don't know what to say, Your Majesty."

Katerina took Teo's hand, caressing it with her fingers. "I hope in time you will learn to call me by a different name."

Before Teo could respond, Ana turned to Helena. "Mother! Why did you tell me the boy was yours when he was actually born to the queen?"

"I didn't say that, love."

"You did! You said you bore the child yourself."

Helena shook her head. "No, honey. I bore the child in my arms to the orphanage. That's what you kept asking about—the identity of the girl who brought the baby. It never crossed my mind you'd think the boy was mine! How could he have been?"

"Um . . . Hanson?"

"Oh my goodness, Ana, no! What he did to me was embarrassing, but when I married your father I had never been with a man."

Ana's cheeks flushed. "I'm sorry, Mother. I just assumed . . . "

Though Ana was flustered, Teo couldn't help but tilt back his head and laugh. He felt as if an unbearable burden had just rolled off his shoulders. Life seemed livable again. Taking Ana's hand, he lifted her from the bench. She turned away from her parents and looked into his eyes, smiling as he drew her into an embrace. "My sweet Ana," he said, overjoyed and relieved. "We're free to marry after all."

Ana's face glowed as she gazed back at Teo. "And this time I say yes!"

"Not so fast," Katerina said.

Teo and Ana exchanged apprehensive glances. Slowly they turned their heads to stare at the Queen Mother. She arched her eyebrows as she regarded the two lovers.

"As happy as I am for you, the ramifications here affect much more than your romantic future. Remember, I didn't marry into the royal family by catching myself a prince. I too am from an ancient line of kings."

Teo felt Ana tense in his arms. Her lips made a little pink O as her eyes flicked up toward him. "Teo! You have royal blood running in your veins!"

Katerina nodded. "And Piair has abdicated his throne—which means you, Teofil, are the rightful king of Chiveis."

✦   ✦   ✦

Shaphan the Metalsmith handed Teo a wooden box with a brass clasp. "I have to tell you, it looks pretty good," said the olive-skinned man with the wavy hair.

Teo smiled at his former student and close friend. "I'm sure it does. I have complete confidence in you."

The affirmation made Shaphan beam. Teo knew the young metalsmith looked up to him and craved his approval. *I wonder what he'd think if he knew I'm the heir apparent to the Chiveisian throne?* Teo wagged his head in disbelief and tried to dismiss the thought from his mind.

After thanking Shaphan profusely for his work, Teo took his leave and went to meet Ana in the street outside the hotel. Despite his best efforts, the idea of being the heir apparent kept returning to him. He laughed as he recalled the look on the Warlord's face when the Queen Mother informed him that one of his own captains—one of the youngest and most insubordinate—was actually the king. Although the general had bowed stiffly to Teo at the news, he didn't appear to begrudge it. The Warlord's unease seemed to emerge more from surprise than distaste. Teo couldn't help but sense that the old soldier respected his prowess in battle and his leadership skills. In the end, of course, the commander of the Royal Guard would serve the Kingdom of Chiveis no matter who the regent might be.

Ana stood on her tiptoes and waved at Teo when she spotted him on the street. He hefted his rucksack over his shoulder and greeted her affectionately. Slipping her arm into his, she strolled beside him toward the Warlord's Bureau. It wasn't long before the impressive government building appeared up ahead.

"I came here the day after I met you," Teo remarked. "I had to report how the outsiders attacked us at the bluff in the river bend."

"I remember. You said you had documents to file." Ana nudged him with a playful grin. "And a companion to see."

Teo tsked. "I meant Maurice, you know."

"I know that now. Back then it wasn't so clear."

"Did it bother you?"

Ana cocked her head and chewed her lip for a moment, then admitted, "A little."

Teo and Ana ascended the granite steps to the main door of the Warlord's Bureau. The clerk inside waved them through, having been alerted to their coming. Teo had arranged with the Warlord to pay a special visit to one of the army's prisoners.

The steps down to the dungeon were steep and slippery. Teo supported Ana with one hand and grasped the railing with the other. The jailer at the bottom handed him a key. "Fourth door on the left," he said.

The cell was dim as Teo unlocked the door and peered inside. He could see no one, so he stepped through the low portal to let his eyes adjust. Ana followed close behind.

"Who are you?" growled a voice from a shadowy corner.

"You know who I am," Teo replied as he stepped into a shaft of light, "but there's more that needs to be said."

A slender young man with dark hair was chained to the wall. He looked drawn and tired, though he hadn't been abused. "Why are you here, Captain Teofil? To gloat? Rub it in? Fine! Do your best. I don't care."

Teo squatted at the man's side. "I would never do that."

"What do you want then?"

"I want your friendship, Piair."

"Friendship?" The disgraced king scoffed and waved his hand. "That's going to be a little difficult, I think. We've been enemies since the day your foreign god drew Astrebril's wrath upon my father and sister."

Ana came and knelt beside Teo. "That's not what happened. The High Priestess rigged it to make it seem like a divine act. She had discovered a powder that would explode when ignited. Those deaths weren't the act of any god. It was treachery and propaganda."

Piair remained silent for a long time. Even in the gloom Teo could see his jaw clenching and unclenching as he wrestled with his thoughts.

"You know it's true," Teo said, trying to nudge Piair off the emotional fence. "She was a master of underworld tricks. She would kill anyone to preserve her power. Free your mind from her grip."

"Easier said than done," Piair muttered bitterly.

"Important to do nonetheless," Teo replied.

Anger flared on the young man's face, though Teo sensed despair behind the rage. "What good will it do me? I'm a reject—a failure of a king!"

"Deu can turn failure into victory, brother."

Piair glanced sharply at Teo but did not speak.

"That's right," Teo said, "I used the word *brother*. Perhaps you think that sounds strange. I thought it was strange too when I discovered a secret about my family not long ago." Piair looked interested, so Teo went on. "I was raised as an orphan near Toon. But I've just learned that my father was the esteemed Professor Maurice. And I think you'll be even more surprised to hear who my mother is."

Piair's eyes narrowed. "Tell me."

"She is the Queen Mother Katerina. You and I are half brothers, and I am destined to inherit the throne of Chiveis."

Recoiling, Piair glanced between Teo and Ana to determine whether this was some kind of cruel joke. When he saw it wasn't, he scooted back into the shadows with his forearm shielding his body. "Why are you telling me this?" he cried. "What's going to happen to me? Am I destined for the executioner?"

"Not at all. I've thought of an even worse fate for you." Teo smiled gently. "I have decided to restore you as king."

The dungeon fell silent. Its three occupants stared back and forth, each waiting for someone else to speak. Finally Ana reached out and patted Piair's hand. "Your Majesty, you have been given the gift of a second chance. Teofil is offering you a full pardon. You can start over as an innocent man."

"No," Piair whispered. "It's not possible. No one does that."

Teo leaned forward and met his half brother's eyes. "There is one who does—Deu, the creator of heaven and earth."

"But why would he do that for *me?*"

"Because that's the sort of God he is. He brings life out of death. He gives mercy where it isn't deserved. He grants forgiveness to the repentant sinner. I've received such grace, and now I offer it to you. I have no interest in being king of Chiveis! But, Piair, I truly believe you can become a great ruler like your father before you."

The young man sucked in his breath at Teo's words. "You . . . you think so?"

"I do. The opportunity lies before you to become a righteous king who does justice and brings blessing to his land. You can achieve this if you'll sever your ties to the wicked gods and bow to the Eternal One."

"Tch! It'll never happen, Teofil. By now Deu's price for my loyalty will be far more than I can pay."

Teo shook his head. "Christianism doesn't work like the priestess's religion. Deu's affections don't have to be bought with a bribe. He sent his Son from heaven to proclaim his love for the world. Though evil men killed him, he overcame the grave. Whoever believes in him will receive eternal life."

"Deu has a son?"

"Yes, Your Majesty," Ana said. "His name is Iesus Christus, and he is the helper of kings. Let me show you."

She turned and rummaged through Teo's rucksack. Withdrawing the *Versio Secunda Chiveisorum*, she opened its silver-embossed cover. "Teofil and I have brought you a gift from the Beyond. Listen to what Deu says in his second Hymn." Ana cradled the Sacred Writing in her arm and flipped a few pages until she found the passage she intended to read: "'And now, you kings, conduct yourselves with wisdom! Receive instruction, you judges of the earth! Serve the Eternal One with fear. Rejoice in him with trembling. Kiss the Son, lest he be angry and you perish along your way; for his anger is quick to blaze up. But blessed are all those who trust in him.'"

Ana raised her eyes from the text. "See? Deu will judge evil, yet he stands ready to bless those who come to him."

Piair ran his fingers through his tangled hair. "But I spurned him so long! Surely it's too late for someone like me."

"You can come to Deu at any time," Teo replied. "Our sister did."

"You mean . . . Habiloho?"

"Yes. Just before she died she embraced the Creator God. Her final wish was that you do the same."

"Habiloho thought of me?" Piair asked, awed.

Teo nodded. "I was with her as she lay dying. She wanted you to know how much she loved you. She said you should reject Astrebril and bring Deu to Chiveis."

"Take up your throne again," Ana urged, "but this time rule according to the Sacred Writing. Instead of by the sword, let it be by the Word that Chiveis lives."

Closing the Secunda, Ana offered it to Piair. He took it in two hands and stared at its ornate cover. The silver tracery glinted in the light from the dungeon's sole window. Warring emotions battled across the young man's face, reflecting the turbulence within his soul. He remained silent for a long time as he gripped the precious book, yet when he finally spoke it was with conviction. "Very well," he said. "I shall follow Deu as my God. And this book will become an heirloom of my family forever." Piair glanced up at Teo. "I mean . . . *our* family."

"Then I think you will also need this, Your Highness." Teo reached into his rucksack and removed Shaphan's wooden box. After unfastening the clasp, he lifted out a golden object: the royal crown of Chiveis, restored to its original perfection.

Piair gasped at the sight. "That can't be the same one! I thought I destroyed it!"

"You did. But we know someone who fixes broken things."

Teo held out the crown in his fingers. Piair lowered his head. As Teo laid the circlet on his brow, the young king choked back a sob. "Th-thank you," was all he could manage.

"It looks good on you," Teo said, then squeezed Piair's shoulder and grinned. "Just take better care of it next time, okay?" The young king looked up and met Teo's eyes, nodding gratefully through his tears.

"What can I do for you?" he asked. "If I'm to be the king again, you shall rule with me! You can be governor of whatever territory you wish. No, even better! The Warlord is about to retire. You shall take his place, Teofil!"

Teo shook his head. "Rulership is best left to those with the right skills. I'm not called to be a politician. However, I do have one request."

"Name it, and it shall be done."

"Let Chiveis build a new city at the bend in the Farm River. According to the maps of the Ancients, a city once stood there called Bern. Now let New Bern rise in its place. It will be our point of contact with the Jinevans. Those people are prosperous. We could trade with them. Many of them have become Christiani, though I think their mayor still has a lot to learn about the actual practice of the faith. Let's join with them and help them. We can build roads and river ports between our two kingdoms."

"An excellent idea! And I shall name you mayor of New Bern!"

"No, I have something else in mind." Teo turned toward Ana. "How about if you tell him?"

Ana's face lit up as she addressed Piair. "We'd like to build a temple of Deu at New Bern, using the sacred architecture we've seen in the Beyond.

It would have pointed arches that uplift the soul and colored glass to admit the light of heaven. We know the perfect place for it—a bluff above the river bend, with the peaks of Chiveis in the distance."

"And I'd like to be the shepherd of Deu's flock at the temple," Teo added, "if you're willing to allow it."

"Willing?" Piair exclaimed. "Of course!" He paused, cocking his head. "But is that really all you want?"

Teo reached over and grasped Ana's hand, then faced the young king and nodded. "Yes, my lord. To open the Sacred Writing before the people of Deu is the highest calling I can imagine."

❖   ❖   ❖

The sunshine filtering through the leafy canopy reminded Teo of the light in an ancient basilica. Towering beech trees served as the imaginary building's pillars, while their intertwined branches formed a shimmering green roof over the natural hall. Lines had been staked out to mark the walls of the future temple, and a cornerstone had been laid at their juncture. Everything about the setting atop the bluff in the river bend was delightful. The day was pleasantly cool and calm. The sky was dotted with puffy white clouds. A songbird chirped happily nearby. It was Midsummer's Day in Chiveis—the perfect day to marry the most beautiful woman in the realm.

Teo stood beneath an arbor draped with white roses and greenery. He clasped his hands behind his back as he waited next to Marco, Shaphan, and Brother Thomas. Though the men were dressed in expensive new tunics, Teo wore the dress uniform of the Royal Guard: a high-collared blue jacket with red piping and brass buttons, dark trousers, and smart black boots. Behind a cloth-covered altar, the Papa faced the spectators seated on benches in the forest clearing. Sol stood ready to translate the Papa's words from Talyano into the Chiveisian speech.

Marco leaned over and spoke to Teo out of the corner of his mouth. "You sure you don't want to back out, *amico?*"

"Are you kidding?" Teo whispered back. "I've been waiting for this day for three years." The reply drew a chuckle from the dark-haired seafarer.

Off to the side of the clearing a young woman began to play a harpsichord, accompanied by another woman on a flute. As the elegant, lilting
canon filled the forest cathedral, Vanita Labella appeared from behind
a curtain at the rear of the seating area. She carried a lovely bouquet of
wildflowers, and her glamorous updo was held in place with a jeweled pin.
Wearing a strapless pale-green gown, she glided down the center aisle
toward the waiting groomsmen. As she reached the front and started to
turn, she flashed Teo a brilliant smile and a wink. Teo couldn't help but
grin back at the saucy aristocrat who had become Ana's best friend. Vanita
was followed down the aisle by Ana's cousin Lina and her aunt Rosetta,
both of whom wore the same green gowns. When the bridesmaids had
reached their appointed positions, the two musicians ended their song
with a flourish.

Now a hush settled on the crowd as the notes drifted away into the
trees. Teo stared at the curtain at the far end of the aisle, hardly able to
breathe. His heart hammered, and his knees felt weak. Every head turned
in anticipation. Then, as the harpsichordist began to play a triumphant
wedding march, the curtain parted, and Teo beheld his bride.

She wore a white linen gown with lace at the sleeves. The V-necked
dress was fitted through the body, creating an hourglass shape that flared
below the knee. A string of jewels adorned her throat, and pearl drop earrings dangled from her ears. Ana's honey-blonde hair had been styled so
that a golden braid encircled her head like a tiara, interwoven with the
delicate white blossoms of ehdelveis that also graced her bouquet. As her
father escorted her down the aisle, she fixed her eyes on Teo and smiled
demurely, her lips forming the shape of a heart. Not once did she break
off her intense gaze. Teo blinked moisture from his eyes and exhaled the
breath he had been holding. After all the dangers, all the trials, all the
fears—at last he and Ana would be together forever.

The wedding march crescendoed as Ana reached the altar. Releasing
her father's arm, she kissed him on the cheek, then took her place at Teo's
side. The couple turned to face the Papa, who lifted his eyes and spoke
over their heads to the watching audience. "*Relinquet homo patrem suum et
matrem,*" he intoned, "*et adherebit uxori suae, et erunt duo in carne una.*" Sol
translated the Old Words into Chiveisian for the benefit of the crowd: "A

man shall relinquish his father and mother and adhere to his wife, and the two shall be in one flesh."

The wedding ceremony was simple and succinct. The Papa offered a brief meditation on the importance of marriage in the plan of Deu, then took the couple through the sacrament of holy matrimony. At the appointed time for the vows, the leader of the Universal Communion asked Ana if she received Teofil as her lawfully wedded husband.

"I do," she said, staring at Teo with her blue-green eyes. He gazed back, exquisitely aware of the adoration bursting from his bride.

"And do you, Captain Teofil, now take this woman as your beloved and cherished wife?" the Papa asked.

"I do," Teo replied.

"What pledge do you give of your perpetual fidelity?"

"This ring."

Teo brought out the ring he had asked Shaphan to make. Its diamond was a gift from Count Federco Borromo, and its gold band was inlaid with a silver metal. Ana glanced up at Teo from beneath her eyelashes when she saw it.

"It's beautiful," she whispered.

"I had some very precious steel put into this ring. Can you guess where it's from?"

Ana gave a little shrug.

"An arrowhead that was used here exactly three years ago."

"Oh! That's perfect!"

A joyful radiance lit up Ana's face as Teo slipped the ring on her finger. He met her gaze and said, "Anastasia of Edgeton, I give you this ring as a symbol of my eternal vows. With all that I am and all that I have, I honor you." Abruptly Teo spun toward the crowd. "And I want you to do the same," he announced.

At Teo's signal two guardsmen approached from behind the trees, carrying a tall, cloth-covered object. After setting it down on an X marked with chalk, they removed the cloth and stepped away. A collective murmur escaped the lips of the spectators. The object was an intricately carved pulpit of rich cherrywood.

"Today I want to tell you the story of an exceptional woman," Teo said. Then, with the clarity of a teacher and the passion of a lover, he began to spin a tale of Ana's undaunted courage. He told how she had crossed the kingdom's highest mountains to venture into the Beyond. There she fought against ferocious wolves. Stared down the length of an arrow at her enemies. Held her head high in the face of insults and lies. Brought great men to their knees with her noble spirit. Found the grace to forgive when she was betrayed. Poured out her life so that others might live. And most beautifully of all, Anastasia of Edgeton had been unwavering in her one supreme goal: to find the Sacred Writing of Deu and bring it home to the land she loved.

"Therefore I offer this pulpit as a gift," Teo concluded. "Not a gift to Anastasia, but in honor of her. I give the gift to *you*, the good people of Chiveis. On this very spot, where my future wife saved me from the claws of a bear, I now promise to proclaim the Sacred Writing in a manner worthy of the sacrifices she made to bring it here."

Having finished his speech, Teo took a step back, expecting a thoughtful silence to descend on the place. Instead the crowd burst into thunderous applause. Grinning, Teo turned toward Ana. Her cheeks were flushed pink, but she was smiling too.

"All rise," the Papa cried, and the congregation stood. "Ladies and gentlemen, I present to you Teofil and Anastasia of Chiveis, joined this day before the Eternal One as man and wife!"

The harpsichord and flute began to play, so Teo and Ana linked arms and walked down the aisle to the cheers and well-wishing of their friends. The Queen Mother and her son Piair sat on the front row in full regalia, while Stratetix and Helena sat opposite them. Almost the whole town of Edgeton had turned out for the event, along with many Royal Guardsmen, including the Warlord. Several foreign guests were in attendance as well: Mayor Calixte from Jineve, Count Federco from Ulmbartia, and even Vlad the Nine-Fingered, with whom the Warlord had worked out a non-aggression pact. Though Vlad looked uncomfortable with his hair slicked down and his rough garb exchanged for civilized clothing, his attendance at the wedding was a sign of mutual good faith between the Chiveisi and Germani.

Teo and Ana reached the rear of the seating area and headed for a heavily laden banquet table. The wedding ceremony had been kept simple, but the party afterward was intended to be a grand affair. White streamers had been strung among the branches, and wind chimes added their tinkling melody to the musicians' songs. Every kind of food was available, from roasted meats to full-bodied cheeses, from fresh summer fruits to sweet pastries. Sparkling wine flowed freely, and kegs of the best Chiveisian beer had been set up on stands. No one had an empty plate or cup except when going back for more. A festive mood permeated the forest clearing as the guests celebrated with the newlyweds.

Teo smiled as Count Federco walked up, looking handsome in a tailored jacket and crisp shirt. Bard accompanied his commander, and so did another Ulmbartian at the wedding, the elderly Sol with his long white hair tied back in a ponytail.

"I can't thank you enough for throwing open the Citadel's gate and saving my neck," Teo said as the count approached. "I owe you one."

Federco gave a hearty laugh. "Not at all! I was just paying you back for the time you barred a door and saved my own skin! Now we're even."

"Didn't I once tell you it's good to have friends in high places?" Sol asked with a grin. Teo chuckled in agreement.

Federco turned toward the bride with a polite dip of his head. "Anastasia, I remember the day you attended a ball at my chateau. I thought I had never seen such a lovely vision in all the world. And yet today I daresay your loveliness has reached new heights."

"Thank you, Count," Ana replied graciously.

"I couldn't agree more," Bard said. "You look stunning. It has been so great to see you again this past month. I'm going to miss you when I return to Ulmbartia."

"I'll miss you too, Bard. You were kind to me when I was a stranger."

Teo held up his hand to intervene. "Hey, don't forget. The expedition blazed a path between our two kingdoms. Now we can tame the wilderness and secure the passes. We might see each other again someday."

"I'll drink to that," Sol said, raising his glass. "And look here, Teofil—Chiveisian brandy."

"Is it as good as I promised?"

"Even better than grappa," Sol acknowledged.

The three Ulmbartians moved on as Ana's parents approached with Shaphan and Lina. Helena cradled a baby in her arms.

"Oh!" Ana exclaimed. "Let me see my little niece!" She took the infant in the tiny pink dress from Helena. "Hello, little Anastasia," she cooed, tickling the baby's chin.

"Rosetta is thoroughly enjoying her new grandbaby," Helena remarked. She slipped her arm around Ana's shoulder, then caught her attention with a mischievous gleam in her eye. "Maybe you and Teofil should provide me one too."

"Mother!" Ana cried, her face turning red.

"Never hurts to try," Teo said with a laugh.

After chatting a while longer, Teo went to the beer barrel to refill his mug. When he returned, Ana's family members were gone and Vanita had taken their place. She was in deep conversation with Ana.

"Marco has decided to get into shipping," Teo overheard Vanita say as he walked up. The idea was intriguing.

"Where?" he asked.

Vanita turned toward him. "He wants to start a trading business between Chiveis and Jineve. The route between the two kingdoms is mostly by water. It'll be perfect for him."

"For him?" Teo asked, raising his eyebrows. "Not you too?"

Vanita's face fell. She shook her head. "I'm going to stay here in New Bern, so I'll still see him. But when Marco asked me to marry him I had to say no. He hasn't yet become a follower of Deu."

"I'm sorry, Vanita. I'll pray for him."

Ana touched her friend's shoulder. "So will I."

"Thank you both," Vanita said, then quickly brightened. "But never mind me! Today isn't a day for sadness. Look, the show's about to begin."

A short distance away near the lip of the bluff, several workers were making adjustments to a series of iron tubes stuck into the ground. The wedding guests began to drift over to a place where the trees parted before an expansive view of the Chiveisian frontlands. In the distance Teo could see the snowy summits of the kingdom's three great peaks rising above the other mountains around them.

A fountain of sparks shot from one of the iron tubes, sending the workers scurrying away. A few seconds later a loud *whoomph* was accompanied by a burst of smoke and a shrill whistle. Everyone waited in expectant silence until . . .

BOOM!

A fierce explosion streaked the sky with a starburst of red and gold. The spectators jumped back, oohing and aahing with delight, though perhaps also with a little residual fear. A second explosion followed the first, and then the sky was filled with fire and thunder and smoke.

"I love it!" Ana giggled, her long-lashed eyes opened wide. "It's so noisy and colorful!"

Teo smiled at Ana's childlike wonder. Though the display in the heavens was amazing, he took more joy watching the expression on his wife's face as the fireworks detonated. The concussions resounded one after the other, each hurling multihued sparks in every direction. At last, after a tremendous climax, the show ended. White smoke drifted across the sky, and all the guests applauded.

"My ears are ringing," Ana said far too loudly.

Teo spotted Shaphan a few paces away and beckoned him over. The young man handed Teo a sack and left the couple alone.

"What is it?" Ana asked as she tugged her ear.

Teo brought out a glass bottle filled with a granular substance.

Ana frowned. "Astrebril's fire."

"Right. We just watched the destruction of all the black powder in Chiveis. Only this little bottle is left."

"What are you going to do with it?"

Teo knelt in the grass and tugged Ana down beside him. He removed a matchbox from the sack, then a book: *The Secret Lore of Astrebril*. "The Papa brought this to me from Roma," he said. "We thought it might help us make a weapon of our own. But we've changed our minds about that."

"Look where it led the Ancients. Let's not start the world down that path again."

"We can put a stop to it right now."

Teo opened the book and sprinkled black powder among its pages.

438

After making a little pile in its spine, he struck a match and handed it to Ana.

"No more secret weapons," he said.

"No more Astrebril," Ana replied, and dropped the match.

◆   ◆   ◆

As the carriage rounded a bend in the trail, Ana let out a gasp. "It's just like I always imagined!"

"I thought you'd like it. King Piair spared no expense. He put the best craftsmen on the job, so the house is really sturdy. It'll last a long time."

"Oh, Teo . . . it's the perfect place to build a life together."

The carriage pulled up near the front door. Teo got out, then reached to help Ana. She lifted the hem of her bridal gown and grasped his hand as she stepped lightly to the ground. The newlyweds thanked the coachman as he drove off, then turned to examine their new home.

The stone cottage sat on the bluff about a league from where the temple would rise. Though it was remote now, Teo hoped one day the house would be within the limits of a thriving new city. A garden had been planted out back, and the window flowerboxes overflowed with bright red geraniums. Not far from the door, a brook babbled into a plunge pool to provide the home with water. The builders had situated the cottage so that it offered a vista across a flat meadow stretching toward the western horizon. The sunset now lit up the sky in a crimson blaze that faded to rosy pink before disappearing into the blue-black depths. In the distance the Farm River was a shimmering ribbon of gold as it made its way toward Jineve.

Ana stepped onto the porch to take in the view. As she glanced around, she noticed a flower-covered mound a short distance from the house, with a headstone. "Teo, is that . . . ?"

"Yes, it's Liber. So we can always remember the gift he gave us. The gift of life."

"That's nice," Ana said, slipping her arms around Teo's waist and laying her head against his chest.

He held her like that for a while, breathing rhythmically with her in the silence. Finally he drew back and touched her chin, lifting her face to meet his gaze.

"How are you feeling about all this? Are you scared? Overwhelmed?"

She smiled brightly. "Not at all. I'm the happiest girl in the world."

"And the prettiest," he replied, then leaned in and kissed her. The touch of their lips was tender at first, just a light caress, but the arousal of passion was quick to follow. Teo felt its primal force crying out for more. He could tell from the way his wife clung to him that she felt the same.

When they parted, Ana glanced up at him with a coy smile. "Teo," she said, "right now I am so glad you're not my brother."

They both laughed at that, then kissed again. Ana clasped the back of Teo's head with her fingers intertwined in his hair. As he curled his arms around her body and drew her near, the powerful desire of a man for his beloved rose up within him.

Ana reached backward and grasped the doorknob. She turned it and kicked the cottage's door open with her heel. "Come inside," she invited, taking Teo by the hand.

"Excuse me, sir!"

The startled couple whirled toward the sound. A lone rider was there, backlit by the setting sun. He wore the garb of a forest wanderer.

"Who are you?" Teo demanded.

"I was told this is where I could find Teofil of Chiveis," the man said in his rough dialect.

"You've found him."

The stranger dismounted and walked his horse close. His only weapon was a sword that remained in its saddle scabbard. "I have traveled many leagues," he said, "but my master has come even farther. He hired me to find you."

"Well, friend, you'll have to come back another time. The Royal Guard can help you for now."

The man fell to his knees, and Teo noticed a bloodstain on his tunic. "Please, sir! My master is wounded! He begs to speak with you right away."

"Perhaps we can aid him," Ana said.

"The best aid you could give him would be to hear his plea. I left him across the meadow when he fell from his horse. He awaits you there."

"Who is he?" Teo asked.

"He has come to Chiveis from a kingdom far to the west. We met by chance in the woods, and he offered me a great sum if I would guide him to you. He is the king of a people who dwell on an island across the salty sea—the Britanni."

Teo and Ana exchanged glances. "What does he want with me?" Teo asked.

"Your reputation has reached him through the gossip of sailors. My master believes in a single God, but the *druidim* of his land started a rebellion. They pursued him and wounded him before he finally got away. Please—you must go! My master wants nothing more than to speak with you."

Glancing at Ana, Teo said, "I should probably check it out. Do you mind?"

"Mind?" Ana shot him a sharp look. "I'm going with you!"

Teo started to protest but quickly realized Ana wasn't going to be dissuaded. She mounted the horse and grinned at Teo from the saddle, her long legs protruding from her white wedding gown. Shaking his head, Teo stepped into the stirrup and swung up behind her.

"Go that way," the stranger said, pointing. "You'll find my master where the grass ends and the trees begin."

As Teo collected the reins, Ana spoke over her shoulder. "Life with you is one big adventure, Captain."

"I'm afraid so. Sorry about that."

Ana turned all the way around to look into Teo's face. "Don't be sorry. I wouldn't have it any other way."

"I know. That's why I love you."

Facing the western horizon again, Ana leaned back against Teo's chest. "I need you to do something," she said.

"Sure. What is it?"

"Hold me."

"What?"

"Just pull me close and hold me."

Teo slipped an arm around her slender waist. "Okay. Why?"

"Because we're going for a ride."

At those words Ana kicked her heels, prompting the horse into a wild run. At first it was all Teo could do to stay in the saddle. Yet both he and Ana were experienced riders, and soon their two bodies merged into one as they caught the rhythm of the galloping horse. Teo leaned forward, holding the reins in one hand and his new wife in the other. Ana's laughter was in his ears, and her golden hair streamed past his cheek. As they raced across the meadow turned orange by the setting sun, Teo could only marvel at the exceptional woman riding with him into the Beyond.

EPİLOGUE

The old Frenchman leaned on his shovel under a dark and noxious sky. Sweat beaded his brow despite the cold winter air. He knew he had expended far too much energy compared to the meager amount of food he had taken in, but it was worth it. His wife of fifty-two years deserved a decent burial.

He shuddered, then wiped tears from his eyes with the back of his dirty hand. Yvette had suffered much during the last three days. Her pain was intense, and the hemorrhaging was messy. Yet she had remained firm in her faith to the end. "We are saints of the Most High," she had said on her deathbed. "We must have hope when others do not."

"The world is bleak, woman. What hope is left?"

"The Eternal One will do a great work," Yvette said weakly. "Believe it, my husband. Believe this too shall pass."

Though Yvette was gone now, her final admonition still rang in the old man's ears. He sighed and walked back to the house.

Two weeks later the Frenchman awoke to the fate he had been awaiting. He felt a tickle on his upper lip, and when he blew his nose, his handkerchief came away red. *Good*, he thought. *Soon I shall see my wife.*

Searching through the empty kitchen drawers, he found a used Ziploc bag. The room was dim now that the skies were perpetually gray and electricity was a distant memory. He held up the bag to the window and noticed a small hole in it. *That probably won't matter*, he decided.

A strongbox in his closet contained papers whose former importance had vanished in the chaotic post-nuclear world. The Frenchman dumped them out and took the box to his desk. A Bible lay there: a leather-bound volume with gilded edges, translated by Louis Segond, the nineteenth-century Swiss theologian from Geneva. A cross and the words *Écriture Sacrée* were inscribed on the cover.

Taking a sheet of stationery, the old man wrote out a note and signed it. After tucking the note inside the Bible, he enclosed the book in paper, slipped it into the Ziploc bag, and wrapped the whole package in cloth and twine. Finally he placed the book inside the strongbox. One of its hinges was loose, so the lid remained slightly ajar when it was closed. Nothing could be done about that now. It would have to do.

The streets of the city were deserted, at least by the living. Here and there a corpse lay in a heap, but the old man ignored the frozen remains. Today was an ash day, so he covered his mouth and nose with a scarf as the white flakes drifted from the heavy overcast. *As if that will matter*, he thought grimly. He hunched into his coat, fighting a losing battle against the eternal winter.

After several twists and turns, he arrived at the cathedral. A single spire topped its tower on the northern side, making it one of the tallest churches in the world. The plaza outside was silent and still. As the old man approached the central door in the stupendous Gothic facade, a crowned Madonna smiled down at him, holding the Christ Child in her arms. The Virgin's peaceful expression reminded the grieving husband of his beloved Yvette.

"Believe this too shall pass," she had said.

I do believe it, Lord! I believe you will do a great work. I believe the Word of Dieu cannot die. Almighty Dieu, accept my final act of faith—and may you somehow use this treasure for your great purposes.

Stretching out his withered hand, Jacques Dalsace opened the door and carried the words of life into Strasbourg Cathedral.

APPENDIX:
CHIVEIS TRILOGY LOCATIONS

Chiveis Trilogy Location	Actual Name *(an Internet search will produce images)*
aqueduct beneath dungeons at Borja's palace	Acqua Vergine, Rome, Italy
Basilica of the Universal Communion	St. Peter's Basilica, Vatican City
bear attack, bluff above the Farm River	site of Münster (cathedral) of Bern, Switzerland
bridge, Lost City	Passerelle des deux Rives, Strasbourg, France
Camarg, the	The Camargue, Rhône delta, France
Camoly	Camogli, Italy
Cassee	Cassis, France
Castle d'If	Chateau d'If, Marseilles, France
castle, refuge after escaping outsiders' village	Rötteln Castle, Germany
castle, Ulmbartian outpost	Ussel Castle, Valle d'Aosta, Italy
chateau, remote, of Count Federco Borromo	near Cannero, Italy. The Count's ruined castle on the island is Cannero Castle.
Chiveis	Jungfrau Region of the Bernese Oberland, Switzerland
Chudeau River	Lütschine River, Switzerland
Citadel, the	near Wilderswil, Switzerland
convent, seaside	near Lido di Ostia, Italy
cove where Teo battles the Iron Shield in the sea	San Fruttuoso Abbey, Italy
Domo, the	Duomo, Milan, Italy
Eagle Pass	Simplon Pass, Switzerland
Eastport, Sessalay	Catania, Sicily, Italy
Edgeton	near Rubigen, Switzerland
Elzebul's Height	Jungfrau, Switzerland
Entrelac	Interlaken, Switzerland
En Vau Calank	En Vau Calanque, France
Farm River	Aar River, Switzerland

Fifth Regiment Headquarters	Belpberg, Switzerland
Fire Mountain	Mt. Etna, Sicily, Italy
Fisherman's Isle	Isola dei Pescatori, Lake Maggiore, Italy
Forbidden Zone	Milan, Italy
Giuntra	near Pavia, Italy
Great Bend in the Farm River	Bern, Switzerland
Great Pass	Grosse Scheidegg, Switzerland
Greater Lake	Lake Maggiore, Italy
Hahnerat Island	Île Saint-Honorat, Lérins Islands, France
High Priestess's fireworks temple	Sphinx Observatory, Switzerland
High Priestess's Temple	Eigergletscher Station, Switzerland
hut on glacier above Obirhorn Lake	Mutthorn Hut, Tschingel Glacier, Switzerland
Jané's house	Alcantara Gorge, Sicily, Italy
Jineve	Geneva, Switzerland
Labella estate	near Novara, Italy
lakes traversed by Teo between Jineve and Chiveis	Lakes Neuchâtel and Biel, Switzerland
Lekovil	Lauterbrunnen, Switzerland
Leman Sea	Lac Léman, Switzerland
Likuria	Liguria, Italy
Lost City	Strasbourg, France
Maiden's Valley	Lauterbrunnen Valley, Switzerland
Manacho	Monaco ("Rock")
Marsay	Marseilles, France
Napoly	Naples, Italy
Nuo Genov	Genoa, Italy
Obirhorn Lake	Oberhornsee, Switzerland
Outsiders' village (Rothgar's home)	Rheinfelden, Switzerland
Padu River	Po River, Italy (Latin: *Padus*)
Painted Chapel	Sistine Chapel, Vatican City
palace of Nikolo Borja	near Villa Borghese, Pincian Hill, Rome, Italy
pass, leading to Ulmbartian outpost (Ana injured)	Grand St. Bernard Pass, Switzerland and Italy
Pon's Height	Mönch, Switzerland
ridgecrest where Ana sacrifices a lamb	Männlichen, Switzerland

Roma	Rome, Italy
Rone River	Rhône River, France
Sessalay	Sicily, Italy
Strait of Mezzine	Strait of Messina, Italy
Tara Mena	Taormina, Sicily, Italy
Tomb of Holy Cecilia	St. Cecilia crypt, Catacombs of San Callisto, Rome
Toon	Thun, Switzerland
Tooner Sea	Thunersee, Switzerland
Troll's Valley	Grindelwald Valley, Switzerland
Ulmbartia	Lombardy, Italy
Vingin	Wengen, Switzerland
Vulkain's Height	Eiger, Switzerland
waterfall Teo is swept over	Rhine Falls, Switzerland (The chateau is Schloss Laufen)
waterfall at University of Chiveis	Staubbach Falls, Lauterbrunnen, Switzerland
Westport, Sessalay	Palermo, Sicily, Italy
White Mountain	Mont Blanc, France and Italy